Nancy Crampton

About the Author

BETH GUTCHEON is the critically acclaimed author of *Leeway Cottage*, *More Than You Know*, *Five Fortunes*, *Saying Grace*, *Domestic Pleasures*, *Still Missing*, and *The New Girls*. She has written several film scripts, including the Academy Award–nominated *The Children of Theatre Street*. She lives in New York City.

Five Fortunes

Also by Beth Gutcheon

Five Fortunes

a novel

Beth Gutcheon

HARPER **PERENNIAL**

HARPER ⬤ PERENNIAL

A hardcover edition of this book was published in 1998
by Cliff Street Books, an imprint of HarperCollins Publishers.

FIVE FORTUNES. Copyright © 1998 by Beth Gutcheon.
All rights reserved. Printed in the United States of America.
No part of this book may be used or reproduced in any manner
whatsoever without written permission except in the case of
brief quotations embodied in critical articles and reviews.
For information address HarperCollins Publishers, Inc.,
10 East 53rd Street, New York, NY 10022.

HarperCollins books may be purchased for educational,
business, or sales promotional use. For information please write:
Special Markets Department, HarperCollins Publishers, Inc.,
10 East 53rd Street, New York, NY 10022.

First Cliff Street Books/HarperPerennial edition
published 1999.

Reissued in 2005.

Designed by Christine Weathersbee

The Library of Congress has catalogued the hardcover
edition as follows:
Gutcheon, Beth Richardson.
Five fortunes : a novel / Beth Gutcheon. — 1st ed.
        p.   cm.
        ISBN- 0-06-17679-2
        I. Title.
    PS3557.U844F5   1998
    813'.54—dc21   97-48926

ISBN-10: 0-06-092995-2 (pbk.)
ISBN-13: 978-0-06-092995-4 (pbk.)

06 ❖/RRD 20

Five Fortunes

For my mother, Rosamound Richardson, who first took Joy and me to Fat Chance when we were too young to need it

And for my mother-in-law, Helen Clements, who has so staunchly supported my recent research

And for the inimitable Virginia Avery—if you know her, no explanation is necessary. If you don't, none would suffice

I am very grateful to friends who have made invaluable contributions to the shaping and grooming of this manuscript: Jerri Witt, Marilyn Yalom, Bob Domrese, Karen Paget, Geri Herbert, David Field, Jeanine Ackerly, Linda Rossen, Sung Ying Cheung, Robin Clements, and Barbara Schragge. Thanks also to Penny Ysursa in the office of the Secretary of State in Boise, and to Mitchell Lester at EMILY's List. For inspiration from fellow travelers: Alida, Fran, and Louisa, Julia Poppy, Jean, Dana, Kitty, Page, Joy, and my sisters. As always, my heartfelt gratitude for the support of my agent, Wendy Weil, and of my editor, Diane Reverand.

S tepping out to the curb in front of the Phoenix airport that November Sunday, Mrs. Albert Strouse, San Francisco matron of impressive age, was met by a welcome shock of heat. There had been a wintry dankness in the wind at home for weeks, which along with the artificial winter of the airplane cabin had settled into her bones. She adjusted her dashing new mango-colored sunglasses and basked.

A young woman in a jacket of a familiar blue appeared beside her. "Mrs. Strouse!"

"Cassie! How are you, dear?"

"Can't complain." Cassie took Rae's small suitcase and led her to the blue minivan waiting in the No Waiting zone. "You're my last lady. Do you mind riding up front with me?"

"Delighted. I'm good with a shotgun."

Cassie held the door while Rae hoisted herself into the front seat.

There were four other passengers already on board, none known to her. They exchanged nods of greeting with her, except for one fat one who either had jet lag or had enjoyed some cocktails on the plane and was slumped in the back with her eyes shut, looking like a failed popover.

Normally Rae Strouse loved a party. Normally Rae Strouse considered three strangers on a bus a festive gathering, but today as the van left the city behind she was just as glad to contemplate the afternoon light on the desert and let The Young behind her get on with their conversation.

1

The Young were apparently two childhood friends, now separated by husbands and children and distance, taking a week together. They were clucking over the guest list, looking for useful kernels of information, hoping they weren't going to regret not going to Aruba. New guests were always anxious about how it was going to be.

"Thirty-four, thirty-five, thirty-six. Thirty-six. Well that's a nice size. Group. That's a good group," said the dark one.

"Look, here's that woman Glenna Leisure. She's in *W* all the time."

"Is she?"

"Yes, you know who she is. She's that one who was a stewardess, she married the leveraged-buyout guy?"

"Is that the one whose co-op got so upset about her Christmas tree?"

"Exactly."

They fell silent as the van sped along toward the violet shadows of the Mazatzal Mountains.

"Is your sister coming with you this time?" Cassie asked Rae.

"No, we're taking a cruise later in the year. Mr. Strouse and I want to show her the Greek Isles."

"That sounds nice," said Cassie.

"We're looking forward to it."

There was another silence.

"A number of your pals from last time are back," said Cassie. Rae nodded. She was such an old hand by now that there were almost always guests she knew from earlier visits. She liked that, but even more she liked meeting new ones. It wasn't so easy at her age to meet new people, and it was important. The old ones kept dying.

The two friends behind her handed the guest list to the third woman, who now remarked, "Mrs. Alan Steadman . . . isn't that Megan Soule?"

Even Rae turned around at that.

"Megan Soule? You're *kidding*!"

"That's her married name," said the third guest. The two friends looked at her.

"Megan Soule, omigod, I *love* her! She was so cute in that movie, with Robin Williams . . . "

"I saw her in concert once. She was incredible."

"I've heard she's a really nice person."

"It says she's from Aspen."

"Well she isn't, but they do have a house there."

"But she lives in Malibu."

"Don't those friends of yours live in Malibu?"

"No, they moved."

The little van whizzed along over the desert.

"Well, this should be fun," said the plump blonde, sounding uncertain.

Forty minutes later the little van turned down an unmarked road winding among tall pines. It crossed an arroyo and stopped before a wooden door set in a high stucco wall. The pines cast deep shadows, and the sounds of the highway above and behind them seemed suddenly far away.

The driver rang a heavy brass bell hanging from the doorpost. It had a deep iron peal. Almost at once a young woman appeared through the carved door. Her name tag said JACKIE.

"*Hello*, Mrs. Strouse, welcome back," she said as Rae was handed down from the van. Rae passed through into a courtyard inside the walls, the first cloister. When the little door closed behind the group they seemed suddenly wrapped in stunning silence.

"Oh!" said the blonde. "So quiet . . . "

It took a moment to become aware that it was not silent at all, but filled with a subtle singing of crickets, of water playing somewhere nearby, of birds, of moving branches. This courtyard was built around a stone pool whose surface reflected trees towering around it.

Inside, the reception hall was airy and light, built in a style that suggested the Southwest missions, but with rather more amenities. The ladies sank into large leather chairs and were brought herb tea. A small woman in a loose belted robe like a monk's cassock brought Rae a pair of sandals. She asked each of the new ladies her shoe size. Jackie appeared with a clipboard and settled on a footstool beside Rae.

"How is Mr. Strouse?"

"About the same," Rae said. "Thank you for asking."

"You're in A-twelve again. Is there anything you need? Do you want to put anything in the safe?"

"I left my tiara at home," said Rae.

"Just as well."

Jackie moved on to the plump blonde, and Rae got herself out of her chair and went out. Her room lay down an outdoor path and through a second open courtyard. Here was an herb garden full of lavender and sage and other aromatics. She entered a third cloister formed around a koi pond.

Rae's usual room was on the east side of the cloister. The door was unlocked, of course. Inside, her little suitcase had been delivered and her raincoat hung in the closet. The dresser was already stocked with clean T-shirts and leggings and shorts and sweatclothes, all in her size. Rae closed the door behind her, creating the first complete solitude she had known for more months than she could bear to think of.

On a redwood bench in the bathhouse, Amy Burrows sat wrapped in a huge white towel and watched her teenaged daughter Jill endure the misery of standing in bra and underpants to be weighed and measured. Several other new arrivals were undressing nearby, chatting and wandering in and out of the shower and steam rooms. The attendant, a friendly little thing in a white nylon pantsuit, slid the small cylindrical counterweight all the way to the left on the top bar of the scale, and then with a shake of her head, moved the large weight up to 150. She slid the small weight to the right again and started ooching it up, as if expressing her faith that surely it would balance in just another pound or two. 160. 170. 180 . . .

She can't be over 180, Amy thought. The cylinder finally stopped at 182 ½.

Jill stepped off the scale and seized her terry-cloth robe. The attendant wrote the facts in a folder with Jill's name on it. It seemed to Jill that the folder should have a different name: "Jill Burrows's Body," maybe, since it seemed to her so remote from her essential self. Essential Jill and Physical Jill should be seen to exist independently. Strangers would have to see big fat Physical Jill as she looked from the outside, because if they didn't she might be hit by a bus. But for people who knew her as a person, Physical Jill should shimmer away like a hologram and they would see, and she could be, Real Jill, the person.

* * *

"How are you holding up, lovey?" Amy asked. "Are you wanting a nap?"

Jill shook her head and wrapped her arms around her upper body in an unconscious gesture she'd developed, as if her innocent flesh needed to be protected.

"Do you want to soak in the hot tub? It's great for jet lag."

Jill shrugged. She pushed her feet into the sandals she'd been given on arrival. Her mother was leading the way toward a room that seemed to be a cone of light. Jill followed, thinking that what she really wanted was her own room, her computer, and about ten Mrs. Fields Double Chocolate Chocolate Chip Cookies.

They'd been here for an hour and, except for the instructors, there wasn't one other person in this place who was under forty. As often happened to her, Jill suddenly saw an image of what she and her mother must look like, as if she were standing quite apart from them both, watching her life as a camera would. She saw her slim and barefoot mother as a sylph or naiad, a pretty woman draped in white cloth tripping along leading Jill, her pet cow, by a ring in her nose.

Laura Lopez sat in the Japanese bath with her eyes closed, feeling the jets of water pulse against the small of her back. She hoped the people attached to the feet clacking toward her wouldn't be wanting to chat. She'd come straight here to the bathhouse when she'd arrived and had spent most of the afternoon immersed in heat. She'd been so numb, and tense and cold and heartsick, that it seemed that all the steam and hot water in the world couldn't soak it out of her. She knew one simple thing: she liked this room, and she hadn't expected to like anything for about the next twenty years.

The room was mostly glass, a sort of dome, and open to the sky. Did it ever rain here? Probably not. It was the desert. The whole building smelled of eucalyptus, a wonderful clean, spicy smell that made her think of Indian healing rituals. Not that she knew much about Indians. Native Americans. Except for the ones who appeared before her in court, and they were usually in need of healing themselves. In the local paper, when their arraignments were listed in the police blotter, it gave the tribe too. Mary Wells, Blackfoot, driving unregistered vehicle and DUI. That was rude, wasn't it?

Other women had come and gone. Some slipped into the hot pool in silence, soaked, and then left. Some, shy, wore bathing suits. Laurie expected to want the room all to herself, but she found that she rather liked it when others arrived, even when they talked, as long as they didn't talk to her. She closed her eyes and listened to the words, or listened to them stir the water, and felt (as she assumed she was supposed to) that she was inside a womb. Maybe it would be possible after enough time in here to leave one's rind of accumulated life in shriveled sheddings on the bottom of the pool, and emerge as pink and cleansed as a newborn.

Laurie opened her eyes just enough to see the bodies these new sets of sandal clacks belonged to. A mother-daughter team, she guessed. The daughter was immense, poor thing. The mother was a blonde with an open, unlined face. Her skin was shining and free of makeup. The mother dropped her towel and slid naked into the water; Laurie saw full breasts and just a suggestion of stretch marks on the belly. This one was healthy, but not a tummy-crunch nut. She looked comfortable in her own skin.

The daughter looked as if it really wasn't her own skin, as if she'd found this uninhabited tent of flesh and moved in temporarily, until she could make more suitable arrangements. She looked to be about eighteen. She had beautiful liquid hazel eyes with long lashes, and a stylish haircut that said Big City. Laurie thought of her own girls, Anna grown recently lumpen in adolescence, and Cara, edging reluctantly toward puberty, still mostly tomboy. Laurie herself had been through both phases when growing up.

The large daughter had now survived her moment of indecision. She hung her robe on a hook, turned her back, and stripped off her underwear. She followed her mother naked into the steaming water, making a little squeak as she did so.

"I love this room," said Amy happily. She was glad Jill had gotten past shyness about being naked in front of that other lady. The other lady had kindly seemed to keep her eyes closed.

"It's nice," said Jill. Her mother had become a talking head on the surface of the water, a head and neck standing on a tabletop of blue. Jill's own body, even the great bulk of it which was submerged, remained attached to her head. Too bad.

At the other end of the pool, the thin lady opened her eyes and scooched down the bench to a tray of filled glasses someone had soundlessly brought. Jill watched as she drained a glass.

"What is that?" Jill called.

"Ice water with lemon," Laurie said.

"Lemonade?"

"Not exactly." Jill made her way down the pool, keeping her knees bent so that she was submerged to her shoulders. She fetched two glasses and floated back to her mother. They drank.

"What *is* it that makes this room so peaceful?" Amy wondered aloud.

"It's a yurt," said Jill.

"I *beg* your pardon?"

"A yurt, there are no right angles. Mongols or someone made them out of skins and poles. They were portable. You feel different in a space with no right angles."

At the far end, Laurie opened her eyes again and looked around her. The girl was right. The lower wall tipped outward at a seventy-degree angle. At about hip level the walls tipped in toward the dome.

"Are they always open at the top?" Laurie called to Jill.

"Yes."

"What happens when it rains?"

"The top is the smoke hole. The rain hits the hot smoke and steam from the fire and evaporates before it gets inside, at least in a Mongol one."

Laurie stared upward at the sky. I like this, she thought.

"How do you know all this, Miss Smart Boots?" Amy asked.

"My anthropology class. We went heavily into dwellings of Stone Age peoples."

"Where are yurts from?" Laurie asked, in spite of her own wish to remain separate.

"The steppes, wherever they are. Siberia?"

"Do yurts work in snow too?"

"I would think," said Jill. "I don't think they, like, move into motels in the winter."

Laurie laughed. "I think I want one of these. But it would have to work in snow."

"Where are you from?" Amy asked her.

"Idaho," Laurie said with her eyes closed.

"Are you?" Amy was delighted. "So am I! Coeur d'Alene."

Laurie opened her eyes in surprise and said, "I'm from Hailey." You never met anyone from Idaho. You never even met anyone who had *been* to Idaho, except to Sun Valley.

"My grandma lives in Coeur d'Alene," said Jill. "We go to visit, and then we go to Sun Valley."

"Did you grow up in Hailey?" Amy asked.

Laurie nodded. "Hailey and Boise." This was enough conversation for her. She reached for a towel from the stack by the steps, and abruptly climbed out of the pool. Amy watched the wan face, the long-waisted athletic body, the sleek, muscled legs. Laurie stopped suddenly at the top step.

"I've been in too long."

"Hold the rail," said Amy. Laurie obeyed. Amy watched her, knowing that if she *had* been in too long, she could easily black out.

Laurie shook her head, trying to clear it. She took a deep breath. She felt ridiculous and pathetically exposed, dripping wet and blind from the black roaring in her ears and eyes.

"You okay?" Amy asked after a minute. The woman, who had a deep Cesarean scar across her abdomen, had straightened.

"Yes," said Laurie, "just stupid." She took a robe from a hook and put it on. She reached into the pocket and found her watch. She put on some Chap Stick.

"See you," she said.

"See you," Amy and Jill answered.

Laurie shuffled out into the cool evening wearing her sandals, naked under the robe. She walked along the pathway on the west side of the cloister, which was built around two swimming pools. She walked quickly back to her room, hurried through it to the small railed porch on the back side with a view of the mountains. There she sat down in a deck chair and cried.

*C*arter Bond was causing problems that Sunday. She had arrived with a suitcase full of tennis clothes and bathing suits. She had no aerobics shoes or hiking boots, and at six feet and 170 pounds, she was too big for even the largest size of sweat clothes provided for the other guests. She was sitting in the Fitness office with Sandra, who was trying to create her exercise plan.

"What would you say is your general level of fitness?" Sandra asked.

"I can bench-press one-fifty," said Carter, sounding aggressive. Sandra noted the number.

"Aerobic exercise?"

"You mean classes? Please."

"Anything that gives your heart an aerobic workout. Jogging, walking, biking, swimming . . . ?"

"I play tennis," said Carter.

"Every day?"

"Lady, I work for a living!"

Sandra smiled. Sandra clearly worked for a living too, and was the first person Carter had met here who looked as if she'd had a decent meal in the last month. She wore stockings and high-heeled shoes, and had long beige-painted fingernails.

"How often are you able to play?"

"Couple of times a month."

"Singles? Doubles?"

"Either."

"And at what level? Would you say?"

"Killer."

Sandra smiled, and wrote that down.

"Any special health problems we should know about?"

"There's smoker's cough."

"Back all right? Knees? Neck?"

Carter nodded. "I'm in a no-smoking room. Where *can* I smoke?"

Sandra had heard this before, and she knew to answer with sympathy.

"There is no smoking here at all."

Carter stared at her. She shifted in her chair and crossed one meaty leg over the other.

"What about the guards? Where do they smoke? I'll hang out with them."

Sandra was genuinely puzzled.

"Guards?"

"All those Mexicans in blue overalls, lurking around the grounds."

"Those aren't guards—they're gardeners."

"You're running a detox farm with no guards?"

Sandra almost laughed. She had never had a guest be so blunt about this before.

"We think of it as a health spa, Ms. Bond."

"Is there an employee's lounge somewhere? I'll smoke there."

"Nobody smokes here. It's a condition of employment."

Carter stared at her.

"Is that legal?"

"As far as I know."

Carter was becoming seriously uncomfortable. She hadn't had a cigarette since the smoker's cell at LAX, a fascist development in California airports. All the smokers were herded into a glass cage so all the clean, pure nonsmokers could look in at the addicts, huddled together inhaling poison gas. Now this.

"How do you get people to put up with this? Why don't they all just vote with their feet and hike out of here?"

Sandra said, "The amount they're paying seems to be an incentive."

Carter hadn't thought of that. She didn't know how much this deal cost, it was DeeAnne's idea. A fiftieth-birthday present. "You need a complete change," DeeAnne had said, and Carter couldn't have agreed more, but that was because she'd pictured a week on her back, poolside, sipping margaritas and reading Patricia Cornwell novels.

"Now. Is there anything you can't eat, or don't like?"

"Plenty. Most of it fish," said Carter.

Sandra noted.

"We have a vegetarian meal plan. Would you like to try that?"

"No."

"Just so you know, there is also a liquid diet that some of our guests enjoy. It's a fast, really. We don't recommend it for more than three days, though, with the level of exercise you'll be doing."

"Pass," said Carter, rolling her eyes.

"Now, what about your calories? How many a day?"

"About five thousand would be good."

Sandra moved right along. "We don't recommend less than a thousand. The nutritionist advises twelve hundred, but you do have the option of fourteen hundred a day."

"I'll take it."

"There will be a name tag, which we ask you to wear all the time, on your breakfast tray. Terri will be your personal trainer; your meetings with her will be on your schedule. A shopper will go into town first thing in the morning to get you some exercise clothes and shoes. She'll bring them to your room. The morning hikes leave at six from the Saguaro Pavilion. What time would you like your wake-up call?"

"Eight."

"I'll put down five forty-five."

"You mean we're supposed to hike on an empty stomach? Don't people faint?"

"I can arrange to have a glass of juice for you in Saguaro, if there is a blood sugar problem."

"Do it."

"There is coffee and tea there in the morning as well, and herbal tea and our special lemonade." Carter made a face. She had tried the "lemonade" in the Saguaro Pavilion while she was looking for the bar. They had a big iced crock of it in there, and ladies were swilling it down like mai tai mix. She was relieved to hear they at least allowed coffee and tea. A week without cigarettes or gin was bad enough, but caffeine would have nailed it. She'd have gone over the wall no matter what DeeAnne had paid.

"Do you have any questions?" Sandra asked her.

"I can't find the TV in my room."

Sandra sighed. "I'm afraid Lalou considers TV one of our modern addictions. The only one here for the guests is in the Saguaro Pavilion. You can watch the news in the morning after your hike; many guests do that. Will you be wanting a newspaper?"

"Who the hell is Lalou?"

"Oh, she's the Founder. The Cloisters is run according to the principles of Lalou and her mother, a famous leader of the health and spirit movement in the twenties. You'll find copies of Lalou's favorite books in your room, and Lalou recommends that for maximum benefit, you just close the world out for the whole week and allow your spirit to heal. Read Zen koans at breakfast, or better yet, let your mind be empty."

"How many newspapers can I have?"

"We offer the *Arizona Republic*."

"I can't get the *New York Times*?"

"We could probably send someone to town for it, but you won't have it until lunchtime."

"Do it."

"I think we're all set, then. Happy hour is at six in the Chapter House, and dinner is at six-thirty. Do you know how to find it?"

"I'll manage."

Carter strode out, feeling silly in the bathrobe that didn't cover her knees. Her craving for a cigarette had grown so bad that she was thinking of ripping one open and putting a plug of tobacco in her cheek. But she decided instead to swim some laps, as many as she could. Maybe she'd bliss out. Or drown.

The Chapter House was a cozy room in which a baronial fireplace warmed the cool desert evening. By six o'clock ladies of varying ages and sizes sat chattering or staring into the fire, and more arrived every few minutes. A few, fresh from traveling, wore street clothes. Most wore the bone-white linen cassocks they'd found in their closets. These were vaguely suggestive of monks' robes, and gave even the most jaded guests, stripped now of makeup, jewelry, and other social markers, an air of freshness and purity.

Amy and Jill sat together, their faces scrubbed and clean after the bathhouse. Jill's hair was wet. Her mother looked around with a welcoming expression, in case anyone should like to make conversation with them. Jill had knocked back her "cocktail," a small cup of some spicy tea flavored with cranberry juice, and was powering down her share of the fingers of jicama that served as hors d'oeuvres.

Amy saw their friend from the Japanese tub, the woman from Idaho, come in. Laurie's hair, now dry, formed a soft ash-gray halo around her face. She had deep circles under her eyes. Amy would have signaled her to join them if she'd caught her eye, but Laurie took a cup of spiced tea and went to a deep chair in the corner.

Laurie hoped no one would speak to her. She felt like a new girl on the first day of camp, watching old-timers greet each other. This whole idea was a mistake. She thought, I wish I hadn't let them talk me into it. I can't explain myself to new people. I miss my children. I miss my husband. I want a drink.

She saw at the edge of her vision the mother-daughter team from this afternoon. And there was the little woman with the huge jewels who had been in her van coming in from the airport. She looked completely different now, with her makeup washed off and the diamonds gone. She looked kind. More real, in some way, than she had in her street clothes.

The door opened and in came a woman with a cap of auburn hair, bright eyes, and a streak of scarlet lipstick.

"Rae!" cried several voices.

"Aha!" Rae cried. Her face lit up as she laughed and embraced old friends. Laurie watched as if she were a fish deep under water seeing a display of fireworks in the sky. It was bright, it was noisy, it had a certain charm, but made absolutely no sense to her. It had nothing to do with the medium she swam in.

The door banged open, and in came a sort of giant woman, so tall that her ankles stuck out beneath her cassock. On her feet were the loafers she must have worn traveling. Everyone else was wearing sandals. The giant stood staring at the table in the middle of the room, where there remained a few cups of scarlet tea and the ruined platter of vegetable sticks.

"This is what they call Happy Hour, is it? I hope somebody brought a flask."

"The tea is delicious," said somebody, handing her a tiny cup. Carter downed it in one motion, and loomed suspiciously over the crudités.

"What's the white stuff?"

"Jicama, jicama," chorused many voices. "You'll love it. Try it, no calories."

Carter took a piece and ate it.

"A little onion dip would go a long way here," she said. Life of the party, thought Laurie. The noisy guy at the bar. She thought about going back to her room and asking to have dinner sent to her there, but just then came the sound of a deep gong.

A young woman in civilian clothes whose body was so thin it looked like a collection of bicycle parts assumed a position of leadership.

"Good evening, ladies. I'm Mandy, and I'm your hostess tonight. As you go in to supper you'll see a temporary name tag for each of you. Please put those on so we can get to know you and the waitresses can give you the right meal."

She opened the door and led the way into the dining room. Amy followed the bright old bird with the cat's-eye glasses, and Jill followed her mother.

They were served a delicious soup of wild mushrooms in broth, followed by grilled fish, some grain called quinoa, and French beans. There was even a parfait for dessert. Laurie noticed that at Rae's table there was much talk, and lots of laughter.

"You know," said a little dark-haired woman, "that looks like a Georgia O'Keeffe." She peered across the room at the painting above the sideboard.

"It *is* a Georgia O'Keeffe; Lalou collects them. They're all over the place."

"It's part of the treatment," said Amy. "Everything you look at is so beautiful, you hardly ever notice you're starving."

"Isn't there supposed to be a movie star here?" asked a woman at the end of the table.

"She's here, but she never comes to dinner," said someone else.

At the head table the girl made of bicycle parts stood up and rang a little bell.

"It's time to say welcome again. I'm Mandy, one of your Fitness Professionals, and I'm looking forward to getting to know you all better. I'd like to go around the room and have each of you stand up and introduce yourself. Tell us your name, and maybe a little bit about what you hope to accomplish this week. Rae, would you start?"

Oh god, thought Laurie.

Rae rose. "I'm Rae Strouse, I'm from San Francisco, and this is my twenty-second visit, so you can tell I don't like it very much. I hope to come out twenty years younger." She sat down.

"I'm Amy Burrows, from New York. I'm here with my daughter Jill, and I hope to lose a few pounds and have fun."

"I'm Jill Burrows, from New York, and this is my first time. I'm with her." She indicated her mother, and sat down.

Some people told their professions. Some people told how many children they had. Laurie half-rose, and said, "I'm Laura Knox from Hailey, Idaho," and sat back down.

The giant said, "I'm Carter Bond from Los Angeles, and I'm here because I thought I was going to Club Med. You think I'm kidding. I don't know about the rest of you, but I am in deep withdrawal at the moment and I'll be lucky to get through the week without committing an ax murder. *And* I hope you've all admired my loafers." She stuck a foot out, to show the juxtaposition of her shoes with her cassock.

Oh good, Rae was thinking, she looks like fun. She surveyed the room with a feeling of warm pleasure. Such jolly old friends, such a lot of new people to get to know!

Amy was thinking of Jill. And thinking of the shit she'd take from Noah if she spent all this money and Jill didn't like it. Fine, she'd accepted that Jill wasn't going to lose fifty pounds and solo with the ABT, but it would be nice if she could find something that would make the girl *happy* for a week.

Jill was thinking that she admired that Carter woman for using the word "withdrawal." There were plenty of heavy people who claimed they ate like sparrows but had cruelly slow metabolisms. Jill was not one of them. To get as fat as she was and stay there, you had to eat a *lot*, and she was now ravenous. It was shocking, in fact, to have to stop eating when everyone else did, and register how little food normal-sized people thought was enough. But at least it was nice to eat without feeling her father's eyes tracking every mouthful she swallowed.

Carter had slept very little, and she had dreamed about smoking. She was so hungry she felt hollow, and she couldn't believe a human being could be so cheerful while uttering the words "Good morning, it's five forty-five." She had had every intention of sleeping through until breakfast, but now that the damn phone had rung, she realized there was no point. If she hadn't slept all night, she wasn't going to now.

She got up and made her way through the dark room, whose ghost shapes of dresser and suitcase and chairs had loomed large in her half sleep throughout the night, sometimes appearing to have turned into appliances, or hunched animals, or large stones. She pulled the curtain cord to let in the cool blue-gray dawn light, and discovered the strange and magical little bonsai garden that her room overlooked. The elaborately gnarled trees looked alive, like dwarfs frozen during a game of Mother, May I? In the center of the garden, there was a rectangle of powder-fine sand. Perfect for putting out cigarettes, Carter had thought last night, stumping past it. A great big ashtray. This morning she noticed that someone—one of the guards, she presumed—had used a rake to make an oddly attractive pattern in the sand.

Now, what was she going to wear? She had a pair of white linen slacks, and of course her tennis shoes. And a tennis sweater and a fancy beaded jacket for evening. She put them both on, the evening one under the one with red and blue stripes. When she'd packed, she hadn't bargained on any dawn excursions. She had thought of sloth, and midday heat. In her dresser she found she'd been given a watch cap and a pair of gloves. She figured this joint must know what they were doing if they were handing out woollies. She put them on and went out.

In the Saguaro Pavilion she found a sleepy group with scrubbed faces holding steaming mugs of coffee and tea and talking quietly. The Movie Star was there in violet sweats looking rather plain and human. She held a cup of herbal tea and stared into space. A number of others reported not having slept well, as if this was surprising in people whose systems had just been abruptly deprived of salt, sugar, nicotine, background noise, and alcohol. No one, Carter noticed, had turned on the television. Carter was itching to, but what would be on? Prayer programs or farm news. She poured herself a mug of coffee.

A Fitness Professional—Carter was beginning to recognize the type—bounced into the room wearing neon-yellow parachute material and a lavender headband.

"Good morning! I'm Helena, I'm leading the Five-Mile Mountain Hike! Three-Mile Mountain and Three-Mile Moderates leave in five minutes! One-and-a-Half-Mile leaves in ten. Five-Mile Mountain! Let's Stretch!" And she bounced out of the room followed by about ten hardy souls, including the Movie Star.

Carter wasn't counting on having to make choices at this hour. She sat still and clung to her coffee mug, and hoped that five minutes was a really long time.

In bounced another Fitness Professional. This was a black one who yelled that her name was Terri.

"Three-Mile hikers, let's go! Put down those mugs, ladies, time to stretch! One-and-a-Half-Mile Hike in five minutes. If you have a medical condition, especially knees, start with the short hike today. Everybody else, let's GO!"

Had there ever been a murder here before breakfast? Carter wondered. Probably lots. Would it be one maddened dieter at a time going over the edge, or would they occasionally rise in a body and tear a little Mandy or Terri to shreds? How long could they get away with it before someone noticed?

She was tempted to wait for the shortest walk, but realized with regret that only four other ladies had failed to rise, and they were all fairly frail-looking. Carter had too much vanity.

Out by the pool, there was a long row of ladies of many shapes and sizes, all wearing violet or navy blue sweatpants and jackets, except Carter. She found she was beside the terrific old trout from last night, the one with the cat glasses who had been here two hundred times.

Terri exhorted them to assume various queer positions designed to stretch their calves, their thighs, their hamstrings. Carter did her best to comply and was surprised at how bad she was at it. There were bursts of embarrassed laughter from time to time from others down the line. The air was beginning to take on the pinks and yellows of full morning, and she could smell jasmine.

"Great! Ladies, Three-Mile Mountain follow me. Three-Mile Moderate, Tanya will be your guide. Let's Go!" And Terri strode off, followed by a gaggle of energetic walkers. The terrific old trout stayed put, so Carter did too. Tanya, in iridescent pinks, rounded up the remaining group and herded them off.

Carter decided to let the trout set the pace. She liked the way she strode out, swinging her fists as she walked, her jaw set in earnest purpose. Carter figured she must be close to eighty.

"I didn't like the sound of a mountain at this hour," Carter said to her.

"I never go up it if I can help it. This is prettier, you walk through the vegetable gardens. You're from Los Angeles?"

Carter was pleased that Rae remembered her. They strode along talking, once in a while admiring the light, or an unexpected vista below them. The mountain, or at least the foothills, were definitely on the program even for Three-Mile Moderates. The surprising thing to Carter was, not only didn't she hate it, she was feeling kind of great.

"I never heard of this place till I got here. My business partner sent me, as a birthday present. I haven't decided yet whether to thank her or kill her."

"I love it," said Rae. "Well, you could probably guess that. It's a week of your life when nothing goes wrong. And you don't have to cook."

"I don't do much of that anyway. Everyone at work's been after me to quit smoking. My mother popped off from heart disease when she was fifty-one."

"How much do you smoke?"

"Pack and a half a day."

"Oh, my goodness. And you're going cold turkey?"

"Looks like it," said Carter.

"Well, hang in there."

They marched along. Rae said, "I quit smoking when I became a dance instructor. I noticed how much you could smell it on your partners. But I never smoked more than half a pack."

"You weren't addicted."

"No, I don't believe I was. I smoked to keep my husband company. My first husband. He was a jazz musician."

"And you're a dance instructor?"

"Oh, no, not anymore. I was a *dancer*, I was on the stage, my dear, in my salad days. What do you do?"

They had arrived at the crest of a ridge, and found Tanya waiting for them. The rest of the group was already there, or straggling in. Laura from Idaho was leaning against a railing and listening to a red-head, very wound up, telling about multiple conflicting diagnoses she'd been given regarding a condition in her abdomen.

"It sounds so frightening," Laurie murmured.

"That's just it, it was terrifying," cried the redhead.

"Everybody doing all right? Anyone getting blisters, need a Band-Aid? Anyone want a section of orange?" Terri and Tanya had produced fruit and Evian from their backpacks. When Carter bit into her section of orange she began to laugh.

"Oh my god. It's so good, it's like a hallucination."

"Fresh air and early rising makes things taste better," chirped the pearly teethed Terri. She was gathering everyone's peels and napkins into a plastic bag that she put back into her backpack. Then, with a rallying cry, she started off again.

"Ooh," said Carter to Rae as they fell into line. "That was *good*."

"It's probably because of the cigarettes."

"I guess that makes sense," Carter said. She thought, Damn . . . am I going to go through with this?

"So anyway, what do you do?" Rae asked again.

"I'm a private investigator."

"You're not!" Rae cried. She had met a lot of interesting women on this mountain, but this was a new one.

"I am, in fact."

"Well, I want to know everything!"

"First I was a public defender—what an awful job. You see everyone at their worst. But I learned the nuts and bolts of what goes on in a criminal trial. What you need in the way of evidence, how to tell when someone is lying, what juries believe and what they don't. My partner, DeeAnne, was a police detective. She had hit a glass ceiling, and I was burning out. We'd gotten to know each other in court, from opposite sides of the aisle, and we decided to make a break for it."

"And you're successful? Well, you must be successful if DeeAnne could afford such a birthday present."

"She's married to a plastic surgeon, he may have had something to do with it. But we have an agency in L.A., and one in San Diego. We're thinking about a third one, maybe San Francisco."

"Do you have a specialty?"

"No, we do everything. But we only hire women."

"Really!"

"Of course. They're more curious, and more patient. As a matter of fact, we only hire big fat women."

Rae shouted with delight.

"I'm serious," said Carter. "Nobody looks at fat women, they can go anywhere. They can sit for hours in a hotel lobby, nobody hits on them. Nobody wonders what they're doing there."

"And how on earth do you locate big fat women detectives?"

"We train them. We're beating the applicants off with sticks. Everyone wants to work for us, and nobody ever quits."

"Have you ever hired men?"

"We did at first. But the women are so good at it. Also, I don't like my people to carry guns. Lot of men have a problem with that."

"But isn't it dangerous? To do what you do, without a gun?"

"I think it's more dangerous with one. But no one has to agree with us. If they don't, they can work for someone else."

"I think I'd like to apply for a job," said Rae, "if you open an office in San Francisco."

"You're not really fat enough, but I can use a good operative in your age range," said Carter. "For instance, can you tell me—what's going on with this one?"

"Which one?" asked Rae. She was on board immediately, ready to be trained.

"This one right ahead of us, on the left." She indicated Laurie.

They both watched as the redhead talked and gestured with her hands. Laurie listened, nodding from time to time. Once she laughed. Sometimes she shook her head and clucked in sympathy.

"Something terrible has happened to her," said Carter.

"You don't mean the redhead?" Rae wanted her to mean the redhead, because she knew the answer, at least partly; she'd heard it last night in the steam room. It started with an alleged fibroid tumor the size of a cantaloupe.

"No, the other one. There's something in the way she holds her shoulders, and something around the eyes . . . and besides, she looks familiar to me. Not to you?"

"I don't think so . . . "

They walked in silence, both now watching Laurie. They were approaching The Cloisters again, coming in from a new direction, one that took them across a parched arroyo. It made a striking contrast with the green of the lawns and a lettuce field in the distance. It gave the place the look not so much of an oasis, which it was, but of a wizard zone like the Emerald City.

They'd caught up with Laurie and the redhead. The redhead was exclaiming "Diverticulitis! Excuse me? And I was about to have a hysterectomy?" Laurie shook her head as if to say, What a world. "Can you believe this?" Glenna Leisure (as her tag said) turned to provide Rae and Carter with an update on the conversation. "Hysterectomy, said the first one, drugs, said the second one, diverticulitis, said the third. Know what it was?"

"What?"

"Ruptured appendix. Ruptured, fucking, excuse my Latin, appendix! I was in the hospital for a month. My husband wanted to sue, but I said, forget it, give the money to me, not the lawyers, I'm going to The Cloisters."

"I hope they paid for your hospital bill," said Carter.

"You bet the farm they paid, and you should have seen the bill. *This* thick . . . I could have died. I almost did." As Glenna went on, Rae and Carter both noted Laurie pulling quietly away from them. She came to a divergent path leading across a courtyard and toward the bedrooms instead of back to Saguaro, and with a little apologetic wave, she left them. Rae glanced at Carter, and saw that this was exactly what Carter had expected. Carter watched Laurie go with a professional curiosity. Something was going on, and she wondered what it was. Rae watched Laurie go with a mother's heart. That kind young woman was in great grief or trouble. Was there any way to help?

*a*my had finished her breakfast, which had been served to her in her room overlooking the koi pond. Having decided to forgo the healing silence of Zen koans in her solitude, she was reading Ann Landers when Jill came in.

"It's pouring rain in New York," Jill said.

"Is it?"

"Yes. They have a page where they tell the weather all over the country."

Jill wasn't used to eating breakfast alone. She had read her paper with great thoroughness, the better to distract herself from how hungry she was. Breakfast had been a little dish of oatmeal, a spoonful of maple sugar, skim milk, and a couple of slices of papaya. She'd dispatched it in about a minute and a half, and now she noticed that her mother had not eaten the squash blossom that decorated her plate. Jill had eaten hers.

"Eight-thirty to nine, I have stretch class, or T'ai Chi. What do you?"

"I always go to Stretch."

"I think I'll try T'ai Chi."

Amy looked surprised.

"Do you know what it is?"

"No. But, why not? What do you do at nine?"

"I have Step or Dance."

"I hate Step."

"I know," said Amy.

When Jill had gone, Amy sat, remembering her lithe little girl in her tutu, dancing a sugarplum fairy in *The Nutcracker*. How she had loved it. When she'd started taking toe, Amy would often see after class that Jill's little feet were bloody and the wads of lamb's wool packed into the hard toes of her shoes were soaked red. Jill never minded. Her teachers had believed she could dance for Peter Martins. Amy wondered now if Jill the elephant even remembered having once been a hummingbird.

Stretch class was very soothing, except that the poor giant woman called Carter, who hadn't brought the right things and was trying to work out in her tennis clothes, split the center seam of her shorts open. The whole class lay on their backs with their feet in the air as New Age music twanged and tinkled, and pretty little Abby cried out instructions with merry zeal.

"Now drop those feet out wide apart, as w-i-i-i-de as you can, and str-e-e-e-tch those inner thighs . . ." and the whole class heard the unmistakable rip. Carter began to laugh helplessly.

"Hold your tuck, ladies, and stretch—hold that tuck . . ." cried Abby as she sprang upright like a cat and tripped to Carter's side. "Are you all right?"

"Oh, perfect," Carter said. "This is my idea of a vacation," and her laughter became uncontrollable. It proved contagious, and all over the room, poses collapsed as glamour girls, rich wives, doctors, lawyers, and captains of industry in their violet and navy sweat suits flopped over giggling.

Amy, prone on the exercise carpet, said to Carter, "You know, my daughter has some sweats that would fit you."

Carter, valiantly stifling her snorts of laughter, rolled over and looked at Amy. She recognized the New York Blonde from last night, the mother-daughter team at the first table. The rest of the class was being exhorted to scissor its legs in the air at a rapid beat, impossibly fast, it would have seemed, except that Abby was doing it with no trouble, and calling instructions at the same time.

"They've sent the shopping fairy to the mall for me," said Carter.

"I'm sure, but in the meantime. They'll be too short, but . . . "

"Well, thanks," said Carter, accepting. She and Amy scrambled to their feet and crept out of the class.

Outside, the morning was growing warm. As they hurried along, Carter still couldn't completely stifle the odd giggle.

"Please excuse me," she said. "I seem to be hysterical. I think it might be nicotine deprivation."

"Makes sense to me," said Amy. "When I quit smoking, I had the most lurid erotic fantasies for about two weeks. It was definitely an altered state."

"That hasn't happened to me yet," said Carter, and she began to laugh again. "Oh god . . . "

Amy began to giggle too. "Yes, this would not be the ideal spot; you don't want to start waylaying the gardeners. Fortunately, when it happened to me, my husband was at home and I managed to channel it into legal behavior."

"Did he know why he got lucky?"

"Heavens, no, he hadn't even noticed the cigarettes were gone. Thank god. Meanwhile I dreamed about the punk who fixes our Volvo . . . "

Carter laughed.

"Here, this is Jill's room. *Is* this it? B12, yes, like the vitamin, we don't want to be found stealing someone *else's* clothes." Amy pushed the door to Jill's room open and they went in.

"Pardon the fact that we hang all our clothes on the floor," she said. "I assume you know that's correct procedure for Generation X. Or Y, or whatever Jill is. Do you have children?"

"No," said Carter. The room had not yet been seen to by the maid, and there were towels and panty hose and shoes strewn around wherever Jill had finished with them.

Amy was rummaging in Jill's suitcase, still full on the luggage rack. She produced a quite enormous pair of green sweatpants and handed them to Carter. Carter held them against herself. Both could see that they were wide enough, but would barely reach below the knees.

"Wait, wait," said Amy. "She has half the Capezio store in here . . ." She produced two sets of leg warmers which, when worn one above the other, would fill in the gap between the ankles of the sweatpants and the ankles of Carter. Amy explained the theory and practice of this, and Carter obediently took off her torn shorts and donned Jill's clothes.

"I think this is rather fetching," she said, surveying herself in the mirror. "Thank you."

"You're quite welcome."

"I think we've managed to miss the rest of stretch class. What are you doing next?"

"I haven't the faintest idea," said Carter. "What is 'Step'?"

"It's like running up and down stairs waving your arms around."

The two were out in the sunshine again, on the path to the exercise studios.

"That sounds horrible. What's the other one?"

"Dancercise. Better music, harder routines."

Carter decided to start with dance, in honor of her unaccustomed leg warmers. "At the end of the week I look like Margot Fonteyn, right?"

"Exactly," said Amy.

Jill was already in the dance classroom when Carter came in.

"If you think these clothes look familiar," she said to Jill, "there's a reason."

Before Jill could answer, Babette, a young woman with a blond ponytail and a bare midriff, pranced in and socked her cassette into the tape machine. "All right, ladies—everyone to the barre, please! We're going to warm up!" In a moment twelve ladies were doing deep-knee bends while trying to follow Babette's balletic arms. Only Jill could do it. Jill could move as if her joints were made of liquid.

Carter was fascinated watching her. As the music got faster, she began to pant and blow. Other ladies were moving their feet while their arms dangled. But Jill seemed to inhale the music through her ears and let it out through her limbs. Babette clapped her hands and shouted, "Whooo!" Behind her, eleven ladies turned red in the face, lost track of the sequence of steps, and reached for towels to blot sweat from their eyes. Jill could move as fast as Babette, and if it hadn't been for her great size, Carter could see you'd have given her points past Babette for grace. This girl was a dancer.

Carter liked the Fred Astaire music best. She dipped and swayed and twirled around the room, quite forgetting, herself, that she didn't exactly embody America's idea of feminine beauty. A little woman in the back row whose tag said RUSTY HAINES changed direction at the wrong moment, causing an entire line of exercisers to pile up in the corner. But Jill, in front, missed the mess and kept dancing. She whirled, she cocked her head, she clicked her fingers off the beat as Babette did.

Babette got a round of applause at the end of the class. She turned and applauded Jill, and so did the rest. Jill blushed, but her smile was radiant.

At eleven, there was a break in the schedule, and everyone gathered outside at the pool. Trays of raw vegetables and fruit had been brought, and cups of hot, spicy, vegetable broth that was said to be rich in potassium, whatever good that was. Carter found Amy and Jill at a shaded table eating carrot sticks.

"May I join you?"

"Please."

"Where have you been this hour?" she asked them.

"I took another Dance," said Jill.

"I've been at Body Shaping," said Amy. "Can't you tell?"

"I did think there was something about you," said Carter.

"I want to hear about T'ai Chi," Amy said to Jill.

"Laurie and I were wave and kelp."

"The lady from the hot tub?"

Jill nodded. "You choose a partner, and one of you is kelp, and the other moves around you sort of bumping or pushing against your shoulder, or your hip, or behind your knee. Like the action of water, making the kelp bend and sway. Then you trade."

"Is this one of those horrible New Age things where you have to fall backward into someone's arms?" Carter asked.

"No, wait. When you're kelp, you keep your eyes closed, because kelp can't see, and you have to wait for the water to move you. What Laurie said is, you realize that the current can move you but after it moves on, you go back to standing. You bend with it, but you never break. You're never defeated. Want me to show you?" Neither Carter nor Amy made any move to get up.

"And who was it, who was your partner?"

"You know—the one from the Japanese bath. The one from Idaho."

"Do you know her?" Amy asked Carter. "The tall woman, with the eyes?"

"She's down at the end of the pool, under the clock," said Jill, and Carter looked and saw that it was the woman who had interested her, last night and this morning.

"I've been thinking she looked familiar."

"We met her in the hot tub. There was a Governor Knox in Idaho when I was growing up. Hunt Knox. I think she must be a daughter."

Carter slapped the table lightly and leaned back in her chair.

"You do know her?" Amy asked.

"Now I do. She's Laura Lopez. She was married to Roberto Lopez."

Amy said, "Oh god. Poor woman—no wonder she looks so sad." She looked down the long pool toward Laurie, who was, as a matter of fact, smiling at something Rusty Haines was saying to her.

"Who's Roberto Lopez?" asked Jill.

"Oh, honey—you know. He was that famous tennis star, he's Mexican. I think he went into politics. He used to be on television, he had that fabulous smile? He advertised some soft drink. He was killed in a plane crash."

"About six months ago," Carter said.

Jill, saddened, turned to look at Laurie.

"And they had a lot of children . . . "

"Five," said Carter. She remembered all about it now.

Carter Bond and Rae Strouse found seats together at Monday lunch. The ladies were served outside at big shaded tables, in a walled garden bright with annuals. Only The Movie Star and her sidekick stayed behind in their chaise longues by the pool and had their lunch brought to them on trays.

The flower beds in the walled garden were perfectly clean of weeds, tidy and well watered, and yet, as Rae remarked, you never saw anyone working in them, as if the sight of actual manual labor being performed outside the window might compromise your pleasure in hopping and sweating. But when did they do the work? At night?

Rusty Haines joined Carter and Rae, along with her daughter Carol. Carter had liked Rusty enormously from the moment she began turning the wrong way more than Carter in dance class. They had spent an hour learning the weight machines in the gym together, and Carter now knew that Rusty was a third-grade teacher, retired, and the reason she wore that dashing head scarf was that she was recovering from brain surgery. The daughter, Carol, was a Beverly Hills attorney. She wore a large diamond on her right hand, but there was never mention of a husband. She must be a hell of an attorney, Carter thought, to be able to take such expensive care of her mother.

Carol had a blissful expression on her face and some sort of oil in her hair. She sat chewing happily on a salad.

"What have you been up to this morning?" Rae asked her.

"I just had a face treatment," she said and sighed.

"Who do you have?"

"Inga."

"She's wonderful, I had her last year."

"Does anyone have Solange?" Carol asked.

"I do," said Rusty.

"My massage woman told me Solange reads palms, but she's not supposed to let anybody know."

"Why not?"

"I don't know. But I'd love to have my palm read!" said Carol.

"I don't think I would," said Carter.

"They never tell you stuff you shouldn't know." Carol had made a specialty of psychics. In her time she had had her tarot cards read, had a Chinese guru in Marin throw her I Ching, had her astrological chart done annually, and spent a good deal of money at a numerologist's.

"Which is best?" Rae asked.

"I don't think it matters, it's about talent." Carol uncrossed her endless legs and turned her chair so she faced the sun.

"And what have you learned?" asked Carter. She had dealt with a lot of psychics, almost all of them bunco artists. But there were bunco doctors and lawyers too, after all. That didn't prove there weren't any real ones . . . suddenly she could picture herself uttering such a sentence to DeeAnne. DeeAnne, sleek and glossy, with her long purple nails, would rock back in her orthopedic chair and hoot, "*What* did they put in the water out there?"

"No, seriously," Carol was saying, "there's a center of spiritual energy, just about thirty miles from here. There are only seven in the world. The Indians knew all about them. So did the Egyptians, there's one where they built the pyramids. I'm going to ask her to do a private reading for me."

"Honey," said Rusty, "you need some sunblock."

"What's next?" Carter asked the group.

"I've got my massage," Rae announced with satisfaction.

Carol consulted the schedule pinned to her bag.

"I've got herbal wrap," she said.

"So do I," said Carter. "What the hell is it?"

"Follow me," said Carol. She started off to the bathhouse, and Carter lumbered after her.

They left their bags and all their clothes in lockers. An attendant gave them each a heated robe. In the herbal room, two more attendants waited. A body was lying on a treatment table, wrapped up so that only its nose was showing. Carter had seen things like this at the morgue.

The attendant signaled to Carter to hand over her robe. She was beginning to get used to being naked in front of strangers, although she had spent her whole high school career trying to sneak out after basketball without taking a shower because she hated how the pretty little ones with their perky breasts pranced in and out of the sprays of water, while great, ungainly Carter stood around feeling like a horse.

She lay on her back on the cot and the attendant folded around her the fleecy flannel sheet on which she was lying. Steaming-hot towels were brought and wrapped around her, then a blanket put over it all.

"Claustrophobic?" whispered the attendant. Carter shook her head no. Later Carol explained that some people fear they are being embalmed, and start screaming.

Carter, however, loved the feeling of being cocooned. The towels smelled of spices, and she thought of mysterious herbs and occult arts, and began to picture herself as Nefertiti. The attendants were her adepts, mysterious healers privy to ancient lore. Her mind slipped its moorings and she had a vision of herself as a slug in a chrysalis, who when unwrapped would have turned to a shimmering thing of beauty. She pictured the sprite on the rock on the soda label, the White Rock girl. She imagined she would step lightly from this shroud, resembling Farrah Fawcett. From there she drifted to a happy thought of Jerry, her ex-husband, asking her to dance. And then, for the next half hour, she slept.

At the Happy Hour, Rae and Carter found each other.

"How are you holding up?" Rae asked.

"I haven't had a cigarette in twenty-nine hours, and I still haven't killed anybody."

"Very good! I see they got you some clothes." Carter was now wearing a navy blue sweat suit of her own, and a new pair of aerobic shoes.

"Yes, but Jill let me keep a pair of her leg warmers."

Carter exhibited her ankles.

"Love the color," said Rae. Jill appeared, excited about her yoga class. She was sure that by the end of the week she would be able to stand on her head. She and Carter made for the hors d'oeuvre tray, where they were allowed one small vegetable dumpling apiece, dipped in some sort of herb chutney.

"We made it through a day. How do you feel?" Carter asked.

"Better," said Jill.

"Me too," said Carter.

The gong sounded. Dressed in a skintight red-knit pantsuit, the night's Fitness Professional said, "Good evening, ladies. I'm Terri, I'm your hostess tonight . . . "

They moved into the dining room, chattering. Jill and Carter found seats together. Carter was pleased when Laurie chose a seat at the end of their table. Tonight they were even joined by The Movie Star's sidekick. She didn't say much. Somebody said she was an agent.

Over the salad they talked of food. A tiny, trim woman whom Jill had met in T'ai Chi announced that she was one of The Cloister's success stories.

"I'm in the book," she said.

"What does that mean?"

"It means I lost more than fifty pounds and kept it off. They keep a book." Jill and Carter stared. Fifty pounds? She must have been wider than she was tall. Now the Success Story knew how the spa chef made everything. The secret of the oil-less dressings, the way to make fat-free chocolate mousse.

Over the salmon the talk turned to politics. This was election week. There was a woman at the next table, someone reported, who was chief administrative officer for the mayor of New York. There was another whose brother was running to fill a congressional seat. The incumbent had gone to prison but was campaigning from his cell.

"Wouldn't you want to be with your family on election night?" Jill asked.

"She gets too nervous," said someone who knew her. "She'll watch it on television."

"Can we watch the returns at Saguaro?"

"Yes, but you have to remember, you're not at home. You're surrounded by Republicans," said a thin dark woman.

"What a relief; I was afraid I was surrounded by Democrats," said another.

"Speaking of television, did everyone see the news tonight?"

"No, what's happened?" voices chorused.

"One of those commuter planes crashed in Kansas."

"How terrible!"

"Do they know why?"

"Were many people hurt?"

"Everyone. Killed. It crashed in a rainstorm, halfway to Lawrence. It just barely missed someone's barn, and it killed a horse."

"Those things scare me to death," the Success Story said.

"I used to have to take those planes all the time," said a small woman who hadn't said anything before.

"Did you? Why?"

"I inherited an oil company, and I had to get to my wells."

It was at around this point in dinner that Laurie Lopez got up quietly and left the room.

*T*uesday morning Laurie was standing by herself in Saguaro, looking hollow-eyed in the early light. She held a cup of something hot, and seemed not to hear the burble of conversation around her. Amy and Jill were talking about the Five-Mile Mountain Hike.

Carter arrived bleary-eyed and made for the coffee.

"Did you sleep?" asked Annette, the woman from dinner with the oil wells.

"Like a rock," said Carter.

After stretching, Carter and Annette struck out together and were joined by the one whose brother was running for Congress. Her name was Courtney, and she could be heard reporting that her mother had ordered her to stay out of the way since the day she'd fainted during a family photo op. "I get *ter*rible stage fright," she cried, apparently rather proud. This was a frailty of long standing. She had thrown up in kindergarten at the Mothers' Coffee while portraying a fringed gentian.

Lagging behind them, Rae walked silently, close to Laurie. Laurie looked ineffably sad, as if everything in the world reminded her of things she couldn't bear.

"I don't suppose it would help if I gave you a hug, would it?" Rae said.

Laurie shook her head and marched on, but Rae soon saw that she was crying. They were climbing toward a ridge through a grove of lemon trees but below them they could see for miles along the dry valley floor. The earth under their feet was baked hard, and hikers could be thrown off stride by pebbles and hard balls of clay earth that rolled beneath their feet like marbles.

Rae handed Laurie a pack of tissues she carried in her waist pack.

"I'm sorry. I guess I miss my mother." Laurie blew her nose. She was trying to make a joke, but her voice was pinched and high, as if her normal range of emotions had been crushed and squeezed into this weak treble register.

"I've got more tissues."

"Thanks, I think I'm okay." She sniffled, trying to turn to something light. "What else do you have in there?"

"Well, let's see," said Rae, and began to root around. "A needle and thread, cough drops . . . some Bufferin . . . here's a bar of soap from the Santa Barbara Biltmore. A little Stolichnaya in case of snakebite . . ." She held up a tiny airline bottle of vodka. Laurie smiled.

"I should just stay in my room till I get over this," Laurie said.

"No, I don't think so," said Rae. "It's always better to see the sky."

They climbed on toward the ridge for a minute or two.

"I lost my husband," Laurie said.

"I know how you feel."

"Do you?"

"Yes. I lost mine too, when I was about your age."

Laurie looked at her quickly.

"It was a long time ago, but you never forget," said Rae.

"No. People say I will, that it will fade."

"Oh, bull," said Rae.

"How did you . . . was your husband sick?"

"No, car crash. It was late at night, and the roads were wet. Somehow the car flipped over. There were no seat belts then, of course. . . . It was hot. The windows were open. His head was cut off."

Laurie winced. After a while she said, "Roberto was in a plane. The engine failed."

"I had two small children," said Rae.

Laurie nodded. "I have children."

"Young ones?"

Laurie nodded again.

"How many?"

"Five," Laurie said in the high voice that wasn't hers.

"Good heavens! No wonder you're worn out!"

"It's not—I have a lot of help."

"I'm glad to hear it, but still . . . "

"I'm very lucky," Laurie said. "My father, and my brother and sister-in-law—we all live close together."

"And cousins?"

Laurie nodded.

"That was always a dream of mine, a big family of kids all tumbling up together. How many cousins? How old?"

They were on the ridge. They stopped to appreciate the scene spread below them. Then Laurie turned toward the path where Carter and her companions were climbing, and slowly started to walk again. Rae moved along with her.

"Mine are . . . seventeen, that's Carlos, then Anna, she's fifteen, then Cara, she's thirteen, and the twins are ten. They have four cousins, three girls and a boy."

"And you're in the same building, or . . . ? On the same block?"

"We live on a ranch. The houses aren't so close in distance, but the kids can ride their bikes or ride horses."

"It sounds like paradise. Where is this?"

"Hailey, Idaho. Near Ketchum."

"I know Ketchum. My son, Walter, has a house there."

"Does he?" Laurie was breathing more normally and seemed almost completely over her crying spell. "We know a lot of the Sun Valley people—what's his name?"

"Walter Keely."

Laurie stopped and put a hand on Rae's arm. She smiled a real, if wan, smile.

"Walter Keely? The campaign guy? You're Walter Keely's mother?"

"Well, yes, I am," said Rae proudly. "I hope you haven't heard anything terrible about him because it's probably all true."

"No, it's—he was a friend of my husband's. They played golf together . . . "

"It's a *won*derful world," Rae cried, and Laurie took note that she meant it deeply.

"Maybe Walter mentioned my husband to you," Laurie said. Here was another dangerous moment, but after a pause, she got through it very steadily, like a skater after a fall, hitting a triple axel. "He was Roberto Lopez, the tennis player."

"That beautiful man!" said Rae. "That smile!"

Laurie smiled herself, and nodded. "Yes. The billion-watt smile. He was really like that too."

"That commercial where he jumps over the tennis net . . ." Rae didn't have to finish the sentence.

"My son Carlos looks just like him."

"And tell me about the other four," Rae said. With something like real savor, Laurie described each one. They had reached the overlook where the group stopped for water. Laurie and Rae were aware that the others had been waiting; the group shepherd was not allowed to lose any of the guests on the mountain. Someone gave them each a section of orange, and with the rest of the group, they moved off again briskly.

"Did you ever remarry?" Laurie asked Rae.

"Oh yes," she said, "after Walter and Harriet were grown. I met Albie on a cruise. I was working and I had a strict rule about socializing with the guests. But after we docked in San Francisco, he started courting me. We've been married for twenty-three years, and they've been very, very happy ones."

"You were working? On a cruise ship?" Laurie didn't exactly know how to ask the next question. Rae couldn't have been the captain. . . .

"I was the dance instructor. My partner and I taught ballroom, and did exhibition dancing in the evenings."

"Like Ginger Rogers?"

"*Exactly* like Ginger Rogers. We taught the samba, that was big." Rae performed a few steps on the rocky path, clicking her fingers as if she had castanets.

"The samba, the meringue, the tango, the Charleston . . . the twist . . . I do them all, divinely. My one regret is retiring before the lambada."

Laurie laughed. "And your husband—is he a dancer?"

"He's a marvelous dancer. After his first wife died, he went on this cruise, and . . . voilà!"

"That's very romantic," Laurie said.

"It was *very* romantic. He's a very courtly man, Albie is. There aren't many like him."

"And how do Albie and Walter get along?"

"Famously. You can understand—Walter barely remembers his real father."

"Does Albie have children?"

"Two. But he always wanted a houseful, and he treats mine as if they were his own."

"He sounds wonderful," said Laurie, meaning it.

"Yes. He really is."

They had arrived back at Saguaro, where earlier arrivals were drinking lemon water and watching the television news. The polls were open in the east, and there was a lot of chatter about pollsters and Contracts with America and Report Cards on Congress and what would it all mean. Courtney and some allies sat waiting for mention of her brother's race. There was a satisfying cry when the camera showed a picture of the brother entering the polling booth.

"Oh look," Courtney screamed, "he has the dog with him!" You could see the candidate's feet beneath the curtain, and beside the feet a little dachshund gazed soulfully at the camera. Then the coverage switched to another state, and someone switched off the set.

Outside the room, unaware of the television, Laurie and Rae stood close together.

"Thank you," Laurie said. "I feel better."

"I'm glad," said Rae. She looked at the younger woman a long moment. "You're going to be fine," she added.

"I know."

"Do you?"

Laurie looked at her. "No—no. Am I really?"

"Yes, you are. Not as soon as you want to be. But you're not going to cry till you blow away, if that's what you're afraid of."

Laurie nodded. That was what she was afraid of.

Rae put a hand on her arm, and then went off toward her room, and her breakfast.

Tuesday lunch was a raucous affair served poolside, with a fashion show. A fancy shop in Santa Fe had sent the latest prêt-à-porter, plus handmade belts and scarves and jewelry from local artisans. The clothes were modeled by the Fitness Professionals, and there was lots of teasing and applause for favorite instructors. The clothes were all available for sale in the spa boutique.

In the break between afternoon classes, when she and Rae Strouse stopped in to check out a hand-dyed silk caftan they had rather fancied, Carter Bond was astonished to learn that about $23,000 worth of clothes had already been bought by a salty little barrel-shaped woman named Bonnie Gray. Carter had followed her around the machine circuit in weight training class that morning.

"Yes, she does that every year," remarked the woman who ran the shop. "She made a lot of money raising Angora goats in the Rockies."

"But doesn't she *live* in the Rockies? On a ranch?" Carter asked. Bonnie had given her the impression that she spent her life in overalls, shoveling goat dung.

"Yes, I think she does."

"Then, where does she wear the clothes?"

"*¿Quién sabe?* Maybe she dresses for dinner." Carter and Rae looked at each other.

"I *love* it," said Carter, who was used to conspicuous consumption in capital letters. Your average Beverly Hills matrons were not shy about announcing the size of their bank accounts by every kind of

semaphore known to woman, from haircut to car model. Here was little Bonnie, without a scrap of makeup or an ounce of pretension, with
fingernails ragged from work, going home with a fortune in evening
clothes to impress no one. "This place is like Oz. Everyone looks like a
normal human, but then they turn out to have a pocketful of magic
pebbles, or keys to a kingdom."

"There's a reason I've been here twenty-two times," said Rae.

"I *guess*."

"I think we may need these sweaters," Rae said, descending on a
rack of colorful clothes. For an old bag, Carter noticed, Rae certainly
didn't go in for Old Bag accoutrements. Rae seized a long scarlet
jacket that appeared to have been knitted of silk ribbons. She handed
it to Carter.

"No, you put it on, I can't wear red," said Carter.

"Don't be silly. Everyone can wear red."

Carter put it on and went to the mirror. She looked at herself as if
she'd never seen this image before. She looked fabulous.

"I think it's particularly good with the sweatpants," she said.

"Got your name on it, honey. I knew it."

"Uh-oh, a bad thing just happened."

"What?"

"I accidentally looked at the price."

Rae put on a jacket made of some kind of Japanese-looking silk.

"I love that stuff, what is that?" Carter asked her.

"Ikat, it's called. It's my favorite thing. Here, this is going to go
nicely with your sweater. "

She took a necklace made of large black beads cut from stone and
bone, and dropped it over Carter's head. "God wants you to wear this,
that's why She made you tall."

Carter went back to the mirror. She looked like a woman with
style instead of the Carter she had fashioned in her adult life, the one
who would never shame herself by trying to be feminine and looking
like a hippo in a tea dress, but who did instead look rather like a cop in
drag.

"Where would I ever wear this?"

"Who cares? You could dress for dinner, like Bonnie."

"I eat Ritz crackers and cream cheese at the kitchen sink for dinner," said Carter. She took off the scarlet sweater and put it back on the hanger. The necklace did not look as good against her sweatshirt.

They sallied out again and back to Saguaro; it was time for juice break. When they got there, they found the group crackling with excitement.

"What's up? What's going on?" Rae cried. If something new was afoot, she wanted to be in on it.

"We took the self-defense class," said Carol Haines. "It was *fabulous*. You've got to do it."

"I was going to Dance-a-thon," said Rae.

"So was I," said Jill, joining the group. She had a glassful of watermelon chunks in one hand and a bottle of Evian in the other.

Every afternoon there were special offerings, classes designed to teach new skills or work different muscles and, most of all, to stop the boredom induced by pop music and starvation. Dance-a-thon was a goofy class taught by a team of tappers and rappers from L.A. Rae took it every chance she got. She loved new dances.

"No, I'm not kidding, you have to do Self-Defense," Carol insisted with the zeal of the convert. "She's a terrific teacher. I've taken Self-Defense, believe me, but this you can use no matter how weak you are . . . "

"Well, that sounds right for me," said Rae.

"Really," said Carol. "I'm going to take it again."

"I think I'm going to Dance-a-thon," said Jill.

"Jilly," said Carol, "you are taking this class if I have to carry you. You young girls, you think nothing can ever hurt you, but we know! Listen to your aunties."

Rae and Carter looked at each other and shrugged; why not?

"Are you doing it?" said Jill, seeming suddenly timid.

"Sure, let's do it," said Rae.

"But isn't Dance-a-thon only this once?"

"I'll dance with you later," said Rae. "Follow me." And she started a merengue step around the pavilion, with Jill following her. Rae pranced over and grabbed a cup of juice and then she and Jill danced out the door and down to the studio where the self-defense class was being held.

The class was led by a small, exotic woman who looked half black, half Asian. In any category she was extraordinarily handsome. She wore loose white pajamas and a black belt. So much was not surprising; what was was the presence of three men dressed like people you wouldn't want to find beside your car in a dark alley. One was large and Latino, wearing blue jeans and a windbreaker. One was white, with bare arms showing a pair of dice tattooed on his bicep. One was either Asian or Indian, with a long ponytail down his back. He looked as if he could easily tear your head off with his bare hands.

The ladies in their sweatpants and leotards sat on the floor to listen.

"My name is Kim," said the instructor. "I know we can't cover much today, but we have enough time to learn one important thing. How many of you have taken Self-Defense before?"

Carol, Carter, and two others raised their hands.

"That's good, that's very good. The thing that is different about this class, what I want to teach you, is something women need to learn that men don't. We were brought up to be good, to be nice, okay? We were brought up to protect puppies and children, we didn't play with guns. When you're faced with someone who wants to hurt you, you have to be ready to hurt him back. It doesn't matter how strong you are, it doesn't matter how big you are, it matters that you want to live and you're ready to fight for that. The man who attacks you, he doesn't expect that. He doesn't expect you at all, he isn't thinking about you, he's thinking about what he wants.

"What I am going to teach you is not to think about *him*. Think about what *you* want. What do you want? You want to live. And you want to not be hurt. To do that, you have to be able to hurt somebody else, okay? That's not easy for us. That's not easy for women. But we *can* learn, okay?"

Jill was looking out the window, toward the pool. "I wonder where my mother is . . ." she whispered to Rae.

"She'd like to take this, wouldn't she?" Rae whispered back. "I think she's in Manicure."

The men were coming forward.

"That's why I have brought my friends with me. This is Lenny, this is Tom, and this is Johnny, my brother." The Indian. "They are all black belts. They all believe that women should not have to be afraid of men, and they have volunteered to be here to help you learn to fight back the only way you really can. Now I'm going to show you what to do if someone comes up behind you and grabs you. Tom."

Kim turned her back to the men, and Tom, the very large Latino, came up behind her and hooked a huge arm around her throat. There was a blur of motion, and in the next second, Tom was on his back on the floor receiving a mock kick in the groin. The women watching gasped, then clapped. Tom got up.

"You think you can't do that?" Kim asked them. "Well, maybe you can't, but that doesn't mean you can't do anything. We're going to go through it again, and break down what to do, and when we are all done, you will each get a certificate of graduation . . . "

"I think if I'm attacked I'll just hold up my certificate," Rae said.

"Okay, watch," said Kim. She turned her back to the men, and Tom again locked his elbow under her chin. Kim said, "First! Turn your head to the side," she demonstrated, "and breathe! You can't breathe with his arm straight on your windpipe, but you can if you turn. Next: hit him where his muscles are tensed." With a knuckle sticking out of her fist, like a child giving noogies, she drove her hand into Tom's clenched thigh. He gave an inadvertent yell, and changed his grip.

"Or *here*," Kim said as she drove her knuckle into the back of his hand where it gripped her shoulder. He let go of her and the ladies involuntarily gasped. "Hurts," said Kim. "Try it on yourself. Now the minute you have the advantage, *follow* it. Kick with your instep, or the ball of your foot, so you don't break your toes. Try for the groin. He'll protect his business but try to come up between his legs and hit behind the balls. That hurts more anyway. Or get your fingers into his eyes. Or bash his nose with the side of your head. Use your neck to punch with.

"Now, ladies, your turn." The three men chose three ladies: Rae, Rusty, and Bonnie Gray. The women allowed themselves to be grabbed from behind, and then they fought back.

"Oh, ladies, ladies, ladies! Such ladies! You are being much too nice! You have to make them understand you want to *live*. Here, I'll show you what. Hit your man in the stomach as hard as you can, and as you do it, yell HA!"

"Ha!" Rae and Bonnie gave the men little punches and squeaked. Rusty couldn't do it at all. On her third try, with Kim urging her on, she managed to land the punch but her eyes were full of tears. "See?" said Kim. "See how hard it is? There is the enemy. The enemy is the good girl inside you. He's trained, you can't hurt him. Now let's go, *hit him*!" Rusty clenched her teeth and rammed a noogie fist into Tom's belly. He never blinked.

"You didn't yell," Kim said.

Rusty roared, "HA!"

"Okay, now what do we do if we're lying down and we're attacked? Say you're in bed, asleep, and the guy comes in the window? You're helpless, right?"

She lay down on her back. Johnny, her Indian brother, was suddenly on top of her, and he covered her so that she looked half his size. And in another moment he was in a ball, protecting the family jewels. Once again, the ladies applauded in amazement.

"Okay, slow motion." They resumed the position. "He's got my hands pinned, right? And he's heavier and stronger than me. Most women don't have much upper-body strength. But you have legs, right?"

She pulled her feet in, bending her knees, and then with a thrust of the pelvis, toppled him off her. "And then you pursue your advantage, ladies! The minute you get a space, you attack! Now let's show you how easy it is: you, you, and you, please." She indicated Jill, Carol, and Glenna. Carol stepped right up. Glenna followed, half shy. Jill stayed where she was.

"I really think I better watch . . . "

"You'll be fine, I promise," said Kim. "You can do it." And then loudly, to the whole room, as she pulled Jill to her feet and led her forward, "The only way you will really believe you can do it is to *do* it. Feel your muscles do it, and if you're ever in that position for real, your *muscles* will remember!"

Glenna was in position, and Tom was on top of her. Johnny took Carol, and Lenny positioned himself over Jill. Carol gave a yell, and Tom went sprawling. Glenna was struggling to get her knees up. Carol, whose voice had an adenoidal quality, was saying insistently to Kim, "But, could I do it again, because I don't understand how I'm going to follow up if I'm under the covers."

Suddenly Carter moved across the room like a tiger leaping, hauled Lenny off Jill and threw him across the room. Jill's eyes were wide and staring, completely hysterical. She was trying to scream, but no sound was coming out. She was shaking her head; in fact, her whole body was shaking, but she couldn't make a sound. The look on her face expressed such agonized terror that it could stop hearts.

"Jesus . . ." somebody said. Rae was out the door, running to find Amy as other voices cried, "Get Sandra! Get her mother!"

Somebody tried to give her water to drink, but she knocked it away. Never saw what it was, Carter thought, just thought it was a weapon. Carter held her and said over and over, "You're safe, you're safe . . ." The class, stricken, stood in a ring and stared until Kim, like the wave brushing kelp, wordlessly turned them away to give Jill some privacy.

Amy ran in, looking white. Rae was with her. Amy had one foot bare and the other, with shell-pink toenails, in a brown paper toeless slipper.

"Oh god, baby . . ." Her eyes met Carter's. Jill was hyperventilating, and both women knew if she didn't stop it, she would soon lose consciousness. Carter was wondering whether or not she was strong enough to carry Jill. She decided she was.

"Can you help me? Get her to my room?" Amy said low, to Carter. Carter nodded. "Come on, baby. Come on, baby girl, it's all right now. I'm here." Jill's eyes seemed to focus a little; she seemed to understand at least that this was her mother. Carter helped her to her feet. "Come on, baby," said Amy, crooning, "you can walk. Let's go." And she could walk. With their arms around her, she was taken out of the room, leaving rows of stunned, frightened faces.

"I have some Valium," said Amy. They put Jill on her mother's bed and Carter pulled a blanket over her as Amy went for her medicine bag. She was back with a pill bottle and a glass of water, and she whispered to Jill, who was whimpering and shivering. Amy slipped the tiny tablet between her lips and whispered, "Swallow." When Jill didn't, her mother stroked her throat the way you do when giving a pill to an animal, and looked at Carter in relief when she felt the throat muscles respond. She held the water to Jill's lips and she took a little.

"Jesus, I wish I had some whiskey," said Carter.

Amy nodded. "For *us*," she said. Amy held her daughter's hand and stroked her hair, and Carter sat on the other side of the bed beside her. After long minutes, during which Amy crooned and sang to Jill, they began to see the rigid muscles soften. She moved her eyes, as if she were seeing out of them. She looked at her mother.

"Mister Lister sassed his sister, married his wife 'cause he couldn't resist her," Amy whispered, barely knowing what she said, but trying to pour Jill's childhood over her head and keep her safe in it forever, although it was too late. Jill made an effort to smile.

"What happened?" Carter asked. "Though I think I can guess."

"She was raped when she was thirteen."

Carter looked at Jill. The beautiful face, bloated and terrified. Lovely hazel eyes, the long lashes.

"In Central Park," Amy said. "In broad daylight, on a sunny Sunday afternoon. She'd gotten a new bike for her birthday. She was riding over to Lincoln Center to a rehearsal. Two kids stopped her. . . . One wanted the bike, and she gave it to him. The other one . . ." She looked at Jill, who was calmer now, holding her mother's hand.

"We know he hurt her and we know he raped her, but we don't really know how, or what it was like; she can't remember. A jogger found her."

Carter took a deep breath. She was used to stories of beastly behavior, but this struck to her core.

"You're looking more like yourself, baby girl. Do you feel better?" Jill nodded. Her mother stroked her hair, then held her wrist and took her pulse. She went on stroking her arms and hair in a soothing way, and talking softly to Carter.

"She had a terrible time. I kept her home from school a whole year. The nightmares were awful. She couldn't be alone. You can't imagine, if you haven't been through it."

"Poor kid. Poor, poor little kid," Carter whispered. "And she still has no memory of . . . ?"

Amy shook her head. "In dreams, but of course . . . they're dreams."

"So, the guys just got away with it?"

"Apparently." Amy took Jill's pulse again. Her color was almost back to normal, and she indicated to Carter that the pulse was too.

"We going to live, kiddo?"

Jill nodded.

"What shall we do now? Do you want to sleep, do you think?"

Jill shook her head.

"Would you like me to read to you?"

Jill smiled and nodded.

"Are you reading something you'd like to hear?"

Jill shook her head. Carter said, "Why don't you go find a book in the faculty lounge, you know what I mean, and I'll stay with her."

Amy went off to the staff library, and Carter got up and turned on some lights in the room. It was growing dark outside.

"Thank you for saving me," Jill said. She seemed to be forcing herself to use her voice, to be sure she still could.

"You're welcome. Now that I think about it, I hope I didn't hurt that kid. I tossed him pretty hard."

"I'm sorry I freaked."

"Don't ever apologize because something was done to you."

"It's still embarrassing."

"He was lucky. You might have torn that little guy limb from limb. Imagine explaining that to the self-defense girl. 'Yo, excuse me, I may have killed your friend' . . . you're standing there beside this steaming heap of bloody scraps."

Jill smiled. "I try to feel angry. My shrink keeps telling me I should scream and howl. She keeps handing me the pillow from her couch, hoping I'll tear it open . . . "

"I've never been to a shrink," said Carter. "I'm the only person left in L.A. who hasn't. Do you like yours?"

Jill shrugged.

"Not so much, huh?"

"Don't tell Mom. Mom thinks she's fab-o."

"And what do you think?"

"She doesn't see that I'm different from her. It's like there's one right answer and I'm not getting it. How come there can't be other right answers?"

"Don't ask me. I'm leading the last unexamined life."

"The only answer is, I have to get mad. What if I can't? What if I can't, ever? I'll always be a great, fat freak? It's not like it's a choice you make. You don't say, like, should I get an Uzi and blow away some guy in the park? No, I think I'll eat a gallon of Rocky Road instead."

When Amy came in, Carter looked at her with new admiration. Five long years of picking up the pieces. Five years of giving up your own life, five years of never blaming the victim. Even when she's a teenage pain in the ass.

"I scored," Amy said. "I got a P. G. Wodehouse. And I stopped in the office and asked them to bring our dinner here. Do you want to stay, Carter?"

"Maybe I'll come back after dinner in my pj's."

"Please do."

Across the courtyard they heard the gong sound. Dinnertime.

"But I was kind of looking forward to the evening program. We're making prayer arrows," she added, and Jill laughed, a real, full-throated laugh.

*a*s Jill sat at breakfast the next morning, someone tapped on the door.

"Come in," Jill called. Sandra from the exercise office opened the door.

"Good morning. How are you?" she asked.

"I'm fine, thank you."

"Are you really?"

"Yes. My mom gave me a sleeping pill after dinner. She used to be a nurse."

"That's lucky."

Jill agreed.

Sandra said, "Kim was very upset about what happened. We all are."

"It wasn't her fault."

"Will you let us know if there's anything we can do for you to make up for it?"

Jill was finished with her tiny muffin and her piece of cantaloupe. She nodded.

Just then, Amy appeared, carrying her tote bag with shoes, bathing suit, books, and bottled water for the morning. She looked at Jill's departing visitor.

"She wanted to see if I was all right."

"That was nice of her," Amy said, a little dryly. She bloody well ought to want to see that you're all right, she thought. You could have landed in a mental ward, and they wouldn't have liked the lawsuit that came next. What she said, brightly, was:

"I'm off to Stretch. Did you sleep well?"

"Perfectly. Thank you. How was your walk?"

"Nice, I'll tell you about it at lunch. Are you going to T'ai Chi?"

Jill understood that her mother was telling her she was late. Her mother was Patience on a Monument when there was a crisis, as yesterday, but she was ready to switch gears, back to Everything's Fine the first second it was possible. Who wouldn't be? Jill got up and began getting dressed.

The T'ai Chi class was going through its paces when Jill found it. Because the morning was so clear and warm, they had moved outside and were arranged in a circle on the lawn. They were finishing an exercise called Accepting the Tiger when Jill arrived and tried to settle into the serene mood she had found in this class the first two mornings.

Solemnly, slowly, each member of the group was rotating in place, trying to experience the world from every angle simultaneously, as a tree does. Jill, whom serenity was eluding, mostly noticed that now about half the ladies had shed their standard issue sweat clothes and were sporting their own exercise gear. There were spandex tights, and one or two fleshless little career exercisers wore thong leotards that go into the crack in your behind, which Jill thought would feel horrible. No fear that with her figure she was ever going to find out. But on the whole, she felt mildly irritated by the glam aerobics garb, not to mention these women, who were twice her age and half her size. In truth, she was feeling fairly pissy this morning. She wondered if it was a hangover from the pills her mother had given her.

"Any questions before we go on?" asked the annoyingly perky instructor. Her clothes were vaguely Chinese, and she wore ballet slippers. The rest of them were in stockinged feet, because it was important to feel the earth with your soles. So you feel *really* grounded. Jill was beginning to wonder how it was that on the first two mornings this whole thing hadn't struck her as a crock.

"I have a question," said the barrel-shaped woman whose tag said BONNIE GRAY. "I'm having trouble accepting the tiger. I keep thinking shooting the tiger would make more sense."

The instructor laughed happily, as if she thought this were not a hostile question. "I'll tell you a story about the meaning of the tiger. There was a Taoist farmer whose best stallion ran away. And the neighbors heard about it and said, 'Oh, bad luck,' but the farmer said, 'Maybe.'

"The next day, the stallion came back, and he brought with him a whole herd of horses. The neighbors all came to see and they said, 'What good luck!' But the farmer said, 'Maybe.'

"The next day, the farmer's son was trying to break one of the new horses, and he fell off and broke his leg. 'Well!' said the neighbors. 'Bad luck!' But the farmer said, 'Maybe.'

"The next day the conscription forces came from the emperor and rounded up all the young men in the neighborhood to go fight a war. But they couldn't take the farmer's son because his leg was broken. The neighbors all nodded wisely and said, 'That's good luck.' But the farmer said, 'Maybe.' That is tiger power. The tiger is a force we must not judge; we must simply accept it. Understand?"

There was a brief silence, and then Laurie Lopez said, "Maybe."

When the class was over, the instructor chirped, "Thank you, everybody. Have a wonderful day, even if it is Black Wednesday!"

"What is it about Wednesday?" Jill asked the woman walking next to her.

"Wednesday is the day everyone hits the wall. We're all achy and constipated, and the instructors hate it. But don't worry; tomorrow you'll feel like a million bucks."

In front of them, Carol Haines caught up with Laurie.

"I've been dying to tell you how much I admired your husband," she announced with the good-natured tactlessness that was her cardinal characteristic.

Laurie nodded, suppressing a flash of resentment. Oh, fine. She supposed they all knew now who she was. But what right had strangers to have any opinion at all about Roberto, their idea of Roberto?

She let Carol talk as she thought about what class to take next. Nine o'clock was the fiercest workout of the day. Laurie was thinking of the boredom of step class, and getting ready to say, "Thank you, Roberto was an example to us all," when she heard Carol saying, "I wanted to kill him with my bare hands, what he took from us. And I hope you're going to fight back. Everyone hopes you're going to run against Turnbull yourself."

The sun seemed to Laurie to be directly in her eyes. It shone on Carol's bright hair. Laurie thought, This woman has no idea . . . she has no idea what it costs me to get out of bed in the morning.

"It's very kind of you—"

"That pig Turnbull thinks nobody could beat him. But *you* could . . . I'm in Washington a lot, I can't tell you how many times I've heard people say that in the last month. 'Laura Lopez would be the perfect candidate. A famous political family, she knows everyone in the state, she's a distinguished judge, and the bastard killed her husband.'"

"Carol . . . I can't . . . I can't even . . ." Laurie began.

"I think you can. Let's talk at lunch," said Carol.

She dashed off toward step class, and Laurie decided to sit by the pool and read a book. She wished she didn't know about that bottle of vodka in Rae's waist pack.

Carter was meeting with Terri, her personal trainer. Terri was muscular, with glowing black skin and long hair in cornrows. She wore strong colors and had teeth so flawless they looked like the capped mouthfuls flashed by the trophy wives you see all over Hollywood. But Terri's were her own.

Terri had interviewed Carter about her "exercise program." The very idea of calling it that made Carter snort. Then Terri had set about testing her flexibility with various contortions, her upper- and lower-body strength, and her percentage of body fat. Now she had her on the treadmill. To Carter's annoyance, this was the moment Terri chose to get chatty. She set the slant of the treadmill up to High, set the speed up to just under Jog, and then asked, "So, are you from Arizona?"

"L.A.," said Carter.

"No kidding! Me too! I'm from South Central."

"You're a long way from home," Carter said, beginning to feel the sweat trickle between her shoulder blades.

"Tell me about it. I've got family there though. My sister and my little niece. What do you do in L.A.?"

"I'm a private detective," said Carter.

"No shit!" Terri covered her mouth with embarrassment, but Carter laughed loudly.

"Sorry. I know a lot of my ladies are doctors and lawyers. I never met a private detective before, especially here."

"I'll bet," said Carter.

"How are you feeling now, by the way? On a scale of one to ten, are you working hard?"

"Five."

Terri adjusted the speed of the treadmill upward a notch. "No kidding, how'd you get into that?"

"I was a public defender, and I got tired of the slime."

"I hear you."

"How about you? What's a nice girl like you doing in a place like this?"

"I played basketball, volleyball in high school. I got a scholarship to college."

"I didn't think there was any money in women's sports."

"This college sent a lot of teams to the Olympics. Coach was training us for that."

"Did you make it?"

"All the way to the last cut, then I broke this little teeny bone in my wrist. How you feeling now, scale of one to ten?"

"Seven," said Carter.

"Hop off a second and let me take your pulse." Carter jumped her feet to outside the moving tread and Terri took her wrist for thirty seconds, watching her stopwatch. Then she readjusted the treadmill and said, "Get back on, and keep walking, we'll cool you down."

"Then what happened?" Carter asked.

"I went back to college, took my degree in Phys Ed. I was going back to the neighborhood to teach, but my mother's asthma got worse. I applied for this job so I could move her out here where it's hot and dry."

"How did you even know about this place?"

"Same way the guys at the Texaco station know about the Rolls-Royce factory. Hop off again, I'm going to take your pulse." Carter did, and was silent again for thirty seconds.

"Okay, get back on. I'll bring you some water. You want a towel too?"

Carter nodded. When Terri came back Carter asked, "Are these jobs hard to get?"

"Very," said Terri. "You can work some very crummy dives in this profession. Most places the showers aren't clean, and the clients are rude, and you have to teach classes until ten o'clock at night. Everyone in our business wants to work here."

"Why?"

"The atmosphere. The clients are happy because they get massages every day and the food's good. The trainers are happy because they get respect, you know? It's not like some storefront aerobics joint where you never get to know anybody and the clients think you're a moron because you're an athlete, and they're a genius because they're a paralegal."

Carter laughed.

"Okay, if you feel like your heart is back to normal, you can hop off any time and I'll give you the news."

Carter pushed the button that stopped the machine. She mopped her wet face and got another cup of water; then she stepped outside the gym to where Terri was waiting in the shade.

Terri showed her the charts on her clipboard.

"The news is pretty good here. You're in the top ten percentile for fitness for your age. Your endurance is good, your heart is strong, returned to resting pulse real fast. You're a smoker, aren't you?"

Carter was startled. "How did you know?"

"You got more winded than I expected, given your general fitness. You had more trouble talking at your peak aerobic rate than we like to see."

"Is *that* why you suddenly decided to have a conversation with me?"

Terri smiled. "How are you doing here without smokes?"

"I can go for about two hours without bringing the subject up. I can go for five or ten minutes at a stretch without thinking about it, which is a lot better than Monday."

"Anyone in your office smoke?"

"No, why do you ask?"

"Just trying to get a sense of how it'll be when you go home. I picture detectives sitting around the office with their feet on the desk and cigarettes dangling out of their mouths."

"Not in my office. In my office they've all got pictures of the kids on their desks and Baby Ruths hanging out of their mouths."

"This sounds like some unusual detectives."

"Yeah, we are."

"Have you got a card or something?"

"I'll bring you one."

Terri promised to meet with her again at the end of the week to design a program Carter could follow at home. Amused at the thought of herself in leotards prancing around her living room, Carter thanked her and went off in search of lunch.

Laurie had spent the whole morning playing hooky. She lay in the warm shade in a quiet lanai beyond the pool and read a novel she'd found on the shelf in Saguaro. She was feeling strangely serene, as if to refuse to do anything that was expected of her, let alone good for her, had been a defiant act, and the novelty agreed with her. She decided to stay where she was and eat lunch by herself.

She had to admit she was feeling better. This morning the world had appeared a sluggish gray. Now it was sepia, as if it had once *had* color, but not much. She noticed that the turkey burger she was eating, on a homemade bun with fresh green lettuce and bright red salsa, was both pretty and delicious. She chewed in silence and listened to the burble of a man-made waterfall across the courtyard.

Meanwhile, at the walled garden tables, everyone was talking about the morning weigh-in.

"I lost two pounds," said Glenna Leisure.

"That's pretty good," said Rae.

"One year I lost four by the middle of the week."

"Which isn't that much, really, when you notice they weigh you first when you're all bloated from traveling."

"My weight changes at least that much in a day," said Carol Haines. "Two pounds? Easy. Depending on the time of day."

"I didn't lose any," said Rusty, looking sad.

"You don't need to lose, Mom," Carol said.

"Did you hear about the time they hired the chef from Le Relais?" Glenna asked. "My girlfriend was here, she said it was awful. They hired this new chef and he said, '*Mais d'accord,* spa cuisine,' and for the first few days everyone said how great it was, how delicious. Then came the weigh-ins and people were *not* losing. They were *gaining.* Finally the guests were so upset Lalou put a spy in the kitchen and, of course, he was loading things with butter and cream. Just loading them . . . "

Everyone at the table was laughing, the thought was so awful.

"When Lalou confronted him, he said, 'But it's so much more delicious, it makes everybody happy'. . . People were fucking homi*ci*dal."

"I wish I hadn't heard this story," Rusty said.

The waitresses were clearing the plates, bringing coffee, and serving little cups of sherbet. Everyone at the table eyed it suspiciously.

"It's frozen banana," said The Success Story, taking a practiced taste. "I make this at home, it has about forty calories."

They dug in. When she had finished eating, Carol Haines said, "You know what we've got to do? We've got to make Laura Lopez run for the Senate."

"Oh, honey," said Rusty.

"No, I'm not kidding. She could beat Jimbo Turnbull. I'm in Washington a lot, and people have mentioned it."

"You *are* in Washington? Why?" Rae asked.

Carol shrugged. "I have clients who have matters there."

"Jimbo Turnbull," said Glenna. "I *hate* Jimbo Turnbull."

"Of course you do, you have a brain."

"Is he *still* in the Senate?" Rae asked.

"You mean after what he did to Ella Steptoe? I know, it's hard to believe."

"No, I mean, he must be older than I am. I thought he was dead."

"Listen. Jimbo Turnbull bounced over three hundred checks at the House bank. He used the Senate postal system to launder campaign money . . . "

"He has a daughter and two sons-in-law on his payroll and not one of them has set foot in the office, in Washington or Boise, in seven years . . ." said Glenna.

"Is this all true?" Rae asked

"Yes." "Absolutely," said Carol and Glenna together. They had both seen the same segment on *60 Minutes*.

"It's disgusting," Carol added. "He pinches women in the elevator, *congresswomen*. He calls Senator Kassebaum 'honey' on CNN, and she's a Republican!"

"I heard that he gave a speech to the Press Club and called Sandra Day O'Connor 'that little girl down at the Court,'" Glenna said.

"He's against the ERA, he's against Choice, and he honestly thinks he's untouchable."

"He's a disgrace," said Glenna.

There was a brief silence. Carol hitched her chair in as if she were confiding a trade secret, although the facts had been discussed in detail in both the *Washington Post* and the *New York Times*. "You know what they're saying in Washington. They're saying if it weren't for Jimbo Turnbull, Roberto Lopez would be alive today."

This got a rise out of them.

"No, really. That plane, that charter company, it's owned by an old fishing buddy of Jimbo's. He leaned on people to cut his pal some slack on the inspections."

"How can he get away with that?"

"There was a hearing, but nothing came of it. They all do it. You know. It was just a courtesy to an old friend, no harm meant, no harm done. They can't really prove what caused the crash, I mean they claim it was pilot error and maybe it was. Maybe there wasn't something absolutely wrong with that particular plane. But the company's safety record was, like, pathetic."

There was another silence. "If we wanted to do it," Jill finally said, "if she wanted to run, how would we help?"

"Listen," said Carol. "There's one woman here this week who raised eleven million dollars last year for a hospital in Los Angeles. There are probably ten right here who know how to do that. This morning I walked with a woman who owns a newspaper chain, and I have a friend in D.C., a policy wonk, who's probably going to get a "genius" grant. You've all got friends like that too. Enough with the Old Boy Network. We've got money right here and we've got power, and we've got brains."

"Right," said Rusty, rising from the table, her head scarf slightly askew and her little withered legs sticking out from the skirt of her bathing suit. She cocked her hip and said in her gravelly voice, "And we've got the *babe* factor." She headed off for her massage.

Jill was wandering around the Beauty Cloister with her schedule for the day in her hand. One of the white-uniformed Beauty people, a pretty woman with blond hair and olive skin, approached her.

"Are you lost?"

"I'm supposed to have a body scrub with Anna."

"She's waiting for you in the bathhouse. Go through the weight room, and turn left."

"Thank you."

"Are you Miss Burrows?"

Jill stopped. "Yes, I am."

"I am Solange."

Solange. Solange? Oh—the palm reader.

"The self-defense teacher thinks perhaps there is something I can do for you," Solange said in a low voice.

"Really?" Jill stood, uncertain, thinking of nights shut up in the linen closet with a flashlight and a Ouija board at Isabelle's house. This stuff was a game, right?

Solange took Jill's schedule from her hand and skimmed it. "I will meet you in your room at five. Your mother will be at yoga, yes?"

Good grief, maybe she *was* psychic. Jill nodded, whether in agreement to the plan or simply assent to the question she hadn't decided.

Solange, the slim Algerian, watched the very pretty, very fat American girl walk away.

Jill lay on a treatment table in the bathhouse and experienced the body scrub. It was a great deal like lying in Wheatena. She thought about whether to meet Solange or not, and couldn't decide. She could hear her father, the Great Pragmatist, the Great Healer, roaring with laughter at the idea.

At the end of the afternoon, Jill went back to her room after the abs class, an experiment she did not wish to repeat (Crunch! Crunch! Crunch, ladies *hold* that Crunch!). Solange was waiting. She had drawn the curtains, and was sitting quietly in the half dark.

"I'm a little early."

Jill nodded, wishing she had picked some of her clothes up from the floor when she'd undressed for her massage. She went to stow her gear in the closet, hoping Solange would think, What a tidy young woman, someone else must have messed up this room. She sat down facing Solange and took a deep breath.

Solange, who had turned on the small reading lamp on the table, sat very quietly looking into Jill's eyes. She didn't blink, so Jill tried not to either. The minutes stretched. At last, Solange looked down and picked up the girl's right hand. She looked at it back and front. She studied the shape of the fingers, the set of the thumb. She turned it palm up.

"You are right-handed." Jill nodded. Solange sat looking at the hand for what seemed another long time. She nodded her head once or twice, and turned the palm slightly this way and that, as if to catch the light differently. At last she said, "Here is the attack. You were— twelve?"

"Did someone tell you?"

"You can see it here quite clearly, where the health line is disrupted. It's a wonder you lived—the break is almost complete. And then this line—very deep. A head injury. But look, the life line is strong for most of its length, and long."

"How long?"

Solange smiled. "Let's just say it's long enough. Longer than mine, for example." She turned Jill's hand sideways, examined the curve of the fingers and thumb. She took up the left hand, and turned it palm upward.

"Interesting."

"What?"

"Let me think for a minute." They sat in silence while Solange looked at the hands side by side.

"All right," she said at last. "Listen. To say that your attacker made everything happen is to give him too much power. The image of him inside you. You don't have to do that. You can demand that the images inside you—the ones that do not serve life and truth—go away."

"Demand of who?" Jill was startled.

Solange's voice was low and warm, hypnotic. "Whoever you pray to. God, Jesus, the god in you. The tiger.

"But you cannot use prayer, or your power, to achieve effects. You can only use it to help you see. You can ask it to show you who it is who wants you to be entombed, alone, looking out at a world of love. Creatures who want you to hold yourself prisoner. You can make them show you their faces."

Jill was staring at her, horrified. The rapist was inside her, and she was giving him life and food and power, and she knew it. She absolutely knew it was true, she had made herself into a house for him.

"What if I can't . . . ?"

"You can," said Solange. "God is something. Evil is nothing. Evil is only denial of life, of love. Evil feeds on fear and uses people the way a toy uses batteries. Denial has nothing and so will use everything it can. All you have to do to defeat it is to give the power to life instead of to the creatures that have gotten so fat and strong."

Jill was staring. She was breathing in slow, deep, long breaths, and listening as if she'd been deaf all her life and was suddenly hearing a bell ring.

"Think of yourself not as a girl alone in a haunted house, but as a much-loved child in a house full of loving people. Aunts and brothers and friends and lovers and angels are in there. Find out who's in there, ask to see their faces. Find out who belongs to you and ask them for help to make the other ones leave.

"Accept your humanity. Spirit chose form for a reason."

Jill spoke in a tiny voice. "What if it won't leave?"

"Find out who put you in jail, looking out at a meadow. Promise yourself the meadow."

"But how can you know those good things are inside me?"

"They may not be. There may be things in the universe that belong to you, that are not yet inside you. You can still ask them for strength. You can still ask them to help you get rid of the things that aren't life."

"How? How do I ask?"

"Be careful not to inflate. Be careful not to give power to anything that shouldn't have power.

"If you're in trouble, you can ask for a ball of light. For yourself, or for anyone who needs it. It cannot intrude, and it cannot take anything it hasn't been offered. But it can give to you, or the person you send it to, whatever life and truth is appropriate. It can take denial or fear away and fill the empty places back up with life."

"Will you give me a ball of light?"

Solange smiled. "Do you need one?"

"Yes. Don't I?"

Solange let go of her hands, and stood up. "It's time for you to find answers."

"But how will I know if I have?"

"You'll know."

She got up and let herself out quietly, leaving Jill alone in the yellow circle of lamplight.

Jill sat going over the last fifteen minutes, recording them in her brain. She felt she had every word, word for word. She had an intense mental vision of Solange's yellow-green eyes. They were deep and refracted, as if they were made out of broken glass. She had the sound of Solange's voice, low and warm, a compelling murmur. She felt she had never been so fully alert and receptive in her life.

She noticed, suddenly anxious, that Solange had said nothing about being paid.

Jill told no one about Solange.

She had no intention of telling her mother. Her mother was not a spiritual seeker, but a lover of the world as it was. She was fearless, cheerful, alive to the moment. She was also a person with no secrets, who would consequently tell anything to anybody. If Jill told her that an Algerian Beauty Person had come to her room and shown her God, Amy would certainly believe her, but she might also share this interesting fact with her gynecologist, or the taxi driver, if the subject should come up.

But Jill would have liked to tell *someone* about the rapist inside her. Not Carter, this would not be her sort of thing. But maybe—Laurie Lopez? To see what she'd say?

Maybe after dinner she could suggest a walk to Laurie, or a trip to the Japanese bath. She'd just ask for a reality check. Did it seem plausible that the power to change and protect and heal might be everywhere, like a virtual computer without monitors and keyboards?

But this evening, Babette their hostess announced that after dessert they would have a karaoke machine.

As the machine was wheeled in one door, Jill saw Laurie go out the other. Most of the other ladies stayed, and Jill did too, because she felt too elated to be alone.

First Terri came in and performed a hip-hop song that all the other ladies had to ask Jill to explain. Then Glenna and Carol got up together and sang "I've Got a Lovely Bunch of Coconuts," with suitable gestures, and then Amy seized the mike and belted a most uninhibited version of "That's Amore." Jill was mortified. When she slipped out of the room, Carter and Rae, arm and arm in their sweat clothes, were singing "Sisters . . . Sisters . . . Never were there such devoted sisters . . ." Apart from the fact that Carter was eight inches taller and thirty years younger than Rae, they were quite convincing.

Thursday was as promised; Jill woke up feeling like a million bucks.

"How are you this morning? How are you?" the ladies asked each other as they arrived, shiny-faced and sleepy-eyed, in Saguaro for their walk.

"Great."

"I feel marvelous."

"I've been hammering down that oat bran, and it finally worked," Carter announced, and the volume of the laughter suggested that she wasn't the only one.

Jill and Carter decided to do the five-mile mountain hike. Glenna Leisure set off with them.

"God, look at that view!" Carter said when they reached the first plateau. Indeed, the morning seemed preternaturally exquisite. The air was clear with just a hint of bite, and the colors of the mountains were mauve and purple, while below them spread the gardens, many shades of green, set in a band of desert.

"I'm going to miss this," she added in a tone of surprise.

"Me too," Jill said, thinking of God, or the tiger, or whatever made stones and plants and hills and color. Color! Think of making color!

Glenna said, "When I get home I get up at this hour and hike, hike, hike around the freezing-cold streets, with the winos in the doorways and the garbage blowing. Then we go to one late dinner party or supper after a play, and bang, that's the end of that for another year. I love to sleep."

"Me too," said Jill. Sleep! Sleep was magic! Full of dreams . . .

Apparently very few people were studying Zen koans at breakfast, because at lunch everyone seemed to have read the Jimbo Turnbull story in the paper that morning. Senator Turnbull, in the full dignity of his office, had appeared on the Bob Battle show to talk about a bill that the day before had lost in the House by one vote. Bob Battle said he thought it was courageous for a young freshman member to stand against her own party, right or wrong. Turnbull had replied, "Oh, yes, Battle-san, most courageous," and continued to discuss Congresswoman Hong in what he surely thought was a hilarious Japanese accent. Susan Hong was a third-generation Chinese-American from San Diego.

Racist, witless, out of touch was the consensus. Word began to spread from table to table that Turnbull had retired the AHOY award.

"Ahoy?" Rusty asked.

"Asshole of the Year," said Glenna.

Laurie, sitting with Rae, quietly smiled at that. Otherwise she kept her eyes down and took no part in the conversation.

"I was talking to a girlfriend who works at the White House last night," said Carol. "She said the President would do anything to get Jimbo out of his chair at the Finance Committee."

"Your friend works at the White House?"

Carol named the friend, and sailed on. "Hunt Knox was a mentor to the President, they were both governors of western states. Everyone remembers the picture of Hunt's swearing in, with pretty little Laurie beside him in her Mary Janes on the Capitol steps, her hand on her heart. It was in *Life Magazine*."

"I loved that picture," said Glenna to Laurie. "That little dress with the smocking? I had one just like it."

Laurie pushed her feet into her sandals and stood up. "I have my massage," she said.

The massage woman met her in her room every day at two o'clock. She set up her table, draped it in sheets, turned up the heat, and closed the curtains. When Laurie came in, she stripped off her bathing suit and lay down without a word; a crisp sheet, still warm from the laundry, was pulled over her. A cassette was clicked into the bedside tape deck and monks began chanting in Latin. She could smell warm oil, scented with almonds. Strong thumbs went to work on the knots in her neck and shoulders.

*　*　*

Laurie remembered a time when she never had knots of pain in her neck or shoulders. When they were in Boise, and she was maybe eight, and Senator Turnbull came to dinner. Turnbull was a state senator then. She remembered that he smoked a pipe and had a lot of hair in his ears. She remembered that Mrs. Turnbull—Marnie—had been a thin, rabbity woman who looked as if someone had let all the air out of her tires. She stammered slightly, and during the cocktail hour she fretted because her bracelet kept falling off. Laurie remembered wondering why she didn't just put the thing in her evening bag instead of fussing with the clasp and talking about it.

The massage woman found a recalcitrant block around one of the shoulder blades. She changed the position of Laurie's arm. She rubbed in warm oil; she leaned into the muscle with her whole forearm. Laurie remembered that when her mother had told her she had to go to bed, although Bliss and Billy were going to eat dinner with the grown-ups, that Senator Turnbull had boomed, "Now, let her stay, Rachel, isn't going to do her any harm." Laurie's mother had said firmly that rules were rules. But Senator Turnbull had said, as Laurie curtseyed and said good night, "Never mind, little miss. You get into bed and Uncle Jimbo will read you a story." And he had. He'd arrived at the bedroom door with a copy of the *Just So Stories* plucked from the library shelf, and he sat beside her and read about "the Elephant's Child, Oh best beloved, all down the great gray-green greasy Limpopo River."

She knew, even then, that he was her father's enemy. But Idaho was too small a state, in population and politics, for the families not to have constantly met. Jimbo and Hunt carried on a certain raillery that they seemed to enjoy. Laurie's mother enjoyed it less. When poor Mrs. Turnbull finally dried up and blew away, Mrs. Knox sent Laurie in her place to the funeral with Hunt.

The massage woman was working on Laurie's thighs. They were painful after the mountain hike and a double-strength step class. Typical, thought Laurie, thinking that the rules don't apply to me. I can climb five miles and then run a marathon without training. No wonder life's decided to kick the shit out of me.

She could picture Jimbo Turnbull, dry-eyed, probably a little drunk, standing in his big front hall as guests drove up from the cemetery. He had said to her, "So you're in law schoo'. Didn't have pretty girls in law schoo' in my day." Laurie accepted the remark, and made her speech about her mother's respects, and their condolences. Jimbo answered, "But what I don't understand is, why'd you want to go to Harvard with all those pinkos and homos? Don't they call it The Kremlin on the Charles?" This was 1969, and Laurie, whose whole soul was inflamed over Jimbo Turnbull's role among the Senate hawks on Vietnam, was too angry to answer. Her father slipped a hand under her elbow and said, "Well, Jim, she wanted to stay here and go to the university, but I said, 'Don't do that, honey, you'll just be meeting a lot of assholes like Jimbo Turnbull.'" Jimbo roared with laughter.

"I bet you did, Hunt, I bet that's just what you did say." He slapped Laurie's father on the shoulder, and put an arm around Laurie. He lowered his voice almost to a whisper, and said to them, "Thank you for coming. Means a lot to me. You were some of Marnie's favorite people."

When Laurie married Roberto Lopez in 1975, Jimbo Turnbull and his new wife, Barbara, were invited to the wedding, of course. Laurie had dreaded giving Jimbo the chance to make wetback jokes, but he had been utterly gracious to Roberto, and to his family. He had kissed Laurie and told her simply that she was a beautiful bride and he'd known she would be. To Roberto he'd said, "Pleasure to shake your hand. Prettiest serve I ever saw in my life. Take good care of our little girl here." It had taken her a year to convince Roberto that Jimbo Turnbull was not a kindly old friend of the family. Meanwhile, Laurie Knox Lopez and Barbara Turnbull had given birth to their first children within weeks of each other. Carlos and Caroline.

"You can turn over now," the masseuse whispered. The monks went on chanting.

Rae Strouse was feeling so much better than she had when she'd arrived that she had resumed wearing makeup. Her eyesight was no longer perfect, and since she had to take off her glasses to put on her paint, it was probably the case that she used rather more, and more vivid, color than she would have when younger. With her trademark lids of sky blue, a dot of bright pink on each cheek, and a bright slash of vermilion on her wide mouth, she generally looked like a marvelous old parrot. But Thursday afternoon, she'd had her private session with the Makeup Artist in the Beauty Cloister. She emerged looking ready for a photo shoot. She strutted around the pool in her bathrobe, causing a sensation of appreciation.

Rae had enjoyed herself so much that she'd bought all the makeup products even though the girl wasn't on commission. She did this almost every time she came because the staff at The Cloisters was so good and they tried so hard. When she got home, she could give the makeup to Doreen, who looked after Albie. Doreen was too pretty to need makeup, but she studied all Rae's fashion magazines and liked to try new things.

Carter and Laurie and Carol Haines and Rusty had all scrambled to make appointments with the Makeup Artist, and one by one they had all emerged looking alike—the makeup girl had a predilection for colors that became her own blond, blue-eyed beauty, but by no means went with everyone else's. Carter's transformation was the most striking. She looked, in her short no-muss haircut, suddenly "Very gamine," as someone said, "very Audrey Hepburn." This pleased and embarrassed Carter so much that she went into the bathhouse twice to look at herself in the mirror, and the third time to wash the makeup off.

There was such a cry of protest when she emerged, reduced to normal, that she was forced to go back to the Beauty Cloister and buy $87 worth of shadow, liner, powder, and blush. The Makeup Artist had given her a chart with a woman's face printed on it and appropriate colors applied to the paper in the right places, so Carter could do her own face as if it were a paint-by-numbers.

"You'll never use it," Jill teased her.

"I will too, I'm too scotch to spend that much money and not use it," said Carter, but she did wonder exactly when she would bother.

It was Friday afternoon, and one by one Amy, then Carter, then Laurie slipped into Carol's room. The curtains were drawn, and the "Do Not Disturb" sign was on the outside knob. Carol and her mother, Rusty, were already there.

"Isn't this fun?" Rusty asked in her wonderful voice that sounded like pebbles being rattled in a can. "I feel so wicked."

Carol had made Solange an offer she couldn't refuse, if instead of giving Carol and Amy their body scrubs, which were scheduled back to back that afternoon, she would come to Carol's room and read palms.

"I've never had mine done," said Amy, wiggling with excitement.

"I think I'm having some kind of breakdown," said Carter. "First I lose nine pounds and give up smoking, next I'm visiting psychics."

The door opened, and Solange slipped in.

She looked startled to see so many of them.

"Don't be afraid, we're all *sworn* to secrecy," Rusty said.

"Can you do it with people watching?" Amy asked, quick to sense another's distress.

"You must be very quiet," Solange said.

"We'll be like church mice," said Rusty. "Who's first?"

Carol said, "Laurie—you go first." Laurie, who in the last two days had amazed herself by joining in everything, even the water exercises, and feeling better and better, was in a what-the-hell mood. She got up and took a seat at the writing table by the window. Solange sat across from her and sat looking at her hands. She studied first the backs of the hands, then turned both over at once and compared the palms.

Solange said, "Oh, I see you're the one."

"What one?"

"The lady who lost her husband. I'm sorry. And it was a very good marriage. Strong heart, lots of children. It's fortunate that you have such a strong head line, and so much courage." The ladies on the bed looked at each other. Of course there were a dozen ways Solange could have known about her husband's death, and all the children.

Solange was studying the left hand carefully. She looked back and forth between the left and right. She considered.

"You have a very good mind, strongly influenced by your father. You have let your heart rule your head in the last ten years or so. You are a risk-taker, decisive, a leader. It appears that you are going to change careers, or have a dual career. There is a strong line of success, here, but I cannot tell if it is going to cross your life line. See, here? It comes close, and then splits."

"What does that mean?"

"It means it is not decided yet. I see a good deal of travel. You are a person who plans carefully and follows through well. You thrive on independence. You are healthy and will have a long life. But because you have great gifts, you shrink from anything that does not come easily. And because of this, there is a danger you will not use your gifts to their full potential."

Laurie felt as if somebody had just undressed her in public. Solange's eyes met hers. After a long beat, Laurie dropped her gaze and said, "Thank you."

Amy took her place across from Solange. She was all atwitter. A little guilty for not inviting Jill to join them, but excited, and thinking maybe she would hear things she'd rather her daughter didn't know.

Solange glanced at her left hand and then turned to the right. She suddenly smiled.

"What?"

"I've never seen this before. You're not in the army, are you?"

Amy laughed. "Hardly. My father was, in the Korean War."

Solange shook her head; that wasn't it. "This is a very lucky hand. You have well-balanced head and heart lines, very good health, lots of travel, a strong life line with no breaks. You have one child. I imagine you wanted more, but you had her late."

"Yes."

"You will be married twice."

"Will my husband die? Or do you see divorce?"

"I would rather not say. Let me tell you why I smiled. You have a star, here." She tapped Amy's palm on the edge between finger and thumb. "The star is the most auspicious sign there is. It's very rare . . . I have only seen two before in my life. But it's on lower Mars."

"What does that mean?"

"Military victory."

Amy laughed.

"I'm sorry to be silly," said Solange. "There is another way to interpret it, but it's not coming to me. Never mind. It is very good, whatever it is."

"I'll take it," said Amy.

"I see here a career change, and late in life, a lot of success in business."

Amy returned to her place on the bed to applause. Carter and Laurie saluted her.

Next Carter, looking sheepish, took her place at the table.

Solange looked at both of Carter's big, strong hands, backs, and then palms.

Solange asked, "Left-handed?"

Carter nodded. Solange looked relieved.

Carter said, "You'll find the dual career there . . . I'm on my second one."

"Many women have that now. Perhaps most." She studied Carter's hand.

"The marriage line is not strong."

"I'll say," said Carter, and there was laughter.

"But it's clear. You are very strong-minded. You are the kind of person who makes friends easily; you are exceptionally curious and outgoing. I see strong success in both careers."

"Financial?"

"Not so much financial as on your own terms. You are very good at what you do. You are a particularly good manager. Good at leading, good at delegating. You are not reckless, though you take risks. You are not reluctant to let other people shine.

"You have a talent for friendship, and I would say you are a particularly good mother."

There was an intake of breath in the room. The first complete misstep. Solange looked up, unperturbed.

"I don't have children," said Carter.

Solange looked at the hand. "I see a child, very clearly."

"Then you see a medical miracle. That, or I didn't understand the menopause lecture last night." Solange squinted slightly and turned the palm slightly to angle the light across it.

"You have a niece? A nephew? A godchild?"

"Maybe I better get a dog," said Carter.

"Yes," said Solange, "I think you better. And be very careful in your work. There is a break here that could mean illness, but more likely accident. Your work is dangerous?"

"Can be. Is this something that *will* happen?"

"Nothing in the hand has to happen. It is waiting to happen, but whether it does or not is up to you."

Solange told Carol that she was hard-working and artistic, and would change careers; she mentioned no children. She told Rusty that she had a cross, an ominous sign, indicating an injury to the head. That she had healer's marks, meaning she was a kind person, a good listener, who would be a wonderful doctor or nurse, but in any calling would make people feel better just being around her. Rusty beamed. Everyone wanted to know if she saw Rusty recovering or dying, but of course, no one asked.

*   *   *

Friday night at dinner, the conspirators sat together and shared a wicked buzz of elation.

"What do you think, Laurie?" Carol asked. "Are you going to run?"

This again. Laurie thought for a bit about whether it was time for a jolt of reality. She said, "Did you know I ran for Congress twenty years ago?"

"You did? No, I didn't know that. What happened?"

"I got buried. It was the worst thing that had ever happened to me. At the time."

"Oh god," said Carol absently, "I'm sure. But at least you know how to do it. Doesn't it make you want to roar back and stomp them this time?"

It did not make Laurie want to do that. It made her feel like telling Carol she had no idea what she was talking about. But she left it unsaid, because she thought, How do I know what she knows? You probably get knocked around in her line of work too.

Rae was watching closely and thinking it was about time to let up on Laurie.

"This omelette is wonderful," she said.

"Could I have the salsa?" Amy called.

"Certainement, mon général," said Carter, snapping a salute. The conspirators laughed. Jill looked at her mother, questioning. "I'll tell you later," Amy whispered.

a familiar and very bad thing had happened to Jill. Depression closed down over her like a bell jar. When the phone rang in her room at five forty-five, she could hardly stir herself to lift the receiver. She felt as if a miasma of something dark and heavy, like lead in the form of a vapor, had invaded her chest. With every breath she wanted to weep. The room, still full of the dark of night, had become a cell in a nunnery. She had committed herself to a future without light or joy or pleasure, in the hope of a heaven that didn't exist. There was no light, anywhere. Nothing ever changed, nothing would ever get better. No one told the truth, nothing was possible.

There was a knock on the door.

"Sweetie?" Amy chirped. She slipped into her daughter's room.

"It's the most heavenly morning," she said, and pulled the curtain cords. Outside, the world was bathed in silvery blue light and filled with the sound of birds.

"Better hop it, little lamb. We're going to do the Five-Mile Mountain."

Jill thought about telling her she didn't feel like it. She thought about telling her she didn't feel like getting out of bed at all. She thought about the effort it would take to open her mouth and tell her cheery, happy mother anything she didn't want to hear, and she thought that she knew exactly why Solange had asked her mother if she were in the army. Yes, sir, ma'am, General Burrows. Up and at 'em.

Jill, without a word, dragged herself out of bed.

"I'm going to trot on down to Saguaro, I want my coffee. See you there," Amy said, and she went out, exhilarated, into the lambent morning.

Two marriages, Amy thought as she bounced along. God, what light, what delicious air, what a sweet smell of cut grass and eucalyptus. She felt like a child. She had slept like a baby. Her skin was glowing, she had the kind of energy you have when you're eight, and the bell rings at recess, and you tear outside and run and run and run until they make you go back inside. She felt so good, she'd have liked to shout. Of course, she wouldn't, there might be people sleeping.

Two marriages. Oh well. Noah worked too hard, and he knew it, and she suspected he still smoked cigars at the club. She'd told him that if he keeled over from a heart attack she'd never forgive him. You couldn't make men take care of themselves, especially doctors. At least if he insisted on stuffing himself full of red meat and dying young she wouldn't have to live forever as a lonely old widow.

Carter Bond, Carol Haines, and Laurie Lopez were sitting together in Saguaro with cups of steaming liquid in their hands. They watched Amy striding in.

"Hello, ladies! Are we ready?" Amy greeted them.

"We are ready, *mon général*," said Carter.

"Shouldn't it be *ma*? *Ma générale*?" Amy asked as she got herself a mug of coffee.

"I don't think there's any provision in the language for that."

"Never mind. I've got it . . . it's a pants role," said Amy, and she and Carol laughed. "Opera jargon," she explained to Carter. "There are men's roles written for women to sing. The character is a man, but it's always sung by a woman in a man's costume." Carter was looking at her with nostrils flared.

In bounced Fitness Professional Diane, in neon pink.

"Okay, ladies! Where are my mountain five-milers? Wow, big group! All right!" she cried as fifteen ladies followed her outside into the dawn to stretch.

Jill arrived at Saguaro as her mother and friends were striding off into the brush. There were more ladies stumbling into Saguaro. Bunny

Gibson and Rusty Haines were drinking herb tea and talking about Nantucket. Wilma Smythe and Rae Strouse were sitting in silence, trying to wake up. Jill met no one's eyes, and poured herself a coffee into which she put three sugars. There were packs of sugar substitute there, but she ignored them.

She wandered outside with the others when Terri mustered them out to stretch. Halfheartedly she leaned or bent or pointed her toes while Terri, dressed in yellow, shouted and clapped. "Come on, ladies, let's get those hamstrings warmed up! Let's get that blood moving, get your heart started! It's a *great* day!" With a shout of encouragement Terri strode off toward the foothills, hands pumping, and the group fell into line behind her. Jill joined in near the rear, behind two ladies she knew by sight but had never talked to. The ladies were talking about German cars.

Jill dragged her feet along the trail, as if they were two badly behaved toddlers. It took enormous will to keep them in line, when one wanted to kick and the other wanted to stumble and her whole body felt as if it weighed a ton. What a shuck it all was. She had gotten nowhere. She was a big fat sack of dirt and she always would be, and her mother had paid enough for this week to settle the national debt, and what was it? A week. One week. One week could change your life? Come on. In forty-eight hours she'd be back in New York. She had a history paper due, and she hadn't even thought about it. She'd have mountains of e-mail because she was on all these mailing lists; for half of them she didn't even remember why she'd signed up. She'd have 114 messages telling her there was a wrong clue in a double acrostic from last Saturday and she didn't even do double acrostics anymore. Fuck.

She was hungry, too. She started thinking about what she would eat when she got home. Bagels. Ice cream. Peanut butter and jelly on fried toast.

Would any of these old bags ever see each other again? She bet not. She hoped not. So why were they yammering away at each other as if they were, like, friends? Why put all that effort into something with the life span of a fruit fly? What use was anything if it was going to die, sooner or later? Friendships? Marriages? Fruit flies? Anything? Fuck it.

She cried a little. Not from self-pity, but from despair. The more the depression sank in, the more worthless she felt, the more angry and ashamed she felt that people kept trying to save her. Why couldn't they just let her go to hell in her own way? What did they know about what it was like to be her?

She had fallen behind the two ladies with the Audis. She was alone, and feeling rebellious enough to sit down and weep, and maybe stay there for hours until she succeeded in scaring the whole place to death, when she became aware of a slim figure in black sweats, wearing mittens and an orange knit hat. The figure came up behind her and stopped. Jill turned and looked. It was Solange.

"What are you doing here?" Jill demanded.

"I am your shepherd."

Jill thought angrily of saying out loud, Wouldn't you rather be someplace doing parlor tricks? Thank God, Jesus and Mary I didn't tell anybody I thought you had told me something important. Everyone had such a good laugh at my mother, the General. And Carter, Mother of the Year. Imagine the roar if they knew what you told me.

Aloud, she said, "My own *personal* shepherd?"

"There is always a shepherd at the back of the group. I like being up early."

Jill grunted and started walking again. No skeleton found under a bush picked clean by coyotes in her future. Don't want to scare away the customers. She stumped along the path, feeling worthless. Man in the desert knows there is no sea.

Jill felt a hand on her shoulder and stopped walking. She turned to face Solange, who looked into her eyes, squinting with curiosity. Solange's face was sleek and unlined; she wore black kohl or something around her smokey yellow eyes.

"I see," said Solange, looking away from Jill's face.

I bet, thought Jill. They walked on in silence, Jill in the lead.

When at last they joined the group, Jill took the section of orange she was offered and sat down on a rock. She ate the piece of orange in one bite, pits and all. Solange crossed the circle and stood at the other side of the group with her arms crossed over her chest and her back to everyone, looking out over the valley.

Jill was marching along on the downward slope in front of the Audi ladies when it began to occur to her what had happened. First, she had learned that one of the ladies had had a Saab, but the window on the driver's-side door had exploded the week she took delivery, then a string of other annoying things had occurred, and then the brake system had failed when the car had 23,000 miles on it. Next, Jill lost a few seconds of the conversation, and when she tried to bring her mind back to it, she couldn't. She couldn't do a thing with it; it was careening around the heavens like a bumper car. There was an enormous balloon in her chest, as if she'd been pumped full of helium, and she had a terrible sense that she was about to laugh out loud. She was full of mirth. The sky was bright blue and gold. She took off her hat and mittens, warmed to her fingertips by some radiant, tingling sense of lightness. Brilliance. Light. She began to focus . . . it was light. It was light! Her chest was full of light, oh, God, Jesus and Mary, it was like a hallucination . . . the pain was gone, the weight was gone, and her chest was full of light.

At that point, she did begin to laugh, and to run. Then she slowed herself down to a racewalk, because it was important to think.

This was not some minor vagary of mood. This was a freaking class B miracle—Jill knew what it was like when that bleak horror set in. It stayed for weeks. There was nothing in the magic chest of pharmacology that could accomplish what had just happened to her. Her shrink and her mother had tried everything on her—Prozac, Zoloft, Xanax. They worked for other people but not for her. And even if they worked, you had to take them for weeks before they kicked in. This was unbelievable. And it wasn't going away.

Can I trust it, can I trust it, she kept trying to ask as she strode down the mountain. But she couldn't even keep her mind on the question. She was too filled with relief and joy. And hilarity. That meant everything she had learned was real. The hope . . . she could trust it. The work of ceasing to be a house for demons . . . it had begun, she could go on . . .

Oh, the danger. The danger of asking for miracles, the danger of wanting proof once a day. Oh, it was awful to be so addictive, she'd have to get rid of that. How much proof do you need? How much does anyone get? She had just had 1,000 percent more than most people. Never forget it, never forget this. Store this joy, these colors, this light, like juice in a battery, soak it in, keep it. Her feet made a beat as she walked, and she made a mantra to go with it. She felt that her senses had been intensified—sight, sound, and smell; she was able to experience things so acutely that this half hour could be unzipped later and stretched out to last a year.

Oh, the pulsating, throbbing, joy-filled absence of despair!

She waited at the bottom of the mountain. She waited by the path, feeling the sun, unable to stand still. She decided to try to remember how to skip.

All the ladies she had passed on her way down passed her now, going back to their rooms for breakfast. Rae gave her a little hug as she went by. Everyone smiled. The Audi ladies went by, and both looked at her and beamed. At last Solange came along. She was a little behind the last of her charges, so they were out of earshot when she reached Jill.

"You sent me a ball of light!" Jill said, and danced a little jig.

Solange said, "You can do it yourself, you know. You can ask for it yourself, and you can send it to other people."

"How?" Jill was glowing. Oh, what an idea! To be able to do that for someone else!

"You know how," said Solange.

"I don't! Solange, tell me!"

But Solange laughed, and walked on.

Carter Bond proceeded to the Saturday morning final weigh-in with a sense of anticipation such as she hadn't experienced since she was thirteen and checked every morning to see if it was still true that she had grown boobs. In underpants and a towel she danced back to her locker after her turn on the scale. She found Jill ahead of her, pulling on her sweatpants.

"How'd you do?"

"Ten pounds! Ten pounds in one week!" Carter crowed. Jill gave her a high five. "How about you?"

"Thirt-teen. Thirteen pounds and fifteen inches," said Jill.

"Yesss!" Carter yelled. Jill was doing a jig.

"See, it all worked, it's all real," Jill said. "So come to T'ai Chi today."

Carter didn't say no as fast as she had other mornings.

"Good, I'll pick you up after breakfast," said Jill.

"No, I can't. I'm afraid we'll have to do that kelp thing."

"At eight twenty-five. Do I look positively waiflike?"

"Positively."

"I live for the day when people start saying 'Now, don't lose *too* much . . .'"

"I can't believe you're making me do this," said Carter as Jill herded her along toward T'ai Chi.

"Shut up, you'll love it."

"You know, I've really gotten into these sand designs," Carter said, stopping suddenly. They were standing on a redwood walkway, crossing a sunken garden that consisted entirely of three rocks in a bed of powder-fine sand. A wooden rake stood against the walkway.

"It's different every day, have you noticed?" Carter said. "Who does it? The guards?"

"It's supposed to be very Zen," said Jill. "If you contemplate it."

"What I contemplate is, how do they do it without leaving footprints?"

"You really *are* a detective, aren't you?"

T'ai Chi seemed to have some special charge this morning, Jill thought. There was giant Carter, solemnly striving to experience the morning as if she were a tree. There were Laurie Lopez, and Carol Haines and her sweet, goofy little mother, Rusty, and dear Rae Strouse, who must have gotten interested in something else while she was doing her makeup, since she had gummy aquamarine eye shadow on only one eyelid. This week had been like a peculiar boot camp, in which they had all shed their external differences and become a troop of comrades, cheering each other on. Even The Movie Star's sidekick had come out to join them.

Jill continued to turn, and now her circle of women was behind her, and before her was a stand of evergreens, and—well—the driveway, but it was serene and silent, and nature was beautiful, and the women and the trees were all part of one thing . . .

Jill had tears running down her cheeks when she had turned full circle, and she was smiling. The funny thing was, she noticed without surprise, that about three other people were weeping too.

"I see *no* reason," said Glenna Leisure, "for life ever to be more complicated than this."

"Laurie," said Carter at lunch, "when you're President, could I be head of the FBI?"

"I was thinking of Justice for you," said Laurie.

"I'll take it, since it's you asking, but I'd rather the FBI."

"Well, we'll take it under advisement."

"What about me?" Amy asked eagerly. "I can type and speak French and do CPR."

"Chief of staff, of course, *mon général*," said Laurie.

"How about Rae for press secretary?"

"Don't be silly, Rae is a dancer. I will put her in charge of the National Endowment for the Arts."

"And Wilma Smythe—Surgeon General, don't you think?"

"Surgeon General. Are you taking notes, *mon général*?"

"I don't need to," said Amy. "When you've given a dinner for three hundred for the Brearley school auction, staffing the cabinet is child's play."

"Besides, Mom has a photographic memory," said Jill, eyes still closed.

"Do you really?"

Amy nodded. "A little thing, but it is mine own."

"Can you remember names and faces?" Rae asked enviously.

"Thousands of them," said Amy.

"What's Jill going to do when you're President?" Carter asked.

"How about the Pentagon? Secretary of Defense? Baby General?"

"I know what job I want," Jill said. "I've known since second-year Latin."

"What?"

"I want to be the Voice of Reason."

"Me too!" cried Rae. "That would be perfect for me."

"You already have a job," Jill said. Then she explained, "When a Caesar would arrive in Rome at the head of a conquering army, messengers were sent ahead so that by the time he reached the Forum the whole population was out to line the route, and cheering. There he'd be, passing under triumphal arches, leading his legions of soldiers, wagons full of plunder, exotic animals in cages, and the rulers and warriors of the vanquished in chains. And all of Rome is roaring and hailing, and behind him in his chariot, there's a slave whispering, 'Remember, you are only a man. Remember, you are only a man.'"

"Of course, they did not remember for more than ten minutes," said Carter. "My memory is that they had themselves declared divine, right and left."

"I think you would be a perfect Voice of Reason, Jill," said Laurie. "You can ride in my chariot and sleep at the foot of my bed. But it would depress me to be nothing more than a man. You'll have to whisper, 'Remember, you're only a woman.'"

The table burst into hoots and applause. Ladies lunching at other tables turned questioning faces in their direction.

*a*s darkness fell at the end of the last afternoon, the yoga class was sitting barefoot and tailor-fashion (or as close to it as they could manage) on the floor. A cassette player emitted the muffled sounds of waves crashing on a beach.

First they did deep-breathing exercises. These were harder than they sounded. Next they did postures that opened their pelvises or stretched their spines. Honey, the instructor, moved among them, devising geriatric variations on these poses for those whose joints refused. Then came the headstand they had been practicing all week.

Tonight, Jill moved out to the center of the room. The other ladies positioned themselves against the wall and began, as they had been taught, to raise themselves to vertical, upside down. After various false tries, and corrections, they one by one succeeded in unfurling themselves toward the ceiling. When they opened their eyes, upside down, they saw Jill, in the middle of the floor, her body perfectly aligned, holding a headstand with no external support.

Bunny Gibson was the first to curl herself down to the floor and give Jill a round of applause. The others soon followed suit.

"You made it look so easy!"

Jill was very pleased with herself.

"I'm so jealous," said Rae. "Want to see me do a cartwheel?"

"Yes!" said Jill, and Rae started to laugh, since she hadn't been serious.

"Well, all right," she said. "I don't think I've done one in about forty years but . . ." and before Honey, who looked horrified, could stop her, Rae in her violet sweat suit and purple socks took two long steps down the carpeted floor and then turned a very respectable cartwheel.

"Ooh la la!"

"Fantastic!" cried the ladies, clapping.

"Madam, please, do *not* do that again," said Honey, appalled, clearly imagining herself explaining how she came to let her elderly charge break both wrists and her neck.

"I won't," said Rae. "I'm going to quit while I'm ahead."

In darkness and silence, Jill trotted back to her room to dress for dinner. This was the night people washed their hair, put on makeup, wore their jewelry, and appeared as their outside selves. It was like the end of Lent; the fast was over.

Jill was feeling full of merriment. She had stood on her head. She had a ball of light. She had lost an immense amount of weight in one week; she hadn't known you could lose that much in so short a time. Wearing her cassock and her string of pearls, she went out and tapped at her mother's door. There was no answer. Jill put her head in the door and heard the shower running.

She went on to Carter's room

"Come in," Carter bellowed. She was on the phone. She smiled at Jill and beckoned her in.

"So you ran the tags . . . of course. From where?" She made rapid notes in some kind of shorthand.

"Okay, m'dear," she said at last. "I'll be in the office by early Monday. . . . Yes . . . I'll be the one with the rose in my teeth, in case you don't know me." She hung up.

"DeeAnne?" Jill asked.

"Yeah, she called to tell me she threw out all the ashtrays in the office. If I want to smoke, I have to stand outside on the ledge."

"How high up is your office?"

"Twenty-two stories."

Jill laughed. "Guess what I did—I stood on my head!"

"Hey! All right!"

"But I wasn't the hero. Rae got jealous and did a cartwheel."

"No! Did she really?"

"She said she hadn't done one in forty years."

"She's in great shape, isn't she?" Carter said. "How old do you think she is?"

"God, I don't know . . . seventy-five?"

"I think eighty."

"Wow."

"Definite wow. You ready to go?"

"Aren't you going to put on your makeup?" Jill asked.

Carter looked embarrassed. "I have to get used to it at home."

"I told you you'd never wear it."

"What a fresh kid you are."

"Come on. I'll help you."

"What do you know about it? You aren't wearing any."

"Aha! I am wearing *pounds* of makeup as we speak. Come on, come on."

Jill was herding Carter into the bathroom. There she found the bag from the Beauty Cloister, untouched, with the jars and bottles inside in their boxes.

"Here. This is foundation. Shake it up, then put it all over your face. No, stop—here, do this first. Put it under your eyes."

"You're confusing me," Carter complained, but she followed Jill's instructions.

Jill handed her the eye shadow.

"Wet your brush and put it on like watercolor."

"Can you *do* that?"

"Sure. You can get it more subtle that way. Only use this gray—the other colors are too much for you."

"I'll say."

"Now this light one, here." Jill pointed and Carter dabbed at it.

"Now powder," Jill ordered.

"I feel like a complete jerk," said Carter, taking the brush.

"Cover your eyelashes too. It helps keep the mascara from smearing."

"Where did you learn all this stuff?"

"You forget my early stage career, girl ballerina." Jill made her put on a darker powder that brought out her cheekbones, eyeliner, which she only stuck in her eye once, then mascara. Carter blinked before Jill could show her how to blot it, so she had a little line of black flecks on her cheekbones. She looked in the mirror.

"Aaah!"

"Hold still, I'll fix it." Jill went to work with a cotton swab. "Close your eyes." Carter did. Jill powdered her face again.

"Okay, you're beautiful."

"Right," said Carter. The dinner gong sounded.

Amy Burrows, Laurie Lopez, and Wilma Smythe were sitting together near the fire, sipping spiced tea. Amy was wearing her rings, and had blow-dried her hair. Laurie was dressed as she had been all week.

"It's too wonderful not to have to look in the mirror," she said.

Every time someone new arrived, there was reaction and babble. Bunny Gibson came in wearing a spangly sweater over sweatpants, and big earrings. On her bare feet she wore thongs.

"I couldn't change my pants," she announced. "I just this minute had my toes painted."

Jill and Carter came in. There was applause. "Miss Thirteen Pounds and Fifteen Inches!" someone called.

"Yes!" cried Jill, and she did a little Zorba the Greek victory dance. "And look at Miss Vavavoom here." She pointed at Carter.

"You look terrific."

"Really, you look wonderful."

"I feel like a complete dork," said Carter, but she seemed pleased.

Carol and Rusty Haines came in. Carol was wearing a pink sarong and diamond earrings. Her hair was washed and curled and fluffy, and she wore heavy makeup over her perfect skin. Her mascara was so thick it was clumped. She who had been so naturally the picture of health now looked like a very tall doll.

"Oh . . . don't you look pretty," people said, staring at her.

Laurie said, "If you'd looked like that the first time I met you, I'd never have dared speak to you."

"You wouldn't? Why not?" Carol asked.

"You're wearing a mask," said Laurie.

Carol turned to the mirror that hung by the door behind a large arrangement of dried flowers. She stared at herself. She turned back.

"Am I?" she asked the room at large.

"You look so pretty with your hair just pulled back," said Amy diplomatically. "I got used to you like that."

"And you like it better?"

It was clear, everyone liked it better. She no longer looked quite like a real person; she looked more like a decoration. Carol, who had an infinite capacity to be interested in herself, took in this information with apparent relish. She turned again, and went to stare in the mirror.

Dinner was hilarious. The Fitness Professionals awarded prizes for various forms of silliness. There was a video shown of the group in their classes, trying to learn the Electric Slide, prancing up and down in step class, puffing and blowing. Even The Movie Star could be seen in one sequence, struggling to master the hula hoop.

Sue Snyderman nearly started a riot at her table by announcing that if you strapped a vibrator to your hand and then stuck your finger in your ear, it was better than sex. Another group telephoned to the nearest village and ordered three pizzas. They had to go out and wait by the gate for the delivery boy, and when they finally had the pizzas in a stack on the table in Saguaro, they looked at the grease from the cheese and pepperoni soaking the cardboard of the boxes, and nobody would touch them.

Jill and Amy went to the bathhouse for their last soak in the Japanese tub under the stars.

"I hope Carter and Rae are coming, and Laurie," Jill said. But none of the others did come. The stars were very fine and bright, and they drank in the scent of eucalyptus.

"Are you looking forward to getting home?" Amy asked. "To show off your new figure?"

The question made Jill cringe. She didn't want to show off anything, ever. She didn't want anyone to notice her, and she knew what was coming. Her mother constantly calling attention to the new Jill,

Miss Thirteen Pounds Fifteen Inches. It was enough to make her want to gain it all back.

"Yes," said Jill. "It will be nice."

"You'll miss your friends, though," said Amy. "I know I will."

"I wish they'd all get on-line so we could e-mail each other," said Jill.

"I hope you told them so."

Jill had. Amusingly, and probably typically, the only one of the group who was already on-line was Rae.

Laurie sat in her room with only one light on. She had thought of going to the bathhouse, but she realized she would not be alone again for a very long time; the children would be needing her and would one way or another make up to themselves for the week she had been away. She couldn't blame them. She was missing them too, especially Cara with her bedroom full of turtles and hamsters, and sturdy little Hunter, and Xavier with his big solemn eyes. But she knew that what was waiting for her, from the moment she walked into the house, was the weight of all those memories of Roberto. Every moment that she looked at her son Carlos. She realized she was dreading the morning.

Carter was dressed in street clothes and ready to leave; it was full day. She'd gone with a much diminished group for the three-mile mountain hike. Jill and Amy were already gone. Rae had come in to Saguaro to say good-bye, looking urbane in her Adolfo suit.

"You take good care of yourself," Rae said, looking Carter firmly in the eye.

"I will. You too."

"And I'll see you back here next year, the first week of November." Carter laughed. "What an idea!"

"It's a perfect idea. I already signed you up. 'Bye, dearie. Don't take any wooden bullets."

"I won't." Carter smiled, and allowed herself to be hugged. Unexpectedly, she felt rather teary.

There was a knock at the door of her room.

"Come," Carter called. She expected the bellman. Instead, it was the pretty redhead who ran the boutique. She was holding a plastic bag.

"I hope you have room for this," she said.

"I didn't order anything else," Carter said, a little sharply. She had a vision of more bottles and brushes and paint. Enough was enough.

"It's for you, though. If you don't have room, I can ship it."

She handed the package to Carter, and tripped off in her high heels. Carter sat down on the bed and opened the bag. Inside was the red sweater, knit of silk ribbons, and a note from Rae.

> **Had your name on it. I was too cheap to get the necklace.**
>
> *XXX*
>
> *Rae*

Rae's plane banked over San Francisco Bay on its final approach to the airport. She could see the Bay Bridge and the Oakland hills as the plane circled to the south. In an hour she'd be at home. She thought about how beautiful the city was. She thought about how glad she would be to see Winston Churchill. Winston Churchill was her bulldog.

Her driver was waiting for her at the gate, crisp and smiling in his uniform. She couldn't pronounce his Chinese name, but he preferred in any case to be called James. His wife's American name was Doreen.

"How is everything?" Rae asked as James took her bag and raincoat.

"Very good," he said.

"How is Winston?"

"Fine, except yesterday he ate a sponge," James said.

"A whole one?"

"Yes, but he ate it a bite at a time. The car is in the parking garage. Will you wait here while I bring it?" They had reached the main terminal lobby.

"I wouldn't think of it, I need the hike. How is the baby?"

"Mr. Strouse taught him patty-cake!"

"Oh, this sounds fine."

"Patty-cake, patty-cake, cake, cake, cake!" James recited.

The two of them walked briskly through the tunnel to the airport garage.

* * *

95

The Strouse house was a four-story brick affair in the Tudor style; it was not small. It had been built in the 1920s on a level block of Broadway in Pacific Heights, the quietest, prettiest, fanciest part of San Francisco, with spectacular views of the bay and the Golden Gate Bridge. To be on a level block, where you could park your car without fearing you would fall out and roll down the hill when you opened the door, and where the children could Rollerblade or ride bikes in front of the house, was a big attraction in this hilly city. Of course, level rarely meant more than level in front. The ground on which the Strouse house was built sloped down toward the bay so precipitously that the house was actually three stories high in front and six in the back, the lowest level being mostly used for storing garden equipment. There was a small shade garden and a patch of lawn where in the spring and summer there was sun in the afternoon. In the back of the lot was a large ivy-covered rectangular building that housed the indoor swimming pool.

Doreen opened the front door to Rae, her face smiling a welcome. Winston Churchill came rocketing down the stairs and shot across the polished slate floor, his whole body wriggling with joy.

"Well, hello, Winston Churchill, hello, my dog. I'm glad to see you too, yes, I am very glad to see you, you bad hound, did you eat a sponge?" Rae managed to greet the dog and give Doreen a hug at the same time.

Winston finally got himself in control enough to sit still at her feet. He looked up at her with intense joy, his toenails clicking on the stone floor as he tried to be still. Rae gave him a biscuit from her rain-coat pocket, and the dog leaned against her leg in adoration. She patted his head and scratched his neck, and he mooed with happiness.

Her husband, Albie, was spending the morning upstairs in the den. His favorite room had been the library, with its walls lined with books, the vast Persian carpet, and his favorite leather wing-backed chair by the fireplace, but now he tended to stay upstairs unless Rae was with him. The den was a much smaller room, with dark green—glazed walls and deep, soft chairs with needlepoint pillows that Rae had made as they watched television together. Here too Rae and

Doreen had installed baby Scott's playpen, and Albie and the baby seemed mutually pleased and soothed by each other's company.

When she walked down the hall to the den this morning, Rae could hear the television. It was turned up loud; Albie's hearing had been failing. He had surprised her by being rather vain about wearing hearing aids. He had always been a handsome man—slender, with thick brown hair and eyelashes, and a heavy brow ridge and square chin that just saved him from being embarrassingly good-looking. All the same, when it came to it, he refused to wear the large hearing aid that made sense for a man in his condition. He wanted tiny ones that no one would notice. The trouble was, he then didn't notice them either; didn't notice where he put them, or whether he had them in at all, and mostly lost them in the cracks of the cushions. He had no idea of the decibel level he had incrementally achieved. That was the danger of clicking the remote control a few extra times and forgetting you'd done it.

Rae stood at the door of the den, buffeted by the din, and looked at her husband. He was wearing a sweat suit, because it was the easiest thing to get him into, and battered boat shoes. He had a box of Kleenex in the chair beside him, and he was gazing at the television, where there was some kind of war show on, a rerun on one of the zillions of cable stations they subscribed to. There was lots of shouting and occasional gunfire, in which Albie was wholly absorbed. Finally she said, "Hi, stranger."

When he looked up and saw her, an expression of the sweetest joy lit his face. He tried to speak, but quickly turned instead to searching for the remote control, which was wedged between his leg and the chair arm. He aimed it at the television, two-handed, and punched buttons wildly, changing stations, until he happened to strike the Off button.

Rae went in and leaned over him. He put his arms around her and kissed her warmly. "You!" he said at last, beaming with happiness.

"Yes, I'm back. I'm even a little early. And it was a wonderful, wonderful week. We had good weather, and I met amazing people, a sweet little girl about as big around as she was tall, and a giant woman who's a detective, and a dear, brave woman who's a judge, who just lost her husband. You knew her husband, the tennis player Roberto Lopez, remember, you met him in Washington when you both got awards? You'd have liked them all so much."

He was smiling at her, watching her face intently and nodding as she spoke.

Baby Scott had now pulled himself up to his feet by the rail of the playpen, and was dancing and squeaking, wanting Rae to pick him up. She scooped him up and gave him a hug and kiss, and sat down on the ottoman at Albie's feet with the baby in her lap.

"Now, how was your week? Did Doreen take good care of you? Was Winston Churchill a good dog?"

"Oh . . . yes . . ." It seemed his thoughts all crowded up to the front of his brain and got wedged in the door. She could see in his eyes that he had many wondrous things to tell.

"Yes, we . . . well . . . "

"I hear he ate a sponge," Rae said, and Albie cried, "Yes!", grateful that once again she seemed able to read his mind. Rae got up and put the baby in Albie's lap. She sat down on the arm of his chair and stroked his shoulders and kissed the top of his head. He leaned his head against her and took her hand. She knew that he had missed her deeply, and that once he got used to her being back the words would come back to him.

"So you had a good week? Did exciting things happen?"

"Oh yes, we . . . they came for us in a helicopter," he said. "And then . . . "

And then he got lost, like someone starting to tell a dream who finds it has evaporated. She gave it a minute.

"On your show, you mean? A helicopter came?"

There was a pause. He raised his hand as if in protest, then put it to his lips, as he used to do when he meant to say "Now wait, let's think."

"Yes," he said at last. "On our show. A helicopter came . . ." He made a motion with his finger, showing that things had gone round and round, and finally, a little frustrated, made a motion of flapping his hands past his ears. "Everyone's hair blew!" he cried, and looked pleased.

He was out of the dream, now. But Rae wasn't.

Albie came down to lunch; they ate in the sunroom overhanging the garden. It was small and glass-enclosed, and made the most of the cool winter light, turning it into warmth. Doreen brought them tomato soup with lemon slices, and an omelette. Albie ate slowly and carefully, and with great enjoyment. He had gotten properly dressed in a pair of old corduroys and a dress shirt and jacket. He looked ready for a brisk walk with the dog, or an afternoon of bridge.

Rae told him all about her week at The Cloisters. She told him about how they'd tried to talk Laurie into running for the Senate, and about turning a cartwheel. He clapped when she told that story. "Good for you!" he said, and patted her arm. As always, his sweet, positive nature shone; as always, he applauded the best in people, and loved to see others' success.

"Did you go to the club for lunch on Tuesday?" she asked him.

He had to think a little while, but then he found it. "Yes! He . . . umm . . . "

"James."

". . . drove me."

"And who did you see there?"

"Tony, and . . ." He made a gesture with both hands of a round belly.

"Gordon . . ."

"Yes, and . . . someone . . . with the . . . oh . . . Paul!" He had worked hard for that; he knew it would interest her.

"Paul Prescott? He was at the club? How wonderful!"

"Yes, oh, he looked fine. He ate with us . . . Paul and . . . "

"Tony."

"Tony."

"Well, I'm awfully glad to hear about Paul. Remember . . . nobody thought he'd live, and then they said he'd never walk, anyway."

"He was walking! He has a little . . . "

"Limp . . . "

". . . but . . . he looks fine!"

"It's a miracle. I'm so happy to hear it, and Peg must be thrilled. I'll call her later."

"Do."

"Was there interesting mail?"

He nodded. "I put it . . . "

On her desk, she knew. He went down for the mail every day at noon, and carefully sorted it. He took the mail addressed to him to the study beyond his dressing room. He put the mail for her on the desk in her office.

"Did you pay your bills?"

"Yes, he . . . "

"James . . . "

". . . helped me."

"Good."

"All finish, Mr. Strouse?" Doreen was ready to clear. Albie nodded and smiled.

"Would you like a glass of milk?"

He said he would.

"And a cookie?"

He nodded, happy because he was so predictable, and she was a clever girl. That was right. After lunch he wanted skim milk, and a cookie.

In her office after lunch while Albie had his nap, Rae went through her mail. A few letters, piles of bills, piles of appeals for money. She sorted them into stacks.

She listened to all the saved messages on the answering service. There was one from her daughter, Harriet, who wondered if she and Albie would like to come east to spend Christmas with them—Walter was coming. There was a message from Walter saying he wanted to spend Christmas with Harriet and her children but could hardly face trading San Francisco's weather for Mamaroneck's. "Call me . . . " he

added, in a way that made her smile. Walter was not made for life in
the suburbs.

There was a brief message from her sister Velma, in Erie,
Pennsylvania. One of her grandchildren was going to be in SF—she
said "Ess Eff"—over Thanksgiving. Could she stay with Aunt Rae?
Rae was making notes, and turning pages on her calendar. There was a
message from Jean, with whom she served on the board of the San
Francisco Museum of Modern Art, reminding her of a meeting
Tuesday afternoon. There was an invitation to lunch at the club to celebrate somebody's birthday, but she had missed it. There was another
message from Jean pointing out that the club was starting Italian
lessons with a conversation table at lunch to follow; shouldn't they
sign up? Yes. Rae made more notes.

She turned on her computer and picked up her e-mail. She wrote
a note to Jill, whom she knew was still in midair.

> **"Welcome home, cookie,"** she wrote. **"It's two
> o'clock and I'm waiting for my massage, but noth-
> ing happens. What am I doing wrong?"**

She was just ready to attack her stack of bills when Albie came in.
His face was rosy from sleep. He kissed her on the top of the head and
said happily, "How about a . . . "

"Swim."

"Yes!"

"I'd love it," she said, wishing desperately that she could have
another hour of quiet here. How Albie would have loved computers,
especially the Internet! Oh, well.

Together she and Albie took the elevator down to ground level in
the back of the house. They walked across the garden; Albie put his
hand on her arm to stop her, so they could stand still and smell the air.
He never stopped loving the perfume of San Francisco, the smell of
moist earth and cut grass, and on a damp afternoon like this, wood
smoke. He put his arm around her; he was so glad to have her back.
They walked on to the pool house.

Decorously they parted to go into the men's and ladies' changing rooms. When Rae emerged from hers in her bathing suit, Albie was building a fire in the huge fireplace lined with blue and amber tiles. There was nothing like swimming on a gray afternoon in a room warmed and flickering with firelight. Rae chose a CD, a Brahms piano concerto. The speakers were high in the corners of the room, and the music echoed wonderfully through the moist air.

Albie and Rae each had a favorite swimming drill, so many laps of breaststroke, backstroke, sidestroke, and flutter kicks. Rae swam, watching the light of the fire reflected against the ceiling, and the dark leaves of the huge rhododendrons that had grown up around the glass walls outside. From time to time she looked over at Albie, paddling up and down in his lane. He looked content. Doreen had found a moment to tell her in the kitchen, though, that while she was away he had often been querulous and puzzled. Cook had found him holding a fresh can of coffee, turning it over and over in his hands in frustration, unable to understand or remember how to open it. There had been periods when he didn't want to leave the den or change his clothes. He had been depressed.

*C*arter Bond stood in the long-term parking lot at LAX looking at her dented brown Mercury sedan, and thought, What have I done wrong in life to be fifty years old and driving such a piece of shit? Why aren't I speeding along in a little red Miata, with the wind in my hair? As she turned onto Lincoln Boulevard, she sourly watched a lithe blonde in a tiny convertible cut in front of her and zip off into traffic.

She knew why not, of course. She drove a car that was thoroughly forgettable, like an undercover cop's. It had a huge engine and a good, heavy frame; she'd chosen it with a friend from the police garage. He worked on the cars that had gotten punched and bashed in the line of duty, and knew the safety ratings of the front bumpers and the rear bumpers and the weights of the engine blocks, a walking consumer report for people who expect to be in accidents.

"What about a convertible?" she had asked.

"Saab turbo," he said, "or a Beemer. Of course you're dead if you roll either one of them. Saab's peppier in the high revs, and it's engineered to be a convertible. The Beemer's just a sedan with the top cut off."

"I can't afford either one," she had said. "What about a Miata? What kind of safety rating do they have?"

"That would be 'closed casket.'"

"Oh, *thanks.*"

"You'd never fit in one anyway," he pointed out. "If you put the top up, your head would be through the roof."

She'd bought this big, brown, overpowered gutbucket, which was what he'd wanted her to buy. Whoopee.

She was feeling fairly blue by the time she pulled up in front of her house in Santa Monica, coming back to real life with a bump. She sat in the Brown Bomber and looked at her house, with its brown lawn. All the neighbors had green lawns. They had things like sprinkler systems and husbands. Her house was moldering stucco with a tile roof, in the Spanish style. She had bought it with her husband, Jerry, their first home of their own when they finished law school and came down here so Jerry could take a job with O'Melveny. They had moved, eventually, to a fancy house they built together in the Hollywood Hills, with a great view and lots of track lighting for Jerry's evolving art collection. They had rented the Santa Monica house to a nice young family with two little girls who kept a guinea pig farm in the backyard. Looking back, Carter thought it was probably a bad sign that they hadn't sold it. As if they both knew that one of them was going to need a bolt-hole sooner or later. It was hard to tell which of them had bolted, when it came to it. It just made sense for her to be the one to leave. They had designed the new house together, but it was his money that had built it. Carter was putting everything she earned back into her new business at that point, and investigators don't bill at quite as high a rate as partners at O'Melveny. Besides, as she had said at the time, her art collection was smaller. This was a joke for Jerry's benefit, and he had appreciated it.

Carter was not one to get much of a hit from material possessions, especially not art that looked like pictures of the dog's breakfast. When the first thing Jerry did after the divorce was to buy himself an early Julian Schnabel, one of the ones with the broken kitchen plates stuck on the canvas, she knew it was sort of a joint statement, issued for them both: "Why on earth did we ever think we could live together?"

Carter, in a pensive mood, sometimes asked herself that question still. As well as she could remember, it started as a joke at Boalt Hall, with their classmates constantly pointing out that if Carter Bond married Jerry Carter, her name would be Carter Carter. It was hard to tell who was being teased. Carter, the giant, who had to be the first to say she almost didn't go to law school when she learned it didn't have a basketball team, har har har. Or Jerry, who back then was a fairly terrible-looking person. Tall, strong, quite athletic as it turned out, but with full, heavy lips and bulgy eyes behind steel-rimmed glasses, and runaway eyebrows like two chunks of dark shredded wheat on his forehead.

Jerry had come to Berkeley from MIT, where he'd taken a degree in pure mathematics. He was a little short on social skills, and may have been the only person in Cambridge in 1970 not to have noticed there was a war on, or to have heard of LSD or SDS. He was not in with the in crowd in Berkeley either. But Carter had taken a Con Law class with him early on, and noticed that he was freaking brilliant. To her, sex appeal was between the ears.

Time had taken the rough edges off Jerry. He dressed beautifully now, played a savage game of tennis, and hung out with people who could green-light a sixty-million-dollar picture. His little Ukrainian parents were incredibly proud of him. Carter was too. He had really done good, for the Frankenstein of the class of '72. The trappings of wealth were by now so much a part of his MO that it was hard to picture him ever living in such a modest little hovel as this one. She found she could barely remember it.

As she opened the front door and walked into her house, she found that *she* could remember living here all too vividly. There was a certain humid smell, as if someone never remembered to wring the kitchen sponges dry. It wasn't mildew; she paid a nice young woman from El Salvador a goodly sum to be sure the place was spotless. But the house was old. It had been lived in hard. It was full of the ghosts of thousands of meals, almost none of which had been cooked by her. There had been those guinea pigs. Babies had thrown up. There had been diaper pails. She and Jerry had had an old cat with a bladder problem when they'd first lived here, though after a little while Jerry made the cat live out its natural days outside.

She draped her coat over a dining room chair and went into the kitchen to make a pot of tea. The first thing she saw, when she opened the drawer to get out the matches, was a half carton of cigarettes. She'd opened it a week ago and scooped out seven packs to stuff into her suitcase. There it lay, waiting to be finished. There it lay, singing quietly to her. How many thousands of times had she pulled open that drawer and cracked a new pack? How many problems solved, fresh cups of coffee drunk, cold beers opened, books read, letters written, talks on the telephone, were associated with reaching into that drawer and the spicy smell of fresh tobacco?

On the drainboard were the ashtrays that Julia had gathered from all over the house on Thursday, emptied, and scrubbed clean. The big heavy glass one from her desk, the Mexican pottery ones from the living room, the little celadon-green dish she kept beside her bed. To live in this house without those ashtrays in every favorite spot would be ending an era of her life. Imagine sitting down at the table in the morning with the paper and a mug of coffee, but no cigarettes, no matches, no ashtray.

She took the carton of cigarettes and put it in the garbage. Then she brought over the stack of mail that Julia had piled on the dining room table, along with the magazines that had gathered on the front porch and the envelopes on the floor of the vestibule where they had been pushed through the mail slot since Thursday. She stood drinking tea from her tall pottery mug, sorting the mail. She threw junk mail into the garbage. She held magazines over the can and flipped through them so that the blow-ins would fall out now, as opposed to later, into the bathtub, where she preferred to read magazines. She pulled out all the stinking perfume advertisements and tossed them. She threw in catalogues, unexamined. Garden catalogues, Tweeds clothing, expensive cookware, equine supplies . . . what list was she *on*, what had she bought, to make these people think she had a garden or needed a $200 saucepan? She kind of liked the equine supply one and took a minute to check it out before she pitched it. Who was it at the fat farm who'd said the secret of a great head of hair was mane and tail conditioner?

When she was done, she tied the neck of the half-full bag and carried it out to the garage. That way, if her will failed her in the middle of the night and she decided to backslide, she'd have to make a real ass of herself, nose down in trash cans in her nightgown, to get at the cigarettes.

Next, she sat down at the kitchen table (next to the empty drawer) with a pad and paper to check her telephone messages. Her brother, Buddy, had called to say he was going to the track; did she want to go? There was a call from her father on Tuesday. No message; she recognized the hang up. There was a call from the blood bank, wanting a deposit; there was a call from a guy she'd gone out with in March, saying he'd call again. There was an invitation to go to an industry screening with her friend Paul, whom she adored and wished wasn't gay. There was another call from her father on Thursday, who said he was fine but wouldn't she like to come down to La Jolla for the weekend? More hang ups. Were any of those from Harold, whom she'd broken up with two weeks ago for what might actually be the final time? A friend in the DA's office left a message saying he'd heard some new O.J. jokes, she should call. The last call was from DeeAnne, saying welcome home.

Carter called her father and told him where she had been. He said fine, but would she be coming down for the weekend? She said she'd let him know. She called Buddy and got his machine; he was at the track, of course. She called Paul and told him where she'd been and had a good laugh with him. Paul told her the movie she missed had sucked; they made a dinner date. She called DeeAnne and got *her* answering machine; she was probably with her family in Palm Springs.

It was two in the afternoon.

Ordinarily, on a sunny Sunday, she'd have put on shorts and settled herself in the backyard with an ashtray, a cold beer, and the Sunday crossword. But she had just thrown out the cigarettes, beer was fattening, and her friends had convinced her that sun was the enemy. She was going to feel like a jerk if she went outside to sit in the sun swathed in protective clothing.

She drank a glass of bottled water and ate a tomato that Julia had left to ripen on the windowsill. It was still only 2:20.

She could go to the Safeway and stock up on low-fat ice cream and popcorn cakes, but that wasn't going to get her through the night. What a bummer not to be able to pop up to The Cloisters' gym and put in some time on the treadmill, or go down to the Japanese tub and hang out with whoever happened to be in it. Then it occurred to her— she did belong to a gym. She *could* go put in some time on the treadmill. It would be different. It would be co-ed. It would not smell of eucalyptus. But it was better than sitting here reading the label on the ketchup bottle, thinking about what was at the bottom of the trash can.

She went. The gym did not smell anything like eucalyptus and the music was at a merciless volume, but she took earplugs and a book, and race-walked for forty-five minutes. Then she put herself around the weight machines in a circuit, using low weights and a lot of repetitions, causing all the muscle builders to have to reset the machines when they got onto them after her. She knew they rolled their eyes. She used the leg press last and set the weights up to 150. She pressed two sets of 20 and left the weights set there to give the guys a surprise, and then went to the showers.

Home again, she felt full of energy. She felt, to tell the truth, better than she had in years. It was just this business of getting through the hours she used to spend eating and smoking.

One of the things she had almost chucked with the junk mail, but had not, was a colorful offering from a computer on-line service. She was pretty sure it was the one Jill had talked about. Curious, she carried it into her office and sat down before her computer to study the contents. She was extremely skeptical. She used her computer to pay bills and keep her case files, and every time she had tried to teach it to do something new and amusing, all the old systems, which she really needed, stopped working. They refused to print, or couldn't find abstruse files they needed in order to run, or they froze and the machine claimed to be out of memory. This usually maddened her, since it took valuable time to straighten out, but it occurred to her that at the moment, time was what she had.

She thought she had a modem, but wasn't sure—the machine was a castoff of Jerry's. Somewhere he had given her about eight pounds of books telling what she had and how to work it. These she found, and after a while she found a command that would get the computer to examine its own innards and tell her what was there. Among other things, it found a modem. She liked this diagnostic thing; it would go a long way toward solving the country's health care problems if you could install them in people.

Next she discovered she needed a telephone wire and a double jack. She had a drawerful of that sort of thing—she knew her way around a telephone pretty thoroughly, given her line of work. After an edifying quarter hour crawling along the floor behind the desk, she had the modem hooked into the telephone line in the wall. Next, she poked the disk into the slot, and holding the instructions in one hand, typed the things it told her to type.

Fancy graphics appeared on the screen welcoming her to her own computer, and telling her what it was doing. It was Installing. It was Running Setup. It was adding Artwork. It was finished. The book in her hand now informed her that she had to reboot in order for the machine to adjust to the changes it had made in its brains. She did this. She then tried to start the on-line program, and got a message saying "General System Failure. Abort? Retry? Quit?"

She quit. She started the system again and tried to start her word-processing program. The same thing happened. When it happened a third time, she took a deep breath, and was glad she didn't keep a gun in the house. Instead she went outside, walked to the next-door neighbor's, and rang the bell.

"Hi, Carter," said Bill, a muscley little internist who had moved in with his family a year before.

"Is Teddy home?"

"No, he's at a soccer game. Why?"

"I've turned my computer into a paperweight. I need a teenager."

Bill understood. "I don't think he'll be home until after dinner."

"If I can't figure it out by then, I'll call him. Thanks."

"Anytime."

She went back to her office and spent a maddening half hour poring over manuals. She called tech support, but got a machine that said

they were available during business hours, Monday through Friday.
The last thing she wanted was to blow business hours on a computer
that had worked fine before she ruined it. On the other hand, she
couldn't pay any bills without it.

She called Jerry.

The phone rang for a long time, and when he answered, he was
out of breath.

"Sorry—did I get you out of the pool?"

"Hey! You're back," he said, sounding pleased.

"Did you call me? I didn't get the message."

"I didn't leave a message, I'm too shy. Where were you?"

"You won't believe this."

"I'll sit down."

She told him.

Jerry roared with laughter. "Which one?" he wanted to know. Jerry
was an aficionado of fat farms? She told him which one, and he loved it.

"You? With the Rodeo Drive crowd, drinking potassium broth?"

"DeeAnne tricked me. She was afraid I would have a heart attack
like my mother if I didn't stop smoking."

"I'd thought about that myself. So, did you want to show me the
new body?"

"No, I do not. The computer and I are having a family quarrel."
She explained what had happened.

"I think you just need to rewrite the config.sys file."

"Why? It was fine before."

"The Install program has changed it and now you have to change
it back."

"To what? From what?" The silence on the other end of the line
meant Jerry was trying to calculate the odds that she could understand
the answer to the question if he told her what it was.

"I better come over," he said.

"Tell Graciela I'm sorry to bust up your Sunday."

"I have to get dressed, but I'll be right along."

"Thanks."

* * *

Jerry arrived in forty-five minutes. He was wearing white shorts and a crisp blue and white dress shirt, and driving his Eddie Bauer–model forest green Explorer.

"Thanks for coming," Carter said at the door.

"Whoa, look at you!" He stood back and gave her a once-over, head to toe. This made her blush.

"Can you really see a difference?"

"You look *great*! Look at this, you're all . . ." He made an hourglass shape with his hands. "And I love the hair . . . "

"I didn't do anything to the hair."

"Are you sure? You look very—chic, somehow."

Carter socked him on the arm. "Chic—what do you know, chic? You're a Ukrainian peasant."

He laughed. "My wives teach me these things."

"Not me."

"No, not you. You probably don't even know what a French manicure is."

"I'm proud to say I have no idea."

Jerry was quietly taking in all her domestic arrangements as they walked through the house to her office. She liked that about him . . . he really noticed what things looked like. Of course it was also what drove him nuts about her: she didn't. She noticed all kinds of details like license plate numbers and dents in cars, but not style things. She always meant to sit down with the Design section that came with the Sunday *Times* now and then, but by the time it occurred to her to do it (these moments usually coincided with a sojourn on the throne), Julia had already thrown it out.

Jerry sat down at the computer and turned it on. It went through its boot routine.

"Now, try to make it do anything, and it will tell you it's lost its mind."

Jerry typed a DOS command and the machine obediently showed him a string of numbers and letters.

"Okay," he said, apparently talking to the machine. Carter

watched. Maybe it was talking to him now after pretending to be dead because it recognized its true owner.

"Let's try this. First we'll save this . . ." He typed some more. "Then we'll try this . . ." He typed some more. "Then we'll have a look at the autoexec.bat."

When he had finished he pushed the Reset button, and sat waiting for it to run its routines.

"I'd forgotten how slow this thing is," he said. "It might be faster if we rearranged your memory . . . "

"Don't touch it! Just make it work and then don't change a god-damn thing, ever again."

They were now looking at a screen with little pictures all over it, the pictures standing for programs.

"I'll be damned, there it is," said Carter. She was pointing to an image with the letters of the program she had been trying to install. Whatever had been clogging the works had been sent skulking back into its hole.

"So, shall we give it a try?"

"No, first I have to see if all my real programs are back."

Jerry brought them up, one after another. Everything worked fine. All files were in order. Carter finally relaxed enough to pull over a chair and sit beside him, looking at the screen.

"Okay," she said. "Let's see."

Jerry clicked at the new program and up came a screen with new pictures all over it, and a voice cried, "Welcome!"

"Hola," said Carter.

"There it is. All you have to do is choose a name for your e-mail address, and sign on."

"What kind of name?"

"Anything you want, as long as no one else is using it."

"Are you on this thing?"

"Certainly."

"What's your name then?"

"JC9999."

"What does it mean?"

"Nothing. JCarter was taken, JerryC was taken, and LittleBoPeep was taken."

She laughed. Jerry looked at his watch.

"You're all set. I've got to go. Graciela has people coming."

"I really appreciate it. You take good care of me."

"I'm a very nice guy. Ask anyone in Century City." Jerry's reputation in the legal community was that he never slept, never made a mistake, and never showed mercy.

When he was gone, Carter settled down in her office with the instruction book in her hand again, and began the process of setting up an account. It was so simple it made her suspicious. She didn't trust the computer when it pretended to be her friend.

Finally she got up her courage and typed a letter.

> Yo, Jill—
> Wow—it's big in here!
> I feel so modern I may decide to go downtown and
> have something pierced.
>   Love, Auntie Carter

She pushed a button that said it would send the mail, and a message appeared saying it had been sent. Then she sent a message to JC9999, saying:

> Thanks for the service call. If this works I may
> never go to the post office again. Is everyone on-
> line? Even your mother? What's her handle? And
> what's Graciela making for dinner?

She sent it, and then began poking around to see what there now was in this box on her desk besides mail. She clicked the picture that said Newsstand, and found herself looking at a list of periodicals ranging from the *San Jose Mercury News* to the *Wood Turners Times*. Suddenly, a window opened in the middle of her screen, and in it appeared: From: JC9999

> **Salmon in egg sauce. She's trying to kill me. And my mother IS on line, but she never picks up her e-mail. Maybe she will if you write to her. Her handle is 1Rugelach.**

Underneath there was a space for an answer. Carter wrote:

> **That's the scariest thing that ever happened to me. What IS that?**

She waited for a second or two. Then this appeared:

> **It's called Instant Mail. Any two people on-line at the same time can talk to each other.**

She answered:

> **Does the telephone company know about this?**

He wrote back:

> **The question is, does God? I finally understand the term deus ex machina.**

She replied:

> **I have to hang up now, this is too frightening.**

The message came back:

> **'Bye, kiddo.**

Carter, smiling, went back to her electronic Newsstand, and wasted hours reading long reviews of new bicycles, and then discovered a magazine for survivalists. After she'd read all about how the U.S. government was *pretending* that the Soviet Union had collapsed as part of a plot to disarm and enslave its citizens, she spent a long time reading the classified ads for weapons to buy or build. Then she composed an e-mail message for her former mother-in-law.

*a*my had always been a favorite with the assistants in Noah's office. She shopped for the birthday and Christmas presents Noah gave them. She attended their children's bar mitzvahs and first communions and sent copies of *Bartlett's Quotations* when they graduated from high school. Noah was a shaman in the kingdom of the very sick, a man who worked alone against evil at the cellular level, assisted and attended by women at work and at home. He had male colleagues but he always said his best friend was Amy.

There was a twelve-year difference in their ages, a difference that sometimes felt like a generation. Amy had to remind Noah not to call the nurses his "girls." Amy had to hint strongly on their fifth wedding anniversary, as they lunched on a flowered terrace in Italy with all of Florence spread like a carpet below them, that if he hadn't stopped talking about his first wife by their tenth, it would be their last. He made the cut, but barely. Amy and Jill lived always with the shadow of Noah's two brilliant sons from his first marriage whether he spoke of them or not. These boys had scored in the fourteen hundreds on their college boards; would Jill? If the boys both went to Harvard and Jill didn't, it must be Amy's stupid genes that made the difference.

There were, on the other hand, distinct advantages to Amy's position. Many of Noah's colleagues openly envied him his juicy young wife. Amy was fun-loving and socially fearless. She once got up from the table, marched outside, and dived into the pool in her evening clothes in the middle of a stultifying suburban dinner party given by a world-famous oncologist. The (to Noah) wholly unexpected result was that the host began to view Noah with respect for the first time in their long acquaintance, and never failed to send his love to Amy when he and Noah met.

Noah liked the fact that men flirted with Amy and that she gave it right back to them. It was clear that she liked men, and sex, and equally clear that she was as straight as an arrow, a woman who kept the bargains she made. If there was ever a testing undertone to the flirting, to see if any part of her was serious, she never went anywhere near it. At a party she liked to listen, and she liked to laugh, and women liked her as much as men did.

Amy was a great cook, while Noah's first wife had been fond of saying that what she made for dinner was reservations. Amy enjoyed people so much that she once tried to get Noah to allow her to list their apartment as a Bed and Breakfast, since they had an open guest room, but Noah said no because he couldn't stand it if people tried to talk to him when he was reading the paper. He did, however, allow her to rip out their nice 1930s Gramercy Park kitchen and put in a restaurant stove and an island with two dishwashers and something called an "appliance garage." After the dust had cleared he said it was the best money he'd spent in his life. They started having friends in to dinner two or three times a week, sitting on stools in the kitchen chattering while Amy fed them prosciutto wrapped around chunks of melon or fig, and then produced platters of hot, fresh asparagus and perfect racks of lamb. It wasn't just that they had friends to dinner, it was that they had friends.

Noah became a wine buff. He installed a "cellar" in their storage room in the basement and laid down cases of cabernet. He gained about twenty pounds. He learned to stop deflecting the men's conversations to politics and sports while the women talked about children and schools and relationships. These younger men, the husbands of Amy's friends, had all had as much therapy as the wives had, and the wives mostly had high-powered jobs just as the husbands did. Noah liked this. It was new, and it was fun. Some of these men enjoyed laughing at themselves, and had regular lunch and squash dates with each other during which, it appeared, they voluntarily talked about their feelings. Some had weathered professional upsets, some had frankly never hit the marks they had expected to when young. One had had a terrifying bout with melanoma and become quietly spiritual. One had fallen down an alcohol well and managed to climb back out, and was sometimes very funny about the things he had learned in the process. Noah began to see the social advantages of occasionally stepping down off your dignity.

Noah's fifty-ninth birthday fell two days after Amy and Jill got back from the fat farm. She had given him a surprise party for his fifty-fifth, which apparently *was* a genuine surprise to him, even though you would have thought he'd have noticed the homemade pelmeni for sixty people that had gradually displaced almost everything else in the freezer. The next year she took him to the opera, but it was Benjamin Britten, and he had hated it. The next year she had tickets to a hot musical, but when the day came she was in bed with a fever of 102 so not only did they not go out, they didn't even sleep in the same room that night. This broke her other favorite birthday tradition of surprising him with some unusually inventive sex.

She had planned all year to recoup the loss on his next birthday, but somehow the whole evening had fallen flat. She had very good tickets to the show they had missed the year before, but he told her only after they were seated that he had seen it already, while she was in Idaho visiting her mother. This rather hurt her feelings, and as a result, the business she'd planned for afterward, with the black and silver bustier, didn't come off perfectly either. This year she had started early, planning a surprise he would definitely not have experienced before. That was where her long friendship with Noah's nurses came in.

Noah had been in surgery early in the morning, a sloppy business that should have been simple, and he resented it. He had looked forward to telling his patient in the recovery room that the tumor had been encased, that he had gotten it all and could virtually promise no recurrence. Instead he had encountered a spongey mass of a color and consistency that meant the worst possible news. He had refused to go in to talk to the patient until her young husband, whom he had personally urged to go on to work, could be found and called back to the hospital.

The morning had ended with an equally upsetting peer review of a colleague who had been letting interns perform his surgeries unsupervised, yet listing himself as the surgeon of record and billing accordingly. What were people thinking of? Sometimes it seemed to him that people in his field just took a dose too much of being treated like gods and lost their minds.

In that mood, the last thing he expected or wanted to find when he walked into Consulting Room #2 to meet his first patient of the afternoon was his wife, stark naked except for her stockings and garter belt, fetchingly arrayed beneath a sheet on the examination table.

Amy managed to stop crying before they got to the Plaza. "What makes me so mad is, you were so damn late the chocolate was melting all down my legs!" she said. "I don't know how you keep patients if you treat them like that!" Then he wouldn't take her word for it that he truly had no more appointments for the afternoon, but insisted on cross-examining both his receptionist and his nurse before he allowed himself to be taken hostage, blindfolded, and led down in the freight elevator to a limousine waiting by the service exit in the basement.

The Veuve Cliquot in the car and the basin of chilled caviar waiting in the suite had improved his mood, but Amy was still so annoyed that instead of proceeding with Afternoon Delight, she decided to tie his wrists to the headboard with her garter belt and pace around threatening to whip him with a hanger. Neither one of them found it very sexy, but she was finally mollified enough to proceed with the program, which included lovemaking (during which they accidentally broke the arm off the desk chair), a nap, a bubble bath, dinner from room service, and a visit from a pair of masseuses.

"You are the most incredible woman," Noah whispered when they were finally on the way to sleep. "I can't imagine what you'll do for a sixtieth."

"Put a lump of coal in your stocking," she said. But she was happy again.

Laurie flew from Phoenix to Salt Lake City, where her brother Billy was waiting for her with the family plane.

"Hello, Fats," he said. "How was it?" He gave her a kiss.

"Can't you tell by looking?"

"I wasn't sure what four thousand dollars was supposed to look like."

"It was good. I stopped losing weight, at least."

"And you slept?"

"I did. After the first night or two."

"You look better."

She nodded. "How's everything at home?"

"Everyone's fine. The twins and Melanie have taken over the tree house, and now they feel like really *big* kids."

"Did Cara and Tessie kill each other?"

"They tried. Then they fell in love again. They're out riding together now."

"That's good news."

They were walking out to the airstrip where the Cessna was waiting.

Billy was the same height as Laurie, compact and muscular. He looked like what he was, a man who spent most of his life outdoors. Billy and Laurie had the same blue eyes and were going slightly gray in about the same way; they had always looked as if they came from the same genetic stock, while their older brother, Bliss, was larger and softer and beginning to run to fat.

Billy moved more fluidly than his sister although he was two years older. Outdoor work had kept him supple. They had both been downhill ski racers in their teens. She was good, but Billy had been Olympic class. He would have gone to Grenoble if he hadn't been in Vietnam.

"You want to drive?" Billy asked her. Laurie shook her head. She hoisted herself into the copilot's seat and studied a high system of cirrus clouds as Billy went through his preflight routine. They wheeled out onto the runway to await clearance for takeoff.

"Anna missed you a lot. She spent a lot of time with Cinder." Cinder was Billy's wife, who was to Laurie the first sister she'd ever had. Anna, at fifteen, was Laurie's worry child, the odd one out in her little fatherless family. Carlos, the oldest, would never question his position in the universe. The twins were the babies and had each other, and thirteen-year-old Cara had an all-absorbing love-hate bond with her cousin Tessie. But Anna was a loose marble. She wasn't athletic, like the rest of them. She was musical, unlike the rest of them. Her father's death had hit her especially hard.

"Did Carlos get his history paper done?" Laurie asked as they moved into position for takeoff.

"Yes. With only one all-nighter."

"Typical." She made a face.

Carlos seemed to regard planning ahead not as an aid to efficiency or a guard against disaster, but as the death of possibilities. Laurie and Roberto had laughed about it. Laurie didn't laugh easily anymore. Instead she tended to weary herself fretting over qualities in her children that might bring them unhappiness or failure. She wanted to *make* them see things as she did.

Cinder would say gently, "We could do so much better at living their lives than they do," and they would smile. But Laurie knew that this will to make the children do things her way was becoming a monster that was hard to cage. If she could be in five places at once, she'd follow every one of them around all day, nagging. She knew what Cinder thought. Cinder thought she ought to get a life.

Billy throttled up, and the little plane scooted down the runway and into the sky. Billy loved flying. Laurie didn't, though she kept her license up in case of emergency. Of all the family, only Roberto had never learned.

The weather was crisp and cool, but snow was still a long way off. The sky was huge. After some time, she'd lost track of how much, Laurie saw they were flying over one of the national forests.

"Is that Wasatch?"

"Caribou," said Billy. "We're in Idaho."

Caribou. About seventy miles from home, then.

"You know what they said at The Cloisters?"

"What?"

"They decided to run me for the Senate against Jimbo Turnbull. It was kind of a goof we all got into."

Billy frowned slightly and adjusted something on the dashboard. He looked intently into the middle distance.

"One woman whose friend works for the President said I'm even on some list at the White House."

"What kind of list?"

"Longshot list, I think."

Billy smiled.

"Some list of people who might by some stretch of the imagination be able to beat Big Jim."

Billy nodded slightly. There was silence for a little.

"Well, since you bring it up."

Laurie looked at him.

"Since I bring it up, what?"

"I've had the same thought myself. So has Cinder."

"I hope you're kidding. I *had* my fifteen minutes of humiliation, remember?"

"It was eighteen years ago. Get over it."

"Why?" She was stung, but Billy took the question literally.

"First, everyone wanted Bliss in seventy-six. Everyone thought Bliss was the next JFK. Second, Idaho wasn't ready to send a woman to Washington. Now they'll elect Maryellen Beckwith, for god's sake."

They hit a patch of turbulence and Laurie noticed, as she had often before, that not only was Billy not troubled, he rather liked it when unseen currents batted the plane around. She scooped up a pair of sunglasses that had hit the floor and pushed them into the over-stuffed cargo hammock where they should have been stowed in the first place.

When the plane stopped lurching, Billy said, "Look. You need a new dream. So do the kids. You had a happy family dream, and you lost it. You need something to put in its place, and you need it right now."

"It wasn't a dream."

"All right, but it's gone. You need something to fight for."

"I feel as if I've wandered into a tough love seminar."

Billy flew his plane.

"It seemed insane to me," Laurie said after a while.

"Well, let's look at the plus column. There's Dad and Bliss and Roberto, the Famous Political Family factor. There's the sympathy vote. And the Moral Outrage vote, all the people who are sick of see-ing insiders and celebrities get a different deal from the rest of us. You'd be a hero to a lot of people if you fought back. Including your children. And including me."

Laurie stared out the window. "But you like underdogs," she said.

"I do." He smiled suddenly. "I can't help it . . . I'm from Idaho."

"This is nuts. A woman? A Democrat from Blaine County? Against an entrenched incumbent? A widow leaving her children to eat worms and fall out of windows while she runs for office?"

"The kids are the most important reason to do it."

"Well, that's a novel approach." There was a pause. "You don't know what it feels like to stand around your headquarters on election night watching those numbers coming in, saying, 'Nah, no thanks, we pass.'"

"Laurie, it isn't personal."

"It's the most personal thing in the world."

"Fine, you're right. Does it feel worse than sitting around in your house feeling the way you do now? If your kids all grow up to be alco-holic John Birchers, don't blame me."

"If I don't strap on my chamber pot and gallop off to get throttled, I'm a bad mother?"

"If you teach your kids that the only fights worth taking on are the ones you know you can win, yes."

Laurie felt tears start. If she could have spoken without crying, she'd have said "Dirty pool." It was one of the things Roberto always said. He'd had so much to overcome, he'd tilted against so many windmills, winning and losing, while she who always had the odds in her favor hated the smallest failure so much.

"Look, the kids can speak for themselves. And if they wanted you to run, they would tell people so. Meanwhile, you know everyone in the party, and they know you. You've served on the school board, you've run for judge. You've won everything you ever tried for except the congressional race."

"You don't know how much I hated that."

"Yes, I do."

"What would Bliss say?"

"No idea. No, I take it back. He'll say, 'Laurie? Why not me?'" They both laughed. Bliss was a lawyer in Boise. He'd been in and out of state politics, but was never willing to drop everything and go for it; he was making too much money. Yet he always talked as if any day now he was going to.

"What about Dad?"

"You can ask him yourself in half an hour," said Billy.

There was a silence.

"What do you *think* he'd say?"

Billy said, "I don't know what he'd *say*. I know it would be the best thing that could happen to him."

They landed at Friedman Field and walked to the farm truck Billy had left there. To the north, suddenly jutting from a wide plain, were the stark and beautiful Sawtooth Range. They drove southeast in the bright afternoon. The aspens were almost bare; the streams were low compared to their rushing spring levels. Laurie rarely traveled this road without thinking about the day Billy had brought home Roberto

Lopez, the famous tennis star. She had loved to think of what this magnificence had looked like to Roberto, seeing it for the first time. It had made her see it with his eyes ever after, instead of her own, as if time had stopped and their first meeting were just about to happen.

The twins were outside with their cousin Melanie playing mumblety-peg when the truck pulled into the yard. Hunter and Xavier, too young to be cool, dropped their jackknives and ran to her, crowing. Laurie wrapped them in her arms, and was suddenly overjoyed to be home. The boys had a million things to tell her. She gave her niece a kiss and went toward the kitchen door with the boys dancing around her.

In the kitchen, she found Cinder with Anna. Cinder was tall and rail slim, with huge brown eyes and her hair pulled out of the way and held with whatever came to hand. Sometimes it was a rubber band, sometimes one of the children's scrunchies, sometimes a bandanna or a pair of sunglasses on top of her head. She was utterly natural, never wearing makeup or taking any care with her appearance except to be shiny clean. She was the most naturally beautiful woman Laurie had ever seen. Cinder had absolutely no idea that it was true and would have been supremely uninterested if she had been told.

Cinder wasn't a touch person. She greeted Laurie by smiling at her, and the warmth in her eyes said all that needed to be said. Anna came to her mother to be hugged. Soon Cara and Tessie came flying in from the barn where they'd been building a clubhouse in the hayloft. Carlos was at home "doing homework," said Cinder, in a voice that let Laurie hear the quotation marks. She meant that she was sure he had the boom box up to top volume playing Pearl Jam, and was wandering around the house in his boxers, eating cold cereal and reading the funnies.

Laurie sent the littles upstairs to pack up their stuff. Anna was already ready. Carlos had taken Laurie's car when he'd gone home, so the bags and small children were put in the back of the pickup, and Cinder drove them to Laurie's house, with Anna between them in the cab.

"Can you stay for a cup of tea?"

"How about a walk?" Cinder said. "I haven't been out of the house all day."

"Great."

"Can I come?" Anna asked.

"Of course, Puddleduck."

"Anna."

"Sorry. Anna." She added, "I'd like to stop and see Dad. Have you seen him today?"

"No, not since Friday," said Cinder.

"I have," said Anna.

"Really?"

"Yesterday. I helped him put straw on his garden."

"Did you indeed. You good person."

"We ate his last tomato." Eating the last of Hunt's summer tomatoes was a great honor.

When Laurie had changed into blue jeans, they set off for Hunt's cottage. They found him reading the *New York Times*, for which he drove all the way into Hailey every Sunday.

"Well, here's the world traveler," he said, giving Laurie a kiss. "How are things?"

"Things are better," she said.

"You look like you've had a rest, anyway."

She nodded. "Do you want to come for a walk with us?"

"No, you go along. I have to write a letter to the editor," he said, gesturing at his paper.

Hunt watched them go out through the backyard toward the mountains, and saw that Laurie was indeed holding her back straighter. She was talking to Cinder with some of her old animation. Anna, with her lanky straight hair and her lumpy hips paced along beside the women, listening passionately to their talk.

Hunt watched them for several minutes, then went to the phone to call Geri. Geri was one of their friends up in Ketchum who had come years ago to attend Sun Valley in the season, and had ended up staying for good. It was she who had ordered Hunt to send Laurie to The Cloisters, and damn the expense.

* * *

Cinder wanted to know in vast detail what they had done all day down there in Arizona, and Laurie described it. Anna laughed about the water exercises. Cinder was worried that Laurie hadn't gotten enough food.

"Did you make friends? Tell about the people." Anna was intent, as Laurie described the detective, and The Movie Star, and the woman whose friend worked for the President, and Wilma Smythe, the ER doc.

"Just like on television!" Anna cried. Laurie found herself saying, "You'd have loved to hear what they said about your father, Puddleduck."

"Tell me!"

Laurie did, and somehow, although she had not meant to discuss this with the children at all, she found herself saying, "In fact, they thought so much of your dad that they said I ought to run for the Senate. In his memory, to carry on for him. Wasn't that nice of them to say?"

Anna looked at her, electrified. She was an avid reader, and she'd spent much of the past year filling herself on tales of American heroines. "Mom! You'd be like Carrie Nation!" Laurie and Cinder laughed.

"Yeah, in Idaho, I might be."

"Or Billie Jean King!" This was Anna's highest praise. Anna's favorite bedtime story, which she'd made Roberto tell her over and over, was about the time Billie Jean had beaten the socks off Bobby Riggs.

"So this sounds like a good idea to you, huh?"

"Of *course*! We'd all campaign for you! I mean, we'd have to miss some school . . ." Anna was an earnest child with more passion than sense of humor. "We'll all help! The twins can make posters, and I can help with your speeches, and Carlos can drive!"

Cinder said, "Perfect!"

"And what about Cara?"

Laurie knew that Cara could fall down a well as far as her sister was concerned, so she looked forward to hearing what she was going to be allowed to contribute. But Anna was ready for her.

"Cara and Tessie will sing your jingle. That's what they do all day anyway."

"My *jingle*?"

"Of course—you'll have ads on television, won't you? And we'll all be on them? You'll have a jingle . . . "

Laurie was very moved, and very amused. She put an arm around Anna.

Cinder said, smiling, "So, Anna . . . it sounds like you're all set."

"Yes!" said Anna. "Of course!"

"But what if I won," said Laurie. "Would you want to live in Washington?"

That stopped Anna for a minute. "*Washington*? Not Boise?"

"Uh, no. I meant the kind of senator who goes to Washington."

"That's even better!" exclaimed Anna doubtfully. Laurie knew that at this point she had less than no idea what she was talking about. Washington was in the east. It was hot there. Anna was just starting high school. If she was a loner here, where everyone had known her from birth, what would happen to her in *Washington*?

"So," said Cinder to Laurie, "are you in? Are we going to do it?"

"Of course not," said Laurie. "It was just something we talked about. I mean—Washington? I hadn't even thought about it."

"Why not?" Anna demanded.

"Honey, because. Listen. You're all in school. You can't be traveling all over with me. It's hard and it's boring. I'd be gone all the time, and Cinder would have to do all the work I usually do. We can't expect other people to do our jobs for us."

Cinder said, "Oh, I don't mind at all. You know that."

"See!?" cried Anna.

Laurie stopped walking and looked at both of them. Cinder and Anna had, unconsciously, drawn together. She looked at their faces, Cinder's so fine-boned and wide-eyed, with deep laugh lines, and Anna's, so young and unfinished, all smooth flesh. Cinder looked like a beautiful animal, a filly or a fawn; Anna looked like a piece of fruit. But they were wearing the same expression.

"But . . . no, but my god, think about it. Think of the money I'd have to raise. Think of all the . . . setting up offices . . . getting the party to support me . . . "

"I doubt that's a problem," said Cinder.

Laurie gaped. "Of course it's a problem . . . I'm a woman. I lost a big race once and said I'd never do it again. I haven't paid my dues . . . "

"Honey—Roberto paid your dues for you," said Cinder.

It caught Laurie by surprise, and her eyes filled with tears. Her daughter looked at her, full of conviction. Cinder, dear Cinder, looked at her in that calm, unsentimental way she looked at everything. Neither of them looked away, or backed down. Finally Laurie said, "And then . . . after all that, all that money and work, I'd lose."

She expected them to protest, but Cinder was way beyond that.

"Oh, I don't think that matters," she said.

*I*t was the Monday before Thanksgiving, and Rae had spent a lovely morning at the club having an Italian lesson. This had included lunch, over which they said things in Italian to each other like "This is my fork." Rae's great triumph of the meal was managing to announce in correct grammar, "Today is my anniversary." People wanted to ask what festive plans she and Albie had for the evening, but no one could think of the vocabulary words. Jean tried to slip into French, but was scolded by the tapping of a butter knife against a water glass.

It was lovely weather, cold, bright, and windless. Rae put the top down on her little car as she drove home, and enjoyed the sense that, really, all was right with the world. Maybe she could take Albie to Rome after Christmas, and dazzle him by saying to people in Italian, "This is my fork."

When she pulled up in front of the house on Broadway, the front door was standing open, and the garage door too, with Albie's car halfway up the driveway. It was stopped at an angle, rear outward. Something was definitely not right.

Rae ran up the walk. Doreen met her at the door; she had been crying.

"Oh, Missus . . ." she said. She looked terrible.

"Is Mr. Strouse all right?"

"He isn't hurt, but . . ."

"What happened?"

"He tried to drive away. James heard the garage door open, and went right down . . . "

Albie hadn't driven in six months. He'd been embarrassed when he met a friend downtown and accepted a ride home, forgetting he had left his own car in the Sutter/Stockton Garage. Soon after he had parked the car at Laurel Village and then been unable to find it again; Christine at the bank had had to call Mrs. Strouse to come get him. Gradually he had fallen into the habit of letting James drive him when he wanted to go out.

"Then when we heard a screech, *so* terrible . . ." Doreen started to cry again.

"But what happened?"

"The dog was screaming . . . "

Suddenly, Rae understood. Albie going down the back stairs with his hearing aids out. Winston Churchill trotting fondly behind him, unseen and unheard. Albie focused on the now unaccustomed task of backing the car up the drive, while Winston Churchill gamboled about, trying to show that he wanted to go too . . .

"Where is the dog now?"

"James took him to the vet, but . . . "

"Did you see him?"

Doreen nodded, weeping. Rae could see, it had been ugly. Then, as if disturbed by the level of distress in the house, Doreen's baby began to wail, and apologizing, Doreen ran for the kitchen.

Rae stood in the front hall with an awful, sickening sorrow. The poor, loving, innocent dog . . . her poor husband . . .

She hurried upstairs. Albie was sitting in silence in the den. Rae went in and sat beside him. She took his hand.

He looked up at her sadly and then smiled a little. "You," he said.

"Yes, love. I'm here. I think something bad has happened?"

He nodded. He seemed too miserable to speak, and yet she knew he would try. It was so terrible for him to be walled up with confusion and sorrow, apart from her, when they had shared so much.

"You were going out?"

He nodded. His mouth worked, a new sort of tic he had, born of frustration.

"You wanted to see someone?"

He shook his head hard. No, that was wrong.

"You wanted to get something?"

He nodded.

"Something you left somewhere?

No.

"You wanted to buy something?"

Yes. He did. He wanted to buy something. Now she was stumped, because she couldn't imagine what he could need that he didn't have. It could be anything.

He struggled. He pointed to his forehead, he frowned painfully, he shook his head. With his hands and shoulders he conveyed something lost, wrong, something that didn't connect.

"Word . . ." he said.

"You couldn't find a word." He nodded, miserably but vigorously. He waited for her to go on, but she couldn't. He couldn't find a word. But what word? Was he going out to find something that would help him show what he meant?

He tried to illustrate something with his hands. It made no sense to her. He quivered with sad frustration. Clearly he could see the thing in his mind, but he couldn't put it into *her* mind.

"Oh," he said, as if it were more than he could bear. He got up and went out into the hall, and she followed him. Agitated, he paced the hall, stopping to study the pictures. There were hunting dogs, and a pair of eighteenth-century prints of the Roman Forum.

Searching, he opened a door to an unused bedroom.

"There!" He pointed to a Chinese vase on the mantelpiece.

"Vase?" Rae said, and then understood it all, with a sense that her heart was breaking in two pieces at that exact moment. *Flowers.* He knew it was their anniversary, and he wanted to buy her flowers. He couldn't think of the word, but he knew how to drive to the flower store.

"Oh, love," she said, and put her arms around him. He clung to her, so grateful to have finally been understood, so horrified at what had happened. Rae cried a little, trying hard not to. Poor dog, sweet, loving, dumb dog. Poor husband—what angry God had done this terrible thing to such a man? This fine, kind man with his lively mind, his sense of humor, his dignity . . .

"Come here," she said. "Come here." They sat down on a little loveseat that filled a bay window in this unused room. The November afternoon light came through white voile curtains in a thin stream. Albie's eyes were red-rimmed. Deep in sorrow, he held both her hands.

When she had composed herself, Rae said: "You are the dearest man I have ever known, and every day I'm allowed to share your life is a happy day for me. You have made me feel loved and safe, you have loved my children. . . . Thank you for the best years of my life."

She kissed him, tenderly, and he kissed her back. (It was one thing he had not forgotten how to do.) When she looked at him, tears were streaming down his face. She added, "And I never in my life met a man who could do a better cha-cha-cha."

She produced a handkerchief, and dried her own eyes, and handed it to him.

"If we go to the store together, will you still buy me flowers? I have a feeling I'm going to want something *very* expensive." He nodded.

They went downstairs, and while Albie found his coat, Rae stopped in the kitchen to talk to Doreen. Bertha, whom everyone called Cook, was making dinner, and Doreen was with the baby.

"Is James back?"

"No, Missus." Doreen feared, as Rae did, that the longer he was gone, the worse the news.

"Maybe Winston Churchill needs an operation?"

"Yes, maybe. I'm glad James is with him. I'm going to take Mr. Strouse out and make him buy me some flowers as an anniversary present," Rae said.

Doreen and the cook both nodded. They were so worried for her, knowing how she loved that dog.

Rae and Albie then drove off in her little red car, top down, and when they came back, Rae had an enormous armful of long-stemmed French tulips. Albie came out to the kitchen with her to watch her show them off to Doreen and Cook.

"Aren't they beautiful? Can you imagine, in November? I think they're the prettiest flowers I ever had. Don't you think so too?" She turned to Albie. He bobbed his head.

"Doreen, would you just put these in some warm water while I go up and help Mr. Strouse get ready for his nap?"

She took her husband's arm and left the kitchen.

When she came back downstairs a half hour later, James was back. She knew by his face the moment she saw him.

"He's dead," Rae said.

James nodded. His eyes were full of tears as he said, "His back was broken. He was bleeding inside. He was so good and quiet. . . . He kept looking at me with his eyes . . .

"They came out after a long time and said he should be put down. I called, but Doreen said you had gone out. . . . He was in terrible pain. I hope I did the right thing."

Rae's eyes and throat ached with tears. She didn't want to cry in front of them. Finally she was able to say, "Did you . . ." and that was all.

"Yes, I held him. They gave him a shot. He looked at me with his big eyes. He showed the tip of his tongue, the way you say he is throwing a kiss . . . "

Rae looked down at the floor and tears flowed. After a while she put her shoulders back, lifted her chin, and produced her handkerchief. "Thank you both. Let's not mention this to Mr. Strouse. Please put the dog dishes away. Find his chew toys. Bring his bed down from my room."

"I didn't bring him home," James said, trying to ask a question. He knew that an earlier dog was buried in the garden.

"No, that was right. We just won't mention him again," she said, and went out.

When Mr. and Mrs. Strouse came downstairs for their anniversary dinner, they were two of the handsomest old people James and

Doreen had ever seen. They had dressed. Mr. Strouse wore black tie, a bright red cummerbund, and a pair of velvet smoking slippers. Mrs. Strouse wore a long dress of teal blue satin. They had danced in these clothes. Rae wore a diamond bracelet Albie had given her on their tenth anniversary. Albie had a red rose in his buttonhole.

They sat in the big library to have their cocktails. James had laid a fire for them, and brought in their cocktails on a silver tray. Mr. Strouse had his vodka martini with two olives, and Mrs. Strouse had a glass of Dubonnet. The cook had made hot cheese puffs for hors d'oeuvres, and Albie showed that he considered this a great treat. They sat by the fire, and Rae chattered to her husband about her Italian lesson, and what she had eaten for lunch, and then she amused him by saying silly things in Italian. Still, underneath was a current of pure sorrow. When they had finished their drinks, James came in to announce dinner. They walked arm in arm into the dark-paneled dining room.

The table was beautifully set for two. Rae's flowers were in the center, and candlelight gleamed on the dark wood. They sat together at one end of the room, and James served them their soup, cream of spinach with mushrooms, which Albie loved. He murmured his pleasure when he tasted it.

"Remember the Waltz Night on the ship, when we met?" Rae asked Albie, suddenly smiling. "Remember . . . we had barely met, and you told me a poem?" She began to recite:

> *"Pa was broken-hearted . . .*
> *When the dancing craze got started,*
> *And he found out that his shoes*
> *Were full of feet . . . "*

Albie did remember, and smiled. "A song!" he said.

"That's right, not a poem. A song. And you went on for verses . . ." He nodded. Verses and verses. He had been famous for it.

Together they tried to remember more of it. "Something something something, Something dancing something . . ." and then together, triumphantly, "I can dance with everybody but my wife!" and they laughed.

"But *you*," he said.

"Yes. You can dance with me," said Rae. "We could dance, from the first minute. You spun me around on that Waltz Night. And you told me poems and made me laugh, and I had to tell you I wasn't allowed to canoodle with the passengers."

He blushed. That was true, that was true. He remembered. They both remembered. They held hands across the table as James cleared the soup plates. He brought in two beautiful, delicate dinner plates, and solemnly passed the dishes, first to Rae, then to Albie. There was a platter of standing rib roast, sliced thin and garnished with watercress. There was asparagus swimming in butter. There was corn pudding. They ate in quiet companionship. This was Albie's favorite menu.

When James had cleared their plates, Rae fumbled in her evening bag and produced a little present, wrapped with a green ribbon of real silk.

"Happy anniversary, dear heart," she said.

Albie smiled. He put the box to his ear and rattled it. He put it down again and peered at it. Slowly, he opened it. It was a watch, rather oversized, with a digital face and a black plastic strap. Albie looked up with a puzzled smile. He *had* a wristwatch, and a gold pocket watch. It was in his pocket now. Rae put out her hand for the new watch, and pushed a button on its side. It spoke in an electronic voice: "Eight twen-ty-five. P.M." Albie clapped his hands.

"For when you don't have your glasses." Albie pushed the button himself. The watch told him the time. He strapped it onto his wrist.

James brought in dessert plates and finger bowls. When their plates were piled with airy meringue floating in custard and James had left the room, Albie shyly produced a wrapped package from his pocket. Exclaiming with wonder, Rae unwrapped it. Inside was a necklace of marble beads, which she knew at once he must have managed to order in secret from a catalogue.

"It's the prettiest thing I ever saw," she said. "All my favorite colors. . . . It will go with everything. Why, I never had anything like it. I may never take it off." And she fastened it around her neck, along with her pearls. "Thank you, darling."

"Happy . . ." he said.

"Anniversary." He nodded and smiled his sweet smile.

They finished their dessert, and James brought them demitasses in the library. As they sat in front of the fire, Rae hoped that no one would mention the dog until enough time had passed that it seemed a bad thing from the dim past, and caused him no pain or shame.

They went to bed together in Rae's room, and held hands together in the dark. When she was sure Albie was asleep, Rae allowed herself to feel the pity for Winston Churchill, and sorrow for herself, that she'd been holding in all day and evening. It was hard to hold it in and grieve alone.

Sometime in the night Rae realized Albie was no longer in bed, but he often went back to his own room if he grew restless.

Toward morning she woke again with a sense of unease. It was not yet fully light; dawn came so late on winter mornings. She sat up and looked around the room. Everything was in order, except that Albie's slippers were beside the bed. That was unusual. He was a creature of habit, and when he went from room to room he put his slippers on.

She got up and went quietly through the dressing room to Albie's bedroom. The bed was untouched.

She went back to her own room for a robe and slippers. Quietly, not wanting to wake Doreen and James, she went down the front stairs. Everything was silent and as it should be.

The fire in the library had burned all the way to ash, and the room was cold.

She went to the living room, which they rarely used, and on to the kitchen, to see if Albie had come down for something to eat. But the kitchen was quiet. There was no sign that anyone had been there since the cook had gone to bed.

She went back into the front hall, about to go up to the den, when she felt a draft. Following it, she went past the front stairway, and saw that the little door to the back garden was off the latch. Immediately she went out, and down the steps.

The morning air was very cold; she could see her breath. The air was filled with the smell of dank earth, and moss. There was no wood smoke on the breeze at this hour. It was a cool, dark, green and woody, slightly rotting smell. She was careful on the steps going down, holding tight to the iron rail. The moss on the stone made these treacherous and the last thing she wanted was a broken hip.

There was no one in the garden. There was heavy dew, which would have been hoarfrost if it were just a little colder. She went on toward the pool house.

There were no lights on in the building, but as she now expected, the door was unlatched. Her heart felt like lead in her chest. She went in, and was struck by the wall of humid warmth and the smell of chlorine. She stood in the thick darkness and called: "Albie?"

The sound bounced and echoed around the room as sounds do across water. There was no answer. She was gripped by a numb sensation of being suspended in time. She didn't want to move. But finally she forced herself to turn on the lights.

The room flashed into brightness. It took a moment for her eyes to adjust. Then it was only a matter of walking a few more feet until she could see that he was there.

He was naked. That was the surprise. She'd been fearing he'd gotten confused, and come here, and drowned by mistake. But he would have been wearing his nightclothes. For a moment then, she pictured him mistaking the time and coming to swim. But if so, why was he not wearing his trunks?

Then she saw the pajamas, on the stone bench on the other side of the pool. They were carefully folded, in exactly the way he liked it done. Everything about them said deliberation. Then she understood. It was the only kind of message he could leave her.

She sat for perhaps a half hour alone with him. She didn't look at the bottom of the pool again. She just sat, breathing the humid air, alone with her love for the last time. She quietly cried.

When she felt she could, she got up and went back to the house. She went up to her bedroom and washed her face and brushed her teeth. Then she called James on the house phone.

He was instantly awake, and alarmed. Rae said, "I'm sorry to have to wake you so early, James. I'm afraid I need you."

"I'll be right there," he said and had almost hung up.

"No, wait, please. Please call Mr. Walter and ask him to come here as quickly as he can. Then put on some water for some tea and then . . . please call the police."

There was an intake of breath. "And I shall say . . . ?"

"Ask them to send someone. Mr. Walter will be here and know what to do. And then please bring up the tea."

unt had been invited to dinner at the big house for a family summit. The girls had cooked and the boys had washed the dishes; now the adults were caucusing in the living room. Cinder and Billy were sitting on the couch while Laurie sat alone in what had once been her father's armchair. Hunt paced around the room. He reached into his shirt pocket twice, looking for cigarettes.

"You were a great campaigner, I remember that," he said a couple of times.

"Do you think the party would endorse me?"

He looked out the window. "I think they would. They don't have anyone else to put up against Jimbo, that I've heard, except that fella up in the panhandle, what's his name?"

"Prince," said Billy.

"That's it."

"Who is Prince?" Cinder asked.

"Some carpetbagger, made a lot of money building shopping malls somewhere. He moved to Sandpoint and retired, but he seems to think Sandpoint doesn't know how lucky it is to have him."

"What about raising money?" Laurie asked. "How much would it take?"

"At least a million, probably twice that," Hunt said, and Laurie flopped back in her chair like a rag doll. "I told you, times have changed."

"A couple of *million*? For a state with one million people?"

"Be glad it's not California. There it would cost you twenty." Cinder whistled.

"How does anyone raise money like that?"

"There's a lot of money right around here, you know," said Hunt. "Even if it does wear flannel shirts and ride around in Jeeps."

"You mean Sun Valley."

"Sun Valley. Sandpoint. All over the state. Skiers, fishermen. They may not vote here, but they love Idaho, and some of them are even Democrats."

"And some of them are even women," said Cinder.

"And Boise's changing," said Billy. "All those computer people. A lot of them have lived in the outside world. They know Idaho's part of America."

"Let me ask you this," Hunt said. "If you won, is it a job you want? You like being a judge."

"I do, but it's lonely."

"Is it?"

"Much more than being a small-town lawyer. I used to know everybody in the district. All the lawyers, I'd either worked with them or against them. Now no one can forget that sooner or later, they may appear in my court. I could live without it."

Hunt got up and paced around. Laurie, Billy, and Cinder exchanged covert glances. They could see he was loving every minute of this.

"I'd need a lot of help, Dad."

"I know you would, I know you would. Now what about the children?" Hunt asked. "Have they been polled?" He turned to his grandson, who had brought a dining room chair into the room and was straddling it backward. "Are you the duly-elected Speaker, Carlos?"

"Yes, sir, until Christmas."

"What are you authorized to say?"

"Our committee is unanimous, sir."

"Very commendable."

"Our decision is Go, Mom."

"Is it? Well, that's very interesting. Do all your members understand what that means? Your mother would be very, very busy for long periods of time. She would be gone altogether for long stretches."

"We plan to go with her, sir."

"That's often not possible."

"We went through it when Dad ran. You ran for things and Mom and Bliss and Billy survived."

"A national campaign is different. And when I was running for office your mom and uncles had their mother at home."

"We have Cinder." Carlos didn't look at Cinder when he said this, since everyone knew she was shy about displays of affection. But all the grown-ups saw that her color rose and she looked at the floor for a while.

The younger children, including the cousins, had finished in the kitchen and filtered in to listen. The twins and Melanie sat on the floor. Anna sat on the arm of her mother's chair. Tessie and Cara lounged in the doorway. There was a silence that stretched, and in it Laurie had the strangest feeling (and she learned later that she was not alone) that Roberto had entered the room.

Suddenly Carlos said, "I'll tell you what Dad would say. Remember the time we went to Mexico for Christmas, and on New Year's Day, on the Sea of Cortez, Dad wanted Mom to go parasailing?" Carlos looked at his mother, who remembered the day vividly. He looked at his grandfather. "Cara and Anna and I had all been up, and Dad wanted Mom to do it with him. She was scared, she said, 'I can't, I'm a mother.' And Dad pointed at these little, tiny people, little dots in the sky, dangling from a parachute thirty-five stories above the ocean, and he said to her, 'Hey, what's the worst that could happen?'"

He had reproduced his father's accent and brilliant smile so perfectly that everyone in the room laughed. No one could ever resist that goofball courage in Roberto, but also they felt a little unhinged, joyous, as if for a very brief moment they had him back. The room fell quiet again very quickly.

Hunt said, "I'm waiting for the punch line. Did she do it?"

"Of course!" "Yo!" "Yes!" The children all answered at once.

Hunt turned his whole body away from the fire, and took a good look at his daughter.

ALBERT STROUSE, SAN FRANCISCO PHILANTHROPIST, DEAD AT 83

ran the headline on the *New York Times* obituary. The account, which ran twelve column inches, went on to describe his rise from department store clerk to manager to founder of The Surplus chain of clothing stores, now to be found on every continent except Antarctica. It mentioned his work with the OSS during the Second World War, his love of sports, especially the Cal Bears and the San Francisco Giants. It dwelled at length on his service on a score of boards and the work of the Strouse Foundation. It mentioned his first marriage to Ruth Rose, his children, Albert, Jr., and daughter Eloise, and six grandchildren. It mentioned his second marriage to the former Janet Thigpen Keely, known as "Rae." It said that he had died at home, after a long illness.

S imilar notices ran in most of the major papers across the country, and the *San Francisco Chronicle* carried an even longer version, with a very jolly picture of Albie dressed as a singing milkmaid during a performance at the Bohemian Club. None of the notices mentioned the nature of his illness or the manner of his death, and for that Rae was intensely grateful.

In the long day while she waited for the children and grandchildren to arrive, she and her son, Walter, had begun the task of going through Albie's papers. They found that he had been preparing for death throughout his life. He'd left a file describing exactly where all his real estate records, bank accounts, insurance records, investment and tax papers were, with names and telephone numbers of agents and executives. It was the work of a man who would have been horrified to fail in protecting and providing for his loved ones.

Rae noticed that the last changes in this folder were dated three years ago. She cried only once, when Walter found a more recent paper that had been tucked under the blotter. On it, Albie had been practicing writing his own name.

The obituary asked that in lieu of flowers, donations be sent to the Strouse Foundation. Mountains of flowers arrived at the house anyway. Rae had the tulips Albie had bought her carried upstairs to their bedroom. The rest were stationed around the library and the living room, and the perfume was becoming bewildering.

Letters began to arrive in piles, and the phone rang constantly. Rae and Walter took turns answering it.

"Carter Bond?" he asked, with his hand over the mouthpiece. Rae reached for the receiver.

"Hello, dearie," said Rae.

"Kiddo, I'm so sorry," Carter said.

"Thank you. He was a wonderful man. I'm sorry now that you'll never know him."

"I'm sorry too. But I'm a little worried about the spook part."

"It was only during the war. I thought it was rather dashing."

"Tell me the truth though . . . how are you?"

"I'm all right. I've been doing my grieving for a long time, and now it can end."

"I'd worry you were being brave and noble if I didn't know about that cartwheel."

"I *am* being brave and noble, and it's a relief to be able to admit it."

"So what's the drill right now? Who's with you?"

Rae described the schedule for the next few days. Albie's children and Rae's daughter would arrive, with grandchildren. The funeral was to be at Temple Emanu-El the day after Thanksgiving. It was wrong to wait so long, but it was taking time for the family to arrive, and it seemed equally wrong to make people who wanted to be there choose between honoring Albie and giving thanks with their families. Everyone would be gone by Saturday.

"And then what will you do?"

"I have no idea."

"Okay," said Carter, "I'll call you Sunday."

"Thank you."

When she hung up, she was smiling. "Who was that?" Walter asked.

"One of my fat-farm buddies," said Rae.

Amy called, and so did Laurie.

"Mother, it's Laura Knox Lopez," Walter said, curious.

"Dearie," said Rae, taking the phone.

"I wish I were there to give you a hug," said Laurie.

"I wish you were too. And then you could talk to Walter about your campaign."

Laurie laughed. "You are relentless."

"He's right here, do you want to talk to him?"

There was a pause, and then Laurie said, "Sure."

Rae handed Walter the phone. Walter listened briefly, then said, "This isn't a joke, is it?" After another beat he gave a shout of laughter, slapped his hand on the tabletop, and said, "I'm in. I'll see you in Boise on Monday."

Rae was watching him with a wide smile on her face.

"What on earth goes on at that place?" Walter asked her.

"She's going to do it?"

"She is."

Rae shook her two fists in the air, the gesture Albie had used to cheer hooray.

The second morning Rae even got sympathy e-mail.

Pretend this is fancy letter paper with a blue monogram, said the text on the screen.

I'm so sorry about your husband. I don't know

**what else to say. You're going to miss him. Write
back if you want. Love, Jill.**

Albert Junior and his wife, Cordie, flew in from Boston. They
installed themselves at The Clift. Their three children were all at different colleges and so all arrived at different times throughout the day.
James was deployed to the airport repeatedly to meet them.

Albert Strouse, Jr., was a nice person, but a conventional one. His
father had sometimes remarked dryly that they had sent Bert to Yale
and he'd never gotten over it. He had been an athlete in his youth.
Now he worked as a stockbroker. He worked hard, but found it slow
going. He often wished for the nerve to take early retirement, but his
father had contempt for men who lived on their private incomes, so
Bert soldiered on.

Bert had respected and loved his father without ever being much
like him. Albie had loved people and games and sports and politics
and travel and history and action. Bert liked systems. What made Bert
happy was new electronic equipment. The latest Loran for his boat,
for example, and a big, thick manual on its operation.

Bert's children were also mysteries to him. His daughters,
Susannah and Mary, took after their mother. They were plump, sunny,
and popular, and viewed their father as a somewhat comic figure.
Their brother, Harton, had arrived from Kenyon this afternoon with
his hair a vivid shade of green. This had set off a clatter of mortified
yammering from parents and sisters.

"You're going to your grandfather's funeral with green hair?!"

"Yes? So?"

"Harton!"

"Harton, whatever possessed you?"

"I didn't go, like, I think I want green hair, Ma. I was trying to
bleach it."

"Well, what happened?"

He shrugged. "I'm not a hairdresser."

"But why didn't you fix it?"

"Dad, chill. It will grow out."

"You mean you're going to your grandfather's funeral with green hair?"

And so on. His sisters thought this was *too* funny.

Bert's annoyance over Harton's hair was made very much worse by the fact that the children of Rae's daughter, Harriet, were all well-groomed, apparently sane, and exhibited easy good manners. Bert's children tended to huddle together and talk only to each other, as if adults belonged to some alien species that needn't be acknowledged.

Bert's sister, Eloise, arrived with little Trishie at dinnertime Wednesday, and took over one of the guest rooms at the Broadway house. Her son, Strouse, had arrived by bus from Oregon during the afternoon.

Eloise Strouse Threadgill had been in tears much of the last two days. She had worshiped her father, and had never forgiven him for out-growing the idyll of her childhood, when nothing in the world had been more important to him than she was. Her mother had been busy with the stores, and her brother, Bert, had regarded her as about as interesting as pond slime, but Albie had somehow managed to be an unfailing source of patient concern. Eloise was therefore disoriented when, after her mother's death, her father had remarried and commenced a new and apparently joyful life in which his grown daughter not only did not occupy the position of the sun, she seemed to have entered an orbit in his universe somewhere in the neighborhood of Mars.

Eloise had never seen this state of affairs as appropriate, let alone permanent. She believed that the intended state of the constellations was the one she had first encountered as a babe in arms. Eloise as center of universe, father rotating patiently within reach, always ready and waiting to turn in her direction. But he had failed to return to his assigned position, and her relations with him had gotten strained. She had developed a strong, sulky resentment at Albie's failure to be pre-occupied with her needs, although she had a husband of her own, and a circle of friends, and soon two small children.

Eloise found in time that her husband failed, as her father had, to provide the ceaseless interest in her that she believed was in order, and her marriage slowly and tediously foundered. When she decided to forgive her father for failing her so she could turn to him in her exciting hour of need, she found to her horror that he was no longer completely there. Or he was there, but no longer completely her father.

She had not been much comfort to him or to Rae during the long years that had followed. When she talked to Albie on the phone, and he grew confused, or forgot things he had known only minutes before, she felt acute embarrassment, as if she had walked in on him in the bathroom, or were overhearing him talking in his sleep. She thought of him as "not himself," as if that meant the affection and duty owed to a father were thus canceled.

It didn't help Eloise to cope with her present despair, when her daughter, young Trishie, had thrown a tantrum about being dragged up to San Francisco to the funeral of a grandfather she had barely known. To Trishie, Albie had been a kind of horrifying old specimen with huge ears who would ask her the same question he had just asked five minutes before. Peoples' ears definitely got bigger as they got old. Trishie was royally pissed because she had a big part in the Thanksgiving play, but now she would miss it, and she could have stayed with Chelcie while her mother went to the funeral, but her mother didn't listen when she explained this.

Harriet Keely Goetz and her family were staying with Walter. There was not really room for them all at his apartment, so they spent most waking hours at the house on Broadway.

Mealtimes gradually took on the aspect of a camp kitchen for an army on the move. Friends came and stayed, the grandchildren all had jet lag and arrived for breakfast at lunchtime, and were ready for lunch as the cook was serving dinner. Fortunately the kitchen was set up for entertaining on a grand scale, but Rae ordered Doreen and James to lower their standards at least to allow paper napkins. James went to Costco and bought three dozen Wolfgang Puck frozen pizzas, and Cook roasted a ham and a huge roast beef so that sandwich production could be maintained around the clock.

It was, thus, an ill-assorted and subdued family group that gathered together on Thursday night to observe Thanksgiving. They filled the whole long dining room table, and spilled over onto a spare table covered with white linen and set up in the hall. Bert said a blessing, and then he and Walter stood at the sideboard carving the turkey while Doreen and James passed vegetable dishes. The young had been allowed to sit together so the cousins could renew acquaintance and the step-cousins could get to know each other. The middle-aged sat at the other end, surrounding Rae.

Bert and Cordie talked about what on earth Harton had done to his hair. Rae said not to worry about it; she was sure Albie would have liked it: "He liked things to be modern."

Cordie tried to share parenting woes with Harriet and her husband, Leon, but the Goetz's difficulties seemed so innocent and minor compared to Harton's hair and the Strouse girls' addiction to shopping that it was hard to get a good grudge session going.

Then Eloise, who'd had about eight tumblers of wine, began to cry, and Bert, sitting beside her, put a hand on her shoulder. Rae, on her other side (and always prepared for maternal emergencies), produced a clean handkerchief.

"I wish it had been some other way . . ." Eloise managed to say.

"I do too," Rae said. "I wish he could have just said to his doctor, 'It's time for me to go.'"

"But it wasn't time . . ." Eloise cried. "His heart was strong . . . he enjoyed his food, he wasn't in pain . . . to *drown* . . . " And she cried some more.

The young, at the far end, were beginning to keep up a steady buzz of conversation. The ones who had seen *Pulp Fiction* were describing it frame by frame to the ones who had not. They were paying no mind to what their elders were talking about. This was good, Rae felt. She had no desire to find herself conducting a seminar for fifteen.

"He *was* in pain," she said quietly. "He was in pain knowing that his illness was destroying the man he had been. He didn't want to be remembered as something pitiful."

"So what are you saying?" Eloise demanded. "Are you saying it *wasn't* an accident?"

Harriet and Walter looked at each other. Finally Rae said, "It was certainly not an accident, and he wanted you to know that."

"He wanted *me* to know that?"

"He wanted it known," Rae corrected herself. "He communicated clearly." She explained about the pajamas while Eloise and Bert and Cordie listened and stared at her.

Bert sat back in his chair and folded his hands in his lap. His wife had leaned forward toward Rae. One hand covered her mouth.

"But *why?*" Eloise wailed, finally. "Why would he do that? He had his pleasures, he was warm and safe . . . "

Rae for one instant wanted to lash out at her. He was warm and safe? That's what you'd say about a baby. He was a man, not some father-shaped dummy who owed it to you to keep breathing.

Instead she said quietly, "He had killed a creature who loved him. How would you feel? He was not willing to go any farther in that direction. He'd woken up day after day to find more and more pieces of himself missing. I think he always had some kind of line in mind that he would refuse to cross."

There was a silence. It went on so long that even the children began to fall silent and glance curiously toward their elders.

"You think he'd been planning to kill himself all along?" Eloise asked, and it sounded suddenly very loud in the room. Now all the children were listening.

Rae said, "Yes. I think he must have been. He wasn't afraid of death. Or perhaps I should say he used to speak of it as he did almost everything else in life. That it would probably be more interesting than advertised, if you looked at it the right way."

Eloise stared at her. Cordie had taken her husband's hand; she thought Rae was probably completely right.

James came in at that moment and said that coffee was ready in the living room.

Carter told DeeAnne she'd hold the fort over Thanksgiving. She had closed the office for the day itself, so that she and her brother, Buddy, could drive down to La Jolla to have Thanksgiving dinner with their dad. Carter had offered to bring a turkey from the fancy deli near her house, but her father had said he wanted to cook for them.

When they arrived, Carter was touched to see how carefully he had tried to do what their mother had always done when entertaining. The table was set with the clean white damask cloth she used at holidays. There were cocktail peanuts in the same leaf-shaped dish she had always used. There was a glass bowl filled with tiny sweet gherkins. There was a plate of shrimp, boiled and peeled, and a small bowl of red cocktail sauce and a shot glass filled with colored toothpicks for spearing and dipping the shrimp.

There was a disturbing smell coming from the kitchen, however, and when she went to investigate, Carter found that her father had accidentally pushed the Clean button on the stove instead of the Bake button, so that the scrawny little chicken he was trying to roast had been cooking for two hours at about eight hundred degrees. They had hot dogs and cranberry sauce for dinner, and played some canasta, and she was home in time to take over a surveillance in the evening. The surveillence was an insurance company job; a guy was claiming complete disability after a minor traffic accident, but so far they had photographs of him putting up a swing set for his daughter, changing a tire, and mowing his lawn. Yesterday, Mae Ruth had gotten a good series of him in the supermarket checkout line and then in the parking lot, carrying two sacks of groceries, one of which contained a twenty-four-pound turkey.

Friday morning Carter was in the office manning the phones and reading case files. Mae Ruth and Candy were out in the field. DeeAnne was at the beach with her husband and kids. Leesa was working on a missing person case; the client, whose husband had been declared dead seven years before, looked out the window of a city bus while on a visit to San Diego and saw him walking down the street eating a Dove Bar. Not unexpectedly, the woman wanted to have a few words with him.

Carter was about to make some calls on a case that had gone cold, a noncustodial-parent kidnapping. She looked up to see a very pregnant young black woman with a toddler on her hip making her way through the office. It took some maneuvering; the woman was not small in the first place, and she was carrying a lot of extra humanity. And as usual, there were stacks of phone books, zip code directories, piles of files, and boxes of detritus around various desks in her path. Private investigators were not the tidiest bunch.

The young woman reached Carter's desk. She held out a card she had in her free hand, the one not balancing the baby. It was one of Carter's own business cards.

"Is this you?"

"C'est moi," said Carter. "Take a pew."

The woman sank into the oak office chair beside Carter's desk, shifting the child around to perch on her knee.

"I'm Shanti," she said.

Carter reached a hand to her, and Shanti shook it. Shanti's skin had a glow of health, almost a sheen. She wore a loose dress of kente cloth and her hair was in glossy cornrows.

"Where are we here, about seven months?" Carter asked.

Shanti nodded.

"And who's this?" Carter peered at the little girl on Shanti's lap. She made a face that made the little one suddenly smile.

"This is Flora," said Shanti, bouncing her knees.

"Hello, Flora." Carter reached out her hand and the little girl clutched a finger, shyly, and then giggled.

"Shake hands," said her mother. "You know how to shake hands." Flora shook her head. "Well, then, can you give her five?"

There was a long moment of apparent paralysis. Carter, giving the child a cool gaze, held her palm up flat. With a little swagger, Flora gave it a slap.

"All *right*," said Carter. Shanti smiled and patted Flora's back.

Carter sat in neutral. The first meeting with a client told a great deal, and since people who hired detectives often wanted something very different from what they claimed they wanted, it was important to listen carefully and jump to no conclusions. What she saw so far was an attractive, confident woman who was sizing her up with equal care. Maybe this wasn't a client, Carter thought suddenly, maybe it was a job interview. She'd never taken on a new hire who was seven months pregnant, but so far Shanti had all the earmarks of a good one.

"So, Flora," said Carter. "You're going to have a brother? Or a sister?" The little girl gave a tiny nod.

"Have you picked out a name for her?"

Shanti said, "If it's a girl, we're thinking of naming her Fauna."

Carter looked at her quickly to see if she was kidding, and then laughed loudly. Flora wriggled off her mother's lap, and careened across the carpet to where she had spotted an open box of thick rubber bands on the floor beside DeeAnne's chair.

"Is it all right if she wanders?" Shanti asked.

"Sure, there's lots of trouble she can get into." But Flora had settled down and emptied the rubber bands onto the floor, and looked as if she could keep herself busy right there for quite a while.

"Terri sent me your card," said Shanti.

Terry Chihuly? Terry Chihuly was a retired cop Carter often used when she needed some extra muscle.

"Terri Johnson. She met you in Arizona?"

Terri the fitness babe! From The Cloisters.

"Got it," said Carter. "She said she was from L.A."

"Yes, from my block."

"So, what's up?"

"I grew up in the house where I live now. Terri lived two doors down. We used to play hopscotch and jump rope in the playground on the corner. Rode our little tricycles. Evenings, the dads would barbecue by the basketball court and afterward, when the babies went to bed, the dads would play dominoes on the sidewalk. Sitting out there in their lawn chairs. It was nice, you know? Now I'm trying to raise a family."

"I'm with you so far."

"There aren't any more dads. There are lots of babies, but their fathers are in the joint, or running with gangs, or dead. Babies can't play in the playground because the sandbox is full of glass. Junkies want it that way; they don't want no kids around there. Only kids in that park are the ones whose parents are there too, nodding or drinking."

Shanti did a little pantomime of a junkie slumped on her seat after shooting up. "Yo, Mom. Great," she said, straightening up. "Flora— what did you put in your mouth?" Flora looked sheepish, then fished a pencil eraser out of her mouth. Shanti put out her hand, and Flora obediently toddled over and presented the slobbery pink thing. "Thank you so much," said Shanti. Carter handed her a tissue, and the wet eraser went into the wastebasket.

"Last week, a fifteen-year-old girl was shot on the next block. She got in the way of a turf dispute." Both women looked at Flora, who had pulled a Seattle telephone directory into her lap and was turning the pages while softly chattering, reading herself a story. There were apparently a lot of baby bears in Seattle.

"You could move," said Carter.

"Right. I could move to another neighborhood, where I didn't grow up and don't have any memories, and I don't know anybody. And if the dealers and the junkies and the crackheads aren't there now, then they will be next week. Or else it's the gangs. Or I could move someplace white, where we'll be *real* welcome."

"There are a lot of mixed neighborhoods . . . "

"I know it. But my neighborhood used to be just as nice, and this pisses me off."

"Are there others like you on the block, who want to fight?"

"Hell, yes. We've got an association. We've got cameras. We put up a banner that says that the neighborhood is watching . . . "

"Does that do any good?"

"Dealers don't care, and the junkies don't care. But the guys in fancy cars coming in from outside the 'hood to score . . . they don't like it at all."

Carter was impressed. "Good point. I bet they don't."

Shanti reached into the soft woven bag she carried. First she pulled out a small square picture book, and looked at it, surprised. "I've been wondering where that was. Flora? Look, here's Mr. Frog." Flora scrambled to her feet and came to fetch the book. She took it back to her nest and began vivaciously telling Mr. Frog's story to her friend the telephone book. Shanti then produced a thick envelope from a FotoXpress shop. Carter opened it. It was a stack of photographs, about three dozen, of drug buys. They were taken from different houses at different times of day. Four or five dealers appeared again and again, and several customers became familiar. A few of the pictures were taken at dusk; the rest were in broad daylight.

"We've got twenty dealers on the one block," Shanti said.

"I see the problem. What do you do with the pictures?"

"We give them to the police. Once in a while they bust someone, and either he's back the next day or somebody else takes over his territory. Police got enough to do going to burglaries and murders. If you just call them up and say, "This shit is ruining our lives," they say, 'Maybe later.'"

Carter riffled through the pictures again. She put them down and looked at Shanti. "How can we help?"

"How much do you know about how street dealers work?"

"Probably not as much as you."

"You got three people, at least, working in sales together." Shanti picked up the pictures, and pulled out one of a kid of about fourteen talking to a man in a black T-shirt with a shaved head. She pointed to the kid.

"This one's the steerer. He's on the street, bopping and humming his little drug tune. 'Smoke, rock, smack.' He sings it to the wrong person, nothing happens. Can't bust him, he isn't carrying. He says it to the paying customer, customer says, 'Yo,' steerer says, 'My man's over there.'"

Shanti pulled out another picture, this one taken with a telephoto lens, of a scene in a vest-pocket park, a dreary patch of concrete with a ruined basketball hoop at one end and a row of benches along a fence. A man in a porkpie hat with a deep scar on his cheek was looking at something in his hands. The man with the shaved head had turned half away from him. One hand was in his back pocket.

"Bust this one," she pointed to the porkpie hat, "and you find a lot of cash, and maybe a vial or two, or a little junk. Not a lot more than a user would hold. Hardly worth carrying him to the station house; he'll just be out on bail in an hour. But you watch him, and pretty soon, he goes to get more merchandise from his holder."

She took out another picture. This time you could see two men with their backs to the camera, seemingly looking across the street. One was the porkpie hat, and the other was another kid, this one about seventeen.

"Holder keeps the stash. Course, he doesn't keep it on his person. He might keep it on top of the wheel of a parked car. Or in a bag inside a garbage can. Once you know where it is, you can call the cops. They come in and take it away."

"And arrest the dealer."

"You *don't* arrest the dealer, man. You don't want to do that. You want to leave him right there on the street to explain it to his suppliers. You arrest him, man, you protecting him. People he work for can't blame him if he gets busted. But if he keeps losing the drugs, man, he has to pay for them, and if he can't, he seeks early retirement."

"This is very smart," Carter said.

"Thank you. There's a problem though."

"Let me guess. The police."

"You get Mrs. Aaron Spelling calling up, 'They dealing drugs in my garden again,' you get a fleet of cop cars in two minutes. Shanti Amos calls them up and says, 'There's a stash of crack in a wheel well right outside my window,' they say, 'Oh, my goodness, there *is*? What was that address again?' And they show up next week."

"I see." Carter stretched her long legs out and recrossed them. She opened her desk drawer, looking for a pack of cigarettes. She closed the drawer again.

"We can't be taking the stash ourselves," Shanti said. "They know us all, they know where we live. What we need is people they don't know, who come quick when we call, and then disappear. Dealers have enough trouble doing business on our block, they'll take it somewhere else."

Carter sat thinking. "This would not be the safest thing we ever did. Just guessing."

"We can pay."

"I'm delighted to hear it. Let me get some more information from you so I can talk this over with my partners. Your name?"

"Shanti Amos."

"Age?"

"Twenty-four."

"Married?"

Shanti shook her head no.

"Living with?"

"Flora."

Carter smiled.

"Employment?"

"I work for the power company, in billing."

"Who looks after the baby?"

"They have a nursery. I usually bring her with me. I work at night, so she's mostly asleep."

"What do you have for family?"

"My parents are dead. I have a sister, but I don't know where she is."

Carter looked at her sharply.

"What does that mean?"

Shanti was direct, as always. "I haven't seen her in a few years. She was using the last time I saw her. I imagine she's on the street, but I don't know where."

Carter was taking notes. "You live in the house you grew up in?"

Shanti nodded.

"So if your sister ever wanted to come home, she'd know where to find you?"

Shanti, looking away from Carter this time, nodded again.

"How old is she?"

"Nineteen."

"Name?"

"Delia Amos."

"Maybe you should just hire me to find Delia. Then you could all move to a better neighborhood."

Carter had been partly kidding, but she saw at once that she had crossed an invisible line, and wished she could take it back. Shanti just looked at her with a cool expression.

"Sorry," she said. "Can I ask you one more question?"

"Yes."

"Why did you choose us?"

"Terri thought you would take us seriously. Not rip us off."

Carter nodded. "No, we won't do that. But I'll have to talk to the others. We're not exactly a democracy here, but we don't just order people to do things we know are dangerous. The ops have to agree. If you give me your number, I'll let you know on Monday, and we can talk about terms."

Shanti gave her the number, then stood up and put out her hand to say good-bye. Carter shook it.

"Flora, time to go," Shanti said. Flora scrambled to her feet and made her way back to her mother. Shanti picked her up, and Flora, now back on eye level with her, studied Carter gravely.

"You made a bracelet," Carter said. Flora had about thirty rubber bands on her fat little arm. She looked at Carter with her big brown-marble eyes from under long black lashes. She looked worried that she would have to give the rubber bands back.

"Next time you come, will you make me one?"

Flora thought it over and then nodded gravely. Shanti, watching her daughter's face, wore a slight smile.

"Great kid," Carter said to her.

"Are you a great kid?" Shanti asked Flora. Flora was at once overcome with embarrassment, and hid her face.

"I'll call you Monday afternoon," Carter said.

"Thank you." Shanti picked up her bag from the chair and made her way out. Carter stood watching her. When she was about halfway down the room, Carter saw Flora lift her head slightly and peer at Carter. Carter winked at her.

*a*my had given up nursing when she married Noah because he wasn't used to having a wife who worked. But after Jill was born she had semi-accidentally developed another career as a photographer. It started with studies of baby Jill, but she had a real eye, not to mention a way with babies, and had soon found herself in demand to photograph children's parties and make formal portraits of other peoples' children. When one of her friends' daughters developed mile-long legs and a neck like the stem of a peony, Amy made photographs of her wearing vintage clothing in improbable combinations. The girl acquired a modeling agent and began to have a vogue, and Amy began to get calls from other models, and then from a magazine editor or two to do fashion shoots. That all ended the day the police called from Central Park to ask if Amy had a thirteen-year-old daughter named Jillian who carried a purple backpack.

The next two years had been agony for everyone. There were endless medical appointments, and even more endless visits to healers of broken spirits. It had been hard on the marriage, for sure. Noah felt neglected and angry, and Amy felt helpless. She even had to stay away from the police department from fear that one of the tabloids would discover her identity and publish Jill's name; miraculously they had confined themselves to calling her "Girl X."

Briefly Amy had hateful feelings about all men, including Noah, which she knew were irrational and yet were hard to suppress. She went back into therapy, and things got better in the marriage even though Noah wouldn't go with her, but Jill seemed completely frozen and stuck. Then Jill came unstuck in an unwelcome way; she began to encase herself in layers of lard until she became a stretched-out balloon version of their daughter. This put a new strain on things. Noah was a very physical and competitive man and he cared very much about the beauty of his wife and children. Jill sensed her father's withdrawal from her, and she withdrew from him in retaliation. That left both of them relating to Amy as if Amy were the fulcrum in a badly designed machine.

Jill's therapist suggested she move to a new school. It would be easier for her in a place where no one had known her before to get used to accepting the person she had become after the attack. It helped in some ways, although at first she was very lonely. Neither of her parents had any idea how much time she spent on the Internet pretending to be a cast of invented characters.

Meanwhile Amy, restless and lonely herself, and wanting a challenge that wouldn't defeat her, volunteered to work on Jill's school's charity auction and ended up running it. When the dust cleared and she had raised $24,000 more than the evening had ever netted before, a couple of the other moms on the committee suggested that they go into business together.

Amy discussed it with Noah.

"Who's going to pay you to organize parties when New York is full of full-time volunteers?"

"We don't think that's a problem."

"What was the matter with photography, if you want a hobby?"

"I don't want a hobby, I want useful work. Getting the bookings depends on contacts. And word of mouth. One job leads to another. I've been out of the loop for three years, everything's changed."

"Well, go back to doing portraits, then."

"Noah—how many people do you know who want a big, formal portrait of their sixteen-year-old? With the braces and the pimples and the ring through the lip? Five-year-olds, yes. Young brides, yes. But the home-baked portrait and birthday party business is going to be a little slow with our kids at this age."

"But it's not as if you need the money. Why not just do it for fun?"

"I don't know. Would you take out peoples' ovaries for fun if nobody wanted to pay you?"

The rest of the conversation had gone badly. Two weeks later she came to Noah with a very professional business plan and asked him to lend her her share of the start-up money. He wrote a check. Within six months she had paid him back with interest, which annoyed him because the business was a succès fou and he would just as soon have had equity in it.

Amy was the client wrangler and food expert. Paige calculated costs, bid the jobs, and wrote the contracts. Elizabeth designed everything from invitations to decor. Noah had been just about dead wrong about all the full-time volunteers they would have to compete with. It seemed that all the former volunteers were working now themselves, and were too busy to plan their own children's weddings or their companies' picnics.

Amy was immersed and happy, although a wise friend had remarked that "you're only as happy as your unhappiest child." She was always fitting her work hours around Jill's schedule, always alert to the tone in Jill's voice on the phone, and her partners were aware that she had to limit the jobs she could supervise on school nights or weekends.

Thanksgiving morning, Jill went out jogging and ran into her friend Clara on Twentieth Street, walking the family's incontinent dachshund. The streets were almost deserted, as if the holiday had had the same effect on city life as a neutron bomb. Clara was a friend from Jill's building. This morning her attire and grooming suggested a certain inner emotional disarray.

Clara was younger than Jill, attending a school that required you to show four semesters of community service on your transcript in order to graduate. You could intern at a museum after school or cook hamburgers in a hospital coffee shop or tutor dyslexic kids, or any number of other things, but Clara had, one way or another, failed to follow through on any of the commitments she had made and here it was almost second term of junior year.

"My dad is all, like, 'I work my butt off to send you to that fancy school and you're not going to graduate, yadda yadda yadda.' Happy Thanksgiving." Clara had persuaded him that if she served dinner at the Tompkins Square Soup Kitchen on Thanksgiving Day she was going to get extra credit. Then she'd applied a bottle of blue food coloring to her platinum hair and drawn black lines an inch wide around her eyes, hoping to look so weird that the soup kitchen would beg her not to come back.

"You've got to come with me," Clara said, pleading. "I'm afraid of Big Lee." Big Lee, the soup kitchen's director, was a man who had spent enough nights outside in bad weather to have very little patience with these conscripts his board forced him to put on his work roster. He had actually called the school to complain when Clara signed up to work Thursday dinners in September and then never showed up.

"I thought Rosella was doing this with you," Jill said.

"No, she got some teaching job. Speed-reading for the blind or something. Can you believe I'm going to miss my own Thanksgiving dinner, and my dad goes, 'Serves you right'? What time are you eating? Is your mom cooking?"

"No, she's working today."

"She *is*?"

"Someone's silver wedding, I think she said. It *had* to fall on Thanksgiving. She says her partners always do the evenings and weekends and she could do this for them. We don't leave for the country until five o'clock."

"Where are you going?"

"Greenwich. My brother's house." Jill made a face.

"What's that like?"

"Perfect," said Jill, looking as if she were sucking lemons. "The babies are perfect, their noses don't even run. My sister-in-law is a marathon racer; she's as hard as a rock and weighs seventeen pounds. She's always making these Cuisine Minceur recipes just for me. We all get along so well they even invite my dad's first wife."

"Gross," said Clara.

"Yes. Betty chats away with my mother while she dandles her perfect little grandchildren and I sit there like the Elephant's Child. I'm sure it makes my mom feel like dog doo on a stick."

The soup kitchen turned out to be a trip. They were drastically understaffed for the day, and Big Lee was so amazed that Clara had finally shown up, he didn't seem to care what she looked like. "Can my friend work too?" Clara asked, unnecessarily. They were both hustled into the kitchen of the Lady of Mercy church, still offering Masses in English and Lithuanian. They were put to work cutting mountains of carrots and onions and celery. There were four huge turkeys roasting, two in each oven, and a woman named Martha Missirlian was boiling a hundred pounds of potatoes.

At one point there was a great pounding on the door of the parish hall.

"Somebody get that, that's the bread!" Big Lee shouted. Nobody moved and the pounding continued. Jill put down her knife and ran to the door.

The sidewalk was filled now for three blocks with discouraged-looking people waiting in the cold. There were men and women but no children—the homeless families were fed somewhere else. At the curb stood a van with the engine running, and the woman who had been hammering on the door shouted at Jill, "Come on, honey, hustle—I've got two more stops to make."

She unloaded four plastic laundry baskets filled with dozens of long loaves of breads of every description. She dove back into the van and reappeared with shopping bags filled with unmatched dinner rolls. She dropped these onto the sidewalk and shouted, "Happy Thanksgiving," then jumped into the cab of the van and roared away. Jill half-expected the line of hungry people to descend on her and tear the bread apart, but they stood quietly watching.

"You never met Cassandra before?" asked a young black man. He was tall, wearing oversized blue jeans and a dirty gray sweater. "You want some help with that?"

Jill said, "Definitely. Thank you."

The young man took up two of the baskets while Jill picked up the bags of rolls. "Lead on, MacDuff," he said. A homeless guy quoting Shakespeare? Jill thought. What a trip.

The last baskets of bread were waiting for her on the sidewalk when she rushed out for them. The turkeys were being carved, and Clara, who hadn't a clue what she was doing, was trying to make gravy. Martha Missirlian was now heroically mashing her potatoes.

When everyone from the sidewalk was sitting inside with a plate of hot food, Clara and Jill were sent in among them with a huge coffee urn on a serving trolley. They passed up and down the rows handing out steaming cups, and offering milk and sugar. Jill came to her helper, whom she thought of now as MacDuff. He was sitting with a rheumy-looking white guy who looked like a defrocked priest or school principal. MacDuff had a paperback book sticking out of the pocket of his sweater. Both had filthy nylon bags at their feet. MacDuff's looked like a bowling bag.

"What are you reading?" Jill asked MacDuff, and he pulled out the book to show her. *The Sound and the Fury*, by William Faulkner.

"Have you read it?" the older guy asked Jill.

"Yes, I have."

"So has he—he's half-memorized it. He's our reader. He's even got a dictionary in his bag." MacDuff now leaned over to open his bag and produce a paperback Merriam-Webster.

"If you were carrying everything you owned in a bowling bag, would *you* carry a dictionary?" It was a routine of theirs, it seemed.

"That's a very good question," Jill said.

Much later, at the groaning board in Greenwich, Jill repeated this question to the family, but no one seemed interested in the answer. They seemed to wish she would shut up about homeless men with dirty bowling bags and the woman with her hundred pounds of potatoes. Fine, thought Jill. Watch this. And she began to eat and eat and eat until she could tell without even looking up that her half-brother's fleshless wife was frightened she might burst and splatter herself across the tablecloth.

*T*emple Emanu-El was packed for Albie's funeral. Walter and Bert gave eulogies. Eloise sobbed. Little Trishie made a cootie catcher out of her memorial program.

Scores of people came back to the house for lunch and there were speeches and fond remembrances, and tears. By the time the last guests had gone and the washing up was finished in the kitchen, it was dark outside. The cousins and step-cousins had split into two groups. Half had gone to the Kabuki to see *Pocahontas* for the eighth time, and the other half were upstairs watching a video of *The Terminator*.

Rae gave Doreen and James the night off. She sat in the library with Bert and Walter in the early dark of the winter evening. Harriet and Cordie were in the kitchen putting together a bowl of pasta and some salad. Eloise came in looking gray.

"Did you sleep?" Rae asked her. Eloise nodded, sunk in misery. The fire crackled, and Bert sat across from Rae in the chair where his father had always sat.

"Where's Leon?" Eloise asked suddenly.

"Gone," said Walter. "He couldn't get anyone to cover for him for another day. It's the holiday."

Eloise nodded, looking blank, as if she weren't sure what that sentence meant but wanted to seem to understand.

"Someone could put on a record," Rae said after a while. She felt like hearing something full of feeling, maybe some Brahms.

There was a long stillness. Walter thought maybe Bert would like to choose something, not knowing that Bert wouldn't know Brahms

165

from Bo Diddley, and wouldn't like either one of them. Eloise got up and went to the cabinet where the records were kept. After a while she put on the Kingston Trio.

Cordie and Harriet came in from the kitchen. They had the air about them of two who have found common ground; they moved like a team, relaxed and content.

"We can eat any time," Cordie said.

"We just need ten minutes for the pasta, everything else is ready," said Harriet.

"Well, why don't we open the bar," said Bert. "Harriet, what can I get you?"

Harriet asked for a beer. Bert and Walter went to the pantry and soon were back with a tray of glasses and bottles and a bowl of gold-fish crackers. The passing of drinks and crackers filled a few more minutes. Then it was quiet again. Everyone was either filled with emotion or drained from it. With the funeral over, the fact of death could begin.

It may be that Bert was one of those people who, when feeling sorrow or edginess or some emotional upset he can't quite recognize or name, distracts himself by picking a fight with somebody. In any case, into the music and the crackling of the fire, he said, "Rae, how long has this Oriental couple been with you?"

Rae sighed. She was counting her blessings tonight. "They *are* wonderful, aren't they? I guess we've had them ... almost three years now."

"Bert. Asian," said Eloise.

Bert looked over at her. He was looking a bit thick.

"Asian. Oriental's a rude word."

"No it isn't. Oriental. It means from the east. China's the east, isn't it?"

"It's west from here. Unless you go the long way for the Frequent Flier miles."

Bert gave that some thought. He looked at his sister and felt vaguely, globally, irritated.

"What is it I'm supposed to say?"

"Asian."

"Fine. Asian."

"They're quite a pair," Rae said. "Remarkable people."

"How did they come to you?" Cordie asked, eager to stop her husband bickering with his sister.

"I was at a gas station on California Street. James was changing my oil one day, and we got to talking."

"You know," said Bert, "that never happens to me."

"It doesn't?"

"No. I just about never find myself having a chat with the Chinese guy who's changing my oil."

"Well, think of what you're missing," Rae said.

"They *are* marvelous, James and Doreen," said Cordie, wondering if there were some way she could get her husband to go away and take a nap.

"But I mean, what did you talk about? Explain it to me," said Bert.

Walter, who was liking Bert's tone less and less, went quietly to sit beside his mother. Walter was a wiry man with dark hair and huge hands and feet. He looked as if his body was supposed to be thicker to match his joints but had been burned off by nervous energy. He was quick, intense, and funny, not a natural mate to Bert's stolid self-importance.

"I asked him if he could figure out why my windshield wipers wouldn't squirt anymore. The dealer had looked at it twice . . . "

"And could he?"

"Yes. He followed all the tubes and discovered the dealer had squashed one underneath when he changed the battery. But that took a little while. So while we were under the hood, I asked him where he was from, and he said 'Hankow.' I never met anyone from Hankow, did you?"

"No," said Bert. "I never did."

"Is Doreen from Hankow too?" Cordie asked. "Are they childhood sweethearts?"

"No, she isn't, that's the whole point. They came to San Francisco with the diplomatic corps."

"What do you mean?" Bert interrupted. "You mean the Chinese mission brings its own mechanics?"

"No, of course not. James is a diplomat. I believe he was quite a rising star. Doreen was stationed here too, and they fell in love."

"Is *she* a diplomat?"

"No, a translator. But she's from Canton, so even though they were married, they were going to be sent back to their home cities, five hundred miles apart."

"You're kidding."

"Not at all, that's the way it works. You work in the province you grew up in or you don't work at all."

"That's how they keep people from the poorest parts from pouring into the cities where the money is," put in Walter. Bert stood up abruptly and went to get himself a refill.

"Cordie? You ready?"

"No thanks."

"Walter? Rae?"

Walter declined. Rae said "Yes, darling, thanks." Bert refilled her glass and went back to his chair. Eloise then got up and flounced dramatically to the bar to refill her own glass. Her brother ignored her.

"So what happened?" Cordie asked.

"They petitioned the government. No exceptions could be made. So they decided not to go back."

"They went underground," said Bert.

"Yes. I don't know exactly how. Went to friends, at first, and James got the job at the garage. Doreen was working as a tailor and cleaning houses . . . "

"I thought his English was awfully good for a mechanic," said Harriet.

"I was impressed he was such a *good* mechanic, in the circumstances," said Rae. "Anyway, I asked him to bring Doreen to meet me, and they were right away so sweet with Albie . . . I don't know what I would have done without them. And I'm so glad now to have a baby in the house."

"But they *are* illegals," said Bert.

There was a silence. Walter had seen this coming a long way off; he didn't think his mother had.

"Yes, I guess they are," said Rae. "Of course, the baby's a citizen."

"I don't know how you can say you 'guess.' They're here illegally. It's not as if there hasn't been enough publicity. You've got Zoë Baird, my god, you've passed Proposition 187! This isn't something you have to guess about," Bert brayed.

"Now hold on," said Walter. "Let's allow that this is an issue on which people of good faith might disagree." He felt an almost imperceptible touch on the back of his elbow from his mother.

"I don't think so, no," said Bert. "It's a matter of respect for the law. I don't see how people of goodwill can disagree, when law-abiding people wait for years to be admitted to this country. It's unfair to reward people who flout the system. The issue is whether we have a right to control immigration at all. If we have that right, then the only way to do it is eliminate the profit motive."

"I don't follow you," said Cordie.

"It's like this stupid 'War on Drugs.' War on Drugs, don't make me laugh. What are you going to do, station border guards every four feet from Alaska to Maine? Ridiculous. The only way you stop people importing drugs is eliminate the profit they make by doing it. The only way you stop people flouting the immigration laws is eliminate the profit in doing it. Don't let them work when they get here, and when you find them, send them back."

"That's a lovely attitude," said Eloise. "Here you sit, with your trust fund, and your passport. Nobody ever tried to tell *you* that you and Cordie had to live five hundred miles apart. Fine, you and Cordie can get married, but you have to live in Hillsborough all your life and she has to live in Philadelphia. At least I wouldn't have a nephew with green hair right now."

"Have another drink, Eloise," said Bert.

"But, really," said Cordie to her husband. "I understand the principle, honey, but these are real people. They were like family to your father. It's not so simple."

"It *is* simple. You cannot take in every person who wants to come here, no matter how good their reason is. The aquifer can't support it. China's a bad place to live, so is El Salvador. I'm sorry. You can't just have entire populations deciding they don't like where they are and they'd rather be here. Use your head!"

"This is very troubling," said Rae.

"I'm glad you recognize that," said Bert. He looked now quite satisfied, since he'd upset everyone in the room and especially his stepmother.

What an odd form of grieving, thought his wife.

Walter, who had campaigned fervently against Proposition 187, was dying to leap in and put up his dukes, but he resisted.

"What troubles me most," said Rae slowly, "is the disrespect for the law. I think you've got a strong point there, Bert. I'm glad you brought it up."

"Thank you," said Bert. He was looking more and more comfortable. Cordie, Walter, and Harriet were looking more unhappy. Eloise said, "This is a disgusting conversation. Daddy's dead, Bert. This is his funeral day. Why is this the way you want to observe it?"

"It came up," said Bert.

"No, it's all right," said Rae. "I think it's just as well. As Eloise said, James and Doreen were as sweet to Albie as if he were their own father. I can't go back to the days before I knew them, and decide what was right to do then. I know them now. They're very dear to me, and I have to deal with what is, not what should have been. But I think I have a solution."

"Good," said Bert.

"What is it?" said Walter.

"I think I'll adopt them," said Rae.

For about five minutes, all hell broke loose. Bert roared, Walter applauded, Harriet laughed, and Cordie and Eloise blithered. Rae remained thoughtful. After a while she said, "I see your point, Bert. They're married, so I only have to adopt one of them. I'll adopt Doreen."

"Rae—you don't *know* them! They're Chinese! If you adopt them, they'll be—they'll be—"

"Yes, that's right," she said. "They will."

"No, that's not what I meant!" he yelled. "I meant, you'll be at their mercy! You're a very rich woman, in case you forgot, and they'll be . . ." He began to hyperventilate. Rae remained calm.

"But I believe I do know them," she said. "That's the point. And I can't have them being deported. What would life be in China for them now? And yet, I can't have you as unhappy as you are with the present situation, Bert. I have to make it right."

Walter never looked at his mother, but inside he was thinking what a jerk he was to fear that Bert could be too many for her.

The conversation raged on for another half hour, when Bert took the whole scotch bottle and got in the car and left.

"Don't they have any scotch at The Clift?" Walter asked.

"He hates paying for those little bottles out of the minibar," said Cordie.

"Well, everybody, how about supper?" said Harriet.

"What a good idea," said Rae. And the family group that was left retired to the kitchen where they ate spaghetti and salad and had quite a pleasant evening.

When Walter left the plane in Boise on Monday morning, he didn't know what to expect. He'd had politicians send junior staffers to drive him, he'd been met by the candidate himself with a brass band, but of course that was Punch White in Louisiana, and if there was one thing no one had to explain to Punch, it was the value of the photo opportunity.

In Boise he found a tall woman with a rich mass of brown hair, wide blue eyes, no makeup. She was wearing a long skirt, a tweed jacket, and flat shoes. He held out his hand to her.

"Hello. Walter Keely."

"Yes," she said and smiled. "Hello. Laura Lopez."

Laurie realized now that they had met before. She remembered the high forehead and the strange pale eyes. They fell into step together.

"Was the flight full?"

"Almost empty. It seemed to be all day-trippers from Silicon Valley. Hewlett Packard guys."

Laurie nodded. "Boise's changed so much from when we lived here."

"And that's good for you," Walter said.

"Is it?"

"Yes." They stopped to wait at the luggage belt.

"Excuse me—Mrs. Lopez?"

There was a very pretty young woman wearing a Hertz uniform standing at Laurie's elbow.

"I just wanted to tell you how much we loved your husband."

"Thank you," said Laurie. She shook the young woman's hand. Walter watched closely.

Raw nerves. Emotions close to the surface. Not good. She may not be up to this.

"Let's go to The Idanha," he said. "I'll buy you lunch at Peter Schott's."

"I love The Idanha! I used to go there with my father when I was little. He'd sit in that sunroom right over the street, and smoke and shake hands with anyone who came through . . . "

"Let's go. I'll buy you a cigar."

Walter's bag appeared, and as they headed out to the parking lot Laurie said, "Tell me about your mother. How was the funeral?" They fell into easy conversation.

The Idanha, six stories of the finest architecture downtown Boise could imagine in 1901, was still boastful of having entertained President Taft, President Roosevelt (T., not F.), John and Ethel Barrymore, and Buffalo Bill. Walter was a regular here. He liked the feeling of a room crowded with such ghosts.

Today he asked for "someplace quiet," and he and Laurie were given a small table in the back where they ordered pasta and hot tea. Walter studied the woman before him. Extraordinarily handsome. Clear, intelligent eyes. Something shy in the manner, none of the born politician's brashness. The intelligence was a plus. The height was a plus; he wondered if he could get her into high heels. She'd be close to six feet if he could. She had a long, delicate nose, slightly uptipped, and great cheekbones. She should be photogenic.

"Let me get the basics out of the way," he said, dumping packets of sugar into his tea. "University of Idaho, then Harvard Law, right? Then . . . "

"Private practice in Hailey."

"And you met Roberto . . . when?"

"My last year of law school, at Christmas. My brother met him skiing and brought him home."

"But you weren't married right away?'

"No. I had a beau at law school."

Walter laughed. "A beau, I like that. Anyone I should know about?"

Laurie hesitated.

"I have to know," Walter said. "I have to know everything."

"Sorry. Of course, I realize that." She named a newly appointed member of the President's cabinet. Walter hooted.

"How did they miss *you* in the confirmation hearings? Everyone making snide remarks about why he's single?"

Laurie said rather formally, "It was a long time ago. There was nothing improper."

"Nothing improper . . . Laurie, come on. Unbuckle it."

"I mean, we were both free, and it was our business."

"Yeah, but what was he *like*?"

Laurie finally smiled. "Adorable."

"Well, what happened?"

Laurie forked some tomato from her plate and took a long time swallowing it.

"I don't really remember," she said. "He went east, I went west. I started seeing Roberto."

Walter stopped eating and looked at her, hard. "I have to know everything," he said again. "I don't want to go into this with a bucket tied to my foot."

"It was a long time ago," Laurie said.

He gave up. "Okay. So Roberto . . . "

"Came to visit one Christmas, then again in the summer. He and my brothers played tennis. He spent some time at the ranch."

"He was pretty glamorous."

"Yes, but I was used to that. Dad was not exactly low profile."

"True. Then. Elective office?"

"The school board in Blaine County. The run for Congress in seventy-six. When the twins were finally in school full time I ran for district judge."

"And won. Easily?"

Laurie nodded. Walter noticed the brief hesitation. Ah, it's immodest to boast. She'll have to get over that too, if she can. If she can't, good night.

"The first year was a special election to fill a vacant seat. Two years later I ran to succeed myself."

"Big margin the second time?"

"Yes."

"Good. And Roberto's campaigns? You helped?"

"Yes, all I could."

"Good. And who in the party have you talked to so far?"

"I spent an hour with the state chair this morning."

"And?"

"He seemed delighted."

Walter nodded, chewing. He was pleased, but he'd expected as much.

"We'll make a list of key people you should call on right away. Like tomorrow. But I think you'll find all of them pleased. Do you fish Silver Creek?"

Laurie smiled. "Do you?"

"It's my favorite thing in the world. I come up every August for it. Float downstream with your lunch in your pocket. Never care if you catch anything or not. Sometimes I forget to cast."

"It's a great state," Laurie said.

"It is. It's a *great* state."

The waitress came to try to sell them dessert. Walter ordered some pie. While he ate, he talked about the steps that should be taken first. Ask key people for support, rent an office, start rounding up volunteers. File a statement of candidacy with the Secretary of State. That had to be done as soon as she'd spent $5,000, which she'd probably do just setting up an office, so might as well get on with it. Then file campaign disclosure papers.

"How are your financials going to look?"

"A little thin. Roberto had life insurance, but it wasn't huge, and he had some campaign debts himself. I own the house we live in. The land belongs to a family corporation."

"Who's in it?"

"Dad, Bliss, Billy, and me. If the ranch makes a profit after upkeep and taxes it goes to pay Billy and Cinder and the hands."

"Money of your own?"

Laurie shook her head. "We live in a beautiful place. That's our luxury. I do have some savings, and a Keogh."

"Kids are in public school?"

"Yes."

"Good."

"You all through here?" The waitress was back. Laurie and Walter both leaned back in their chairs to make room for her to clear.

"We'll talk about strategy as we go along, but the first thing you're going to do is raise a lot of money."

"Damn."

"I knew you weren't going to like that."

"No, I'm not. How much?"

"At least a quarter of a million. You'll probably need at least two million by the time you're done. The more you raise, the more you'll attract, and the earlier you start, the better chance you'll have of scaring off other candidates."

"Dad *said* two million. I hoped he was wrong."

"No, not in this climate. I know it sounds like a lot, but I think you can do it."

"I'm glad *you* do."

The waitress came back with their check, and Walter paid it. Then he leaned back in his chair.

"Before we go any farther down this road, I want to know from you that you are absolutely sure you want to do this. I think you can win, if you can take the pressure. But I don't know you very well. Can you stand the press, can you stand the lack of privacy, can you take the schedule, can you do what you have to do to make people give you money? What kind of fighter are you?"

There was a long silence.

Finally Laurie said, "Could we go out and walk?"

"Good idea."

They retrieved their coats and went out into the flat, windswept streets. It was a bright, cold day that smelled of snow, though none had fallen yet this year. The high western sky arched over them. Boise was a city whose edges could be sensed, meaning even downtown you had a feel for the flat land under the pavement and the prairie out past the city limits. A few blocks to the north the hills rose, bristling with new houses for the computer people who were pouring into town. Out along Warm Springs Avenue were the "mansions" of the founding families. It was a stone's throw from Main Street to the Boise River, which cut through the heart of town. In the summer, as people went about their city business, the Boise River was full of tourists, bobbing along in the sun in inner tubes.

Walter and Laurie started to walk toward the river, but were discouraged by the wind. They turned instead toward the capitol, the great domed building where Laurie had spent so much time as a child.

"Now I'm going to shock you," Laurie said. She took a packet of cigarettes from her pocket and lit one.

"By god, you *do* shock me. Will you please promise you won't do that any place there might be a human with a camera, ever again?"

"I promise. The children would kill me if they knew. I started again when Roberto died." She dragged deeply and the smoke mingled with the frost from her breath, making a very satisfactory white cloud.

"Oh hell," said Walter, "I'll have one too." Laurie offered him the pack and her box of matches. Breathing smoke like a happy dragon, Walter added, "If that's the worst thing you have to tell me, we're going to be all right."

"It isn't."

"Oh," he said.

They were almost the same height as they paced along in the early afternoon. There were few people about; lunch hour was over.

"I had an abortion," she said.

"When?"

"The spring I finished law school."

"Oh my god. You mean, you and Mr. Cabinet?"

"No, it wasn't . . . no, he never knew. It was . . ." she took a deep breath and stalled. She dragged on the cigarette, then stopped to stub it out on the sole of her shoe. She put the butt into her pocket. "Don't let me forget that," she added, touching the pocket.

"It was 1972. You had an *illegal* abortion."

"Yes."

They crossed Bannock Street to the capitol building. They paced around it and on past the Joe R. Williams Building, a glass-faced office building that handsomely reflected the dome of the capitol in its own mirrored surface, as if paying its respects.

"Okay," said Walter finally. "I've got to ask you some questions."

"I know."

"Where did you have it?"

"You're not going to like it."

"Tell me."

"Washington, D.C."

Walter groaned. "Washington!? Couldn't you have gone to some country where they don't speak English?"

"I didn't have a lot of choices. It was not a baby I could have. I couldn't face my parents, I couldn't marry the father, I was almost out of time when I realized what was wrong, because I had an IUD . . . I doubt you can imagine the panic. Or despair. I had one friend who knew someone."

"Did the man know, the father of it?"

"Yes."

"What was his attitude?"

"He was angry I wouldn't marry him."

"And why wouldn't you?"

"He had a commitment to somebody else. That I hadn't known about."

"I'm not getting the picture."

She was very reluctant to say more, but she did at last, speaking carefully.

"We'd gone out for a year, my first year in Cambridge. We'd broken off four or five times—it was a mess. He was brilliant but angry, and I wasn't used to it. I didn't know what to do. Except never see him. And I hadn't, for over a year, and then—I can't explain. One thing happened. There were reasons, but they don't change anything. The price was terrible."

Walter looked at her, but she looked at the sidewalk as they walked. Clearly, still a painful subject, even after many years.

"Do you know where he is now?"

"No idea."

"And you're not going to tell me his name."

"Correct."

"Would he have any reason to want to hurt you?"

This gave her pause. "I don't think so. He loved me. But I don't know."

They walked some more.

"You're not exactly reassuring me," said Walter.

"I'm doing the best I can."

"And Mr. Cabinet?"

"He just knew that all of a sudden I was gone."

"Well, didn't he . . . "

"He was gone too. School was over, we were done."

"You were having an affair . . . "

"We were having a romance."

"What's the difference?"

"There is one," she said.

They walked on. After a half block, in which Walter realized that he was not going to get Laurie to tell him any more than she had decided in advance to say, he said, "Tell me about the doctor. Doctor?"

"Yes. It wasn't a clothes-hanger deal."

"Do you know what happened to him? Him?"

"Yes, him. There weren't so many women doctors in those days either. If there had been, there probably wouldn't have been so many clothes hangers."

"Well? What happened to him?"

"He was finally caught . . . somebody turned him in." She paused.

"It was a terrible experience, worse than I can tell you. But he was a decent man. He didn't even charge that much. He was trying to do the right thing."

"Did Roberto know?"

"Yes."

"Anyone else?"

"My brothers. My brother Bliss got the money for me. And Billy helped put the pieces back together all the rest of that summer. I came pretty well apart."

"So, now four living people know, if we don't count the doctor. How old would he be, by the way?"

"Oh god. He looked so old to me then, but he was probably . . . fifty."

"So he could be alive."

"Yes, but he didn't exactly take my social security number."

"So now five people know."

"Cinder knows."

"Six people know. Plus me. I guess that's seven."

"Yes."

"I suppose you know Ben Franklin said three people can keep a secret if two of them are dead."

"We've kept this one a long time. And it's a secret I share with a lot of good women."

They turned a corner and started back toward The Idanha, by unspoken agreement.

"I take it," said Walter dryly, "that you will be a Pro-Choice candidate."

"Does that mean you think I can go ahead?"

"It's going to add to the white-knuckle factor for the select few of us, but yes. I think it's a risk worth taking."

"What would happen if it came out?"

"I don't know," said Walter. "I don't think you'd enjoy it. Nor would your father, or your children, or the men you were seeing at the time of the pregnancy."

They walked in silence until they were in the car.

"So," said Laurie. "Do you want to go back to the airport?"

"Hell, no. Let's go talk to Hunt, and get to work."

Laurie gave him a quick smile. When they were out of town, Walter added, "Thank you for telling me now. I've known candidates who would have let me read it in the paper."

"You're welcome."

Laurie drove, feeling an odd sense of apprehension and elation.

The Monday after Thanksgiving, Carter and DeeAnne met with all the ops to discuss current and future business. Carter made the case for Shanti's vigilantes. "It will be dangerous," she said more than once. "This is gang territory."

"I *hate* those guys," said Leesa. "Dealers. Posers. Jerks who think going to prison or dying young makes you a man."

"Can't be any more dangerous than the freeway," said Mae Ruth.

The yes vote was unanimous.

Two nights later Carter was in the basement of the Good Hope Baptist Church, with Shanti and Flora. Almost fifty of Shanti's neighbors were sitting on folding metal chairs, drinking coffee and holding notepads. They were mostly women, though the minister of the church was there, and a number of the church wardens. Shanti gave Carter the cast of characters as people arrived.

A tall green-eyed man wearing a Lion of Judah emblem ran the local video store. There was a man in his sixties who owned a fried chicken franchise, and a Hispanic couple who owned a bodega. There was also a lone Korean who ran a grocery store two blocks down; Shanti had urged him to come but was surprised that he had.

"Who's the one with the hat?" Carter whispered. She watched a matron in a flowered dress and a regal air take a seat in the first row. People came to pay respects as if she were the matriarch of the gathering.

"Aunt Sallie Spear. The church organist. She's lost three sons on the street," Shanti explained. "They were all she had."

"She's not your real aunt?"

Shanti shook her head no. "Her grandnephew, Titus, is Flora's best friend. There's eight . . . no, nine women here who are raising their grandkids, because the parents are dead or in jail."

"Who's this now?"

"That's Thomas Magee. He's like the mayor of the square. He used to court my grandma."

The old man walked slowly, and his head wagged slightly from side to side, as if his neck were on a spring. Someone gave him a chair so that he too could sit in front. He wore large pink hearing aids, the color once designated as "flesh."

The minister called the meeting to order with a prayer, and then Shanti spoke. She announced that she had copies of a legal guide to fighting street drug markets, anyone interested should see her. She reported that a citizen's group ten blocks away had gotten the housing court to shut down a crack house by filing a civil suit against the landlord. She repeated what had obviously been discussed before, the way to turn in a dealer. "You got to describe the dude from hat to shoes, man, and get it right, or else they don't have 'reasonable suspicion.' They're not *allowed* to stop him and search him if you just say 'little black dude, the one that's always out there dealing by the basketball hoop.'"

"I don't want to call The Man at all," said a woman wearing a purple dress and matching lipstick. "I just go up to the guy and say, 'Get the fuck off my block!'" There was applause and laughter.

"I hear you. But *you're* the one they're going to hurt if they start having serious business trouble. We've got a new plan." And she introduced Carter.

Carter started by establishing her credentials, then she explained the drill. There would be a regular rota of watchers monitoring the block. All the watchers would have her cell-phone number. When anyone knew where a drug supply was stashed, she would call with exact details. "We'll come as quick as we can and leave as quick as we can. If we have to poke around looking for the stuff, it puts my people in danger, so help us.

"Next: Shanti has a petition we want you all to sign to get the incoming service to the pay phones in this neighborhood cut off. That will keep the customers from calling to place their orders."

"Numbers guys aren't going to like it," someone shouted from the back row, and there was laughter.

A young woman nearby answered, "Why not get them to change to rotary phones, so they can't page the fucking runners on their beepers?"

"That's a great idea," said Carter. "You need someone to bird-dog it. After you send the letter, you've got to call every day, be polite but firm . . . "

"I'll do that," said Aunt Sallie Spear. There was a stirring of approval. There was no doubt in anyone's mind that if this woman said she'd get it done, it would get done.

"Three: you've got to put pressure on the merchants who allow dealing in their stores. If they're afraid, offer to work as a group to keep the police responding to calls. But if they refuse, make it clear that you will boycott the store until you close it down."

She told them to work as a group, avoid confrontations, and try to stay anonymous.

"When the police see you're serious, they'll start answering your calls," she added. She hadn't expected quite so many people to laugh. But the main thing, everyone understood, was that if the dealers kept losing their stashes, the suppliers, or their enforcers, would start taking care of the problem themselves.

*a*lbie Strouse had made a point of informing his family of the provisions of his will, so it came as no surprise. The Strouse Foundation got a bequest equal to half the estate. Bert and Eloise had been amply provided for during his lifetime, and the grandchildren had trusts that would pay for education and travel. He had set up a similar trust for Rae's grandchildren, per stirpes, in case Walter married. He had given Harriet and Walter $10,000 each on their birthdays every year, and they had known that this would go on only for his lifetime. There was also a trust set up for Rae's support, more she said than she could ever use, that would revert to the Strouse Foundation at her death. The rest of the estate, except for bequests to James and Doreen and other servants, and some jewelry and furniture left to Bert and Eloise, went to Rae outright. It amounted to quite a few millions. The number of millions was a surprise, but the real surprise was a letter, filed with the will, sealed and addressed to Rae.

October 16, 1988

Dear wife,

If you are reading this, we have already said good-bye. I can't guess how far in the future that may be, but I know my memory is failing and I believe I see where I am headed. I want to make clear (and I enclose my doctor's report, dated and witnessed) that I am very much in my right mind as I write this.

I want to leave you with a wish. Although I hope we will
have many more happy years together, it seems wise to com-
municate it now. I have thought about this from all angles
and am not likely to change my mind. Nevertheless, it is not
an instruction, or in any way binding on you. You will know
when the time comes what is right.

If it happens that it pleases you to fall in with this wish, it
will affect our descendants, and for that reason, I will explain
myself more for them than for you; I believe you will understand without much explanation.

As you know, my father's parents came from Russia, from a
town whose name I do not know. My grandfather wrote only
Russian and Yiddish; my grandmother could not read or write
in any language. If there were ever family letters or diaries,
they were not passed on, because my generation couldn't read
them. My grandparents were very proud of having come here,
and they wanted their children to be Americans. That is how
the name of the town we came from was lost and the name of
the family, for that matter. My grandfather, who loved music,
renamed himself after the composer of waltzes, but he spelled
it his own way, so no one would think he was pretending a
relationship. Late in life he was reunited with his brother
Hymie, who had settled in New York. Hymie had renamed
himself Harley Shore. Harley, Grandpa never understood;
Shore is easier. It's a family full of poets. (And dancers!)

The Shore cousins have prospered. And I have had luck
beyond all expectations, as I don't have to tell you. What I do
have to tell is, I was especially lucky to make my fortune
when I was a grown man. Already a person, I learned my
lessons from my parents and my grandparents, not from the
way the world treats you when you have a certain kind of
bank account. I've seen the children who grow up with that,
and I am not impressed with the result.

I do not know much about my family's history, and I do not
expect my distant descendants to know much about me. I
have not been a practicing Jew. I haven't really been any

kind of Jew, but I am the son of my fathers, whether I know their names or not. From them I have learned to be grateful for what life has given me. More important, I know that true charity is not conducted in public in exchange for recognition. The gift that feeds the giver is done only in sight of God. I'm enough of a Jew to know that.

I do not believe that I made millions of dollars because I am smarter than everyone else. There are hundreds of thousands smarter, harder working, more deserving. I made money because it was a boom time after the war, and because I was lucky. I knew my business, like hundreds of others; I had some good ideas, like hundreds of others. I worked hard; so does the man who tends our garden. California happened to be giving away great educations in those days. My idea happened to take off. Other people had good ideas that didn't. I've been lucky financially but that doesn't make me beloved of God. If I'm beloved of God, the proof is that I've been lucky in love.

In my grandmother Sunny's house, we always met for Shabbes evening when I was a boy. She sent me down to O'Farrell Street for challah every Friday, and every Friday night, after Grandpa said the blessing, she tore a piece of bread from the challah, and burnt it in the candle. That was the offering. It meant, "We have enough. We remember the needs of others." Then the bread went around the table. Each one tore off a piece, and you said out loud one thing from the week that made you happy and then you had to say one thing in the coming week you hoped to improve.

This is the Sabbath evening of my life. This is what I want to say. I don't think there is anything wrong with being rich. There have always been rich and poor. But in the old world, you couldn't get rich and forget so easily that the poor are your neighbors. Rich and poor, you were all side by side, and if the village was sacked you were all going to suffer together.

I love America. I have had a wonderful life. But here the rich get so rich, you don't know anymore that the poor are your

neighbors. They *aren't* your neighbors. They live out of
sight, and it might as well be a different planet. The gap is
too wide. I think it is wrong for everyone. In my grandfather's world, you were rich if you had a house, and plenty of
food, and enough clothes, and your sons went to school. You
could also have a gold watch and a diamond for your wife. If
you had ten times as much money as you needed for that,
you didn't then have ten houses and ten gold watches. Here
we have ten houses.

While I was making this money, it seemed so lucky, I didn't
know when my luck might turn sour. I was also brought up
to put something aside for a rainy day. So I did, and it's a
good excuse. But if Grandma Sunny were here, I'd burn my
piece of challah now. And my wish for the future? I wanted
to leave this choice to you, so you would never, ever feel I
hadn't taken care of you or the family. But if, as I think, you
have enough to live as well as you want for as long as you
may need it, and if you agree that our children already have
enough to ruin them several times over, it is my wish and my
gift to you that you should give the rest away.

The letter was signed and witnessed, as was the enclosed doctor's
report.

Rae took off her glasses, and looked across the fireplace to Andrew
Simon, Albie's young attorney. Andrew had been one of the witnesses,
and it occurred to Rae that this explained, in small part, why Albie
had suddenly stopped using his old friend George Livermore, the
senior partner. Albie wanted to be sure his lawyer would outlive him.

"I imagine you have some questions," Andrew said.

"Well, yes, I have." Rae poured herself another cup of tea and
handed the plate of cookies to Andrew. "What if I had died first?"

"If you had predeceased Albie, similar letters would have been sent
to Bert and to Eloise. After the bequest to the foundation, the
remaining estate would have been divided equally between them, and
each would have had the choice to follow his wishes or not."

"That would have been interesting," said Rae.

"He thought so too, but he hoped it would work out as it has."

"And have you notified Bert or Eloise?"

"No. My instructions were to leave that to you. You can show them the letter, you can leave it with your own will, or you can keep the whole thing to yourself."

"And did he tell you what he hoped I would do?"

"All he said was that the foundation is doing the public good works. He didn't want any Albert Strouse Memorial hospital wings. Though you're free to build some, if you want to. He just hoped you would have a whale of a good time."

"Honey," said Rae, "just watch my smoke."

Yo, Auntie Carter! (Jill typed into her computer).
Laurie did it! She's in! Mom is PSYCHED. . . . Me too!
Que pasa avec toi?
    XXX,
    J.
**P.S. The reason you can't see me is I have lost
another EIGHT pounds. You?**

The news that Laura Knox Lopez had declared herself a candidate for United States Senate was getting a big play in the national media. Was this another Year of the Woman? People invoked the career of Lindy Boggs, who had served in the House with such distinction after *her* congressman husband was lost in a plane crash. There was a joyful rehashing of Senator Turnbull's unreconstructed views on such totems as affirmative action and the environment, of his maddening sexism, and especially of his behavior during the savage confirmation hearings of Ella Steptoe. That still enraged women of both parties, even years after the fact, the *Times* reported.

Jill and Amy had done a war dance of joy around the breakfast table when they'd opened the paper.

"What's this?" Noah said, looking up in surprise from his soft-boiled egg and his *Wall Street Journal*.

"Our friend! We told you! We made her run for the Senate!" Amy handed him the paper, and put her hand up for Jill to slap. Noah skimmed the article.

"Oh god," he said wearily.

"What? Isn't it great?"

"Look at Carlos, Mom. He really does look just like his father." Jill was leaning over the paper, studying a picture of Laurie going into church on the arm of her eighteen-year-old son.

"You must be kidding," said Noah.

"What do you mean?"

"Jimbo Turnbull is chairman of the Senate Finance Committee."

"I'm aware of that," said Amy.

"We're in the deepest budget doo-doo of the century, and that meatball in the White House was smoking catnip during Econ.#1 or something. There's not a chance in hell he can cut the deficit without stalling the economy. We are never going to get this under control without Jimbo Turnbull. You have no idea."

Amy stared at him, and then said, "Exactly when did *you* become the policy wonk?"

"What do you mean?"

"What do *you* mean I have no idea? I read the papers too, you know."

Noah put down his paper and looked at his wife. Amy was wearing her sweat clothes and no makeup, having just finished following her Step Class video in their bedroom. His daughter was wearing huge floppy clothes in about thirty layers, but this was because Sherpa chic was her idea of what to wear on the street. Their wide-set hazel eyes, so alike, with their long thick lashes, stared back at him.

"Sorry," he said. "It's just an expression."

"What is?"

"'You have no idea.' I'm sorry I said it."

"You know what?" Amy finally said. "You have been trying to provoke me for months. I don't know why and I don't care, but I do have

an idea. I am going to support Laura Lopez any way I can, and I hope
that doesn't present a problem."

"I don't see why it should, as long as we don't talk about it," said
Noah. "I don't really think a bunch of amateurs are going to scare Jim
Turnbull much." He brushed imaginary toast crumbs from his lap as
he stood. "I'll be home at the normal hour." He left the kitchen.

There was a long silence during which Amy didn't move. Jill
gnawed uncomfortably on a piece of dry toast.

Going down in the elevator, Jill's thoughts were jumbled. To avoid
thinking about her father's bad humor, she was composing a mental
telegram to Laurie saying, Remember, You Are Only a Woman.
Outside, she wrestled with the zipper of her parka as the December
wind struck her face. Christmas was coming. It smelled like snow. She
wished they were going skiing, but they were going to Mexico instead
because warm weather was better for Daddy's heart. Before the
Christmas break she had two ten-page papers to write, and she was
worried about her father. He had angina, which he refused to talk
about but which she'd looked up at the college library. She thought
worry was changing his personality. She wondered if it was only
health, or was he worried about money? Why else would you pick a
fight with your beloved wife over a budget in Washington that you
couldn't do anything about anyway?

As she rounded the corner onto Park Avenue South heading
toward the subway, hurrying to get out of the wind, a dark figure suddenly stepped into her path, and she nearly screamed.

"Good morning," said the figure. A tall black man, filthy anorak.

She ducked her head in what was supposed to pass for a civilized
nod. She hurried past him and crossed the street, although it meant
she was no longer protected by the lee of the building. Calm down,
you dumb shit, she said to herself. Calm down. This is the world, this
is not your dreams. Every single man on the street is not planning to
attack you.

She glanced back across the street, half ashamed of herself, and
hoping the man had not taken her fear as rudeness. She saw he was

wearing a grimy sweater, not an anorak as she'd first thought. No help against this wind. And she saw he had a paperback book sticking out of his pocket.

It was MacDuff, the homeless man from the soup kitchen. He was standing around on a freezing December morning outside her apartment building. He didn't seem to be coming or going. He seemed to be where he meant to be. She was terrified.

he first week of the surveillance, Carter took the night shift and Leesa took noon to eight. The Association couldn't afford round the clock, and they figured even drug dealers had to sleep sometime. Leesa used a ratty-looking van with windows painted black; inside she had seven or eight changes of clothes and a dozen hats and wigs. Every time she stepped out of the van she looked like a different person. She kept the van on side streets and waited for her phone to ring.

Her first call came from a woman on the north side of the block. A holder, a boy of about fourteen, had just put his stash into an over-flowing trash bin outside her window. It was in a white paper bag from a doughnut shop. Leesa was able to drive past and pluck the bag without ever getting out of the car. She parked a block away and walked back to watch the panic on the kid's face when he came back at a jog, having been beeped by his dealer, and found the bag gone.

They were not all so easy. Twice the holder came back before she could collect, and once the car described by the watcher was gone when she got there. Working in daylight was tricky, but there was euphoria when, by the end of the week, she had scored eight times.

You could feel things changing on the street, even the first week, Shanti reported with excitement. Word was spreading among the members of the Association that the plan was working. More people signed up to be on watch, and more people joined to stump up their share of the money. One dealer beat up his holder in broad daylight and they were both arrested. The holder was let go, but the dealer was carrying crack vials, wads of cash, and an unregistered pistol. Immediately the Association started a letter-writing campaign demanding that the District Attorney's office take the case seriously. To their surprise, in the second week they got a respectful reply.

"So we'll see," Shanti said. Carter could hear that she was full of righteous pride.

Carter, on the night shift, used the Brown Bomber; she kept a collection of hats and jackets in the backseat. Because it was dark, and the dealers had a tendency to shoot out the streetlights, she was protected by the same cover that covered them, and had less need to disguise herself. But by the second week, word was out. Holders were not going far from their stashes, and they were not leaving them unwatched. The police seemed to take an interest; black and whites cruised the streets more frequently. Dealers who had always worked the park were moving into side streets, requiring mobilization of new watchers. Shanti was ready for them.

he day Laurie's candidacy was announced, Walter was due at his mother's house to have dinner and talk about Albie's letter. He arrived carrying the *New York Times*, the *Wall St. Journal*, the *Washington Post*, and the *San Jose Mercury News*.

"I figured you'd have seen the *Chronicle*," he said.

"Well, indeed I did, and I tried to talk to the candidate, but her line was tied up all day, so I talked to everybody else. Let me see. Are there pictures?"

Walter had led the way into the library. Rae looked at his tall, slightly stoop-shouldered frame and thought how exactly like his father he carried himself. He had his father's strong nose and deep-set, almost yellow, eyes. His thick ash-blond hair was from her side of the family. Walter's father had been almost bald when he died, and Walter was older now than his father had ever been.

Walter settled Rae in her favorite chair and lit the fire James had laid. Then he handed her the papers in turn, opened to the coverage of Laurie's announcement, and watched as his mother quickly read each piece.

The *Mercury News* carried the same smiling picture of Laurie surrounded by her children that the *Chronicle* had run; that must have been the one sent out with the press release. The *Times* ran a picture of Laurie in black, head bowed, walking up the steps of a church on the way to her husband's funeral. She was on the arm of her son Carlos, who *did* look just like his father. The *Washington Post* ran the funeral

196

picture and also a picture of Laurie, age about six, in a dress with a bow sash, shaking hands with President Truman. Governor Hunt Knox, dark-haired and bulky in a double-breasted suit, stood, smiling, beside her.

The Washington paper reported the reactions to the news at the Capitol. Democrats were pleased. Senator Turnbull's office declined to comment.

Rae laid aside the last paper. "Of course, I don't want to miss a thing. Can I stuff envelopes? I could go door to door, and talk peoples' ears off?"

Walter smiled. "I have big plans for you in this race, Mother, and I may send you door to door. But the first thing we need to do is raise money."

"Why don't I just give her some? I've got quite a bit."

"That's true, you do."

"How much would she like? Why don't I give her a hundred thousand?"

Walter roared with laughter. "Because I don't want to visit you in jail. You can't give more than a thousand dollars, it's against the law."

"Oh!" Rae was quite indignant.

"Excuse me, can I get you something to drink?" James had appeared at Rae's elbow.

"I think I'll have a negroni."

"Can you make a negroni, James?" Walter asked.

"Certainly," James said proudly.

"No, why don't we have champagne?" said Rae. "It's a great day."

"That's a fine idea. But wait a minute, James, as a man about to become a citizen, can you explain campaign contribution laws to my mother?"

"Certainly," said James again. "You may contribute one thousand dollars per candidate. You may give up to twenty thousand dollars to a national party committee or five thousand dollars each to any other political committees. But you may not give more than a total of twenty-five thousand dollars in one year."

"Thank you," said Walter.

"You're welcome."

"Well, at least," said Rae, "I can give Laurie a thousand now and then another thousand in January."

"No," said James. "The thousand-dollar limit is per election, not per calendar year. You may give another thousand for the general election, if she wins her primary." He went out to find champagne.

"I'm going to love having James for a brother-in-law," said Walter.

"Yes, I think he'll be a great addition."

James returned with a bottle and two champagne flutes on a tray. He opened the bottle expertly. He poured the wine and left the bottle behind him as he went out.

"To Laurie," said Rae. Walter echoed this, smiling, as they clinked glasses. "And confusion to the enemy," she added.

They sat quietly. "Mother, what exactly is going to happen after the adoption? Are they going to stay on? Are they going to call you 'Mother'? How do you picture it?"

"This has been worrying Bert a good deal, I must say. He expects they'll start putting something in my food, so I'll go quietly mad, but I've pointed out that I'm worth much more to them sane and alive than in any other condition."

"Have you discussed it with them?"

"Not very much. Doreen says how grateful they are and I say not a bit, don't mention it . . . I thought I'd wait till you got back, and we'd think it through."

"They probably will want their own house and all that. I would. I *do*. But it ought to be made clear. Is she to be your daughter in name only, to satisfy the law? Or what?"

"I don't see that it can be in name only. If I adopt her, I adopt her. But it isn't like bringing home a baby. I was thinking what we really ought to do is ask *them*."

"Aren't you smart," said Walter. It had been fretting him that he was going to have to work it all out, the way he planned a campaign.

"Maybe now would be a good time." She rang the little handbell that stood on the table beside her chair, and James appeared.

"James, could you and Doreen join us for a few minutes? Would it be convenient?"

"Of course." In a minute or two he was back with Doreen, who blushed and apologized.

"I'm so sorry . . ." She gestured at her blue jeans.

"Don't be silly, it's your day off. They're very becoming. Would you like some champagne? Walter can get some glasses."

They declined to drink, with much thanking and embarrassed shaking of heads.

"Please sit down, then."

They chose chairs side by side, facing the fire and perched on the edge of their seats.

"Is the baby safe with Cook?"

"He is sleeping."

"Good. Well, we'd like to talk about your future," said Rae. They nodded.

"Have you thought about it?"

They both nodded again. They were serious now, shy and quiet.

Walter said, "You might like a place of your own. You can start to think about more suitable jobs. You might want to start your own business."

James and Doreen looked at each other. Doreen looked at her sneakers. James said, "Doreen is planning to go to medical school."

"When we save enough money," she added quickly.

"I always wanted a doctor in the family!" said Rae. "So you have university credits?"

"Four years at university."

"You'll probably have to take some courses here, to get the premed requirements squared away," said Walter. "Once you have your papers, you can have your credits transferred. Or maybe you don't need them. Maybe you just have to take entrance exams. And there's UCSF right here. Or Stanford, of course, if you don't want to stay in San Francisco."

"So expensive," said Doreen, shaking her head.

"You don't have to worry about that," Rae said. "Mr. Strouse set up a fund to educate our children and grandchildren." She suddenly laughed, then settled herself down. "I don't think the trustees will object, do you?" she asked Walter.

"Not a bit. It's set up for all your descendants."

Doreen's eyes widened and she and James looked at each other. It was as if they had been talking like kids of their wildest dreams, but not really until this moment understood that something was going to happen.

"I think you'll be a wonderful doctor," Rae put in. "And what about you, James? I don't suppose you want to go into the diplomatic corps?"

"No. I want to work for justice in China. I want to help those who are trying to change things. More fairness. More freedom to choose your own lives, like here. I have many friends in China who are doing this work. They need support. They need money. And they need United States people to understand what they are trying to do."

"I like the idea of a democratic firebrand in the family," said Walter, "but this doesn't sound like a job description."

"No, of course," said James. "I would like to go on working here, if that's all right. If you would like me to. I will need money while Doreen is in school."

"You don't want to move out?"

"Oh no!" they cried together. "It's so pretty here, and so quiet . . . safe for the baby . . . "

"We're used to big families, both of us," said James. "All ages, living together. We would be very lonely if we moved out, just by ourselves. We would miss Cook. We would miss you."

"Well, I'd miss *you*. I couldn't be happier," Rae said, and her smile was very broad. James and Doreen stood, wanting to be alone and talk to each other.

"We better . . . ", "The baby . . ." they said at once.

When they had gone, Walter began to laugh.

"So you're not losing a houseman, you're gaining a doctor."

"She should finish her training right about the time I'll be ready for her," said Rae. "I hope she goes into geriatrics."

They sat enjoying the fire and drinking champagne.

"Not to change the subject, but we better talk about Albie's letter," said Walter.

"Yes."

"It's fairly clear that he's left you free to give the money in ways that institutions can't. To find where there's need that isn't being served by other programs."

"*That* shouldn't be hard."

"No, I agree, not to find the need. But how to do no harm. I can't help but think of the boy who won the Hero medal."

"What boy?"

"Funny—I thought you told it to me. Must have been Albie. It's this: A young man in Cleveland. He was walking on the beach of Lake Erie one evening when he saw somebody drowning. He dove in and saved the man's life, and got his picture in the paper. Then he was given a Citizen Hero medal, and flown to Washington to meet the President. It ruined him. He quit his job and spent all day every day wearing his medal, pacing up and down the beaches of Cleveland, waiting for somebody else to start drowning, so he could do it again. True story, I checked."

They sat silent for a while, watching the fire.

"According to Maimonides," Walter said, "the truest form of charity is to help someone to help himself."

"I'm all right so far," said Rae, with a slight tip of her head toward the kitchen wing of the house. "I hope."

"The second highest is to give in secrecy. The ideal would be that the giver doesn't know who received, and the one who received doesn't know who gave."

"But how do we do that?"

"What if we look not for people who need help, but for people who are helping? There's a pair of young doctors out in the Sunset giving away medical care. They have supplies to buy and rent to pay . . . "

He handed her a clipping.

Rae read it. "I *like* this," she said.

"It's going to take some research. And it's got to be done discreetly. Whatever you decide to do, you're going to need a front man. If anyone finds out the money is coming from you, you'll have every con artist in America on your doorstep with a begging bowl."

This Rae already knew. Forget Maimonides. She'd seen plenty of
that at the Strouse Foundation.

"I was hoping *you* would . . . "

"I'd like nothing more," said Walter. "*The Millionaire* was my
favorite show. I used to practice writing John Beresford Tipton all
during high school math."

"I know you did, I saw your notebooks. Did you put Albie up to
this, by the way?"

Walter laughed. "I didn't have to. But we both agreed, the person
you really wanted to be was Michael Anthony, who knocks on the
door and says . . . "

"You must have laughed your head off when you read the letter,"
said Rae.

"I cried, actually. The point is, I can't be your Michael Anthony,
I've had my picture in the paper too many times. No, you've got your
man. James."

"James!"

"He's a diplomat. He's discreet as a tomb. He's a raging human
rights champion, he'll love this."

uring the third week of December, somebody broke a stained-glass window at the Good Hope Baptist Church. Plywood was nailed up, and on Sunday the collection plate overflowed with money to replace it. Carter decided the night shift should work in pairs, with one to pick up the stash on foot, the other to pace along in the car in case of trouble.

One night just before Christmas, Carter was reaching into the wheel well of a pickup when DeeAnne, driving slowly up the street with her lights off, turned on her high beams and leaned on the horn. Carter wheeled around to see a little fat boy freeze in his tracks, exactly like a deer in headlights. Carter began to run toward him and DeeAnne followed, leaning on the horn. The boy ran for his life.

In the car, sweating, Carter said, "I bet you made that poor little bugger shit his pants."

"I better go back and switch cars," DeeAnne said. "Every enforcer in ten blocks will be looking for this one."

"I'll stay here. Give me the cell phone."

"You sure? It will be quiet for a while, after all that racket."

"Customers are paying for an eight-hour shift. I'll be all right."

DeeAnne gave her the phone and promised to be back in an hour with coffee and food.

Carter was walking toward the avenue when her pocket began to ring.

"Carter? Shanti. Are you all right?"

"I'm fine. We were just giving you your money's worth."

"You want a cup of coffee?"

"Do you drink coffee at this hour?"

"I drink it anytime."

"I'd love it. Thanks."

She walked around the park to Shanti's house. When she rang, Shanti turned off the porch light and opened the door. She had Flora on her hip. She led Carter into the living room, which was bright with kente cloth and crowded with ferns and cactus.

"Miss Flora! Are you awake?" Carter asked.

Flora was in her jammies, and awake was not really the word for it, but she nodded.

"The sitter just left," Shanti said. "I left her home tonight because she's had a little sniffle. But Miss Watchdog always hears me open the door, no matter how deep asleep she is. Because I missed you all evening and you knew I needed a hug, isn't that right?" Shanti nuzzled her daughter.

"Did I wake you up with all that honking, Miss Flora?"

Flora looked across at Carter, her eyes wide. Shanti laughed. "You heard that honking, didn't you, little bear?" Flora nodded.

"I've got to get you back to bed, little bear. Can you say good night to Carter? No? You can't say good night?"

"Can you give me five?"

Carter held up her hand, and the little girl gravely reached out and gave it a slap. As she was carried away, Flora peeped at Carter over her mother's shoulder.

When Shanti came back with two mugs of coffee, Carter was looking out the window.

"Look at that asshole," she said. There was a white man wearing a tan suede jacket and loafers with tassels walking into the ruined playground. He stopped under one of the few functioning streetlights, uncertain what to do. Out of the darkness two large dark figures started toward him, walking purposefully, as if to music. The tasseled loafers went to meet them.

"He come in the Jag?" Shanti asked, settling down beside her. There was a vintage XKE parked halfway up the street.

"Good guess," said Carter. There weren't a lot of $70,000 cars in this neighborhood. They drank their coffee and watched as the white man moved into the blackness across the playground with his two escorts.

A phone rang. Shanti stood up. "No, it's mine," said Carter. She reached into her pocket. The call was from a watcher one block over on a side street. A kid had just left his stash in a wheel well and gone off running, probably to make a delivery to the park. If she could get there fast, she could pick it up before he got back.

"See you later," Carter said to Shanti. She was on the street, moving quickly through the darkness, around the corner and onto a quiet street of bungalows. Some of the yards were well kept; others were weed filled and littered. She could see some lights on behind window blinds, but most of the houses were dark. Behind at least one of those windows was her watcher.

The car where she was to look for the stash was parked in front of a house covered in tar paper that had an imitation brick pattern printed on it. One of the front windows was boarded. There was a stereo system playing somewhere with the bass thumping, *pump-pump-pump.* Carter walked quickly, all senses alert. Nothing was moving on the street in front of her, but she had a fleeting sense of footsteps behind her. She stopped suddenly. The sound, if there had been any, stopped too. She figured it must have been a sort of echoing off beat from the stereo, an illusion caused by her own footsteps against the pulsing of the drum machine.

She reached the blue Oldsmobile and, without stopping, swept her hand in under the right rear fender and pulled out a paper bag. She scooped it into a long inside pocket sewn into her jacket. The bag felt soft and heavy. This could be quite a haul.

The next thing she knew she was belly down on the sidewalk with blood pouring out of her nose. Someone huge was on top of her, pinning her hands to the sidewalk. She could smell sour sweat. She whipped her head straight backward as hard as she could, bashing the back of her head into his face.

With an angry scream he drew away from the source of the blow, shifting his weight enough to allow her to flip onto her side. This threw him further off balance. Moving with speed and force, Carter brought the toe of her shoe up between his legs and smashing into his groin right behind his testicles. She barely heard the howl as his body whipped into a protective ball; she was springing to her feet.

It was a big guy wearing gang colors. The heavily muscled upper body suggested a lot of time spent on weight machines, and she doubted it was at Jack La Lanne's. Everything about him suggested a recent sojourn at one of the charm schools run by the penal system. She found her tear gas canister and gave him a shot in the face.

"Bitch!" he roared as the pain spread into his eyes and nose, rendering him blind and agonized.

"If I were really a bitch, I'd have broken your leg, asshole." She searched him for weapons as he writhed and wiped at his eyes; she found a huge switchblade. "That's cute," she added, putting it into her pocket. Surprisingly, he didn't have a gun.

"What's the deal, your parole officer took away your piece?"

He didn't answer. She suspected that the unflattering truth was that he hadn't expected to need it. She was a woman. He probably thought he was born with all the equipment necessary. She reached into a pocket for her handcuffs, and realized with horror that they were in DeeAnne's car. Fuck. Maybe she *should* break his leg.

"Stop wiping your eyes, asshole, you're making it worse."

The guy was in worse pain from the tear gas than from anything else that had happened. She could see now, accustomed to the light level, that his nose looked mashed to one side, and blood was pouring out. No wonder the back of her head hurt. Not to mention screaming pain in her chin and elbows where she had hit the pavement. She hoped she hadn't cracked anything.

"On your feet, stud," she yelled. She held the gas canister aimed at him with two hands, as if it were a pistol. It was probably empty, but he didn't know that. Snorting with anger and pain, he got up. He didn't look as if he felt very comfortable in the midsection.

"Undo your belt and hand it to me."

He protested. She roared, "HURRY UP!" She knew he could barely see, and she wanted him secured before he felt in the mood to try kick boxing.

He took off his belt, and she took it from him.

"Undo the fly."

"Maa-an . . ." he yelled.

She clicked open the switchblade beside his ear, so he'd be sure to hear it. Swearing, he unsnapped and pulled down the zipper.

With the belt she swiftly and harshly tied his hands together behind his back. She pulled his pants down so that they shackled his ankles. He yelled a string of obscenities unflattering to women. There was a keening note to his rage, the raw edge of humiliation.

Jerking the bound hands upward as a warning, Carter ordered, "Take off a shoe."

"Can't take off my fucking shoe if you got my hands—"

She jerked upward again, harder. With another string of blue language, he used the toe of one shoe against the heel of the other to take a shoe off. She kicked it away.

She could tell by his breathing that the agony from the tear gas was beginning to abate. His eyes were probably tearing less, and vision returning.

She pricked the point of the switchblade against the exposed butt of his briefs. "Into the street, stud," she ordered. Feeling the knife point, he started shuffling.

She made him walk down the middle of the street under the brightest arc of the streetlights to protect herself from anything coming at her from the darkness between the houses. He shuffled and cursed. She held the knife with one hand and with the other reached for her cell phone. This she found in two pieces in her pocket. She swore. But up near the corner she saw the shade in a lighted second-story window go up a little. Her watcher had seen it all.

By the time she got her guy down the street and around the corner onto Shanti's block, she could hear the sirens rolling toward them.

"That will be your ride," she said. Her guy called her a string of very unpleasant names. "By the way," she replied as the police car sped into the street, "nice underpants." They were Ralph Lauren.

The police were both white, both male. They leaped out with nightsticks ready, although it was fairly clear that the suspect was not presenting any danger. Please guys, Carter thought, no Mark Fuhrman stuff.

"Not bad," said the first one, looking at the overall picture presented by her captive.

"You got a license for this shit?" the second one asked, rather aggressively. He was pointing to the purple stains the tear gas had left on the guy's shirt, dye that shows up under light so that if an attacker is sprayed, but escapes, he is marked.

Carter had her PI and tear gas licenses ready.

"What happened?"

"Assault with a deadly weapon," she said, handing over the switchblade. "I'll be glad to press charges."

"I kind of like this rig," said the first cop, who was looking over the prisoner.

"Will you let me pull my fucking pants up?!" roared the object of their attention.

They took their time getting him re-dressed and putting the cuffs on him as they asked Carter questions.

"What about my shoe?" asked the guy.

"Oh," said Carter, "did you lose a shoe?"

"Guess he lost a shoe," said the cops, and opened the door to the backseat. As they drove away, Carter looked up and saw Shanti smiling at her from the darkened front window of her house. She didn't want to direct attention to Shanti, since she hoped and expected that there were plenty of witnesses to that last performance, both friendly and not. But she certainly hoped Shanti had enjoyed it.

She sat down under a streetlight to wait for DeeAnne. Somehow she wasn't worried that anyone else would mess with her tonight.

*a*my had experienced this month of December as a set of thumbscrews, clamping down tighter and tighter. First, Christmas. It was the most frantic time for her business, and she added to that an unwillingness to give up the family traditions of the holiday. She insisted on doing elaborate stockings for Jill and Noah, filling them with presents she used to buy and hide throughout the year but now seemed to have to do all in one week. There was the holiday wassail party she had given every year since Jill's first Christmas. It got bigger and bigger, because everyone who had ever been invited was on the list, and they came with their now huge children, people she once had seen almost daily at school plays, or on crossing-guard duty, or serving hot lunch, whom now she saw only this one time in the year. Every year she said to Noah, "This is the last time, this is ridiculous," and every year people were so appreciative and effusive about it that she told them all to save the date, of course they'd be back next year.

There were the Christmas cards to send. She and Noah used to divide the list and sit in the den for a couple of evenings side by side, addressing envelopes and writing notes on the cards to absent friends. But Noah never had time anymore to help. He barely had time this year to look at the cards that came to them. She stuck them up all over the mantelpiece and bookcases in the living room and den and figured he could read them in January before she threw them out.

And this year there was this man whom Jill believed was stalking her. Amy hadn't seen him, but really, the whole thing was too much to bear. Just when Jill seemed to be turning the corner. She was getting out more, she was still losing weight, and she didn't spend nearly as much time holed up with that damn computer. Amy had talked to the police about the stalker, but even she could see there was nothing they could do. The man didn't threaten. He didn't even speak to Jill. He just watched her.

Still, this litany of pressures being loaded onto her shoulders explained everything and nothing. She loved Christmas. She complained every year and then thrived on it, the cooking, the news from old friends, the parties, the sight of the little boys she had pushed on swings now wearing blue blazers and experimenting with eggnog. The little girls Jill had played dress up with now in slinky black dresses and makeup, saying "like" and "actually" four times in every sentence and running off to Jill's room to giggle and gossip.

Something else was wrong. Noah's uneven temper, his angina, the excruciating pressure of his job. Sometimes he'd be in surgery at seven A.M., not get home until eight o'clock that night, and go straight into the bedroom to read medical journals for two hours. It was too much for a man almost sixty. He insisted he was deeply happy, and certainly they'd had times in the last month when she felt they'd never been so close. But they needed a real rest, a real break from work, from cold, from New York, from everything that had been so hard for the past five years. They needed a month alone together in some part of Tuscany where no one else spoke English and the phones didn't work.

Ten days in Mexico with Jill and the Kneodlers would have to do. The bedroom was covered with suitcases and tissue paper in preparation for the departure when the phone rang. Amy needed a suitcase for her own clothes, another for Noah's, a carry-on bag with some extra underwear and a bathing suit for when the airlines lost the rest of the luggage, and a whole separate case for the Christmas presents.

Amy could hear Noah in the den, his voice low and tired. She heard him hang up and trudge toward their room. Now what?

Noah stood in the doorway, and Amy stood in the middle of the room holding her new filmy nightgown. Suitcase or carry-on? Carry-on.

"Joe Casey's mother had a stroke this morning," said Noah. Joe

Casey was one of Noah's partners. His mother was eighty-eight, in a nursing home in Florida.

"I'm so sorry," said Amy. "How bad is it?"

"Bad."

"Poor thing. I'll put her on my prayer list."

"You're not understanding me. Joe Casey was going to be on call for the practice this week. It was all arranged six months ago. Instead he's going to Florida. I can't go to Mexico."

Amy dropped the nightgown onto the bed. "Noah—no! We've planned this for months!"

"What do you expect me to do?"

"I'm sorry. I didn't mean to be mad at *you*, but. . . . Can't anyone else do this? You need the time off, Noah. We *need* it."

"Everyone else is already gone. I'll find someone to cover for me. Rod Greene owes me a favor; he's divorced and I think he was staying in the city . . . "

Amy sat down on the bed and struggled to adjust to the disappointment.

"Why don't we all just stay here, then? We'll have a quiet Christmas at home, and maybe get away together the second week."

"Don't be silly. We've paid the deposit. Freddy and Dagmar are counting on us. You and Jill go ahead, and I'll be there in a day or so."

"The airlines are booked solid. And how do you know you can get someone to cover for you?"

"Amy, please. Just keep your voice down. I'll do the best I can, all right?"

They took off in a snow squall and landed in bright heat in central Mexico after an endless layover in Fort Worth. Dagmar and Freddy were feeling very festive after having had several margaritas on the plane. Amy was at least reading a good book, and Jill seemed happy. All four of them stretched in the heat like lizards and took off their sweaters and winter socks while they waited for the luggage.

Only the suitcase full of Christmas presents had been lost. After a lot of palaver in Spanish with the airline people, and more with the rental company that didn't have the car they'd reserved, they piled into taxis and were off to the Cancun Royale.

"It's lovely," Amy said to Noah on the phone that night. "Jill has a tennis lesson in the morning, and the food is wonderful. We have our own little cottage thing overlooking the beach." Noah said it sounded perfect and that he hoped to arrive tomorrow night. If not, the day before Christmas without fail.

"We've arranged to go see the Mayan ruins that day—do you want me to put it off? In case you get delayed?"

"No. I'll get there. I've always wanted to see them."

All the next day they lay in the sun, walked on the beach, waited for word of Noah's arrival. The airline called periodically to say they were tracking down the Christmas presents. Then again to say they had found them; they'd gone to Australia. Then again to say they would deliver the case to the hotel by morning. Which they did not.

There was bad news on the Mrs. Casey front. She was in a coma, but holding her own. It didn't look like Joe would be back before New Year's. No luck tracking down Rod Greene. "How will you ever get on a plane at this time of year?" Amy asked, depressed.

"Don't worry. I'll stand-by. If worse comes to worse, I'll charter one."

The next day they did a lot of sight-seeing, and Freddy took a windsurfing lesson from a gorgeous young German named Hans. "'Keep still da feet, Fritz! Iss not a discotheque!' he kept yelling at me," said Freddy. He had enjoyed himself and gotten a hell of a sunburn.

"Remember not to put ice in your drink, sweetie," Amy said to Jill.

"I think it's margarita time," Dagmar said, and she swam off to the bar, which sat in a thatched hut on a Disneyesque island in the middle of the pool. Dagmar wore a large straw hat and sunglasses even while swimming.

There was no word from Noah and no answer at home when Amy called. She expected him to walk in the door any minute throughout the night, but he hadn't.

The trip to the ruins was disappointing. Amy was upset that Noah was missing it, and kept thinking she should have stayed back at the hotel to be there to greet him. Their guide had arranged a lunch stop for them in a place that seemed less restaurant than private home, a slatternly tin-roofed affair that Jill enjoyed because there were monkeys in the yard, but which worried all the hygiene-minded grown-ups. The ruins themselves were magnificent and so was the number of tourists issuing from vast silver buses, and the riot of languages in which people were crying either "Hold still" or "Smile!" When they finally got back to the hotel, the suitcase full of Christmas presents had arrived, but not Noah. Amy learned at the desk that there was a snowstorm in the Northeast.

Noah finally called after dinner. He sounded worn out.

"The airports are a mess. People are sleeping on the floors at LaGuardia. I think I'll take the train out to Greenwich in the morning and spend the day with Louie and the children."

"Yes," said Amy, "do that. I don't want to think of you traveling on Christmas Day."

At Christmas lunch the hotel featured green and red salsas and candy cane swizzle sticks in the margaritas. Dagmar pronounced this a disgusting taste sensation. Conversation was rendered impossible by the mariachi bands that cruised through the rooms serenading each table no matter how earnestly you begged them to stop.

"Why *did* Noah choose oncology?" Dagmar demanded as they lay beside the pool in the late afternoon. Midday tequila had made her cross, and she'd run out of patience with Amy's temporizing about how dedicated Noah was and how hard it was on him.

"He said that when he was starting out, it was the field that seemed to be making the most progress," Amy said.

"Does he still feel that way?"

Amy sighed. "I don't know. So many other things have changed since then."

"I just can't imagine taking a knife and cutting into a living human being," said Dagmar peevishly.

* * *

Noah finally reached them by lunchtime on the twenty-sixth. He had brought presents for everyone, and seemed to be in a wonderful mood. Amy began finally to relax. She watched Noah's color deepen in the sun and the tension lines disappear. The nicest thing of all was his present for Jill—a beautiful winter coat of silvery faux fur, said to be made of recycled Coke bottles.

"She's so pleased," Amy whispered to him in bed. "You were really listening to her." Jill and her friends were deeply opposed to the killing of sweet little beasties for their pelts.

"I always pictured giving her a mink when she went off to college."

"I know you did, but she'd have hated that. How on earth did you find such a beautiful thing? You don't even know what avenue Saks is on."

"I have my methods," Noah said. "By the way, what avenue did this come from?" He was appreciating the filmy nightgown.

"I have my methods too." She kissed him, perfectly happy again.

*I*t was broad daylight when Shanti was killed, three days after Christmas. She had been sitting in her front window watching Flora playing on the floor with her new Mighty Morphin Power Rangers. A rusted Buick drove slowly down the street outside her house; inside it a young man in the backseat took careful aim with a rifle and shot off the back of her head.

A watcher saw it happen. Carter got the call as she was on her way to West Hollywood on another job. She got to Shanti's house one step behind the ambulance and two steps before the police.

There were people gathered on the street outside the house. Somewhere was the sound of a woman sobbing. Carter pushed past them and ran up the steps.

Two medics had brought a stretcher with them to the living room. Shanti was still sitting on the couch, or rather, slumping forward and to the side. Carter stood in the doorway, staring. She was swept by a wave of anger and grief, followed by nausea at the smell of so much blood.

"Who are you?" Two cops with guns drawn crowded into the room behind her, one of them barking questions. Carter turned to stare at them. Guns drawn? Who are *you* assholes?

The medics were talking to each other softly, and moving with a deliberation that showed there was no need to hurry at all for this patient anymore.

"Who are you? What are you doing here?" she was asked again,

215

more aggressively. She showed her PI license and said, "Friend of the family."

"You surveilling her?"

"I said *friend of the family*," she said louder. "And she was a client."

"What's her name?"

"Shanti Amos."

The second cop had spotted Flora, sitting in the corner. She had flattened herself into the shadows when the first of the big white men crashed in.

Carter now realized that whoever had arrived first, probably the fire department, had had to break the glass in the door to reach the inside lock. It was a good thing Shanti hadn't had the double locks on, they'd have chopped the door down, with Flora sitting on the other side, watching those hatchets crashing through the wood.

The first cop nudged the second and pointed to the baby. Both men stared at the wide eyes, the blank, terrified expression.

"Must of seen the whole thing," said the first one.

Brilliant, Sherlock, thought Carter. With every passing second her desire to scream or weep was growing.

The first cop took a step toward Flora and then it was Flora who was screaming. She howled terrible wordless sounds, the loudest noise she could make as she stared at the big white man who was starting to come for her. In a second Carter was on her knees between Flora and the uniform. She held out her arms, not knowing if the baby would let her pick her up. In a swift motion, Flora wrapped her arms and legs around Carter and clung fiercely, still shrieking, and Carter stood up and turned around, so that it was she who faced the police and the body on the couch, not the baby. She could smell the sweet milky smell of Flora's skin, and from across the room, the reek of blood.

"So what is this, a drug thing?"

"Looks like it," said one of the medics.

"She dealing? Or using?"

The cops were clomping around the apartment, looking out the window at the street, then back at the body.

"It was an execution," said Carter. She carried Flora to her bedroom, found Flora's pink backpack, and started stuffing things into it. She took some clothes from the drawer and a small teddy bear that looked worn with love, and crammed them in. She remembered Flora sitting on the floor of her office reading a picture book to herself, and she grabbed a few small books from the shelf. Flora clung to her so hard that Carter didn't even need to hold her. She could use both hands to pack.

One of the cops appeared at the door.

"The ME's on his way. Could we talk to you, please?"

"I have to get this child out of here."

"I'm sorry, you can't leave until we ask you some questions."

"No, *I'm* sorry," said Carter. "You know who I am, you know where to find me. I'll be happy to tell you anything you need to know, but not here, not now."

"I can't let you leave . . . "

"You can't make me stay, except by force, and what goddamn good would that do you or this child?"

The cop stared at her, nonplussed. Carter was nearly as tall as he was, and looked to be in considerably better shape. And she was holding a baby.

She walked past him and out the door. On the steps she nearly collided with the medical examiner, who looked extremely surprised to see her, or any civilian, leaving the crime scene.

On the street, most of the rubberneckers had melted away when the police arrived. Carter was careful not to meet anyone's eye as she marched out. In a day or two someone would come to her for Flora, but anyone who spoke to Carter now would be making himself, or herself, a moving target for whoever had killed Shanti.

Carter set Flora on the front seat of her car, close beside her, and started the car.

"This is my car," she said. "I'm going to take you to my house. No one is going to hurt you." Flora stared at the dashboard and clutched the pink backpack. Carter pulled out and drove.

*   *   *

It was only when they were inside her house with the door shut that Carter got a good look, close up, at Flora. She had blood on one hand, and on her clothes. She must have gone to her mother to try to wake her up or comfort her. Carter could imagine the bewilderment, giving way to fear . . . but no, she couldn't. How could you imagine a thing like that?

She asked Flora if she would like to change to clean clothes. Flora shook her head, very slightly. She asked if she wanted some lunch. Flora shook her head. Of course she didn't. She wanted only one thing in the world, and it was dead in a living room sixteen miles away.

Carter found herself just looking at the child as if, if she looked at her long enough, she would guess what Flora was feeling and then finally she could do something that would make it better. But Flora was very still. Her eyes moved. Her little body sat quiet in the chair where Carter had put her, and once in a while, for a second or two, she looked at something. Cased the room. The rest of the time she stared at Carter. As if she would vanish. Or the back of *her* head would explode and she would slump over and never move again. Or if she just stared at her hard enough, Carter would produce her mama.

Carter went to the phone. She intended to call DeeAnne, but when the flutey voice of the receptionist answered, she found she had called Jerry's office.

"Mr. Carter, please."

"Mr. Carter is in a meeting. Who is calling?" said the secretary.

"It's Carter Bond. Would you tell him . . ." Then she paused, and to her astonishment, began to cry. Mortified, she hung up, and sat hunched over the telephone in the kitchen, shaking with tears.

The phone rang.

"Carter?" It was Jerry.

"Yeah, I'm . . ." She put her hand over the phone and took deep breaths. It was so long since she'd cried she had no idea what you could do to make yourself stop.

"Jerry . . ."

"I'm here."

"Hold on . . ." In another moment or two she was ready to try talking again. "Okay, I'm back."

"What's going on?" His voice sounded anxious.

"I'm sorry . . . I hope you're keeping clients waiting. What do you bill at now, two hundred a minute?" Her voice was ragged.

"Three. Now, what's happened?"

"I killed someone this morning."

There was a silence. "Do you need a lawyer?"

"I think a priest."

There was a pause. "I better come over."

"No, you can't do that. You've got a client there."

"Fuck 'em. It's just a movie star and his 'people.'" That at least made Carter smile.

Carter watched Jerry park and come up the walk. She'd been sitting at the window, holding Flora, waiting for him. The minutes had seemed preternaturally slow to pass, as she lived again and again through the moment of walking into the room and seeing that brave young woman so still and painfully bent on the couch, with her blood all over the back of her furniture.

Jerry was wearing an impeccable blue suit that seemed to give grace to his broad-shouldered figure. He walked quickly, looking at the spot right before his feet, as he almost always did. Carter thought it was because he dreaded looking people in the eye and having them imagine they'd been invited to speak. Jerry only talked and listened to exchange information. The idea of talking just to talk, talking to establish a bond, to pass the time, to disguise social unease, seemed to frighten him.

The door opened, and Carter stood waiting for him with a small caramel-colored child on her hip. She had lost even more weight in the last few weeks, and she looked unstrung.

He kissed her on the cheek. "You didn't mention you'd given birth," he said. Flora, at the sight of another huge white man, had buried her face in Carter's shoulder, much as she once had hidden against her mother when she'd first met Carter.

Carter led Jerry into the living room, explaining as briefly as she could about the drug sting, and the night she "arrested" the enforcer.

"It's gang territory. They know everything. They have members as young as ten. So we moved into their market and fucked it up, and when they tried to stop us I *dissed* this guy. I couldn't have done him worse if I'd cut his nuts off in the street. He knows who saw. Or worse, he doesn't know, so he has to guess, so it's like *everyone* saw. I thought Shanti would get such a charge out of it. Then I changed the cars and rearranged the schedule so they never saw me again, and I thought I was so smart. But they were smarter. They couldn't kill me, so they killed the person who hired me."

They sat in silence for a moment. Jerry just breathed, and looked at her.

"She was almost eight months pregnant . . ." Carter said, and started to cry again. She was exhausted. She couldn't remember being hit so hard by anything, maybe since her own mother died.

"Carter. He jumped you. What do you think he was planning to do to you?"

She shrugged, "Rape me. Kill me. Something along those lines."

"So?"

"I know. It just doesn't help."

"What would?"

She thought for a few minutes. She knew this was not an idle question; Jerry didn't ask idle questions. She thought of a range of things, from a neck massage to a week in Acapulco to a shot of Valium. Flora shifted a little on her lap, and Carter realized that the exhausted baby had finally gone to sleep.

"Tell me what to do. I can't make my brain work."

Jerry leaned back in his chair and recrossed his long legs. He exposed an expanse of shin, and Carter, who never noticed such things, suddenly realized that even *she* could tell that for dark gray socks, those were very fancy socks.

"All right. First. Don't go back to that neighborhood, ever. That case is over."

Carter didn't say anything.

"God, Carter . . . you weren't *going* to try to go on with it, were you?"

She shook her head, more to say I don't know than to say no.

"Next, tell me about this baby. What about the father?"

"I have no idea."

"Do you know anyone who would?"

Carter thought. "I might be able to track him down, but not without going back there."

"Or the father of the baby she was carrying?" Carter just shook her head. She didn't know if it was the same man, or anything about him.

"How about relatives?"

"Her parents are dead. She has a sister on the streets."

"Do you know how to find *her*?"

"I hardly think she sounds like a candidate for motherhood, at the moment," said Carter.

"I wasn't suggesting that. I'm suggesting that you find out who owns the house. If there's a will. That sort of thing."

"Oh," said Carter. She thought he was telling her it was absurd for her to try to take care of this baby, even for a day.

"In other words, the *baby* needs a lawyer."

"She might," said Jerry.

The doorbell rang. Since Carter had a babe in arms, Jerry got up to answer it. He was soon back with a uniformed policeman, the one who had ordered Carter not to leave Shanti's house, and a man in plainclothes who had to be from Homicide. Introductions were performed.

"Forgive me for not getting up," said Carter. She indicated chairs, and Jerry too sat back down. The detective got out his pad. "You are a private investigator, Ms. Bond."

"That's correct."

"And you were employed by the deceased."

"That's correct."

"And you are?" he had turned to Jerry. "Her lawyer?"

"Friend of the family."

The cop rolled his eyes.

*I*n the first week of January, the whole Knox family drove up to Sun Valley. Ketchum was a four-block traffic jam, so full of day-trippers that all the restaurants and galleries and even the gas stations were packed. Hunt insisted on stopping for the out-of-town papers and then Cara and Tessie just wanted to pop into a clothing shop for a minute, "Just a *minute*, pleeease, we promise," where their classmates had caught sight of Demi Moore with her children. While they were gone Anna decided to hop across the street for a latte, she'd get it to go, it would really be one second. The whole detour cost them a half hour.

The town glittered with new snow, and as she waited in the car, Laurie found herself envying the designer sunglasses worn by a mannequin in a window who was also decked out in a bright yellow ski outfit so sleek it looked like a wet suit. She thought of the thick, stiff clothes she and her brothers had first learned to ski in, of the hand-me-down wooden skis with bear-trap bindings, of the feel and smell of heavy wet wool that went with a day spent falling into snowdrifts. Her children were going to spend the day on the mountain with Billy; she and Hunt and Cinder were going to Walter Keely's house to watch videotapes of some focus groups their pollster had conducted just before Christmas. Reactions to The Candidate. This was a new development since the last time she had run, and she doubted very much she was going to like it. She wasn't a woman who even liked to look in the mirror for more than the time it took to be sure she didn't have spinach in her teeth.

They dropped the children and Billy at the slopes with a maximum of confusing instructions about money, watches, mittens, goggles, and where and when to meet for lunch. The twins were mad to go snowboarding; they had offered to teach Billy, and to Cinder's dismay, he had accepted. Carlos was in charge of the older cohort. Anna wanted to go with the grown-ups but Walter had vetoed this, so she got out of the car with the others, ostentatiously carrying a book.

Walter's house was all stone and glass, and he had a huge fire and coffee waiting when they arrived.

"How were things in town?" he asked, pouring coffee.

"Jammed."

Hands wrapped around warm mugs, they followed Walter into his screening room.

The house had been built by a movie actor who had looked like he would become a star but proved instead to be space debris. His celestial arc had intersected Walter's entry into the real estate market, after which he dipped beneath the horizon and into erratic orbit, occasionally seen by the naked eye on the airwaves in Japan. Walter had left the actor's fancy plush chairs and couches in place, but replaced the movie screen with a very large television. He had the first tape cued and ready.

"The groups were shown a video of your speech at Boise State in December. I thought you looked terrific that night, the talk went well, and the Q and A was especially good. Yes?"

Laurie nodded. She had revised the speech a couple of times since then, but it was a good event. The audience had been very warm and she felt she'd done well.

The tape began. On the large screen there was a wide, bare room with institutional tables and folding chairs set up in the middle, a floating island in cold space.

"This is the parish hall of the Methodist Church in Pocatello," said Walter. "They've been told who you are, and shown the tape. This is a broad-spectrum group, men and women, young and old, working to middle class. This particular group is all white; in the next tape there's a better ethnic mix."

They were watching some eighteen people drinking coffee and helping themselves to a pile of doughnuts on a platter that was going the rounds of the table. A bouncy young man named Brad from the pollster's office was leading the group.

"Please feel free to be perfectly frank; we want your honest reactions. Any feelings about what you've seen?"

The group stared at him and chewed.

"I thought the speech was pretty good, myself. How about you?"

Gray-haired man in a flannel shirt: "I thought she talked awful fast."

Brad: "Good. Thank you, that's helpful. Other thoughts?"

Middle-aged man with thick glasses, wearing a ski sweater: "I thought she was impressive."

Brad: "Impressive. Thank you, can you say more about that?"

Glasses: "She seemed intelligent. Decent. I believed what she said."

Brad: "Good. Very helpful. Could we hear more about that? About what her message is?"

"She was stiff, though," added Glasses.

There was a little silence. In the screening room, Laurie twitched uncomfortably. Walter smiled at her. Hunt was deeply absorbed in this new phenomenon.

Young woman with very short hair and a runny nose: "Change," she said. "And she talked about character."

"*Yes!*" said Laurie to the young woman on the tape. She relaxed a little.

"Yes, well, I'd like to say something about that," said a woman with short, permed gray hair. She had a firm little chin and a mouthful of doughnut.

Brad turned the group to her. "Yes, please." His gesture said, You have the floor.

"I don't think much of a person who goes out running around when she has five children and they just lost their father. I don't think much of that character." She quivered with emotion.

Brad: "Thank you, any more to say on that subject?"

The one with the perm seemed to have clamped her mouth shut, afraid to be punished for saying something mean. But a fat young woman at the end of the table wearing a blue cardigan with little pearl buttons over a man's T-shirt jumped into the silence: "I don't know about character either. I mean, so she lost her husband and he was a politician. Does that make her one? I think she's, you know—I think she thinks because we liked her husband we should vote for her. But what's she ever done?"

The earnest short-haired woman spoke up warmly: "She's served on the school board. She's a district judge . . . "

Blue Sweater: "Yeah, but a judge, so what? She sits on a bench? It's not like she works, like a lawyer . . . "

Earnest Young Woman (hotly): "A judge *is* a . . . "

Brad: "Thank you. Interesting comment. How about the rest of you? Do you have a feeling that Judge Lopez is riding on her husband's coattails?"

A heavy-set man in a brown parka spoke up. "I don't think so at all. Her father was governor. She's been in politics plenty. I think she's entitled to do this if she wants to."

Gray Perm: "You'd vote for a woman who would leave her children at home after their father died?"

Brown Parka: "I wouldn't let that stop me. It would depend on whether I liked her message."

Brad (smoothly): "And do you like her message?"

Brown Parka laughed. "I have to wait and see about that. I think Jim Turnbull's done us a lot of good. I'd have to wait and see." He wheeled around to speak to the woman with the perm. "But she's got a right to try it if she wants to. Having children doesn't seem like an obstacle to me. She knows her own business."

The woman in the perm and the fat one at the end of the table looked cross and stared into space. There was another silence. Brad seemed temporarily boggled.

A woman of about fifty with long hair coiled around her head decided her moment had come. "I thought she was inspiring. You know my generation—I feel pretty cynical about politics. Vietnam, then Watergate—but I trusted her. I think she's real. It's a typical thing politicians say, but I *believe* she wants to run because she believes in service."

Brad: "Thank you. Is that a message the rest of you heard?"

Gray Perm: "I heard Choice for women."

Brad: "And is that something you like?"

The woman with the gray perm looked nervously at a thin watery-eyed man sitting beside her, presumably her husband. She took a breath. "Yes, I like that." The thin man whipped his head around and stared at her. "And, I'm a Christian. I believe it's up to the woman, that's all right with me. But this is a woman who *chose* to have five children . . . "

Brad: "Yes, thank you. How about politics as service. Anyone else hear that message?"

There was some murmuring. The young woman with the short hair raised her hand high. About half the other people in the room raised hands, or nodded. Brad looked around waiting to see if someone else would volunteer.

Brad: "Okay. This is all very good. How about appearance, now. Do any of you have feelings about the candidate's appearance?"

There was another pause. The fat woman at the end asked, "You mean—whether she's pretty?"

Brad: "If you think that's important. Anything at all you'd like to say about whether the candidate's appearance seems appropriate. Or is there something that puts you off?"

The woman who'd first mentioned Choice said, "I thought she was fine. I liked it that she didn't dress in a suit like a man."

Blue Sweater: "I thought she looked like a schoolteacher."

Brad: "Yes? And is that good or bad?"

The fat woman in the blue sweater shrugged. She didn't seem to know. Her face had settled into a look of displeasure.

The man with thick glasses said, "She looks like her father."

Brad: "Thank you. Anyone else think she looks like her father?" Many did. "And is that good?" Many heads nodded.

Brown Parka: "I don't know. I didn't live in Idaho then, but wasn't he kind of a blowhard? Big God and Country guy?" Several people perked up and got ready for a lively deconstruction of Hunt Knox's career, but Brad derailed them.

A young blond man who had a shopping bag on his lap said, "I didn't like the way she talked."

Brad: "I see. You don't mean the message, but . . . "

Blond man: "Yeah. I didn't mind what she said but the way she talks. It was, I don't know, like . . ." He shrugged. "She has a conceited way of pronouncing things."

"I really didn't like her hair," said a sparrowlike woman who hadn't spoken before.

Brad: "Thank you. Can you say more about that?"

Sparrow: "There was that piece that would fall in her face, and she pushed it back. That bothered me . . . "

Walter stopped the tape. "From here it pretty much unravels into a referendum on hair spray. There's more constructive Appearance stuff on the next tape, but let's stop here and see how we're doing. Laurie?"

Laurie was sitting still with her arms crossed over her stomach. She didn't say anything. Cinder watched her.

"I think that's amazing," Hunt said. "Isn't that amazing? You can't go out and meet all the people the way you used to, but you can find out what they're thinking like you never could before . . ." Laurie turned to look at him. He'd heard himself called a blowhard, and all he thought was, Isn't this interesting?

"I feel sick," she said.

Walter was expecting this. "Do you need something? Alka-Seltzer? Pepto-Bismol?"

"I don't know. My stomach hurts. That woman with the frizzy hair, and the fat one—they *hated* me." Hunt turned to look at her.

"Laurie. You can't take it like that. It's a game, you know that. It's just a game. The more information you have, the better you'll play."

"I know but . . . finding out what people really think of you? And finding out you're pouring your guts out and they're thinking about your *hair*?"

"Or not thinking at all," said Walter. "You have to see that. There are people who have no idea what a judge is, and yet they're going to vote. And when they do, you want them to have heard one simple thing about you that's true. Two at the most."

"I have to talk as if they're third-graders, and they're judging *me*?"

"Yes. Of course." Hunt and Walter both looked at her.

"Can I get you more coffee?" Walter asked Laurie. She nodded. Hunt got up and paced around. He couldn't wait for the next tape. What idiotic thing would people say next?

"I feel like the only person in the whole room who really got it was the one who talked about trust," said Laurie.

"And Watergate? She doesn't count," said Hunt. "You've got her before you're out of the gate, she's your core group. The campaign is about the undecideds. The guy in the brown parka. The little woman who didn't like your hair."

"Oh god," said Laurie.

"You didn't think you were just going to preach to the choir, did you?"

Laurie didn't answer. Of course, she rather had. She pictured audiences who agreed with her and trusted her.

"Laurie," said Cinder. "It's not you they're talking about." Walter had come back in with the coffeepot and sugar and milk on a tray.

"Of course it is."

"It's an image. They don't know you. I know you. I'm right here with you. They're looking at a thing on the screen. They're going to see all kinds of things that aren't there because of who they are, not who you are. You have to make a separation in your head. The thing on the screen will run for office. You'll always be safe at home with people who know you."

"Could you do that?" Laurie asked.

Cinder laughed. "Of course not. I'd be awful at it. But I believe you can." The two looked at each other, and much passed between them without words.

"Well," said Hunt. "Are we ready for the next one?" Clearly *he* was.

"Oh, sure," said Laurie after a while. "Bring 'em on."

Walter popped the next tape in and said, "This group is in Idaho Falls. It's a little younger, a little more urban." He pushed the Play button.

E loise Strouse Threadgill was late for lunch. She had slept late, and then the phone had rung as she was halfway out the door, and then the pool man had stopped her to talk about why there were so many mice getting sucked into the filtering system. He had about six little waterlogged bodies laid out on a paper towel, with their tiny pink hands all pitifully curled. They were tiny, the size of her thumb tip. Eloise thought they were voles, not mice, but whatever. It certainly didn't matter to the pool, or to the voles.

"I'm so sorry," she said as she slipped into the booth at the restaurant.

"That's all right, I went ahead," said Carol Haines. Eloise saw that there were two chopped salads and a glass of wine and a Perrier on the table, and Carol was halfway through the Perrier. Eloise took a grateful sip of her wine.

"Have you been waiting long?"

"No, traffic on Santa Monica was brutal. I just got here myself. Love those earrings, by the way."

"Aren't they cute? I found them on Melrose."

"You keep saying you'll take me; I don't know any of the good places down there anymore."

"Just tell me when," said Eloise. They were crunching away on their salads, dressing on the side.

"Who is that over there, is that Jean Simmons?"

Eloise put on her glasses and looked across at the women at the window table overlooking Rodeo Drive.

"I think it is. She looks great, doesn't she?"

"Great. So what's going on?" Carol tore a piece of bread off the half loaf in the basket on the table, and gnawed on it.

"Butter?"

"No."

"My stepmother wants me to come up for the weekend. Bring Trisha, never mind that she's got a horse show. To celebrate."

"Celebrate what?"

"The adoption of the Chinese houseperson who looked after my father."

"The *what*?" Carol was bug-eyed.

"Didn't I tell you? It's official this week. I am about to have a new sister. And brother-in-law, and nephew. I think Rae may be a sandwich short of a picnic, I really do. The only thing I like about this whole deal is it's making my brother shit green."

"Wait a minute. What's your stepmother's name? Rae?"

"Yes?"

"Was your maiden name Strouse? Rae Strouse, *she's* your father's gold-digging fan dancer?"

Eloise was staring at her. This was not the round of sarcastic groaning she'd looked forward to.

"This is too much, this is *so* funny! Rae Strouse is one of my fat-farm buddies! She called me this morning, as a matter of fact. I think she's the greatest."

It was Eloise's turn to gape. Carol Haines was a high-powered lawyer and Eloise was a divorced Beverly Hills housewife, a category of person with which that township was unusually well supplied. Eloise was always aware that in the subtle algebra of friendship, what Eloise brought to the table did not equal what Carol did. Therefore Carol said to Eloise whatever it occurred to her to say, because in the end, if something derailed the friendship, that would mean that many more lunch hours in which Carol would be free to eat tuna fish at her desk and keep working, while Eloise was careful to weigh first what Carol would enjoy or approve of, because if something derailed the friendship that would mean that many more days in the year when she had nothing at all on her schedule except waiting on Trisha and talking to the pool man.

Rae was a buddy of Carol Haines all of a sudden? You could almost hear the gears stripping in her conversational machinery as Eloise adjusted to this fact.

"She is, she's one of my fat-farm buddies," said Carol, who was perfectly capable of performing two sides of a conversation herself, and thus never minded when a companion was struck dumb. "I thought she was the greatest. She did this cartwheel in yoga class? She was just neat fun, she was like our den mom."

"She *is* quite a piece of work," said Eloise weakly. She was suddenly hit with a ghastly thought: did Rae say such slighting and nasty things about her stepchildren as they had been saying about her for twenty-two years? And if so, would Carol remember? "What did you call her about?"

"She called me. We're forming a political action committee."

There was another tiny gap in the conversation. "Do you see our waiter? I'd love one more glass of wine," said Eloise, shifting so suddenly in her chair that she almost fell off it. A political action committee? What the hell was that? Since when was Rae into politics?

"A friend of ours from The Cloisters, Laura Lopez? She's going to run for the Senate, and we're all going to help her."

Carol waited a moment for Eloise to press for details, but Eloise had locked eyes with a distant busboy and was waggling a perfect crimson fingernail in her empty wineglass while assuming a pleading expression. Carol carried on, content if unbidden.

"I think it will be great fun. It's like EMILY's List, you know? Don't you write them checks every time you turn around?"

"Absolutely," said Eloise, diving into her fresh glass of chardonnay. "How do you plan to raise the money?" What she really wanted to know was, who was Emily, and why didn't Carol introduce her interesting friends to Eloise, but she was too savvy to ask a question like that directly.

"What we'll do right away is give parties to raise money. Rae says her house will work for that, so we'll do one in San Francisco first. Her son, Walter . . . well, you must know Walter, he's your . . . "

"Yes," said Eloise. "And it's a lovely house."

"Knows tons of political people. So he draws a couple of heavy hitters, and Rae has beautiful food and flowers, and we'll have a topic for the evening. Rae thinks Walter can get the First Lady to come, and you have fifty people and charge them a thousand dollars each, and after dinner there's a talk about health care. Or something."

Eloise said, with absolute sincerity, "That *does* sound like fun." In fact, for the first time in years, it sounded like something amusing to do for which she herself possessed a few of the necessary qualifications. Unlike the things she'd been trying lately. Like taking up ballet. Or becoming a movie producer.

Then she caught another thought on the chin. Walter knows the *First Lady*?

"Then we'll do one here. This is a *great* town for rich Democratic women. Rich Democrats, period . . . "

A problem occurred to Eloise. "Does it have to be only for Democrats?" She and her brother had voted Republican for years, though they had never told their father that.

"Not at all. There's plenty of common ground. We'll get Dianne and Barbara, and maybe Barbra or Jane will come . . ." Hollywood always called famous people by their first names. Even if you'd never met them and never hoped to. It was like living in Detroit and expecting the guy on the next stool to know what you meant by Chrysler.

"What we talked about this morning is where to give it. My house in Hancock Park would have been *perfect*, but . . ." Carol had lost it in the divorce wars. Not that she had minded especially.

Eloise said, "Well, *my* house . . . "

Carol put down her fork. She looked at Eloise with wide eyes.

"*Your* house! Your house is *per*fect! Remember that gorgeous Christmas party you and David gave . . . ?"

Did she remember? She had insisted on buying the house *because* it would be so great for parties. And she'd given some doozies before

David stopped coming home at night. Wouldn't David come unglued if the First Lady came to *her* house?

"Are you serious now?" Carol asked, putting her hand on Eloise's arm. She was excited.

"Completely. I'd love to help."

"Oh god, this is going to be lots of fun. I can't wait to tell Rae! This is *so cool*! Do you mind?" And she pulled out her electronic Filofax, and flipped open her cellular phone.

"Hello, Rae? Sweetie, it's Carol again. You won't believe who I'm having lunch with!"

Jill's homeless person seemed to have disappeared during the ten days she was gone. She came out of their building in the mornings, onto a street glistening with snow, and her nerves tightened as she turned the corner onto Park Avenue South heading for the subway. But morning after morning, there was nobody there.

"It was probably just a coincidence that he ever found you, sweetie," Amy said. "You didn't encourage him, did you? People don't keep on with that sort of thing if they don't get anything out of it. You handled it right, and he's gone."

"I hope so, but I still think maybe I should move." Jill thought about those flat brown eyes, the way they stared at her. She could not work out if MacDuff had been trying to frighten her, or wanting to hurt her, or wanting something else she couldn't imagine. His face was a mask, like the head of a stone god. The only part that seemed to be living tissue was the strange yellowish whites of his eyes.

He always had the book in his pocket. He didn't have the bowling bag anymore; now he carried a blue nylon sports bag with a Pepsi logo on it. All December, in spite of the fact that the weather had turned bitter, he had worn that dull gray sweater. It couldn't have been much help against the wind.

"I did check with the housing office about a dorm room," Jill said to her mother.

Amy put down her grapefruit spoon. Jill had been talking about moving up to the Barnard campus, but Amy didn't think she'd ever do it.

"Do they have anything?"

"They think so. Some people always move off campus at midyear. They said to check back at the end of the week."

"Well, dearie . . ." Amy was feeling something she hadn't expected. She was thinking about the breakfast table, alone with Noah. She was thinking of mid-afternoon, with no Jill coming through the door with news of the classroom, or the subways, or the shops on Prince Street, or what was showing at the Angelika. "What are the rooms like?"

"Probably horrible." Jill looked at her watch and got up. "Have a good day, Mum. Where will you be?"

"I don't know. Shopping this morning. Probably here, this afternoon. I feel like cooking something."

"Great. Keep warm."

Amy went shopping. She went to Saks and went up and down the escalators. She looked at all the spring clothes, and ordered a couple of dresses for those benefit things you end up at every season even though you swear you're going to stay home in your bathrobe and watch a movie.

For lunch she bought a big soft pretzel on the street and ate it slowly as she walked home, enjoying the salty warmth in her hand and in her mouth, while the still air was so bright and sharply cold. Noah was scornful of people who ate on the street, as if it were akin to giving birth in a hedgerow. Eating was an intimate function and should be done in private. Noah ate only sitting down, and only at mealtimes.

She did cook when she got home that afternoon. Something was making her feel mournful, so she took the opportunity to reproduce her grandmother's recipe for a very sticky tray of cinnamon buns. The whole house smelled like the house in Coeur d'Alene when Jill came home.

* * *

Friday the Barnard housing office said they had a single room available in Reid Hall, and Sunday Jill moved out. She had her sound system in a cardboard box and her clothes in an old steamer trunk that she would use as a coffee table. Her computer was packed in a box full of Styrofoam. With the printer it took up most of the back-seat of the taxi, and Jill sat in front with the driver. Amy offered to come with her and help her move in, but Jill said she would be fine. She'd call her as soon as she had a phone hooked up. Amy stood on the sidewalk and waved as the car pulled away. She had no idea she would feel so bereft; she had always imagined that Jill's being well enough to leave home would be cause for celebration. All these long five years, when she'd felt so hemmed in by Jill's fragility, she hadn't guessed how much she would miss the confinement if it were suddenly whisked off like a bell jar.

"I don't know what to do with myself," she said to Dagmar on the telephone. Dagmar was home in bed with the flu. "I'm sitting around the house trying to figure out how long it will be till we have grand-children."

On the other end, she heard Dagmar blowing her nose.

"At least you have a business."

"I know, but . . . "

"Don't tell me, I know all about it. You have three choices. Join a board, take a lover, or learn a foreign language."

"Another one? I'm still working on French."

"Or take up the piano."

"How about pottery? They have classes at the Art Students League."

"If you're going to do arts and crafts at least do something useful, like goldsmithing. I don't want to start getting clay ashtrays from you for Christmas. Why don't you get a dog?"

"A dog! You know, that's a great idea? Did you ever have a dog?"

"We always had mutts. Knowing Noah, you better get something really chic, like a bichon frise."

"I wonder if Barnes and Noble is still open, I can go get some dog books."

She did get the dog books, but not the dog. Noah was completely opposed. "They either shed, or yap, or soil the carpets."

"Not if they're well trained . . . "

"And what about when we travel?"

"There are kennels. Or pet sitters. Besides, when do we travel?"

"We just went to Mexico. And then the guests arrive and the dog gallops up and smells their crotches . . . no. Really, Amy. I am fifty-nine years old and my last child just left home. Let's just have some time by ourselves, shall we."

It was a long week for Amy. It took Jill until Wednesday to call to say she had a phone and an answering machine. Amy worried night and day until she heard from her. When she finally did call, it made Amy feel silly. Jill sounded fine. She had made new friends on the hall. She had found some girls who had even more CDs than she did, and they were making mixes for each other, whatever that meant. She had met a boy who loved computers. She was joining a feminist dance troupe.

"What is a feminist dance troupe?"

"It's women dancers who refuse to be prevented by conventional stereotypes of feminine beauty from using their bodies to express themselves."

Amy tried to deconstruct this sentence by herself, but gave up. "I'm still not quite . . . "

"We're all fat," said Jill. And then she roared with laughter. Amy laughed too, although it occurred to her that compared to her weight at maximum blimpage, Jill was a good deal less fat than she had been.

"And do you give performances?"

"Yes, I think so, though I don't know that anyone comes to them. Some of us refuse to be constrained by conventional ideas of technique as well as other stereotypes. We have a lot of fun though."

"You sound great, lovie."

"I think things are pretty good," Jill agreed.

Business was slow in January, and Dagmar was still at home living on a brew of lemon, ginger, and garlic, so Amy had no one to play with. She accepted an invitation to a lunch party up on Beekman Place, a bridal shower.

"Is there a theme?" she asked the bride's godmother.

"The boudoir," said Elayne with a giddy laugh. Amy knew how to shop for that. She was thoroughly versed in the best places to find silk charmeuse, not rayon, trimmed with real lace.

On the Friday she took a taxi to the restaurant. It was a little French one, new to her, dark and cozy, the kind of charming neighborhood place New York used to be full of. The party was at the back of the restaurant, where two tables were dressed with place cards and party favors. Amy knew about half the guests, none of them well.

The bride-to-be was sweet and not very pretty. She was dressed in a Chanel suit, or copy, and looked as if she'd much rather be mucking out a stall someplace. She was a very good sport when, over dessert and champagne, she had to open the presents.

As the black teddies and slinky pink nighties emerged from frothy wrappings, Amy slipped off to the ladies' room. She was thinking of the far-off day when perhaps she would give such a party for Jill. She happened to glance in the mirror over the bar as she turned to rejoin her table, and for a very long moment her heart ceased to beat. She could feel all color draining from her face and her hands began to shake. She remembered thinking that this might be the end, she might be going to slip to the floor with a heart stopped cold and die there by the waiter's station.

Then her heart began to pound, and she flushed so hot that her ears were filled with a roaring. She thought she might pass out from boiling heat rather than silent cold.

In the mirror over the bar she could see in profile a couple at a side table. They were leaning over their glasses, their foreheads almost touching. They held hands; they murmured to each other and smiled and smiled, and from time to time the man would kiss, very gently, a knuckle of the girl's hand. The girl brushed his cheek with her finger-tips, a gesture so full of tenderness that it made Amy's throat ache. The girl was twenty-something, a brunette with wide black eyes and lush, loose hair; she was model-beautiful. The man was Noah.

Amy walked back to her place at the table and assumed a smiling face. A primitive reptile part of her brain enabled her to nod and laugh when the group nodded and laughed, to turn her attentive face to the bride-to-be and seem to watch with interest as yet another package was unwrapped. She drank an entire glass of ice water without know-ing she had done it. She swallowed and swallowed, as if the heat of the pounding blood in her head had burned her throat dry.

When she felt marginally calmer, Amy lifted a finger to catch a waiter's attention. She whispered in his ear, and gave him a lovely smile and a twenty-dollar bill. Then she watched.

The waiter went to the bar, and then to the table where Noah sat with his inamorata. He presented Noah with a perfect martini, straight up, in a chilled glass. He spoke a few words, smiling, and with his head gestured to the back of the room. Amy watched Noah raise the glass and turn to offer a smile of thanks to the giver, expecting to find a former patient perhaps, or an old colleague. Even as far away as she was, she could see his face change color as he saw, instead, his wife, waving hello.

He whipped around in his chair, giving her his back again. He put the drink down as if it were poison, and began talking fast to the young lady. Amy bet she knew the scenario. The girl had been told that the wife was old, ugly, bedridden, deranged. The wife didn't understand him, hadn't loved him for years, but wouldn't give him his freedom. The last thing he would want on the face of the earth was the wife and his mistress face-to-face.

Amy slipped from her chair and whispered to her hostess that she'd been taken ill. She would call tomorrow, don't get up, please explain to the others later. Then she walked, smiling pleasantly, through the bar, toward the door. As she approached her husband's table, the young brunette's eyes locked on hers, her face full of surprise and fear. Amy might have had some sympathy for her if she hadn't been so full of rage. But steadily, smiling, she held the girl's eyes.

As she walked past the table, she dropped her wedding rings into Noah's martini.

Hunt Knox had been wrong about the candidate from Sandpoint. Lloyd Prince was not just a transplant with a big ego. He was a millionaire many times over who had had a religious experience he wanted to share.

"He sounds like a zealot," said Hunt. It was a meeting of Laurie's war machine.

"No, he's not, or at least he conceals it well. He's an interesting mixture of things, and he's also smart, and very attractive," Walter said.

"Does he have an appeal beyond the Christian right?" Laurie's brother Bliss had agreed to be campaign treasurer, and he was beginning to realize it was going to take more time than he'd thought.

"It's early days," said Bunker Elwies, the campaign chair. "We know he's serious, at least. He's made a pledge not to take any special-interest money. He's spending his own."

"Don't we call that 'trying to buy a Senate seat'?"

"Certainly *we'll* call it that . . . "

"He's for balancing the budget, he's for prayer in schools, an anti-abortion amendment, and absolutely no gun control."

"What programs does he want to cut?"

"All of them, except environmental ones. 'God Helps Those Who Help Themselves,' but Mother Earth can't help herself."

"Why is this guy a Democrat?" Cinder asked.

"He *was* a Republican," said Lynn Urbanski. "He switched parties down in Orange County to run against Bob Dornan."

"So it's the same deal here?"

"Exactly. He didn't expect any Democratic competition. The last serious race against Jimbo was Puck Brown in 1984."

"Would the party support him?"

"To some extent."

"He doesn't care if they do or not. He's rich."

"How rich?"

"I told you. Very. And he's willing to spend it."

"It's going to force us to spend a lot of early money," said Laurie.

"Yeah. Well." Welcome to the real world.

"Could someone please explain this guy to me?" said Hunt. "Why here? Why now? He's not from Idaho."

"He was in a head-on collision he never should have survived," Lynn explained. It was a story she knew well, part of Prince's press kit. "He was visited by an angel while he was trapped in the wreckage waiting for the Jaws of Life. The angel told him he was being spared for a reason. This is the reason. That's the best explanation I can give you."

"An angel," said Hunt.

"That's right."

"Bright nightgown? Wings?"

"He couldn't see him. He had too much blood in his eyes," said Lynn.

"Aiyiyi," said Hunt, and fished in his pocket for absent cigarettes.

"So the message is Christian self-reliance; clean, simple living; and a pure environment."

"So he walked away from this wreck? What was he driving?"

"He didn't walk away. He's in a wheelchair."

"He's in a wheelchair?"

"Didn't you know that?"

"We're up against a handsome born-again zillionaire Yalie in a *wheelchair*? Aiyiyiyiyi." There was another silence. Finally Hunt asked, "How are his numbers?"

"Name recognition isn't high, but he hasn't really begun to spend yet. His numbers are real good up in the Panhandle, where he's known, good among the Greenies, and surprisingly high among transplants."

"I thought those computer people were all cappuccino liberals," Hunt said.

"No, it turns out the cappuccino liberals move to Oregon. The ones who want school prayer and elk hunting with assault weapons move here."

"I have to go," said Laurie. "I have a fund-raiser in Lewiston."

*Y*ou have reached the offices of Dr. Morris Fischbein," said Jill's answering machine. "Dr. Fischbein is with a patient. Please leave a message at the sound of the tone." There was a beep.

Jill was sitting in a half lotus on a cushion on the floor. She had turned herself to the window so that the morning sun would shine on her eyelids as she meditated.

From the machine's speaker, she heard her mother's voice.

"Hello, Jilly—I'm sorry I missed you, and—"

Jill had practically fallen over the phone.

"Mummy?"

"Oh, honey! You're there!"

"*I'm* here," said Jill. "Where are *you*? I left three messages!"

"I'm so sorry. Have you been worried?"

Jill, who had been frantic, didn't answer at once as she absorbed the fact that her mother was once more at the other end of the phone line, where she was supposed to be, and not dead in a ditch somewhere.

"Oh, well," said Jill. She was recovering.

"Is everything all right with you?" Amy asked her daughter.

"Yes, sure. If you're all right. But are you and Daddy out of town or something?"

"You haven't talked to him?"

"No."

Amy gave a short laugh, which sounded to Jill a little bleak.

Amy took a deep breath. "I've left your father."

"What?"

"I'm sorry I didn't say good-bye. It was a little sudden."

"What do you mean, say good-bye? Where are you?"

"I'm in Idaho."

"Mother!"

The two were silent on the line at opposite ends of the country, listening to each other breathe. Jill, who had been standing over her desk, now carried the phone to her bed and sat down with her back to the window, as if she wanted to huddle over her feelings and sort them out without even the sun seeing them.

Jill said, "What happened?"

Amy described the tryst at the restaurant. "I probably shouldn't tell you this. He's your father. But I didn't want you to think I had left you for no reason."

Jill was silent. In a way, she really didn't want to know any more about this than she had to. But . . .

"How long will you be gone?"

"I don't know."

"Well . . . I guess I can understand that."

"Your father doesn't know where I am, by the way, and I don't want him to. I want to decide what to do about this without him pressuring me."

"Okay."

"Does that make things too hard for you? You may want to go home, or spend time with him. You wouldn't be able to be completely honest with him."

"I'll deal," said Jill.

At the other end of the line, in Coeur d'Alene, Amy became aware that her elderly mother was on the stairs and would soon be in the kitchen. "I can't talk much longer, love. I'll call you soon though, and you can call me anytime. You have the number at Granny's?"

Jill said she did, and sent her love to her grandmother. They said good-bye.

*   *   *

A girl named Lesley who lived at the end of the corridor appeared at Jill's door. She was from Edinburgh, and she called Jill Jillian.

"Can I come in? I heard your phone ring. Was it your mum?" Jill nodded.

"Is she all right?"

"She's fine. She's left my father."

Lesley plumped down on the bed. She was holding an empty mug, probably looking to borrow some instant coffee or a tea bag. Lesley's mother seemed to have an imperfect idea of what was a passable amount of pocket money for a student in New York City. But Jill didn't mind Lesley's borrowing. It made a good excuse for her to visit, and everyone knew that Jill had a virtual grocery store of herbal tea and ramen noodles in her room. Jill seemed to be living on air-popped corn and green Chinese dieter's tea, a powerful diuretic known to have killed at least one young mother in California. This was thought to be a bold improvement on the meals you got on the food plan.

"Does she do that often?" Lesley asked. "Leave your father?"

"No," said Jill. "I don't know why not, though."

"Is she coming back?"

"She doesn't know."

"What do you think?"

Jill shrugged. "I can picture it going either way."

Lesley was thoughtful. "Is it a shock?"

"Yes."

What would happen if her mother didn't go back? They would get divorced? Where would they live? That is, where would her mother live? And would that, then, be home? How could it be?

"Are you freaking?" Lesley asked. Jill realized she had been completely lost for some time, maybe a minute. She took a deep breath.

"No. I think I need to get outside. I think I need a long walk."

"I wish *I* could take a walk. I have to write ten pages on Cindy Sherman. You don't have any diet cocoa, do you?"

Jill did. She gave Lesley a packet and then burrowed in her closet for her snow boots.

* * *

When she opened the door to the outside, the bright expanse of snow seemed blinding. Cold air stung her eyes and nose, and burned the inside of her lungs. She walked happily toward the gate out to 117th Street, but when she turned the corner to strike out toward Columbia, she walked almost directly into a dark figure. She opened her mouth to scream and strained to make a sound, but could not. It was MacDuff.

*a*my had gone directly home from the restaurant Friday afternoon, packed a suitcase, and taken a taxi to Kennedy. From there she had taken the first flight to Spokane and spent what remained of the night in an airport motel. She woke early, still on New York time, dressed in corduroy slacks and snow boots, and rented a car as soon as the agency opened. She was at her mother's kitchen door before Retta had finished breakfast.

The house, which had once been full of Amy's skis and skates and bikes, and of her father's hunting rifles and fishing gear, was now largely a domain of stacked magazines, *TV Guide*s, and remote controls for the giant TV. Amy and Noah had had a huge satellite dish installed for Retta one Christmas. Amy had been afraid it would be too complicated for her mother, but when she and Jill arrived at winter break, they found that Retta could ring variations on it that even Jill didn't understand. Retta's mother had been born in a sod hut in North Dakota, and she thought a lonely old age with only the sound of the wind for company was the shits.

Amy's bedroom had been made over into Retta's sewing room, to an extent Amy would never have discovered had she not appeared unannounced. Obviously Retta had to rearrange things for days to make the two bedrooms ready for Jill and Amy when they came for their scheduled visits. Amy was now sleeping in a bed cleared of piles and piles of patterns and fabric, and her night table was the cabinet of the sewing machine.

On her first night at home, Amy had wanted to take her mother to the Resort on the Lake for dinner. Retta said, "Oh, hon . . . I always go along with you because you and Jilly like it, but, tell you the truth, I'd rather stay home. I'd have to get into my girdle to go to the Resort, and when I get there they won't let me smoke my pipe."

"Your what?" Amy thought there had been an odor of smoke in the house.

"Riley next door, he gave me a little pipe and some cherry tobacco. I like the smell of it. Reminds me of your daddy."

"Daddy never liked to see women smoke," Amy said, remembering a most painful New Year's Eve when she was seventeen, and her father had smelled cigarette smoke on her sweater when Johnny Kalmbach brought her home.

"Well, he's not here to see, is he?" said Retta calmly. "Riley said he always enjoyed smoking a pipe with his mother, and now she's gone he gave her pipe to me."

"I didn't know Riley was still next door—his house looks all closed up."

"Oh, that's just till he gets home. He's down at the state hospital."

"Has he been sick?"

"No, just mental."

"Well, *Mother* . . . " Amy could hear herself taking the tone she took with Jill, when Jill took the subway home from SoHo after midnight instead of taking a taxi as she'd been told to. Riley had gone mental and he was right next door; what if he came over here with an ax? He was a big, shambling, loose-limbed man, plenty strong, Amy guessed, in spite of his age.

"Oh, hon. It's nothing. He's just like he's always been, only from time to time a little more so. His mother used to remind him where he was and that would snap him back, but now he's alone so he gets a little out of orbit. I always know when it's time for him to go away for a rest."

"You do? How?"

"Most times, he'll pull all the flowers out of his window box and start planting Triscuits."

* * *

The first night Amy was home, she and her mother ate frozen pot-pies, and then sat in the den together where Retta smoked her pipe and watched MTV. For a day or two Amy jumped whenever the phone rang, imagining it would be Noah calling to beg her to come home. Surely he couldn't be so dense that he wouldn't know where to find her? But she was forgetting that to Noah, Coeur d'Alene was a place to have been from, not a place to think of as home. Noah would be looking for her in Martha's Vineyard, or in Rome; he would picture her staying with glamorous friends and running amok with his charge cards on the Via Veneto. On Monday when she called her lawyer, the young toad who had represented her when Noah insisted on the pre-nup, she found that Noah had been calling him all weekend, *"AT HOME,"* the lawyer added as if it were Amy's fault. Noah had been bullying, demanding that the lawyer reveal at once where his wife was hiding from him.

"Don't," said Amy.

"I won't," said the lawyer, "but I have to tell him that I've heard from you."

"Fine. Tell him he can contact me through you but in no other way."

"And do you want me to file?"

"I want an allowance first. Then we'll talk about an agreement."

"How much do you want?" the lawyer asked.

"Well, the prenuptial agreement said . . . "

"Amy, you've been married over twenty years. The pre-nup is toilet paper. Gone, good-bye, forget it. And New York is not a no-fault divorce state. Now, how much do you want?"

Amy named a sum. The lawyer laughed. "I tell him that, he'll guess where you are. What would you need if you were in Paris, staying at the Georges V?"

Amy named a much larger sum. "Fine," said the lawyer. "I'll call you in a day or two."

"Amy!" Retta called. Amy was upstairs getting out of the shower when she heard her mother calling from the den downstairs. "Come on down, hon, that friend of yours, Laurie Knox, is on the television!"

Amy piled down the stairs wrapped in a towel, just in time to see a story taped at the Boise zoo earlier in the day.

"They just reopened the bird house," Retta was explaining, "and your friend Laurie took her children, and she ran into Senator Turnbull . . ." Amy was trying to shush her mother so she could hear what was being said on the newscast.

The picture on the screen was of the inside of the aviary, newly refurbished, the air filled with the squawk of birds. "Remember how Jilly always loved that big crow . . . "

"Raven, Mother. Shhh!"

". . . Senate hopeful Laura Knox Lopez with her five children, when they were surprised by the arrival of Senator Jimbo Turnbull, with his daughter Caroline," said the newsreader's voice as the tape ran. There on the screen was Laurie with her son Carlos, and two younger daughters, each holding a hand of one of the twins. There were some extra children too. Those must be the cousins, Amy thought as she watched Laurie turn in response to something that was said to her. Then after some bobbling of the camera, Senator Turnbull walked into the shot with his long arm outstretched toward Laurie. Laurie shook hands with him, and then the senator wrapped an arm around her shoulder and turned them both to face the camera. Beside Jimbo, his slim blonde daughter Caroline looked at the camera as if it were a gun pointed at her.

The reporter who had been covering the aviary opening pushed forward with her microphone.

"Judge Lopez, is this the first time you and Senator Turnbull have met since you declared your candidacy?"

Jimbo was way ahead of her.

"This little lady and I go back a looong time," he boomed affably, and the body language of their two poses said that he was the grown-up who had taken this amusing child firmly in hand. "This little lady and I have been friends since she was in pinafores. In' that right?"

"We go back a long time," said Laurie.

"We been friends since she was a little girl, way back when her daddy was governor of this state. And here she is, running for the

Senate, and we're going to have a lot of fun." He gave Laurie's shoulder a squeeze.

"I'm sure we're both going to learn a lot," said Laurie, smiling to the camera. Around her, you could see the children pressing close to her and looking at the reporter. Birds screeched and flapped.

Amy called Information in Hailey and asked for Laurie's number. She was surprised when the operator gave it to her. She dialed again.

"Lopez for President, Anna speaking."

"Hello . . . this is Amy Burrows, a friend of Laurie Lopez. Is she in?"

"Just a minute. Mom!" Anna could be heard, yelling.

Laurie came on the line. "Hello?"

"Laurie, it's Amy Burrows, from The Cloisters."

"*Mon général!* Hello! Where are you?"

"I'm in Coeur d'Alene. We just saw you on the news!"

"You're here? How great! Are you here visiting your mom?"

"Yes—"

"Am I going to see you?"

"That's what I'm calling about. I may be here for some time and it occurred to me that there might be some way for me to help you."

"Be still my heart! You mean you could volunteer for a little while?"

"Maybe for quite a while."

"Are you serious?"

"Very. But I'm afraid I don't know how to do much."

"Come meet Walter."

"I'll be there Wednesday."

"God bless you."

Sitting in her childhood bedroom with the phone in her hand, surrounded by stacks of fabric and patterns and pincushions shaped like tomatoes, Amy thought about Noah. Noah sitting in his romantic hideaway with his doe-eyed girl. She thought about all the excuses she had fallen for, all the signals she'd missed, and she felt completely defective, robbed of home, of love, of dignity. And good and angry. She felt ready for a fight, and hoped she had just found a fair one.

Coleman and Cecily hadn't had dinner at home together in almost three weeks. Tonight would be the same. Cecily would have to spend hours putting the patients' files in order, transcribing notes she and Coleman had dictated during patient conferences throughout the day. Coleman had three grant proposals to finish and a dozen unvarnished begging letters to write to potential donors. On top of it, he was hoping Cecily was pregnant. She'd been more tired than usual lately, and he was pretty sure she'd missed a period, but he hadn't had time in the last two days to ask her. It wasn't the kind of thing you wanted to ask as you passed in the hall. "You pregnant?" "Think so, yeah." "Good. Do we have any Imitrex injectors in the closet?"

"Take a deep breath for me, please," he said to the thin brown boy who was sitting on the treatment table before him. The boy, dressed in a paper gown, looked at him with black eyes. Coleman took a big breath, to demonstrate. The boy copied him as Coleman listened to his lungs. He moved the stethoscope and said, "Again." The whole bronchial area was congested, a mess. He wished he could speak a word of this child's language, whatever it was. Coleman's Spanish was fluent, and he and Cecily were both picking up some Cantonese, but this boy was from the subcontinent. He either spoke no English at all, or had been warned not to answer any questions. It was like treating a sick animal who could only gaze at you.

He handed the boy his shirt and signaled that he should dress himself. Then he walked down the narrow corridor that connected the treatment rooms to the waiting room, a barely furnished storefront space on Valencia Street. Waiting here were two pregnant women, a young mother with a toddler who had a frightening cough, and a neatly dressed Chinese man. It was almost six o'clock, and doctors' hours were nearly over for the day.

"Anybody here speak Hindi? Or Urdu?"

The people in the waiting room looked at him, but no one responded to the question.

Coleman sent the boy with the infected chest off with two pre-scriptions and instructions for his care written in English. He hoped that someone at home would be able to translate for him. Cecily was doing the gynecological exams; Coleman took the coughing toddler. This one was easy; the mother was from Peru. When he had examined them both (the mother was looking a little jaundiced, he thought), written a prescription for the baby and given the mother a handful of antihistamine samples for her dust allergy, he went back to the waiting room. Only the Chinese man was left.

"You can come in now," said Coleman.

In the treatment room, Coleman gestured toward the examining table and said, "Hop up."

Instead the Chinese man sat in a cane chair and answered in sur-prisingly fluent English, "It's all right, I'm not sick."

"Oh," said Coleman. He sat himself down on the rolling stool he used during examinations. "Well, what can I do for you?"

"I'd like to ask a few questions, if that is all right with you."

Coleman nodded and gestured with his large splay-fingered hands. Sure, shoot. This wasn't unheard of. Quite a few people had trouble with the concept of free medical treatment.

"You are Coleman Morrison?"

"Right."

"And your wife is Cecily Buffman."

Coleman tipped his head in assent.

"You have been in private practice four years?"

"Four years for me. Cecily finished her residency two years ago. You must have seen that article in *West Coast* magazine."

"Yes," said the Chinese man. "Was it accurate?"

"Pretty good," said Coleman. "Except that we don't have a receptionist anymore. She's gone back to school to become a pharmacist."

"Your sister?"

"You're a careful reader."

The Chinese man tipped his head and smiled slightly. "I have something for you," he said, and produced from the pocket of his jacket an envelope, which he handed to Coleman. "I know you've had a long day, so I won't keep you." Quietly he took himself off while Coleman opened the envelope.

When he was sure he wasn't going to faint, Coleman walked down the hall and tapped on the closed door of his wife's treatment room. "Cecily, could I see you for a minute?"

"I'm with a patient . . . "

"One minute."

After a brief wait, Cecily opened the door. Her large green eyes had circles under them, but she was smiling; she and her patient, the very pregnant Chinese woman on the treatment table, had been sharing a joke.

Coleman said, "Some man who never told me his name just walked in here and gave us fifty thousand dollars."

I don't know how he found me, Jill typed, **and it scares the living crap out of me.**

Darling, your language, Carter tapped back. **Maybe he's a private investigator.**

Glad you think this is funny.

I know it isn't funny. But I can't figure out what he wants.

Me either. All I did was look him in the eye and treat him like a person.

Stop that. This is not your fault.

I know. But he scares me.

Has he spoken to you? Or touched you?

No. He just looms.

Jill and Carter were in a private chat room on-line. It was mid-February. Jill was missing her mother, who was in Blaine County, Idaho, up to her eyeballs in politics. Carter was at home more than she'd been in thirty years, because she had very suddenly become a full-time foster mom. They liked talking to each other over the Internet because it was quiet, and didn't wake the baby, and because if the other was unavailable you could just leave e-mail and pick up your answer at any odd hour that happened to suit you.

Jill was frightened about MacDuff because he had become the Unimaginable Other that wouldn't go away. He was as different from Jill as one could imagine a member of the same species to be. Big where she was small, male where she was female, black as she was white, as deprived of material things as she was laden with them. She looked at his eyes and she saw nothing she recognized. No hunger, no fear, no hatred, no requests. He was just there, staring at her. What did it mean? Had she somehow conjured a night terror from her dreams and made him flesh?

Carter's concerns were less existential. A toddler needs clothes, books, toys, special food. It gets an earache and you can't give it a shot of scotch. Flora had gradually begun talking again but she got frantic if she woke from sleep and Carter wasn't in the room. Awake, she didn't want to be out of her sight, and she preferred to be touching her. Carter spent a lot of time holding Flora, reading with her, or watching *Sesame Street*. Jerry had brought her two cartons of children's videotapes and Flora watched them over and over and over. DeeAnne bought Flora a little yellow plastic cassette player so that Flora could sit quietly beside Carter's desk listening to *The Muppet Musicians of Bremen* in her headset while Carter worked.

Carter had called the minister of Shanti's church. He remembered meeting her. He said that the neighborhood knew she had taken Flora, and thought it was the safest thing for her, if Carter was able to keep her for the time being. Carter said she'd been expecting to hear from Child Protective Services, or whatever agency concerned itself with orphaned children. The minister said he thought it unlikely. "She wasn't in the system when her mother died. No reason they'd know anything about her." From him she learned more about Shanti's history.

"I never knew her late dad," said Reverend Campbell, "he passed before my time. But her mother was a fine woman. Sang in my choir."

"Did she work?"

"Yes, I believe she was an executive secretary. She worked somewhere over in Century City."

"And Shanti lived with her?"

"Yes, Shanti and Delia both," said the minister.

"What about other relatives?"

"I believe May's people were from Georgia, but they moved to Detroit when she was a girl. She had one older brother, but I don't think he is still living."

"What about her husband's relatives?"

"His mother may be alive. I believe she was from Pittsburgh, Pennsylvania, but I wouldn't have an idea how to find her."

Neither would Carter. The police had taken all Shanti's records, her letters, her address book. They wouldn't release them to a nonrelative. The minister hoped Carter would be able to locate Shanti's sister.

Carter had called Terri at The Cloisters. Terri knew what had happened to Shanti; her mother, homesick for the old neighborhood, kept in touch.

"Tell me about Delia," Carter had said, and Terri sighed.

"Little Delia," she said.

"Why do you say it like that?"

"Oh—little Delia. You couldn't tell that girl anything she didn't want to hear. Tell her she couldn't make mud pies in her Sunday school dress without getting dirty, she'd think that meant *you* couldn't. She thought she'd be able to manage it just fine."

"Did she and Shanti get along?"

"She thought people like Shanti and me were Goody Two-Shoes."

"Would you know any friends she might be in touch with?"

Terri came up with some names of girls Delia had run with in junior high.

"What about boys?"

"She liked the bad ones. She thought she could handle anything."

"What about men in Shanti's life?"

"I can't help you. I think Flora's dad was someone she met through work, but she never talked about him. She really wanted kids; she didn't especially expect Prince Charming to be part of the deal."

That left Delia as Flora's most promising next of kin. As soon as Carter could get back to work, she would lay out a strategy for tracing her. She didn't expect to be out of action for very long.

If in those first few days Carter could have found a more sensible home for Shanti's daughter, who was utterly bereaved, a speechless bundle of nerves and needs, she would have. But Flora became hysterical if Carter left her. The family next door had offered to keep her for a morning so Carter could go discuss the situation with DeeAnne, but the baby's screams followed her down the sidewalk, and she had turned around and gone back. It was as if Carter linked Flora to her mother, and thought that as long as Carter was near, time might reverse and bring Shanti back.

Finding a proper home for an orphaned baby would not in any case be the work of a moment. Carter couldn't bear the idea of delivering Flora to the child welfare system; she would disappear into its maw and Carter feared she would never again know how to find her, how to tell if she was well placed, if she was all right. Or be able to help her if she was not. In the first long days and nights they were alone together, Carter and the baby were in suspended animation. Carter tried to think of what she ought to do, but instead was bombarded with the raw shock of the moment when she had walked into Shanti's living room. Awful images. Smells. She closed down her emotional aperture to a pinprick of light through which she could see the baby, and thought of nothing, as best she could. For a while there would be no tomorrow and no yesterday.

As she waited, almost paralyzed, for enough scar tissue to form to allow her to resume normal functioning, Carter became absorbed in minute changes in Flora's adjustment. She watched for a hint of smile. She sat staring into space, apparently vacant, while inwardly engaged in feeling the little body relax against her into sleep. Something began to happen to her. It was as if she had finally been let in on nature's biggest secret, the answer to the formerly unanswerable question: why would a woman rather have a baby than live her life for herself? Why did parents look at their children with adoration when a stranger observing the same child would want to brain it? Carter woke up one morning to find she was utterly in love with Flora.

She stopped talking about how temporary the situation was. She started studying how to choose a pediatrician, how to manage the baby and work, how to get her adjusted to a baby-sitter in case Flora ever decided to let her out of her sight. She discovered Toys R Us.

Jerry came by about once a week. He had never had children and Carter couldn't imagine he had much interest in them. But he seemed unwilling to allow Flora to remain as frightened of him as she had been the first day he'd met her. He would arrive unannounced after work and sit with Carter while she gave Flora her supper, or they'd put her in a stroller and walk around the block. He made no attempt to bribe Flora or even please her; he just sat quietly, talking with Carter about this and that. After he'd gone Carter would find a stuffed toy or a giant box of crayons left in the front hall. One Saturday he came and took Carter and Flora for a ride in his convertible. This appeared to be a completely new experience for Flora, and she liked it. He drove them out to the beach and sat studying Flora's face as she looked at the ocean.

"Have you ever been to the beach?" he asked her.

Flora looked up at Carter, as if she had a few questions herself.

"I think we ought to take her down, so she can feel the sand."

It was a bright day, but cool. They walked down to the water's edge with Carter carrying Flora. She put her down on the sand, and Flora squatted to feel it.

"Sand," said Carter. "The same stuff you have in a sandbox." Then she remembered what Shanti had said about the sandbox in the playground that the junkies had ruined.

"Do you want to take your shoes off?" Carter asked. "Wiggle your toes in the sand?" Flora nodded. Carter took off her sneakers and her tiny socks, and Flora, standing on sand, obediently wiggled her toes. She looked up, surprised and interested.

Jerry walked a little way and found a seashell.

"What's this?" he asked, and Flora trotted over and squatted to study it.

When she had collected enough shells to fill both of Carter's jacket pockets, Carter said, "We better get you home, little bear. It's time for your lunch." Jerry had offered to stop at McDonald's, but Carter worried that they had taken enough of his time, and declined. He didn't press it.

The next time he had stopped by for a few minutes in the evening on his way to meet Graciela for dinner at Venice Beach, he said; Flora was playing with a toy school bus on the living room rug. When one of the passengers fell out and rolled under a chair, Flora had to squeeze past Jerry to retrieve it. Carter noticed that she put a hand on his knee to balance herself as she went past him, as if he were something safe, like a chair in a familiar room. Jerry gave one of his rare smiles.

One Sunday afternoon in mid-March, Carter was sitting at her computer in the tiny office off the living room when she saw an enormous ancient black Lincoln Continental creep down the street past her door. It stopped, then reversed. Majestically, it pulled into her driveway behind the Brown Bomber. Carter was standing by this time, her face against the glass. When she saw who was inside, she went to the door with a feeling of dread. The longer Flora was with her, the less she wanted to think about a time when she might not be.

The driver of the car was the minister, Reverend Campbell. He held open the passenger door for his companion, Aunt Sallie Spear. Both were wearing their church clothes, prepared for a formal visit. Carter was in sweatpants, none too clean, and an old tennis sweater. Too late to change, or to run the vacuum, wash the windows, or bake a cake. She opened the door.

"We thought you must be at home when we saw your car," said the minister.

"I'm afraid I'm not dressed for company."

"Don't give it a thought," said Aunt Sallie Spear with the air of one who has gotten used to the younger generation, which is not the same thing as being one who would ever be caught in her housecleaning clothes on a Sunday afternoon herself. She was wearing a navy blue dress with covered buttons and a white lace collar, and a hat with a blue veil. The veil was turned back so that it covered the hat, not her face, but it made Carter want to see her with it down. It made Carter want such a hat herself; what a good idea veils were, a hell of a lot easier than all those bottles and brushes Jill had made her buy.

Aunt Sallie led the way into the house. The living room floor was littered with the toy schoolhouse and bus Flora had been playing with, and the little peg-shaped children that fitted in the bus or in the school. Oh god, oh god, the children are almost all white, Carter thought. There's only one little brown one. What's the matter with me, why didn't I think of that?

Aunt Sallie took the chair Carter gestured her to, and Reverend Campbell took another one partway across the room. They didn't lounge or sprawl on the couch. They sat rather stiffly. Carter offered coffee or tea, or iced coffee, or iced tea. Reverend Campbell said, "Nothing, thank you. We've just finished the hospitality hour after the service. Unless . . . Sallie?"

"No, nothing for me, thank you. But you go ahead."

"No, I'm . . . I'm fine too," said Carter, and she sat down. "I was just . . . I'm fine. I'm very glad to see you."

She gave a big smile. Then she noticed that Aunt Sallie had decorously crossed her legs at the ankles whereas she had flopped one great knee over the other, and there was a gap between the tops of her socks and the hem of her sweatpants. She uncrossed her legs and sat cursing her mother for not teaching her anything useful, ever. She smiled again.

There was a silence because finally Carter managed to remember a shred of her training, and kept her mouth shut. If they've come to take Flora, at least don't make it easy for them. Make them say why. Make them make their case.

The silence lengthened.

Finally both her guests began at once.

"Forgive us for busting in . . ." said Reverend Campbell, while Aunt Sallie said, "Reverend Campbell tells me you . . . "

Then they both stopped and looked uncomfortable. Somehow they agreed, wordlessly, that Sallie would continue.

"Reverend Campbell tells me," she began again, "that you asked him about Shanti's family."

"Yes," said Carter.

"And you know that she has a sister."

"Yes, I know. Shanti told me. And since . . . And I've been trying to find her, but the last lead we had put her in San Francisco, and we've had no luck there at all."

"Well, that's the thing, that's what it is we wanted to talk to you about," put in the minister.

"We know where she is," said Aunt Sallie. "She's been seen."

"Where?"

"New York."

"New York!" Carter needed a minute to adjust to this. "Well, no wonder I couldn't find her in San Francisco."

"Yes."

"No wonder." Her callers once more spoke together.

"Can you tell me more? Who saw her? And when? And what kind of shape is she in?"

The minister looked at his hands. Aunt Sallie looked distressed. It was she who pressed on.

"There's a boy who used to go to our church, he was a friend of Shanti's."

"Like a big brother to her."

"He went to New York to get into the music business. He played the clarinet you know, and the saxophone, and something else . . . "

"Flute."

"That's right, flute. He was doing real well, he got into the union, and first we heard he was in the orchestra of a Broadway show . . . "

"Do you remember which one?"

"You'd have heard of it, it was a big show . . . "

"I don't recall the name of it."

"No. Anyway, it closed."

"He's still working, you know, he plays the sessions sometimes."

"But it isn't steady."

"I'm sure it isn't," said Carter.

"So, sometimes when he's between gigs, he drives a cab."

Carter nodded.

"He keeps in touch with some of the boys he went to school with. And he heard about what happened to Shanti. So he knew about that."

"And one night, he stops for a fare, he looks in the rearview mirror, and there she is sitting in the backseat."

"Delia Amos," said the minister.

Carter nodded her head slowly. She was picturing the scene, looking for all the blanks in the information that she needed to fill in.

"So what we wanted to ask you . . ." said the minister, and then stalled.

"We wanted to know if you know how to . . . "

"Or could you help us . . . "

"Find her. Of course," said Carter. And she went for a pen and a pad of paper.

The musician's name was Sidney James, and he went by Sid. He didn't have a phone at the moment but there was a club where he often played, and his friend Bo said the bartender there would take messages for him. Did they know the name of the cab company he worked for? They didn't. It did not seem that it was a Yellow Cab. They assented that it was most likely a gypsy cab. Had Sidney told Delia that her sister was dead? He had tried to. He had said to his fare that she was Delia Amos and she'd said her name was Penny. He had said her sister, Shanti, was dead. And the fare had looked stunned, and then she said she'd changed her mind about going to work, she had to see a friend, and demanded to be let out of the cab.

When they had told Carter all they knew, they sat and looked at each other.

"I'll do the best I can," said Carter after a while.

"Thank you."

"That's all you can do," said her visitors. "We thank you for just the trying."

"Just to know," said the minister.

"Just to be sure that she knows . . ." said Aunt Sallie.

There was another silence.

"While you're here," said Carter finally, the sense of dread returning, "would you like to see the baby?"

Of course they would. It had obviously been on their minds since the minute they'd arrived. How was this giant white woman, who certainly was not a churchgoer nor much of a housekeeper, managing to take care of Shanti's baby?

Flora was just waking up from her nap when Carter sat down beside her on the bed to wake her up. "Hello, baby. Did you sleep well?"

Flora nodded, bleary-eyed.

"You have some visitors. Friends of your mommy. They came to see you."

J ill was reading Simone Weil in her dorm room when the phone rang. (Talk about someone who carried dieting too far.)

"Hello, is this the Voice of Reason?"

"Auntie Carter! Do you need to be told you are Only a Woman?"

"No, I don't. I just had a visitation from all the Baptists in South Central, and they managed to tell me that without saying a word about it." She described her afternoon. "I guess I'll be coming to New York."

"Hooray! Will you bring Flora?"

"That's the tricky part. I can't imagine leaving her, but you don't really see a lot of private investigators taking their toddlers along on jobs."

"It's too bad Mom isn't here—she's great with babies," Jill said. Carter thought she sounded wistful. "But I could help."

"Have you heard of this jazz joint, though?"

"Tell me again?"

"Carla's. Sidney James gets his phone calls there. I'm guessing it's uptown, the way the story was told."

"What kind of person gets their phone calls at a bar?"

"Good question. Might be just living hand to mouth, but many times a person who gets his messages at a bar is a person with a tendency to get a snootful and call Buenos Aires at three in the morning if he has his own phone."

"You should be a detective."

"It's just a guess. But if he's driving an unlicensed cab it could mean his driving record's a tiny bit spotty. It would fit, anyway. Musician's a hard life. All the ones I know drink like fishes."

"I'm pawing through the wastebasket as we speak to see if I have an entertainment listing. That part of the paper. No . . . I left most of it in the library. But I know what I'll do. You know my e-mail friend Colleen? She's a jazz nut."

"Is she in New York?"

"Yes, her e-mail name is Sweet2 after Sweet Basil, the club in the Village."

"Will you ask her?"

"Hold on, now I'm looking in the phone book. Carla's Bunnycuts, Haircare for Children, you probably don't want that one. Carla's, 505 West Fiftieth . . . "

"Where is that?"

"I guess Hell's Kitchen."

"Is that as bad as it sounds?"

"I don't really know. It's probably some trendoid fern bar yuppie suburb by now."

"Is it a club?"

"I can't tell, all I have are the white pages. It just says Carla's. I'll ask Colleen."

Jill had met Colleen in a modern music chat room when she was writing a paper about Charles Ives, and they had, figuratively, fallen into each other's arms. Colleen was a senior at City College. She lived at home with her mother and brother and was a hilarious letter writer. She was, apparently, a night owl; it had become one of the pleasures of the winter for Jill to send a funny note into the void to her last thing before she went to bed, and then pick up Colleen's answer first thing in the morning. She was an Econ major and was probably going to try to go to work on Wall Street, though what she wanted to do was sing.

* * *

Jill wrote:

> **Greetings! Do you know anything about a jazz club,**
> **or a bar with jazz, called Carla's?**
> **XXX Jill**

She sent the letter, then poked around among the Arts and Entertainment section looking for chat rooms for people who liked jazz. Finally she found one that wasn't full, and posted:

> **Is anyone here from New York? Have you heard of**
> **a jazz club called Carla's?**

In return she got a lot of ????? from people who were not from New York. BeBob recommended Carla's rib joint in Brownsville, Texas, very highly. Cool234 said:

> **My husband's from Brooklyn; hold on, I'll ask.**

Jill waited in the chat room while others argued about Gerry Mulligan. Then Cool234 posted again:

> **Carla's is on the west side. Was very hip fifteen**
> **years ago.**

Jill thanked her and was about to sign off when the computer voice, full of brainless joy, exclaimed, "You've got mail!"
She found her return from Colleen.

> **I heard Dave Lahm at Carla's. Magic time. Why?**

Happy, Jill sent back Instant Mail.

> **My friend is looking for a reed player called Sidney**
> **James who's supposed to hang out there. Does that**
> **sound like the right place?**

In a moment, back came:

> **Never heard of him, but it could be.**

Jill answered:

> **I'd like to go see. Want to go with me?**

This felt like a very bold thing to say. Jill knew that Colleen would probably be disappointed when she met her, that she was so young and so fat. But . . . what the hell. Time to come out of the closet.

The message came back.

> **Love to. When?**

> **Tomorrow?**

> **It'll be closed Monday.**

> **Forgot what day it was. Tuesday?**

> **What time?**

> **Six?**

She was thinking it would still be light then, in case the neighborhood was dicey. They could have a drink together or a coffee, and if they liked each other in person, as they did on-line, go for dinner.

> **Great**

came the answer.

> **I'll be wearing the famous silver Coke bottle coat, of which you have heard so much.**

> **Thank God. I was afraid I was never going to get to see it.**
> > **XXX Colleen**

Jill wore her famous Christmas coat, although the weather had turned suddenly warm. There were still patches of gray snow in places, but the damp earth smell of spring was everywhere. She took the subway to Fiftieth Street and started to walk west, enjoying the soft light of early evening. Ahead of her, the sky had the peculiar airy emptiness of light over water. She was heading for the river.

She walked past long rows of tenement buildings, and a grim-looking school building, its blacktop playground surrounded by hurricane fencing. The blocks were long and empty. She watched the building numbers and calculated the blocks still to go, and mentally measured as well the amount of light left to the evening. At least an hour, she thought. Somewhere above her in a room with an open window, John Lennon was singing "Revolution."

She had a small spiral notebook in her capacious coat pocket, and a paperback copy of *Jazz* by Toni Morrison, so she'd have something to read if she was early or Colleen was late. She tried as she walked to remember everything she passed so she could report to Carter.

There were a couple of working girls on the corner of Ninth Avenue. They wore skirts so short they barely covered their underpants (assuming underwear was part of their equipment). One, a beautiful yellowish girl with big purple lips and copper-colored shoulder-length hair, wore fishnet stockings and spiked heels. The other had masses of black hair and scarlet lips. Her skirt was gold and her shoes were leopard skin. Both of them gave Jill the eye as she trotted

271

across the street toward them in her long coat and flat-heeled boots. The second one lit a cigarette with long-fingered hands, flashing endless scarlet nails. As Jill scurried past them, glancing sideways at the strongly muscled bare thighs beneath the gold skirt, she knew suddenly that neither one of them was a girl at all.

(Shoes size eleven at least, she mentally noted for Carter's benefit, along with details of coiffeur and costume.) She checked the house numbers and thought to herself that Carla's ought to be on this block. And indeed, down on the corner she could see a neon sign hanging out over the sidewalk with a neon martini glass that danced from one angle to another, back and forth on the rim of its round foot.

The door to the club was set into the squared-off corner of the building. There was a glass case on the outside wall with a light inside it to illuminate the night's program.

Jill stopped to read the sign. It had "Carla's" printed in red script diagonally across the corner. Typed in the middle of the page were the date, and "Cabaret Night." The light was on inside the case in spite of the almost full daylight.

Looking through the window, she saw a dark-paneled room with a long bar at one side. There were round tables and lots of bentwood chairs, and a small stage at the far end of the room. The bartender, a young white guy with earrings in both ears, was rapidly cutting up limes into half wedges and setting them out with the rest of his fruit in white china bowls. His only customer sat at one end of the bar drinking a glass of beer and reading *The Village Voice*.

Jill pushed the door open. The bartender looked up briefly. A couple at a table, students by the look of them, were leaning toward each other, talking quietly. At the edge of the table were two coffee cups, a full ashtray, and a plate of what had been chicken wings.

There was no one in the place who could be Colleen. Jill took a seat at a table near the door. The room was warm, and she thought of hanging her coat up but decided against that; it was by the coat Colleen would know her.

A waitress with red hair in a near crew cut came to her carrying a menu.

"I'm meeting a friend," said Jill.

"Something while you wait?"

"No, I'll just . . . "

"Water?"

"Yes. Thank you."

The waitress brought her a glass of water, and left her alone. Jill took out her notebook and her novel. She wrote down things she thought a detective would want to know in her little book, and she watched the door, and she watched the clock, and she watched the bartender. A couple came in and took a table across from her. The bartender turned on a television above the bar. The waitress brought bowls of chili con carne to the new couple, who said something, looking apologetic. The waitress went to the bar and the TV was turned off again. The sound system came to life, playing Eartha Kitt. The couple looked happier, and began to eat their chili.

A man in a leather jacket and a Mets cap came in and took a table. A pair of women in matching black jeans came in and ordered tequila. The waitress came to Jill again, and Jill asked for iced tea.

She tried to concentrate on her book. I'll wait until 6:35, she thought. More people came in.

I'll wait for the door to open two more times, she decided.

Almost at once it swung open, and a man carrying a cello case entered and went straight through the room and out again through a door in the back.

The room was filled with smells of food now. The women in the black jeans were eating quesadillas. The light outside was beginning to shade toward violet gray.

The door finally opened again at five of seven and a group of four came in. They looked like Jill's parents; like her mother, anyway. Middle-aged, well-fed, looking for fun. From the way one of the men examined the silverware she gathered they were slumming.

Jill got up from her table and went to the bar.

"Excuse me . . . "

"Can I getchou?"

"Nothing, thanks, I have to go, but . . . "

The bartender cocked his head back. He was a portrait of punk cool.

"I'm looking for Sidney James. I was told he comes in here."

"Not at *this* hour."

"Oh, sorry . . . "

"Sidney be in, two, three in the morning." He looked at Jill. "You're welcome 'a come back then."

She smiled. "Thank you."

The bartender smiled too.

"If it happens I don't get back . . . "

"Yeah?"

Yeah, indeed. What? What exactly did she want? Just to look at Sidney James, so she could report. "Is there any other way to reach him?"

"Not that I know of."

"Does he live near here?"

"I guess he must."

"So this is his local."

The bartender smiled.

"Right. This is his local."

"Well, thank you very much," said Jill, and the bartender smiled again. Clearly, he found Jill cute.

Outside, the sky to the west was streaked with pink. To the east the street made a shadowed canyon between rows of buildings. She had a long block to walk to the avenue; she wondered if the working girls were still there. She wondered, too, what her chances would be of finding a taxi.

The wind was coming up, and the temperature was dropping. It had been a spring day, but it was a winter evening. Her feet made an almost silent *fuffing* sound as she hurried along in her soft boots.

She wondered why Colleen hadn't come. Probably held up at home. That, or she had intuited somehow that Jill was a fat freshman and she never meant to come. It was all right. There would be a message when she got home. Jill would assure her it was no big deal. It *was* no big deal. She'd found out what Carter needed to know. It would have been more fun with a friend, but *que sera*.

The working girls were not on the corner of the avenue. Must have gotten lucky, Jill thought. The wide street seemed unusually empty, but then again, what did she know about what was usual for this neighborhood?

On the sidewalk, half a block down the avenue, a couple was necking. Well, necking was a euphemism. They looked as if at any moment they might consummate an act that Jill's father would find a good deal more boorish than eating in public. The woman, or at least the one in the skirt, was pressed against the wall. She had both arms wrapped around the man's neck, and one leg wrapped around one of his. There was a good deal of heaving going on.

Jill turned her attention to the clump of traffic heading downtown toward her. It was sparse, and she could see no taxis. She waited through a long red light. She looked at her watch. It was 7:10. Too early for the theater rush, surely. Then she suddenly, irrationally, experienced a feeling of being watched, and remembered that you weren't supposed to flash a watch as expensive as this in questionable neighborhoods.

She pulled her hands deep into her sleeves, and scanned the next wave of traffic approaching like a school of fish released downstream. There were no yellow ones. One dark rather ramshackle four door edged over to her lane and slowed as it approached her; a gypsy cab. Jill made eye contact with the driver, but then shook her head. She didn't have the nerve. What if there were no door handles inside? What if she were never seen again?

When the light changed, she hurried across the avenue. She would try her luck at the next avenue, and if nothing happened there, walk toward bright lights and the subway.

She was halfway down the block toward the next avenue when she felt the footsteps behind her. She could not turn to check out her fellow traveler; that would be rude. She could speed up, but it would be too terrible if the feet behind her sped up too. So she slowed down.

The person—a big man, young, with a drooping eyelid half covering a milky-blind eye, caught up with her. She glanced sideways at him for a very brief moment and found, to her horror, that he was looking straight at her. As her eyes met his, her panic meter went through the roof. This was it, this was the face of evil that everyone said she would see only in her dreams. Then the man lurched, throwing her sideways, and she was pinned against the wall. She could feel him shoving against her, and god knows she could smell him. She thought her eyes were open and yet she could see nothing except blackness. And her mouth was open, as she tried and tried to scream and nothing, nothing, nothing would come out.

This is it, she thought. This is it, I'm cracking right now. I am just going to leave this mind and never come back. No more horror.

In her blindness she felt a blade cut the watch from her wrist and at the same time felt a wrenching pain as he yanked the double strand of beads at her neck. He jerked savagely until the strands broke. She howled her silent howl.

And then from somewhere outside her body—but somehow caused by her, her straining, throbbing throat—came a roar of anger. It was a shriek, huge, a howl; it was the sound she had been trying to make for five years.

A split second later some force wrenched the marble-eyed man sideways with such a power that Jill was knocked to the ground with him. His hands had been under her coat, in her clothes, gripping the strap of her small leather purse. As she fell, her head cracked hard against a pipe rail guarding a basement stairwell.

For a moment she saw popping lights and then sight returned, along with throbbing pain in her head and elbow. The thing that had howled was not herself. It was a man—another man, who had the milk-eyed one on the ground. The milk-eyed one was kicking viciously, twisting and swearing. The other one roared and pummeled him. The other one—she saw though she was now nearly blind with tears—was MacDuff.

*a*my had rented an apartment for herself in Boise, a small, tidy, second-floor conversion in a once grand house off Warm Springs Avenue. She'd rented some furniture and a television and VCR, and bought some secondhand pots and pans and one fancy new coffeemaker. In the two months since she had become a campaign junkie she had learned to consider coffee one of the major food groups. It was nearly the only thing she consumed in her little apartment, since she was never there except to sleep and wake up.

Laurie's Boise office was in a wide, low, brick building on the south side of the river. It had once been used for some sort of light manufacturing; you could still see scars and wheel marks where machinery had dug into the softwood floors. When Amy had arrived in the first chaos of setting up Laurie's office, the campaign chair had taken one look at her and announced it was her job to get office furniture for dozens of workers the cheapest way possible, to have a platoon of phones installed, and have the place wired for office equipment. Within three days of her arrival Amy had found an old college beau working for the biggest of the new computer companies in Boise and persuaded him to donate two dozen used computers.

"They were fourteen months old. They can't play CD-ROMs," Amy explained as a mountain of boxes was wheeled in and stacked everywhere. Within a week she had negotiated very favorable lease rates on a pair of jumbo copiers and an industrial-strength color printer.

The office was being managed by a young man who had worked for Roberto. His name was Aaron Jackson but everyone called him Ajax. Ajax understood office systems, he had a brother who could fix anything, and he was thrilled, after years among grandmotherly office workers over at the capitol, to be with the podluscious volunteers who started showing up in droves after Laurie spoke at Boise State.

"You can*not* say 'podluscious' though," Amy had to tell him, twice. Ajax was an earnest, shy, plastic pocket-protector kind of guy who would have been over the moon if anyone called *him* any kind of luscious. It took him a while to understand that a young lady could object to being so admired. But there was no danger that he was going to become addled by the presence of so much estrogen and become a masher. Within a week, Amy noticed, he was beside himself with undeclared love for a pale and desperately timid young creature named Sheila, who had large breasts and a picturesque head cold.

Amy spent a lot of time with Laurie. Usually she went to media events with her because Laurie got sick of delivering her stump speech and it helped her to keep it fresh to talk to Amy in the audience.

"You're a born cheerleader," Laurie said to her gratefully one afternoon.

"Made, not born. It was my job description in my marriage."

"You know," Laurie said, "when you're happily married you don't have much time for women friends. Or you don't feel the need. It's one of the cruelest things about suddenly . . ." She didn't finish the sentence.

Amy thought about Noah, always saying his wife was his best friend. For Roberto, it had actually been true. What had been true in her own marriage? It hurt too much to think about.

She said to Laurie, "This is fun."

"It *is*. And it never occurred to me that it would be."

Amy also went with Laurie to fund-raising events and coached her on how to make calls asking for money, which she was required to do at least an hour a day.

"It's the only way to approach a major donor. Don't worry—they know why you're calling. It won't kill you if someone says no."

"How do you know?"

Amy laughed. "I've done tons of this for Jill's schools. You get off on it after a while."

"If I live through this, you have no idea how I'm going to fight for campaign finance reform," said Laurie.

"Here's your list for today, honey. Dial." It was now clear that even for the primary they would need a major media campaign. They'd been running radio ads from the beginning, but they were going to have to go to television early. Lloyd Prince's numbers were holding and his name recognition was way up. He'd even gotten on the *Today* show by coming out against the Americans with Disabilities Act.

"I'm going to kill myself," Walter had said as they watched Lloyd proclaim from his wheelchair:

"It's insane to spend billions of dollars to redesign the world for the two percent of Americans who are in wheelchairs. A hundred percent of our young people need much better schools."

"But aren't there times when you find it inconvenient yourself to . . ." asked pretty Katie Couric.

"Many. But I think I should play the hand the Lord dealt me, not demand a recount."

"They never even mentioned Laurie's name," said Lynn when the segment was over.

"I'm going to kill myself," said Walter again.

"Come on," Amy said to him. "I'll buy you a drink."

Laurie was right about Amy; she *was* a born cheerleader. Amy was the one who could muster unshaken faith in their ultimate victory when the others lost heart, as happened two or three times a week for one reason or another. She was unexpectedly helpful to Lynn and Walter as they worked on the media plan, and she was useful in dealing with Hunt, who was having trouble remembering that it was Laurie who was the candidate. Hunt Knox's idea of a media campaign, for instance, was that *he* should make a series of television spots, sitting at his desk before a wall of photographs of himself with people like Lyndon Johnson.

"I'll say 'When I was governor you wanted me to do X, Y, and Z, and you weren't disappointed. And you won't be disappointed now if you send my little girl down there to Washington. . . .'"

"That's a great idea, Hunt . . ." Amy would say, and Hunt would beam.

"And then, we could do another one, of me out hunting with the dogs, and I'll say: 'You know me, Hunt Knox, and you know my family and we have always been straight shooters. We understand this state . . .'"

"I'm not sure how that's going to work, Hunt. Laurie's for gun control."

"No, no. Gun control? I better talk to her."

"But it's a good idea for a spot. Laurie's a great shot. She could be out with *her* gun and the dogs, and she could explain that she's licensed to use it for hunting, but she doesn't think she should be allowed to stockpile bazookas . . . "

Hunt looked troubled.

"I don't think this is going to play. This is a western state, it's a sportsman's state . . . "

"But she's going to Washington, Governor. To make laws for New York City, and Los Angeles and Chicago. Not just Hailey."

"What business does someone in Washington have telling someone in Hailey what to do with his guns?"

"That's a good question," said Amy cheerfully.

They did use a clip of Laurie shooting skeet, also some footage of Laurie on skis at nineteen, in a tight crouch, shooting down the last chute of a giant slalom race at Sun Valley, with the announcer's voice cracking with excitement as he shouted her time over the cheers of the crowd.

In March, Laurie maintained an increasingly demanding schedule around the state, and with every week she grew more relaxed and confident. She went to PTAs and canasta clubs and Rotary groups and union halls and Grange meetings and coffee klatches and shopping malls. People were curious to meet her, and the press was eager to cover her. Roberto Lopez was news, Hunt Knox's daughter was news, and any serious challenge to Jimbo Turnbull was news. But before there could be such a challenge there was the weekly war of momentum and public opinion building toward the primary in May.

A third candidate, Carrol Coney, had joined the race. He had recently moved across from Oregon and built himself a house in the Owyhee desert out of 135 bales of hay covered with plastic garbage bags. "A dollar a bale," he told the press proudly. He was very photogenic in his long beard, with tattoos up and down his arms. The Sunday papers loved him. His campaign listed no phone number because, as he explained, he had no phone.

"I set out to put an initiative on the ballot outlawing gun control," he told the press. "But I found out that took forty thousand signatures. It only takes a thousand to run for senator, so I decided to do that." He talked a lot about our brother freemen over the border, Men of Montana, and about Ruby Ridge and Waco.

Laurie was becoming a gifted listener, brilliant at responding to questions. She was good at pacing, comfortable with freewheeling, and she was funny but gracious. Inescapably, as she grew weary of following orders to "stay on message," she began to ad lib. The first time she gave Walter full-blown apoplexy was at a senior citizen's center at Twin Falls. Laurie had joined the line-dancing class, side touch, side touch, with a dazzling smile, her long gray skirt swirling among the pink and turquoise exercise suits. She had joined a widows' grief therapy group, both talking and listening. But in the question-and-answer period at the end of her visit she had taken the inevitable questions about protecting Medicare from marauding Republicans.

Amy and the reporter from the local paper snapped to attention when Laurie said, "You know, I'm from Blaine County, and there are people who'll tell you all the Democrats there are millionaires. I certainly wish we were. But my family are working ranchers, and the last time we had any millionaires on our road was when a carload of movie stars got lost trying to find Sun Valley." This was not the stock answer.

"I do *know* some millionaires because a lot of them ski, and so do my kids. I know a woman who wears a diamond pin that looks like a set of headlights. She brags about buying it with her Social Security money, like she's playing a joke on Franklin Delano Roosevelt. I told her, 'I think that's shocking. You don't need that check, no matter how much your husband paid into the fund, and you can afford to buy your own health insurance. You don't need Medicare. If I'm elected senator, I will fight for a means test so that money goes to people who need it and not to those who can help themselves."

There was a worried silence in the room. "Do you know what that woman did?" Laurie went on. "She sent me a thousand dollars for my campaign."

At headquarters that night, Walter said dryly, "I've known candidates who would have saved that speech for another venue."

Laurie apologized. "You weren't there though," she said. "They understood me."

"It doesn't matter whether they understood you, what matters is what the press can do with it."

Amy, who privately thought Laurie had been perfectly right, was delighted to see that in the next week there was a steady stream of five- and ten-dollar contributions from Twin Falls. They came with notes on lined paper, or sometimes on notepaper printed with old-fashioned flowers, and were mailed in inexpensive drugstore envelopes addressed in spidery cursive handwriting.

HOMELESS HERO read the headline in the *Post*. The *News* called John Henry Howard a "Citizen Hero" and the *New York Times* carried a long story in the Sunday Metro Section. The mayor, who had been taking a beating in the press and the polls for heartlessness toward the city's least fortunate, invited Mr. Howard to Gracie Mansion, presented him with a plaque, and posed for pictures with him on the steps.

Asked by the press if he didn't think a plaque was a stupid present to give a homeless person, John Howard said with dignity that he did *not* think so. He intended to send it to his mother, who lived in Baltimore. He expected she would hang it over her mantelpiece, along with his high school wrestling medals, his father's certificate of thanks for distinguished service that he got when he retired from the railroad, and his sister's summa cum laude degree from Emory University.

The *Times* ran a picture of John Howard in his high school graduation cap and gown. He had an enormous round Afro and an expression of solemn purpose. He had won the science prize, it was reported at the time, and was hoping to go into medicine.

The papers had talked to his high school teachers, his wrestling coach, his mother, his piano teacher, and his sister, an intensive care nurse in Atlanta. He had begun to show signs of erratic behavior when he was a sophomore at City College, they said. There were no drugs involved, that anyone knew of. He'd grown agitated, and then obsessed, especially with the Gulf War. He'd given some speeches about visions he'd had of lakes of burning fire. He'd disappeared from school, and from his night job. He'd turned up in Bellevue.

Twice he had seemed to recover and had gone back to school. Then he'd gone home to Baltimore for a Christmas visit and been stuck for a six-week stretch in which he couldn't get out of bed. After that he had disappeared, and his mother hadn't known where he was until the New York press started calling.

Why had he decided to get involved, he was asked, when he saw the young lady being attacked? It seemed like the right thing to do. Had he heard her call for help? Yes, he said. He had heard her scream. Had his wrestling training helped him in subduing the attacker? He thought perhaps it had. And what were his plans now?

The city was, for the moment, in love with John Henry Howard. He was articulate, soft-spoken, attractive. He was modest; he had a sense of humor. An anonymous donor offered to pay his way if he would go back to college. A church offered him a job as sexton. There were several offers of private security jobs, and a call from a rap singer wanting a bodyguard.

"Have you decided which one to take?" a reporter asked as she checked her watch. This was great stuff, the press pool knew, and they wanted to be sure to wrap it up in time for the evening news. "What are your plans?"

John Henry Howard was entirely composed. "I've given a great deal of thought to what work I am most suited for at the present time," he said. "I would like some warm clothes, and I like to watch people coming and going. The job I would like at the moment is to be a doorman."

Jill was sitting on the couch in the den where her parents used to have their cocktails. She had wept a lot in the last few days, but they didn't seem to be tears of grief. It was more as if an iceberg inside her were breaking up. Every few hours or so there would be another great shivering and cracking and then some huge splintering mass of emotion would start sluicing away, chattering and sharp and painful. But with each storm of weeping she seemed to grow lighter. She seemed to be able to fill her lungs more completely; there seemed to be more room around her heart.

Her father, sitting in his leather chair, looked across at Jill as the segment with MacDuff ended. The swelling on the side of Jill's head was slightly better, though her left eye was purplish and her lips were puffy and cut. There was a bandage around her left wrist where her watch had been. She'd been cut by the blade that hacked through the band, a shallow but dirty wound.

She had begun to cry again when MacDuff said he liked to watch people come and go, but would like to do it in warm clothes.

"You okay?" Noah asked after a moment. He had switched off the television.

She nodded and smiled, although tears were streaming down her face. It was as if she were experiencing two entirely different emotional systems at one time. It was like being a wall that is turning into a river.

"No reason he shouldn't be a perfectly good doorman, is there?" her father asked her.

Jill wondered how she was supposed to know, but decided it didn't matter. No, she shook her head. Wonderful doorman. She'd watched him on the news as she had struggled to imagine him face-to-face, and was no closer to understanding what he was. Why shouldn't he be a Janus, a two-headed doorkeeper, simultaneously looking at the past and the future? Maybe someday he'd be able to get all the way back inside, and go back to being the person he had expected to be. Like somebody else she could think of.

Noah picked up the phone and dialed.

"This is Dr. Burrows. Is Mr. Lewin home yet?"

A pause.

"Yeah, Stu, Noah Burrows. Didn't happen to have the news on, did you?"

A pause.

"No, the gentleman who tackled the mugger . . . yeah. . . . Yes. You could find a place for him in one of your buildings, couldn't you?"

A pause.

"It'll be great PR. I know it's a union thing but I'm sure you can . . .

"Thanks. That's what I thought too. Yeah, we'll get his records and see, maybe there's . . .

"Yeah, let Payne Whitney check him over and see if there's something that would . . .

"No, no reason. I just thought he looked like the kind of fella who could use a break. . . . Yeah. Yeah, I thought so too. No, I don't know, but I'm sure those reporters do, or the mayor. Yeah. Let me know. Thanks."

He hung up and smiled at Jill. She smiled too, apologetic, and cried. She could almost hear his thoughts: tell your mother I'm doing the right thing. Tell your mother I'm taking care of you. But he wouldn't say it out loud. He looked pale and ten years older than he had in Mexico.

*D*ona Reo was a big woman, and this was a good thing. She would probably have been a dead woman several times over had she weighed less. She looked like a pirate, except for when she went to church; for church she wore a dark dress and put in her glass eye. The rest of the time she wore bright shirts and skirts and a green patch over her right socket. Her orange hair she wore cut close to the scalp. Once, in jail, everyone in her cell had had head lice and they had all had their heads shaved. Dona found she rather liked the feeling of air on her scalp, and the stiff velvet texture of the hair itself as it started to grow in again. And it sure as hell was easier to take care of.

She'd lost the eye in a knife fight, the result of a miscalculation she would never have made if she hadn't been beginning to shake and needing to get to her supplier. Of course, if she hadn't been using, she wouldn't have been trying to roll a john in the first place. She wouldn't have been hooking at all. But if she hadn't been such a big woman, she would have lost more than an eye. That guy had looked like he was planning to take out her liver.

The other time being so big had saved her life her friend Mickey had scored some shit for them from a dealer south of Market. The second she took the rubber tubing off her arm she knew something was wrong; this stuff had been cut with something terrible. When she came back into her body, it was morning. Her clothes were stiff with dried sweat and there was vomit all over her sweater. Mickey, however, sitting up on the green couch beside her with his eyes bugged open, had been dead for twelve hours. He was a skinny little dip, and she figured that had made the difference. He hadn't had enough body mass to slow the stuff down, so it had slammed into his heart like a locomotive going full speed into Grand Central.

Quitting had not been fun. But it had been more fun than being dead. When she found she would have to wait over a year to get into a methadone program, she had gotten a friend with a pharmaceutical connection to score her a ton of Valium. Another friend drove her out to Marin and left her in a crappy little motel room near Stinson Beach. There she sweated it out. At first she slept and shook. After several days she began to walk on the beach. By the time her money ran out, she knew everyone in the town, walked miles by the water every day, and had even taken to wading into the water up to her waist, though she couldn't swim, until she felt clean inside and out.

Back in the city she had gotten a job working in a community garden that hired ex-cons. They raised chayote and sorrel and orange peppers and yellow tomatoes and sold these to fancy restaurants. She was grateful for the work and the peace. But she was a woman with big appetites and she'd thought some big thoughts while she was walking on the beach and aching, and before long she had begun to feel restless.

The backers of the felon farm found out that Dona was great at PR. They soon had her leading groups of wide-eyed potential donors around the arugula beds, telling them lurid tales of her days and nights on the street, of the two children she hadn't seen in twelve years, and the way the farm let criminals like her feel connected again to a world that was natural and simple and God-centered, to feel themselves part of creation. After an hour with Dona, visitors opened their checkbooks and then fled home to be sure their doors and windows were locked and their children were safely enrolled in private schools.

But Dona knew she wasn't a criminal. She was an addict. There was a difference, or should have been. She began asking the money people questions about how a thing like this was set up. Whose idea? Who bought the land? Who made it happen? Finally, two of them took her aside.

"We don't have much extra money," was the first thing they said, and she had learned that in the great scheme of things, they actually didn't. One ran a reasonably famous San Francisco restaurant and the other was an architect. Both of these were professions you conducted while unarmed and wearing clean clothes, and that had looked like a lot to her at the time.

"But we have jobs to offer," they said. "Have you thought about your future? We know people who need people like you," said the architect.

But it turned out that Dona did not picture herself in designer clothes, saying, "Right this way, Mr. Coppola, your table is ready." She did not see herself tooting around town in a convertible. She wanted her own piece of ground to garden.

That had been nine years ago. For the past eight years, she'd been the director of The Safe House, a health clinic, counseling service, and needle exchange for junkies. She'd started in a rented space in a church basement in the Haight. She had just a drug counselor and a couple of doctors at first, and a semi-reliable rotation of ex-con volunteers. After a year, the church had burned down. She reopened in a storefront. She exhausted the architect and the restaurant guy but not before she'd squeezed everything she could learn out of them about helping the least appealing of the needy, those with unattractive symptoms whose misery seemed to be self-inflicted. The first two had gotten lawyer friends to serve on her board and file her papers. Those got doctor friends to counsel and volunteer. They got a member of the police commission to run interference for her when she started the needle exchange, which City Hall hated.

Naturally, her biggest problem was raising money. Her clients were junkies. You couldn't exactly send junkies door to door in Pacific Heights. Who would open the door, they look out and see a big spacey guy in dark glasses, twitching?

Sometimes she could afford her own apartment. The last three years she'd been living in a room behind a curtain at the back of the store. She had a cot with a quilt a recovered crackhead had made for her, and a small plaid dog bed filled with cedar chips for Sebastian, an apricot-colored cocker spaniel–poodle mix whose owner had died of AIDS.

This morning, before the center opened, she had to take all her plastic pails of used needles back to her supplier for disposal and pick up the week's supply of fresh needles and pails. Her being able to get there and back was a matter of uncertainty. Her car, a 1972 Dodge Dart, was showing signs of terminal illness. She had bought it at a police auction, one of those deals where you have to make a decision based on what the car looks like from the outside. Always a chance you'll open the hood and find out there wasn't any engine. She called the car Patty Hearst, since she figured it had been kidnapped and forced into a life of crime before the police got it. An ex-con friend had kept it running for her, but Dona knew that Patty was on bor-rowed time.

"Don't fail me now, baby," Dona said as she shrugged the car into a parking spot a block from home. "This would not be the week for it." She never knew when she switched off the ignition if she was ever going to hear the sound of that engine again.

She stopped at the bagel shop on the corner and bought a double latte and a bialy to go.

"How you doin', D?" asked the counterman as he counted out her change.

"I'm sick to death of this rain," she said.

"Tell me about it. I got water in the basement, I can't go down there without hip boots."

"I've got a leak in my roof, back in the back. But it could be worse; where it's coming in is into the shower. The luck of the Irish," she added, and they both laughed. Dona might have had some Irish blood, but if she did, it was not dominant.

There was a clean-cut guy waiting for her on the sidewalk when she got to her door. She was carrying her sack from the bagel shop and a big plastic bag of the needle pails. The needles themselves were locked in the trunk of Patty Hearst. She'd bring them in when she had somebody large and frightening with her to watch her back.

The clean guy was Chinese. They got some clients who came from the suburbs in limousines for the needles, so his fairly expensive clothes didn't surprise her. She didn't ask. She just handed him her bags to hold while she dug in her pockets for her keys. He followed her into the center. She didn't bother to keep him in front of her. If she were going to be robbed and killed for a bialy and a latte, then fuck it. Enough was enough.

"Not officially open yet," she said as she moved around the room turning on lights. "But you're welcome to take a seat."

She gathered up last night's detritus, soda cans and candy wrappers and greasy waxed paper with cold husks of pizza slices sitting on desks and counters. She disappeared into the back to get some trash bags, then emptied all the wastebaskets.

Finally, she sat down at one of the desks and opened her brown bag.

"Can't stand to eat lookin' at a garbage dump," she said. "I got a double coffee. You want some?"

"That would be nice," said the man.

"Clean mugs on the wall." She gestured to a row of wooden pegs from which hung mugs with all kinds of insignia, from "49ers" to Far Side cartoons. The man brought a mug to the desk; she poured half her coffee into it and gave it back to him.

"You using?" she asked him.

"No."

She leaned around the desk and looked at his shoes.

"You're not the police, are you?"

"No."

"FBI?"

"No."

"IRS?"

He finally smiled. "No."

"Good. 'Cause if this country needs tax money from *me*, we're in big trouble. I got to get to work in a minute. Is there something I can do for you?"

"Do you mind if I ask you a question or two?"

"Oh. You the press?"

"No."

"I'm running out of guesses, here."

"Sorry."

There was a brief silence.

"Well, go ahead. I guess I don't need to know who you are to answer questions."

"Why do you do this?"

She leaned back in her chair and looked at him. *Not* the press? Then what?

"You want the ten-cent answer or the five-dollar answer?"

The Chinese man was thoughtful.

"Five-dollar, please."

She took a breath. "Okay. When I was in jail, we used to have people come in and try to give us church services. Are you Christian?"

"No," he said, "I'm Jewish."

Surprised, she let out a belt of laughter.

"Funny, you don't . . . never mind."

The man smiled anyway, but offered no explanation.

"Well, I wasn't Christian. I had been to church with my sister when I was a kid, but the only power I'd found up to then that was greater than me was delivered through a needle."

The man nodded.

"In jail on Saturday mornings these people would show up in the dayroom, where half the sisters are watching *Soul Train*, and five of them are talking on the pay phones, and half a dozen are riding away, on these exercise bikes?" She lifted her feet and pretended to pedal. "Pumping away to nowhere, man, you know? The racket was awful. So in would come these people, and they couldn't set up chairs 'cause we didn't have chairs, we had benches attached to tables 'cause if you have chairs you can hit each other with them. So these people have to get the sisters to stop reading comics and writing letters and get up, so they can make a circle with the tables and benches. I thought it was a scream.

"And every week the Catholics would join in, but most of them didn't speak English, and a couple of my cell mates, meanest pair of bitches I ever met, one was a murderer, man, she always went because she liked to sing. 'Amazing Grace,' eleven verses, she sounded like Della Reese, but she was a *monster*. There we'd all be holding hands, and these terrified amateurs from one church or another would be trying to lead us in prayer?

"I started to go when the Episcopalians showed up, because when they do Communion, they do real wine. You with me? Then an interesting thing happened.

"Here's what it was. We were standing in a circle holding hands, waiting for the wine. And the leader says, 'We going to go in a circle and say a prayer, say whatever you want, and when you're done, squeeze the hand of the person on your right.'

"So I think this will be good. 'Please, God, help me make bail so I can get out of here and kill the motherfucker who gave me up,' that kind of thing. But no. Every one of those women—every one—and this was a group of the sorriest, most fucked-up, forgotten, betrayed, ashamed, guilty bunch of cows you ever saw—everyone of them said, 'Thank you. Thank you, God, for the love of my mother, thank you for the sister who's taking care of my babies, thank you for forgiving me, lord, thank you for my health, my peace, my future, your love.' And when the person beside me squeezed my hand I started to cry. It was as if all my life I'd been looking at people as if I could see them, you know? As if I could judge what they deserved. And all of a sudden I heard the voices of women who didn't feel judged that way. They felt seen by someone who didn't judge.

"And I thought 'I am never going to get clean because some people think I'm a shit criminal. But someone look at me and not judge me . . . someone say to me, 'It's your life. You do the best you can with it. If this is the best you can do, I just want you to have the chance to go your whole journey, whatever that is.' Person say that to me and maybe behind that, I can save my own life.

"So that's the story. You asked for the dime answer, I'd have told you that eighty percent of new AIDS cases come from sharing needles, and no one deserves to die like that no matter what they've done."

"Thank you."

"That what you came for? I'm afraid the paying guests are here."
She waved her hand toward the window where at street level you
could see a row of legs belonging to people lined up outside the door.
Just then the door opened, and then closed again, and a handsome
young man carrying a medical bag came in with a middle-aged
woman. They were chatting in Spanish.

Dona got up and threw her coffee cup in the trash. She held out
her hand for the Chinese man's empty coffee mug.

He took an envelope from his pocket and said, "May I leave this
for you?"

"Sure, thank you," she said, and dropped it into a desk drawer. She
assumed it was some kind of tract, or possibly a misguided sales pitch.
It was not until the next morning, when she was searching for rubber
bands, that she opened the envelope and found a check made out to
the center for $75,000.

*a*s the campaign approached the Idaho primary, and their workdays grew longer and longer, Laurie's team found it increasingly hard to wind down and go home at night. Often Amy and Walter would drift into Lynn Urbanski's office at the end of the evening to smoke cigarettes and gossip. Lynn, a small barrel-shaped woman from Mississippi, kept a supply of red wine "for medicinal purposes"; Walter would touch Amy on the shoulder as he headed for Lynn's office. "Time to visit the doctor." When the door was closed, and Lynn unbuttoned her waistband and Walter put his feet on the desk, they talked about anything in the world that would make them laugh. Amy told stories about Noah's self-importance she had never expected to tell anyone. Lynn did imitations of her dotty Bourbon-swilling parents, and Walter talked with gentle self-mockery about what he referred to as his tragic love life. "I don't blame women for dumping me," he'd say earnestly. "I'm impossible." He would promise to call and never do it. He forgot their birthdays. One lady friend gave a surprise party for him when he turned forty; the guests kept being crowded into closets every time the doorbell rang, expecting to leap out and surprise him. He was working on the San Francisco mayoral campaign and never showed up. He also, of course, talked about his hilarious mother and about the Strouses. Amy was privately developing the most unseemly crush on Walter, so by the time the L.A. fund-raiser rolled around, she was greatly looking forward to actually meeting his step-sister, the famous Eloise.

* * *

Amy paid off her taxi and stood on the Beverly Hills sidewalk for a minute, taking in the street of enormous houses and the April air, gorgeously soft on her skin after the long Idaho winter. She felt as if she'd arrived on a new planet. Housing in Boise was rarely merry, while here in the sunny south Eloise Strouse's house sported a couple of turrets and a curving shingled roof like a Bavarian cottage. It looked as if it were designed for Donald Trump by Hansel and Gretel. As Amy started up the walkway, the front door was opened by a thin blonde with a slight overbite and a lot of gold jewelry clanking on her arms, as if she were usually shackled to some gilded wall.

"Amy?" Eloise said timidly.

"I'm so glad to finally meet you." Amy shook the offered hand. "What an amazing house. This will be perfect." She had walked into the broad front hall.

Eloise was in a panic about the fund-raiser. For weeks she had been convinced that the fancy guests would sneer behind her back at her decorating scheme, eat her food, and exit laughing, having seen her for the frantic, empty, underemployed twerp she feared she was. She watched anxiously as Amy settled into the den, creating a command post.

Amy hadn't been in town for more than an hour before Annelise Jones, the famous but very secretive L.A. party guru, appeared at Eloise's doorstep and swept Amy into an embrace. Before another hour had passed, Amy and Annelise had finished the seating plan for the dinner, deftly avoiding such pitfalls as placing the head of Business Affairs at a major studio beside the Academy Award–winning film editor who was having a lesbian affair with his wife.

"He's the only one in the whole town who doesn't know about it, poor lamb. His wife 'shared' while she was at Betty Ford. No one wants to spoil his happiness; he thinks her depression has finally lifted because of the detox." Eloise could think of about four people she couldn't wait to tell.

"Where are we putting the wife?"

Annelise studied the seating chart and chose a spot.

"Oh, here, no . . . no, you can't put Joe Keller beside Mariko—Mariko's husband did Joe's eyes."

"What's wrong with that?"

"He smoothed out all the wrinkles underneath, the fool, instead of just doing the lid tuck. You can't do that with a man, they come out looking like hermaphrodites."

"Really?"

"Wait till you see him. The rest of this looks pretty good. Oh, Georgette Reuther is coming? How did you pull that off?"

"She's a big fan of Senator Lorenz."

"She *must* be. Georgette never goes out at night." Then Amy and Annelise toured the kitchen, talked through the menu and the wines, and discussed how to position Laurie and the senator for the after-dinner talk.

"The front salon, definitely. Bring those two big chairs from the front hall and put them in front of the piano. Put the guests in semicircles around them, and close the doors.

"But then the waiters won't be able to serve liqueurs," said Eloise.

"Nobody drinks liqueurs."

"But you have to serve them."

"There's room for a portable bar there in the corner—get rid of that credenza thing. Closing the doors will make it feel intimate and secret."

Amy had had an idea that Annelise thought was genius: the invitation had read "Come to an Off-the-Record Dinner—Senator Judith Lorenz, honored guest." Instead of using the event to create media hoopla, they had defined it as off limits to the press. Since people who already live in safe neighborhoods and have enough to eat love being in on secrets with celebrities more than almost anything else, the party had sold out immediately.

Eloise was disappointed about the press, having hoped that her name would be in bold type in the society column, and miffed about the "credenza thing," which she had chosen herself and bought at huge expense against the advice of her decorator. But she was having a good time. The more she followed Amy around, the more she wanted to *be* her in another life. Amy treated Eloise as if she were happy and capable, and to her own surprise this made it, apparently, possible for Eloise to be so. She found they were easily working through a long list of tasks that had to be managed perfectly—flowers, candles, cloak-room, towels and soap for the powder rooms, triple-checking the caterer's arrangements and the rentals. Astoundingly, everything seemed to be going according to plan.

Rae arrived at sunset the next day, and Eloise watched the unaffected joy with which everyone greeted her. Rusty and Carol Haines had come in Carol's Maserati convertible to join them for supper. The five women sat outside in the soft blue Southern California night.

"You are looking extremely rad," said Amy to Rusty, and Rusty preened. Her hair was growing back in.

"I have the cutest girl," said Rusty. "She has about a hundred rings in her nose."

"What girl is this, Mother?" Carol poured herself more coffee.

"I told you, the new one at . . ." She gave it a second and then made a fierce birdlike scissoring gesture with her fingers in the vicinity of her ear.

"Jacques's," said Carol.

"She has a name too. I'll think of it. She wears black nail polish. It looks just as though she slammed all her fingers in a door." Rusty's short hair had been spiked with mousse or gel, and she looked all set for a night of stage diving.

"Well, I love it," Rae said.

"And Carol bought me a Wonderbra," added Rusty. This brought a loud peal of laughter from Rae and Amy.

"Are you wearing it this minute?"

"She's taking tap-dancing lessons," said Carol. "She needed it for her recital costume."

"Eloise, you should have been at the fat farm with us last fall. We did have fun," said Rusty to her hostess.

"I bet you've never even seen your stepmother do a cartwheel," said Carol.

Rusty added, "You better come along with us this year."

"I'd love to," said Eloise. *Cartwheel?*

"Are we all going that week?"

"Well, I *hope* not," said Amy. "I hope that Laurie and I will be otherwise occupied. But Jill says she's going."

"How is she?"

"She sounds great. She moved out of the house, you know."

"Really!"

"Yes. She moved into the dorm in January. She's making friends, and she sounds very cheerful. She's lost an immense amount of weight."

"Good for her!"

Somewhere inside a telephone rang. After a moment a maid came to the door with a cordless phone in her hand.

"Mrs. Amy?"

Amy identified herself, and was given the phone.

"Amy? Walter."

"What's up?" Amy asked him, hoping the sound of his voice hadn't made her blush. With her lips, she shaped the word "Walter" to Rae. "Your mother says hi."

"Hi to her too," said Walter. "And brace yourself. We just heard from Senator Lorenz's office. She isn't in California."

"What?"

Amy gasped, and the others at the table fell silent.

"She *has* to be here, she's in San Diego tonight for the . . . "

"She's in Washington. There's a vote tomorrow she can't miss. Can you get Streisand? Or Susan Sarandon?"

"Streisand?" Amy repeated lamely, and everyone else at the table echoed "Streisand?"

"Willie Brown? Kathleen Brown? Someone?" Walter asked in Idaho.

"What is it?" Carol asked, at Amy's elbow.

"Walter . . . we'll handle it. I don't know how. Tell Laurie not to worry and we'll see her tomorrow. Is Siobhan staffing her?"

"Yes."

"Good. I better get on this."

"Thanks."

They both hung up, and Amy stared at Carol and Rae and Eloise. "A thousand bucks a head, and we don't have a star attraction. This is not good."

Carol said, "We'll never get Streisand . . . "

"Oh god. I was hoping . . . I mean, who likes to go out to these things? Any fool would rather stay home and eat a baked potato in bed. And we need a hit here, we've got media to buy in the next two weeks . . . "

"I think I'll call Megan Soule," said Carol.

"The Movie Star?" Rae and Rusty said at once, in surprise.

"The people tomorrow night, they've already paid, haven't they?"

"It's not just the ticket price. A lot of them are on my prospect list, people we hope will raise money from *their* friends if they see we've got momentum . . . "

"Do you know how to reach her? Megan Soule?" Eloise asked.

"I'll call her buddy, who came to the spa with her." Carol had her electronic agenda out and was punching buttons in the torchlight.

"What is that thing?" Rae asked.

"Address book. Phone book. Calendar." Carol handed it to Rae and started to dial the cordless phone.

"She'll never do it," Amy said softly to Rae.

"I'm afraid you're right . . . "

"I mean, she hardly deigned to talk to *us* . . . "

"And we're so nice . . . " said Rae. "Look what she was missing."

"Babes like us," said Rusty.

"I know someone who knows someone who worked with her. When you work with her on a movie you have to sign a thing promising you won't touch her."

"*What?*"

"Grips, gaffers, ADs, everybody. Heaven forbid you should lay a hand on her shoulder when you say 'Good morning.'"

"But she does give a lot of money to noble causes . . . "

Carol had gotten up and walked a few feet away with the phone. She was talking to an answering machine.

"Yes, Brenda, it's Carol Haines, from The Cloisters? I'm here with Rae Strouse and Amy Burrows and Rusty, my mom. We have an emergency. Could you call me back whenever you get this message? I don't care what time, or fax me and let me know how and when I can reach you?"

And she began reeling off her beeper number, her home phone number, her car phone number, her car fax number, and her home fax number, and was starting on the office numbers when Rae said to Amy, "What about Carter? Maybe she can help."

"She owes us. Imagine missing dinner with us because of the baby."

Rae said, "Don't worry, *I'll* deal with her."

$\mathcal{A}$ my and Rae were on Carter's doorstep at eight-thirty the next morning.

"General!" Carter cried. "Rae!" They exchanged hugs, awkwardly, laughing and bumping into each other.

"All we're missing is the Voice of Reason," said Carter, and Amy said, "I *know*, and I miss her. Oh, isn't this nice!" She had marched into Carter's shambles of a living room, looking around happily, taking in the PlaySkool toys, and the stacks of kid videos, and the ruined packs of playing cards with which Carter had been teaching Flora to play slapjack.

Please don't tell Mom, Jill had written to Carter on the computer after the attack.

Instantly Carter had been on the phone to New York, but Jill still insisted. "I can handle it. If you tell her, she'll come back, and she can't do that to Laurie."

"Laurie will manage fine," Carter had said.

"But it's not necessary. Dad is hovering around, bringing me worms in his beak and stuff."

"That doesn't sound like your dad."

"I know it doesn't. Having Mom leave has really shocked him. If she had to come back because of me, it wouldn't be right. Let her do what she has to do."

* * *

302

Carter had dropped the matter of telling Amy, but she checked in with Jill even more often, and made her tell the story over and over, looking for signs of panic or depression or obsession. She didn't hear them.

"If I were a tree and you cut me down to look at the rings, the year I was thirteen would look like Armageddon. This one would look normal. A mild hurricane, lost a few limbs, no major damage."

She's being kelp, Carter thought as she hung up. She had that exact image, the wave and the kelp. Jill had been hit, but not broken. She was up again and waving in the current. Far out.

Amy and Rae had found their way to the kitchen and were introducing themselves to Flora, who was sitting at her little play table, in her bite-sized little chair. Rae got down on her knees on the floor beside her and chattered goofy nonsense until Flora gravely offered her a Cheerio from the dry pile she had emptied onto the table. Rae thanked her, equally grave, and ate it.

When Carter had produced coffee, and hauled Rae to her feet so they could sit on chairs, Amy said, "Carol thinks she can get through to The Movie Star, but so far no luck."

"Walter's trying to get to Michelle Pfeiffer, but somebody said she's in Mexico on location."

"Jerry plays tennis with Megan Soule's agent," said Carter.

"Does he?" Rae asked.

"Let me give him a call." She looked at her watch, then dialed his car phone.

"Sorry, are you on the other line?" she said when he answered. This was a pro forma question; Jerry was always on the other line. She explained the crisis.

"Give me a couple minutes," Jerry said.

"I'll give you all day," said Carter. "We're desperate."

"It won't take all day," said Jerry. "Tom Lewis owes me, big time."

"So what's on the docket for you today?" Amy said after Carter had hung up. "Describe your life, little mother."

"Flora and I are going to work. I'm doing more of the in-house stuff now, and DeeAnne is more on the street. It's working out."

Flora was standing beside Rae's knee. "Hello, pet," Rae said, and Flora solemnly presented her with another Cheerio.

Rae thanked her effusively, and Amy said, "I guess I've lost my touch, I don't rate a Cheerio."

"Don't worry," said Rae, "no one can compete with me, I'm a dancer."

"Flora, I wish I had a Cheerio," Amy called. Flora was back in her chair. She looked Amy over.

"You gave my friend a Cheerio, and she ate it. If you gave *me* a Cheerio, I would put it in the bank and take it out and look at it once a year. Or I might frame it. I might hang it on the wall with gold letters underneath: 'Sacred Cheerio Presented to Amy by Flora.'"

Flora, looking as if she might actually smile, began studying her pile of Cheerios. Finally she chose one and marched to Amy with it.

"Thank you so much, what a wonderful little girl you are. I will keep it always."

"I'm sure she'll give me another one soon," said Rae.

"Goodness, you are competitive," said Amy.

"So does Flora have her own desk at the office?"

"She shares a desk. My partner Mae Ruth has a daughter who's taking a semester off from school. She comes in to take care of Flora."

"So now she has a whole roomful of mothers?"

"Exactly. And she doesn't even mind if I leave the office, as long as I'm not gone too long. Big progress."

The phone rang.

"Hello, is this Carter Bond?" said the female voice on the line.

"Speaking."

"This is Megan Soule. We met at The Cloisters."

Rae and Amy nearly got whiplash turning to stare as they heard Carter say, "Oh, Megan. It's nice to hear from you."

"My agent tells me you have an emergency."

Carter looked at Rae and Amy with her eyes popped open. They stared back at her. Rae made a thumbs up and rubbed her hands together.

Carter said to the phone, "You remember Laura Lopez?"

"Of course," answered the famous voice. "I knew her husband. I don't know how she's done what she's done. It's the bravest thing I ever saw."

Carter made another surprised face at Amy and Rae. She said, "I agree. Would you mind if I put you on with Amy Burrows? She's working on Laurie's campaign."

"Not at all, I'd love to talk with Amy," said The Voice.

Looking amazed, Carter handed the phone over.

Amy explained the evening and the crisis. She was starting her speech about how much money Laurie's opponent was spending, when Megan Soule said, "There won't be any press?"

"Absolutely none."

"And no one but you and Carter would know I was coming?" Amy looked at the other two, crossed her fingers, and said, "Right."

"You guarantee?" Her voice sounded, Amy told them afterward, almost as if it held a note of panic.

"Personally," she said.

There was a pause.

"I can't make speeches," said The Voice.

"Honey, if all you did was sit in a chair and look gorgeous, it would mean the world to us."

"I can do a *little* better than that. Is there a piano?"

When she had finished giving the address, the description of the back entrance, and the timing of the evening, Amy hung up and said to the others, "I think she's going to do it."

"Whoopee!" cried Rae.

"You *think* so? What do we do if she doesn't?"

"You know—she sounded genuinely terrified. I always thought that was an act."

"Why shouldn't she be terrified?" asked Carter. "I'd be terrified if every time I went out of the house I was greeted by hordes of strangers who thought they knew me."

"She knew us all. She knew which classes we'd taken together. She'd worried about Laurie."

"The thing I want to know," said Rae, "is, has that piano been tuned or voiced in under a century?"

Carter and Amy looked at her.

"You can't just sit down and play if all she uses it for is to hold up picture frames. It'll sound like a load of dishes being thrown down stairs."

"Where do you find a tuner?"

"I have no idea; I get mine from the symphony. But I book way in advance, and I *did* build them an auditorium."

"Annelise will know how to get it done," said Amy. "But listen. We are not telling anyone why. Not Eloise, not Carol, not anyone. Let's get the piano tuned, and then start filing plan B, to tell the others."

"And in case she doesn't show . . . "

"Carter, you start right now finding a baby-sitter," said Rae.

"I don't go to things like that. Especially not alone," said Carter.

"Then find a date."

"You are the most overprotective mother I ever saw," said Amy fondly, when at 6:05 that evening she opened Eloise's front door.

"Et la plus belle!" Rae exclaimed, coming up behind her. "Va-va-voom!"

Carter, blushing a deep pink, stood on the doorstep with an odd entourage. She was wearing the red ribbon sweater Rae had given her and all the makeup Jill had made her buy, and a pair of black velvet pants in a surprisingly slim size, and she did indeed look amazingly glamorous.

"And good evening, Miss Flora," said Amy. Flora, clutching Carter's hand, was wearing a pink dress with a sash and a lace collar, and carrying a Barney.

"This is Romie," Carter said, introducing the plump African-American girl who stood behind Flora holding her jammie bag and her backpack stuffed with toddler supplies. "And this is Jerry Carter." The very tall, heavy-featured man, handsome in a Boris Karloff kind of way, tipped his head to them, and everyone shook hands.

"Is Laurie here?"

"Just got here. She's upstairs changing."

"How is she?"

"Exhausted."

"But all right?"

"You'll see," said Amy. "When it's showtime, she will glow. And Trishie is all ready for you," said Amy to Flora. "Come this way. You girls are going to have your supper in Trish's room and Romie will help you, and you know what Trishie has? A big tank of tropical fish . . . "

To Carter's complete astonishment, Flora was peacefully going off toward the stairs holding Romie's hand. Suddenly she stiffened and turned back to look at Carter. Carter smiled at her and waved.

"Have fun, little one." And Flora went.

"I don't know how Amy does it," Laurie said to Carter. She was putting on her lipstick and looking into the mirror, talking to the image of Carter lounging on the bed. "She was in Idaho for a week, she knew people I hadn't met in living there my whole life. There's an old boyfriend from high school who's turned up; he's mad about her. Half the movers and shakers in Boise are old beaus of hers from college, or married to her sorority sisters. Or they *were* her sorority sisters. And the same thing happened here. She's been in Los Angeles one day; there's nothing she can't get done."

"She's a piece of work," said Carter.

"I've got a great team," Laurie said. "If the whole thing ends with the primary, I'll still feel lucky I tried it."

There was a knock on the door, and Amy came in. She had dressed in a black silk crepe sheath that made the very best of her very good figure, while looking rather demure.

"You ready?"

Laurie nodded.

"How's the headache?"

"Better."

"Are you sick?" Carter asked.

"I'm a delicate flower," Laurie said. "I hate the days I don't get any exercise, and Cara had her nightmare last night, at three in the morning."

Both Amy and Carter knew about daughters with nightmares.

"Well, if you need anything, there will be about eighteen doctors in the house, and Eloise has a pretty complete pharmacy going in her bathroom."

Laurie smiled and shook her head. "I like the concept. I knock back a handful of pills and go down to give my ringing speech on Character."

Laurie gave her ringing speech on Character at the end of the cocktail hour. Standing in the garden beside Carter at the edge of the crowd, Jerry watched with a professional eye.

"She is really good," he said to Carter, who was applauding loudly. "Isn't she?"

"I mean, *really* good. She could go a very long way."

Carter turned to look at him. Jerry was a hard man to impress.

"How long a way?"

"She could go a long way. She could make people believe things they haven't believed for a long time."

"Why, Jerry Carter. You're going all gooey-eyed."

"I'm always telling you, I'm a deeply tender person. I'm just misunderstood."

Partway through dessert a waiter bent discreetly to Eloise's ear. She was wanted in the kitchen.

"Of course," she said, smiling smoothly, knowing that this was it, the disaster she had been waiting for. The plumbing was overflowing. The cook was on fire. "I'll be just a minute," she said to her dinner partner, who was in any case deeply absorbed by the pretty young starlet on his other side, the one with the *belle poitrine* who was married to that sharp Business Affairs fellow from Disney.

Squeezing past waiters garnishing plates with candied lemon peel, Eloise made her way into the kitchen. Beyond a tower of stacking racks holding wineglasses, she found Amy talking to a waiflike creature who on second glance proved to be one of the most famous women in America.

"Oh, Eloise. This is Megan Soule," said Amy with a straight face.

Eloise took the offered hand. The Movie Star was wearing a silk scarf around her famous hair, and a long black raincoat over her evening dress. She was carrying a gym bag. Behind her was a young man in a dinner jacket holding a sheaf of music.

"How nice to meet you," said Eloise, shaking the famous hand.

"I'm sorry to be so stupid—tell me your name again?" Megan said.

"Eloise Strouse. I live here." The Movie Star smiled and looked around at the cooks and waiters who were bashing into each other all over the kitchen while pretending not to stare at her.

"Can we get you something?"

"Oh god. I've already had about five Inderals and I don't think it's doing any good. I can hardly swallow." She also could hardly talk; her voice trembled, as if she might weep.

"They take some time to kick in," said Amy.

"Do *you* get stage fright?"

"Paralytic with it," said Amy, smiling.

The Movie Star looked at her warily. She took several deep breaths. "Is there somewhere I can do my makeup?"

"Right over here," said Eloise. "I'm afraid it's not very grand."

The guests had moved into the room overlooking the garden, the room Eloise would forever after think of as "the front salon." The credenza thing had been removed and a portable bar set up with port and liqueurs and designer waters. Fancy folding chairs with silent hinges and padded leather seats ("Annelise knows how to find these things," Amy said) had been set up forming arcing rows around the two big chairs in front of the piano. There was an immense mass of flowers in a vase on the table beside the chair to which Eloise escorted Laurie. The guests were finding seats, and giving orders for coffee and drinks, and there was an expectant thrumming buzz of talk as people finished their dinner conversations.

"How are you holding up?" Amy whispered to Laurie.

Laurie squeezed the hand Amy laid on her shoulder and smiled at her briefly. "A-OK," she said.

Amy turned and stood facing the guests. Laurie, sitting in the big wing chair beside her, poured a glass of water. For a moment Amy thought of the ashen, depleted woman she and Jill had met in the Japanese tub. She glanced down at her friend, with her high color and straight gaze, her straight, strong posture.

The audience began to draw themselves to order and attention. Amy began.

"Have you all got everything you need? Water? Coffee?"

There was a contented murmur.

"I know you've all had a chance to talk with Laurie Lopez, and there will be a formal question-and-answer period in a little while. But first I have to report a change in the program. You may have noticed a certain absence of Senator Lorenz here tonight. There's a reason. She's in Washington."

There was a buzz and rumble of whispered conversation. Washington. Well, but . . . ? Before speculation and bad temper could settle in, Amy went on.

"She sends her sincere apologies. There was a vote in the Senate late this afternoon that she couldn't miss. In the meantime a friend of the candidate has very kindly agreed to take Senator Lorenz's place."

The accompanist walked in carrying his music, and took his place at the grand piano on the far side of the fireplace. There were whispers and some polite laughter. Oh shit, some wannabe lounge act. But when the next figure entered, there was sudden and complete silence, followed by waves of applause.

Half the people in the room owned every album she'd ever made. Some had seen her on Broadway before she had made her first movie. Every single one of them remembered her first Academy Award speech, for which she was mercilessly teased for years after. And every single one of them knew she hadn't sung in public in over ten years.

Jerry suddenly touched Carter on the knee and left his chair.

No speeches, The Movie Star had said. But she stood in front of them with no microphone and no fancy lighting, a walking symbol, a moving target, for everything people loved and loved to hate about superstars and celebrity.

She stood with her hands folded in front of her. Eighty-some very alert faces looked back, taking in every detail of her.

She's put on a pound or two since her last movie, thought more than one lady, studying the curve of the abdomen under unforgiving silver lamé.

There's a line or two around the mouth, thought more than one plastic surgeon. And the very beginning of a softness along the jawline.

She can't be as young as her publicists say, thought a number of others. Who makes her up for the camera?

She took a deep breath and smiled that amazing smile.

"Unaccustomed as I am to public speaking," she said, and the room filled with knowing laughter, "I *would* like to say one thing," she went on. "I will never forget the spectacle of Jimbo Turnbull baiting Ella Steptoe during her confirmation hearings. Ella Steptoe tried to make a difference and she got hammered for it. I don't want that to happen to Laurie Lopez. I could have sent in my check, but I figured if she's brave enough to take on Jim Turnbull, I'm brave enough to do this."

She let go with a four-minute version of "Mood Indigo," and when she was finished, the applause and foot stamping could be heard on the next block. This was known, and reported over and over in the papers the next day, because by then the house was surrounded by paparazzi. Someone in the kitchen had been unable to resist a bragging phone call.

As the applause boomed, Jerry slipped back into his chair beside Carter. In answer to her questioning look, he tipped his head toward the back of the room, where, turning, she saw Eloise's daughter, Trish, and Romie with Flora in her arms. Flora was clapping with excitement, though Carter doubted she knew why, and Romie was hopping up and down.

"By the time the set was over, the whole kitchen staff was in the back of the room," Carter said. She and Jerry were still talking the evening over in the private darkness of the moving car. They had driven Romie home, a girl considering a career change from dental technician to permanent nanny. Flora was asleep on Carter's lap. Jerry had promised to defend her if she were arrested for not using a car seat. And it was very nice to have Jerry to do the driving. And Jerry to talk to.

He pulled up in front of the house and turned off the ignition. "Don't get out, I can manage," Carter said. Jerry was already coming around to her side. He opened the door. Carter made an attempt to gather up Flora's bags and Barney and then sat, looking puzzled. Jerry leaned over and gently extracted Flora from her armful of burdens. How *do* you get out of a car with both hands full and your arms around twenty-four pounds of baby? Flora woke briefly, then settled onto Jerry's shoulder, and Carter hauled herself out of the bucket seat. Together they walked to the door, which Carter unlocked. She settled the baby's things inside the door and Jerry passed Flora over.

"Thank you, pal," Carter said. She smiled at him in a way that made him duck his head shyly.

"You're welcome."

"Tell Graciela I thank her too, for the loan."

"I will."

"I hope she won't be sorry she didn't come when she hears what happened."

"Serves her right," he said. And after a brief moment, "Good night, then."

"Good night. Thanks again."

She went inside and he heard her lock the door against the night as he shambled down the walk toward his car.

*I*daho. God's country," boomed the baritone voice on the sound track. Lloyd Prince, wearing fishing gear and holding a fly rod, sat in the stern seat of a canoe, his useless legs tucked away out of sight. Behind him was a flooding brook, with soaring mountains and blue sky in the middle distance.

"Like you, I love this state," said the candidate to the camera. "I moved here so I could raise my family the way our founding fathers intended."

He swiveled, whipped his rod two or three times, and lightly cast into the lake. He turned back to the camera.

"My opponent has called me a carpetbagger . . . "

"I did not," said Laurie. "The editor of the *Idaho Courier* called you a carpetbagger."

"Shh . . ." said Lynn Urbanski.

". . . because I didn't grow up in Idaho." He deftly reeled in his line, then turned back to the camera.

"Now we learn that my opponent's campaign is being heavily funded by out-of-state money, from special-interest groups in Washington, New York, and California," Lloyd informed the camera, looking saddened. "People who are in favor of abortion and against prayer . . . "

"In favor of choice, you moron, NO one is in favor of abortion . . ." said Amy.

"Shshsh . . ." said Lynn.

313

". . . who want to have more influence on the senator from Idaho than you do."

He turned to face a second camera, and gave a wide, well-coached smile.

"I want to be your senator, not because I grew up here, but because my children are growing up here. I want to keep this state for them, the way God intended it to be. When you send me to Washington, I'll be beholden to no one but you. The Idaho voters." The music swelled.

The baritone announcer was booming again that Lloyd Prince was going to protect *your* Idaho. As the canoe swung, the camera just caught sight of a wheelchair standing on a dock in the distance. Lynn snapped off the set.

"Well, that doesn't scare me much," said Laurie.

"It doesn't? I think it should. He's spending like a maniac. It's saturation bombing."

"We're going to have to triple our media buys in the next three weeks," Walter said.

"Are the positives ready?"

"Two are. We're working on the last one. We'll keep the 'Lopez Can Beat Turnbull' one running all this week."

"Can we afford it?"

"We need to show well in Washington, no question."

Amy was in her apartment, packing. She and Laurie were leaving for the District in the morning for a major fund-raising dinner. Even more important, they had meetings set up with eight different PACs. Laurie's showing in the polls had been strong in March but her lead was slipping badly now that Lloyd Prince had started heaving money at the TV screen. PACs didn't like to give money to losing causes, no matter how attractive the candidate.

Amy was glad to be going with Laurie for a couple of reasons. She was still better at raising money than Laurie was. Also, Jill was coming down from New York to join them. Amy would be overjoyed to see her, in the first place, and in the second place, it wouldn't be a bad thing at all to put some distance between her and Walter. She'd begun to be afraid that someone—worst of all Walter—would notice her infatuation. She hadn't felt like such a fool since she was in ninth grade and everyone knew she "liked" Johnny Kalmbach.

Amy knew it was some sort of hallucination, like her nicotine deprivation crush on the Volvo mechanic, and she wished it would go the hell away. In fact, it was ridiculous. She'd been ripped from her identity as a happy wife, dislocated and disoriented, and like everyone in the campaign she'd forgotten what it was like to get a full night's sleep. Complete explanation. Sailors on night watch took manatees for mermaids. Amy wasn't used to working closely with a man who was not her husband. Walter was famous as an intensity junkie, a sort of political buccaneer. He might as well fly a skull and crossbones; he was no kind of man for a hearth and kinder type like her. And yet he made her laugh, and she kept thinking about those big knobby wrists and that silly Adam's apple. There was one thing that wasn't silly; the more she thought about Noah, the more she thought you were doomed if you married a man who hated his mother. Walter seemed to really, truly, like women.

That was what she was thinking when the doorbell rang. When she opened the door and found Walter standing there, she thought for a moment she was having an out-of-body experience.

"I brought your ticket," he said. "Sheila Detweiler said you had left it."

"I could have picked it up in the morning" was all she could manage. Her voice sounded absurd to her.

"I know, but you have no idea what self-restraint it's taken me to stay away from this door this long," said Walter.

"Really?"

"Really. May I come in?"

And that was all that was said between them until about an hour later, when they lay in the wreck of the bedclothes, with their own clothes all over the apartment.

"Do you do this often?" Amy finally asked. Her head was on Walter's smooth, bare chest. She had already decided she didn't care what the answer was.

"Not nearly as often as people would have you think. Do you?"

"What?"

"Do this often."

Amy laughed. "I don't even know what 'this' is," she said.

"Don't even think about it," said Walter. "Neither one of us will know until the campaign is over."

Carter was trying to get Flora to eat her supper, but Flora was experimenting with a spirited improvisation of that favorite of parenthood, the Terrible Twos. This is very healthy, Carter chanted to herself. This is a really good sign, that she feels secure enough to do this. "This" was hurling her spinach tortellini overhand at the glass door out to the terrace one little dumpling at a time, and watching the birds jump when they heard the thuds. There were cheese-sauce splats all over the glass panels, and Carter was trying to do deep-breathing exercises as she stooped to clean up the floor. She had no idea what to do about this behavior. She had exhausted reasonable discourse. Swearing like a drill sergeant was what came to mind, but she was pretty sure that wasn't right. If she could get the kids next door to baby-sit for an hour after she had the little monster in bed, she was going straight to Borders Books for whatever had taken the place of Dr. Spock.

Carter had been out of the office all day. Romie said Flora had been as happy as a lark; she had been to the playground, and had a good nap, and watched Mr. Rogers. But the minute Carter arrived to pick her up, she'd started howling, and she'd been behaving like a candidate for the Foundling Home ever since.

Carter sat down beside the baby and took her spoon from her.

"No!" Flora said.

"Yes," said Carter. She filled the spoon with peas and held it to Flora's lips. Flora stared at her.

"If you can't eat like a big girl by yourself, you'll have to be fed like a baby. Come on. One bite for Romie."

There was a long eyeball-to-eyeball negotiation before Flora caved. She ate peas for Romie.

"That's a good girl. You wouldn't want Romie to be sad you wouldn't eat for her. Now one for Jerry."

Lips locked together. The doorbell rang.

"See? That's probably Jerry right now. I bet he heard you wouldn't eat any peas for him and he came to show you his crocodile tears."

The doorbell rang again, aggressively long this time.

"Yes, boohoo, big crocodile tears. Here, take this and *eat*."

Carter gave Flora the spoon and jogged for the door. She was beginning to understand those rants about the spiritual trials of motherhood that had filled the hip women's novels and magazines and so bored her when she was a young lawyer.

On her doorstep stood two large white men in black shoes. In her driveway, blocking her own car, should she wish to make a dash for freedom, sat a late-model American sedan with some government insignia painted on the door; at her angle, she couldn't see the agency.

"Is Mr. Bond here?" It was the taller one, who had little triangular patches of bristle on his neck where he'd missed shaving. Why did the feds always look so much like heavily armed insurance salesmen? The other one was wearing some repellent brand of drugstore cologne.

"There is no Mr. Bond."

"We're looking for Carter Bond," he said with irritation.

"I'm Carter Bond."

The one with the bearded neck looked at her as if it were her fault that he had begun by making himself look foolish. He stepped into the house.

"Mind if we have a look?"

"Could I see some identification, please?" she asked. The first one stepped past her and walked into the living room, saying, "Mind if we look around?"

The second one produced a thing like a vinyl billfold. He flipped it open to show her a badge and a photo ID under plastic, and stepped past her, following his partner. The first one had paced forcefully into the kitchen where, at the sight of him, Flora gave a panicked scream and began to cry. Carter ran.

It took Carter a good several minutes to quiet Flora again. Meanwhile the men had marched into her office. The first one had pressed something on her computer keyboard, causing the screen saver to disappear and the screen to exhibit Carter's check register.

"Do you guys have a warrant?"

"For what?"

"I'm trying to feed my daughter here, who are you and what do you want?"

"You invited us in," said the one with the neck.

"I most certainly did not!"

"I asked if we could come in, and you didn't say no," he said.

"I'm saying no now," she said. Growing frightened, Flora was clinging to her. Carter could feel the spoon, still clutched in the baby's fist and covered with pea mash, wiping the back of her neck.

"This is your daughter?" the second one said. He was staring at the two of them, as if he were about to say something funny.

"What exactly do you want? And could I see your ID, please?" Carter said to the first one. He had taken a textbook on Constitutional Law from a high shelf and was leafing through it.

"You studied law?"

"What the *hell* do you want?" Carter asked, louder. Flora was whimpering.

The first one closed the law book and turned to study her. He seemed pleased that he had her thoroughly angry and Carter was furious that she had let herself be caught so completely with her pants down.

The first one drew a paper from his inside pocket and slapped it onto the desk.

"You filed a lien in the state of Nevada on the property of William Bender?"

"Yes."

"And you knew perfectly well that Mr. Bender owed the United

States government the value of the property in taxes. You are hereby charged with conspiracy to defraud the government . . . "

"That's ridiculous!"

The man turned and looked with interest at her computer screen and, insolently, pushed the scroll button. The screen changed, and there were her check entries for Visa, MasterCard, the dry cleaner, and the housekeeper. She could have spit nails. With the baby in her arms, she couldn't even assume a stance that would cause him a moment's hesitation.

With a reach of her hand, she turned off the computer's monitor.

"Oh," said the tall agent. "You have something to hide?"

"I just think you should show me *your* checkbook first."

"You say this is your daughter?" asked the second agent for the second time.

"That's enough," said Carter. "Out."

They looked at each other and made no move to go.

"Out!" she said louder. The baby was now sobbing.

"OUT! NOW!" she yelled. It took her another five minutes to actually clear them out of the house, and as she watched them smile at each other as they got into the car she wished she could aim one clean punch at either one of them. Clearly, they felt they had done a fine evening's work.

"What?" Flora asked her over and over as Carter tried to calm her.

"Nothing, baby, it's nothing."

"Why?"

"Nothing bad is going to happen."

Flora was not willing to let go of Carter for an hour after that. It took her forever to fall asleep, and in the middle of the night, she woke Carter with a screaming nightmare.

J ill was waiting in the hotel room in Washington when Amy checked in. Amy didn't even stop to take off her coat; she dropped her bags and swept her daughter into her arms, so happy to be close to her again that she smiled until her cheeks ached. She finally stepped back to look at Jill, and all she could do was shake her head.

"You're a sight for sore eyes," she finally managed. "Have you been waiting a long time?"

"No. How is Laurie?"

"Holding steady, but boy, it's hard. The more I see what it takes, the more I wonder how anybody does it. . . . Oh, honeybunch, I am glad to see you!" Amy started to cry.

"Don't start that, you promised."

"I know I did, but I can't help it. You look so beautiful, and I abandoned you, and I've missed you. Tell me everything," Amy said, thinking of Walter and hoping it didn't show.

"I have something to tell you you're not going to like."

"What?"

"Well, first, take a good look. I'm fine, all right?"

"Should I sit down?"

"Yes." Amy sat down on the bed with her coat on, and Jill told her about MacDuff. As the story unfolded, Amy grew still, and when Jill described the attack, she had both hands over her mouth.

"Oh god."

"No, Mom. It's all right."

"How could it be?"

"Everything I had done to try to protect myself failed, and then I was saved because of one tiny thing I did months ago, some mystery I'll never understand."

Amy was beginning to recover from her panic. She couldn't take her eyes from Jill's face. Jill looked so calm. So free of fear.

"Maybe I should have left town years ago," said Amy. "What's happened to him? The hero?"

"One of Dad's wicked Republican friends owns midtown. He gave him a job. Dad's got him doing the rounds of fancy doctors, trying to fix him."

"So Noah knows this whole story?"

"Not about the ball of light. But I went home for a week or two right after the attack. I was afraid I was going to need another stretch in the hat factory."

"And Noah took care of you?"

"He came home early every night. He sat with me in the study, and made me eat, if you can believe it. We talked. One night I made him watch *Clueless*."

"My god."

"I know. The next night, he made me watch *High Society*. He's different," Jill said. "It's really shaken him up. I don't think he knew that you could leave."

There was a silence.

"Show me what you're going to wear to the dinner," Amy said. She stood up and went to the closet. "Jill! You brought this?"

She came out with a long soft dress of black wool crepe.

"Do you mind?"

"But does it fit you?"

"Not the way it fits you. But without the belt, it's okay."

Amy stood looking at her daughter. Size twelve, maybe ten. She looked like a different person. Amy wondered what she'd think of Walter.

* * *

In the middle of the afternoon, Laurie arrived. It was amazing to Jill to see her surrounded by handlers, dressed in a suit with big shoulders. Laurie cut through the chaos in the room to give Jill a hug.

"Thank you for being here, little one. We've been missing you."

"Do you need to be reminded you are Only a Woman?"

"No, I've got that nailed down for the moment. There's a serious chance I'm going to lose the primary. Little one—what *have* you been doing to yourself? You're wasting away! No wait, no wait, I know what I'm supposed to say. Just Don't Lose Too Much!" And they both roared with laughter.

Jill was disappointed not to see more of Laurie, and slightly appalled at the way she was scheduled. She seemed to have no time to herself, and hardly time to sleep. But she enjoyed watching her mother fit into the group around Laurie. They *were* a team. She began to think she'd ask for a summer job, if they were still in the race by summer.

By nightfall, the ballroom of the hotel was as ready as it would ever be, and Jill knew more about the logistics of dinner for three hundred than she had ever wanted to know. There was a rumor the President would drop by during the cocktail hour, and the Secret Service was driving everybody crazy. Jill, already dressed, sat nervously on the bed playing Canfield and waiting for her mother.

Amy came out of the bathroom still blotting her mascara. Jill stood up to be admired.

"Is it all right?"

"Honey. You look marvelous." And she did.

The President did not manage to appear at the cocktail party. But the ladies of the Senate turned out to a woman, and Laurie looked radiant. She was standing in the middle of the room with Senator Lorenz. Jill, nursing a glass of Evian in the corner, saw Laurie change color. A tall man, slim, with thinning dark hair and deep-set eyes, had come in by himself and made his way to Senator Lorenz.

"Well, hello, John," the senator said, with obvious pleasure. The man called John seemed to blush, a surprising and very appealing thing for a man to do. Then he smiled, and that was even nicer. Clearly, he was fond of Senator Lorenz.

"This is the shyest man in the Cabinet," the senator said to Laurie. "And absolutely the smartest. You never go to parties, John. What are you doing here?"

"Laurie's an old friend," he said. Senator Lorenz looked with surprise and interest at Laurie.

The man had turned to Laurie and taken her hand. He held it, and after a moment made a small courtly bow.

"John," said Laurie. She seemed quite tongue-tied.

He said, "It's nice to see you again."

"And you," said Laurie. She was suddenly wearing a huge smile.

*I*t's complete crap, of course," Carter said to DeeAnne. Carter was pacing up and down in the corner closet they called the Conference Room. DeeAnne and Mae Ruth watched her. "Nix has a perfect legal right to file that lien, to be sure he gets paid. They're just pissed that he got there first."

"Well, of course," said DeeAnne. DeeAnne had recently had an eye tuck and the top half of her face was all swollen. She was working out of the Conference Room instead of in the outer office, and she wore immense dark glasses that covered most of her face and made her look like a bug, with her trim little close-cropped head on her long stalk of a neck. To create a diversion from her battered eyes she had painted her lips and fingernails the color of eggplant.

"They've registered the indictments . . . they're in the permanent record. We're all getting our pictures in the paper."

"I hope they spell the name of the agency right," said Leesa.

"This isn't funny!" Carter snapped.

DeeAnne and Mae Ruth looked at each other. Mae Ruth shifted her substantial bulk in her chair. She was wearing a flowered dress, an outfit she favored because she claimed it made her blend in with the furniture. "I can stake a building lobby for hours and nobody knows I'm there. I decide to walk down the hall, they say, 'There go one of the sofas, heading for the ladies' room.'" Her daughter Romie was a suppler, bouncier version of Mae Ruth, but she too would likely be a woman of serious size some day.

"Who's representing you?"

"Oh, Nix is taking care of that. That's not the point. The point is . . ."

"What?"

"The point is, I was planning to file adoption papers."

DeeAnne took a deep breath and let it out through her nostrils. Mae Ruth shifted in her chair again, and uncrossed her ankles.

"Flora? You going to adopt her legally?"

Carter stopped racketing around the room and faced her.

"Yes, I was planning to. Did you think I wasn't?"

There was a silence.

"I thought you were looking for the aunt. Shanti's sister," Mae Ruth said.

"I am. I've run all the arrest records. I've sent her picture to Vice in New York. They haven't turned her up yet."

"I thought you were going to New York yourself to look for her," said DeeAnne.

"I am, if I have to. I thought it would be easier than it's turned out. But in the meantime . . . so what? I mean, so what if I find her or if I don't? Are you saying you think a junkie would be a better mother than I am, just because she's a relative?"

"No," said DeeAnne. "I wouldn't say that at all, I think you're a fine mother. But I do think the sister's got some rights in the case. And so does Flora. I think the time will come when Flora's friends are all going to be having breasts and fighting with their parents and getting into their identities." She pronounced it "I-Dent-It-Ees." "And all the kids who look like Flora are going to have hip young mamas watching *Fresh Prince* with them, and reading to them about Harriet Tubman, and Flora's going to be coming home to this sixty-year-old white woman who's going 'Why you wearing your hair like that?'"

"I never would."

"And she's going to be saying, 'You mean my mama had a sister, who looked like her, and looked like me, and you didn't try to find her?'"

There was a long silence. Carter looked at Mae Ruth, and found that her friend was looking back, full of thoughts she'd been storing on this subject for a while now. She sat down.

"This is a motherless child," said Carter. She was surprised her voice was so steady. "And fatherless."

"I understand that. And I think you've given her a shot at being a healthy human being again someday, where if she'd been hauled off to some foster home she might never have been all right."

"Or she might have been fine . . ." said Mae Ruth. "My oldest girl's husband, he was raised in a foster family and he's a fine young man."

Carter sat, silent. She thought about her own family, with her one brother so much older than she, and with so little in common. She could say that she herself had been practically an only child of older parents, and she was all right . . . (right?) Or she could admit how jealous she had been of her friend Chrissy Cuddeback, with her crowded, noisy house full of brothers and sisters, and how she'd spent so much time with them that she made her mother cry by saying she wanted to take confirmation classes with Chrissy. She hadn't meant to make her mother cry, she just hadn't been real clear on the fact that taking Holy Communion was an issue if your family was Jewish.

"Flora loves me," said Carter.

"Without question," said DeeAnne. And Mae Ruth nodded.

"But I still wouldn't file adoption papers while you're under indictment," said DeeAnne.

"I *know* that," Carter snapped.

Laurie came back from Washington with about half the money she needed for the last weeks of the primary campaign. The PACs were taking a wait-and-see attitude; Idaho was such a Republican stronghold there were only thirteen Democrats in the whole state legislature. If Laurie could beat Prince, they'd get serious about whether she had a shot at Turnbull. Meanwhile, the Republican Senate Campaign Committee had sponsored a negative ad: Laurie Lopez, a very nice woman who ought to be home with her children.

To make matters worse, Laurie had caught a rotten cold on the plane coming back from Washington. She'd been going on four hours sleep a night for a month, eating take-out food and rubber chicken dinners. In the warmth of May, when even in the Idaho mountains the last patches of crusty snow were gone and the shivery aspens were leafing out, an astonishing baby-green color only seen in spring, Laurie's infection turned into walking pneumonia, and her doctor said if she didn't go home to bed and stay there, he was going to put her in the hospital.

The mood at the Boise headquarters was tense. Altogether, there was the unshakable impression in the countryside that Laurie was the candidate of the big city, of overpaid yuppie scum. Even the independent candidate, Carrol Coney, was gaining ground on her; he had taken to campaigning from the back of a mule, town to town, and the press was loving it.

"We have to keep running against Turnbull," Lynn urged many times a day. "We have to ignore Prince and Coney."

"It's getting hard to do, with the numbers Prince is getting. If he keeps climbing at this rate, he'll have us."

Laurie was back on the stump three days after the doctor sent her to bed.

"You look like a dead lily on toast," said Amy.

"I'm on drugs," said Laurie. "Don't tell the children." From that moment on, she didn't stop, that Amy could see. She was up and out at seven every morning, speaking at prayer breakfasts, visiting sewing circles, standing in shopping malls in the rain shaking hands. Prince was invited to give the Boise State University graduation speech. Laurie staged an event at a high school in Grangeville; nobody came.

Turnbull didn't even bother to campaign in person; he stayed in Washington until two days before the primary. But his ads were everywhere. Jimbo Turnbull gets things done. Jimbo Turnbull—when experience counts. Jimbo Turnbull. Jimbo Turnbull. Seniority. Seniors for Turnbull. Jimbo Turnbull, family man. Jimbo Knows You, and He Knows How.

Some of the ads were paid for by Turnbull's war chest, and an equal number by the Republican Senate Campaign Committee. In the last week before the vote, the national press showed up. Laurie finally got some key endorsements, from the *Post Register* and the Lewiston *Tribune*, and she seemed to stop sleeping at all. She was out in public all the time, working restaurants, visiting feedlots, talking with voters at the Iris Show in Nampa, shaking hands.

She had her groupies. There were the middle-aged women who had loved her husband. There were the college kids, in droves. The national press did stories about her political legacy, and the Sunday *New York Times* did a piece on the plane crash that had killed Roberto. Jimbo Turnbull took to calling Laurie Sissy, a childhood name no one had ever used except her brothers. The press loved it, and took to calling her Sissy too, so she sounded like a little girl doing battle with the grown-ups.

On election night, the ska band in the party room for Laurie's young supporters was loud, which was probably an advantage. Next door in the room where the press and the grown-ups were gathered, people were drinking wine out of plastic cups and saying brittle things to each other. The volunteers had been working like animals all day, manning the phones, driving vans of voters to and from the polling places. They could not believe that after all their effort they could fail. But the exit polls were terrifying. Although any number of local races were called within minutes of the close of voting, the Democratic Senate race showed Laurie and Lloyd Prince within half a percent of each other. In rural areas Prince was leading strongly, and in Boise, Moscow, and in Blaine County, Laurie's early numbers were not as strong as they had hoped.

Upstairs in her suite, Laurie sat with the children, and with her father and brothers and Cinder, Amy, Lynn, and Geri.

"Early days," said Hunt, looking defeated. Bliss was drinking vodka. The twins were playing slapjack. Laurie got up suddenly about eight-thirty in the evening and went into the bedroom. When Amy went in a half hour later she was astonished to find the candidate sound asleep. Her skin was burning.

It was twelve-thirty in the morning before all three networks had declared Laurie the winner. When she went downstairs to thank her supporters, there was pandemonium. Her family lined up behind her, even the twins, who had never been up so late in their lives. She made her speech to the campaign workers and press and then went next door and made it again to the young volunteers, a great many of whom seemed to have gotten completely drunk or fallen in love or both. Then Laurie went back upstairs to her bedroom and shut the door.

The next morning she was up in time to do the morning television shows. She spent the day thanking supporters and talking to the print press; she stayed up to do *Nightline* from a local news studio. The day after that she was checked into the hospital and it was ten days before her doctor let her out again. By then, she said, she had an entirely new angle on health care.

And Lloyd Prince had announced that he would run as an independent for the Senate in the general election.

Hello, stranger. wrote Sweet2. The InstantMessage appeared in the middle of Jill's screen while she was reading an article about Rush Limbaugh on-line.

Hello! Where have *you* been? Jill answered.

I lost control of my computer. came the answer.

????? Jill returned.

It's a long story. What are you doing up so late?

I've been on the net, watching elections returns. Jill tapped.

What election? Where?

The Idaho primary. My mom is working for Laura Lopez.

Cool! Did she win?

The results still hadn't posted last time I looked.

It's past midnight in Idaho. typed Sweet2.
Let's go look again. What's the address?

Jill typed in the website address, and Sweet2 answered,

I'll meet you there.

Jill clicked back into the Internet and read a jubilant announcement, entered onto the net by (though she didn't know it) an ecstatic and completely drunk Aaron Jackson.

> **All three networks project that Laura Lopez has beaten Lloyd Prince in the Democratic Primary!!!! She is expected downstairs to address her suporters momo soon.**

Ajax had drunk an entire bottle of red wine since suppertime and been kissing Sheila Detweiler for the last hour, and the combined effect of these stimuli had been to lower his IQ down to around his earlobes.

In New York City, Jill returned to her screen to find a message from Sweet2:

> **That's so cool!!!**
>
> **I am psyched, completely!**
>
> **We should celebrate!!**
>
> **Too bad it's three in the morning.**
>
> **Do you want to go hear Woody Allen play some Monday?**

Jill stopped. This was in fact something she had always wanted to do, but hadn't had anyone to go with. She had had no intention of setting another date with Colleen, but . . .

> **Yes.** she typed.
> **I absolutely do.**
>
> **Cool!** answered Colleen.

*I*n mid-June, Rae's sister Velma died. She'd been in Florida, in a condo in Boca Raton. Rae hadn't seen her in almost a year, but they had been planning to leave on a cruise together in two weeks' time, through the islands of Greece and Turkey. Instead Rae was packing for a hot-weather funeral.

Velma had left no instructions for a service or interment. The family plot in Buffalo where their parents were buried had room for her, but none of the family had been in Buffalo for thirty years. Velma's sons were stolid and silent at the condo where they gathered. Velma's daughter, Cookie, four times married and looking now so much like her mother that it gave Rae a start when she walked into the room, was bereft. She had planned a service to be conducted on the beach at sunrise.

Rae was glad of the company of Leon and Harriet and her grand-children. In the predawn darkness her son-in-law made sure there were folding chairs brought out and placed in the sand, and Harriet, foreseeing how cold it would be at dawn, had brought her mother an extra shawl. Rae could tell that her daughter was annoyed at the cousins and worried that she would be undone by the chill and the early hour. On top of that was the shock of losing the last person on earth who remembered what she remembered about Christmas in Buffalo, when they both believed in Santa Claus.

In truth, Rae *was* cold to the bone and dazed by jet lag; in California, it was two in the morning. But it was lovely to see the sun come up over the horizon of the sea, and sweet, she thought, when the church soprano Cookie had hired sang "Somewhere Over the Rainbow."

Cookie sobbed. Rae was dry-eyed and numb. They all had been given Sweetheart roses to hold during the service, and at the end, they were instructed to go to the water's edge and, silently saying a last farewell, to throw the flowers into the dawn. The surf cast them right back up onto the sand, along with bottle caps and plastic soda can holders and a rim of sticky yellow foam scum, which might not have been exactly the image Cookie had envisioned. Rae insisted that Velma would have liked it. Harriet took her back to her hotel and put her to bed. She slept until past lunchtime.

"Will you go on your cruise by yourself, Missus?" James asked her as he brought her coffee. Rae was having lunch on a tray in the sun in the side garden a day or two after she got back from Florida. She wasn't reading or listening to music; she was just sitting in the sun like an old person, chewing and staring into space.

"I don't think so," she said. "But it's all paid for—why don't you and Doreen go?"

James laughed.

"No, why not? It's a shame to waste it. I'll be fine here, Cook will take care of me. You were going to be on vacation those weeks anyway, weren't you?"

James thanked her, but made excuses. The truth was, he was worried about Rae. He and Doreen knew what it was like to be far away from home and family and childhood friends, cut off forever. There had been many, many nights of tears. Doreen had been unable to visit her father's grave in Canton; she had not even known of his death until a month after the fact. Now it had happened to Rae. She was separated not by distance but by time from a world she missed. She wasn't as lucky as they were; they at least had each other. She had a lot, but Doreen and James talked to each other in quiet voices in the kitchen about what she didn't have.

"It's too much death," James said. "Mr. Strouse. Winston Churchill.

Now the last sister." Doreen nodded. For the first time, they could see at moments the effort it cost her to be gay. When no one was with her, she seemed to be visibly smaller. Her eyes didn't shine. She looked old.

"She may recover," said Doreen, in a way that James knew meant that she also might not. Doreen had a doctor aunt in China. Aunt said she could always tell when a person was beginning to die. She said she didn't even have to see the patient; she could see it in the faces of the relatives.

A week or two passed. Rae was settling into a new routine. It was quieter. Many of her friends had already begun to scatter for the summer. One had a house in southern France and left in May. A number of others moved out to Stinson Beach. Some had houses in Napa. San Francisco was gray and windy in the summer and the wind could grate on your nerves.

"I don't like it," Doreen said.

"You could call Walter or Harriet," James said. "Your brother and sister."

Doreen made a face. "I hear her talk to them on the phone. They don't know anything's wrong."

"My father was ninety-three when he died, and he died happy, but that was different. He had a job," James said. His father had been a master tailor, and he'd kept sharp and busy until the end of his life. Only arthritis in his hands had slowed him down, and it never entirely stopped him.

"That's what *she* needs. She needs a job." Doreen went to the stove to heat water for tea.

"Uh-huh," said James. Doreen turned around and looked at him.

"What?"

"Right. She needs a job."

In the solarium Rae was thinking about The Cloisters. She was thinking she would like to just move there and take the veil. Everything would be decided for her. Every morning she would wake up and her schedule would be planned. Every week a new raft of people to meet would arrive.

But then again, every week the last group would leave, going back out to sea, to be in the midst of life, while she sat on the beach in the dry sea scum, like Velma's roses.

There were moments, increasing in number during the day, when she felt hopeless.

"Missus," said James.

He was standing in the door of the television room. Rae was sitting there in the chair where Albie used to sit. She was wearing bedroom slippers even though it was almost lunchtime. She had not done her exercises yet today, and had not even really finished dressing. It was too early to turn on the television. To turn it on in the morning would be like drinking alone. She was sitting in there, looking at the *TV Guide*, thinking about Albie and about what she would watch this afternoon.

James looked as if he had something weighty to say. He had his hands behind his back and the sort of expression on his face that people wear when they are about to deliver a memorized speech.

"Yes, dear?"

"I have been thinking," he announced.

"Come in, dear. Sit down."

James came in. After a moment, he decided he would sit down. He perched on the edge of the love seat across from her.

"Missus, you asked me once what I wanted to do."

"You said you wanted to be a terrorist, didn't you?"

"Activist, yes . . . "

"Have you changed your mind?"

"No, but I have found something else that attracts me as well."

"Have you!"

She looked at him with the old spark. Aha! Something interesting!

"Yes. I have."

"Well, spit it out. I'm all ears." She stuffed a pillow behind her back and settled into the couch.

"I would like to take you to see something, if you are free."

"Of course I'm free. But will you tell me what it is? Do I need my hiking boots?"

He smiled.

"It's a housing place. Project. In Oakland."

"A housing project. Well, this is very mysterious, James. Am I going to buy it?"

"We will talk about it."

"This is something you turned up in your research?"

"Yes."

"A public project?"

"No."

There was a pause. Rae said, "This is rather fun, like playing Twenty Questions."

"Twenty Questions?"

"It's a game. I'll teach it to you in the car. Should we go right now?"

"Right now would be fine with me if you are not busy."

She looked at her watch. "I don't think we'll get back in time for lunch if we leave right now . . . "

"I thought I would take you to McDonald's on the way home."

"Oh, you devil," said Rae. James had discovered that she loved driving up to the window and buying french fries and a milkshake without even getting out of the car.

On the way, over the Bay Bridge, she explained Twenty Questions to him. She went first, and it took him only nine guesses to discover that she was Patsy Cline. Then he took a turn and she was furious when she asked all twenty questions and wasn't even close, except that she knew he was mineral. "I give up. What are you?"

"A car wash," he said.

"I'm never playing with you again." James was very pleased with himself.

"I surmise you have been to this place before," she said after a while. They had passed the downtown and were heading out toward the piers.

"Yes, I've been here several times. Dona Reo thought we might want to know about it. It's a friend of hers who runs it." Rae liked to have James check back periodically with the people to whom they had given money, to see how it was used, and if it had helped. He had early morning coffee with Dona about once a month now.

After the tour, James bought Rae a Big Mac and fries and a chocolate milkshake. She waited until she had eaten, and gotten the catsup off her fingers and reapplied her lipstick before she said, "Okay, James. I'm waiting for the other shoe to drop."

James was busy with his Filet-O-Fish. "He has an interesting idea, yes? Village life. The very old together with the very young. Everyone responsible to the others. Clear rules, a strong leader. The social contract made visible."

"James, you are so American I'm faint with pride. You've become a Utopian. Now I'm waiting to hear what it is you have in mind for me. Am I going to buy a project?"

"You could."

She looked at him. He was keeping his eyes on the road, picking his way through the Oakland streets.

"I could, but . . . ?"

"You could. But I have spent some little time discussing it with Ralph. His idea is working, but there are frustrations. Those buildings were not designed with his theory in mind. The nursery rooms are low and there's not much light. The basketball court should not be in the middle, where the midnight games disturb people sleeping. The Town Meeting and martial arts rooms should be somewhere light, instead of in basements, which are nasty . . . "

"You mean you want me to *build* a housing project?" She thought she was prepared, but this idea was so big it actually shocked her.

"It would be best," he said primly, "if we are really going to prove something."

She stared at him.

"Well, but . . . but, James! That's a huge job! It would take years! We'd have to find the right site, choose an architect, hire urban planners, I wouldn't wonder . . . "

"I hadn't thought of that," he said. "I suppose we would have to do all those things . . . "

$\mathcal{I}$t was a hot night for June in Los Angeles. Aunt Sallie Spear was eating tuna salad on iceberg lettuce. She had it on a tray in her parlor where she could see the television. There had been another arson of a black church, this one in Alabama. She was watching the pictures of the pastor picking his way through the rubble, followed by a camera crew. You could see a charred triangle of wood sticking up like a stalagmite that was all that was left of the organ. The pastor was crying.

She knew what that was like.

She had taken her girdle off before she sat down to eat. Her hose were rolled down to her ankles. She was watching the President of the United States call for an end to these burnings. The President was sitting in his suit at his desk, signing something. Calling for an end to this cruel and cowardly arson. Good luck to you, she thought. She pushed her food around on the plate with her fork, eating slowly. Each bite was like a chapter in a story she was reading. When the plate was empty, and the news was over, there would be nothing to do with the long hot evening until it was time to climb the stairs with her girdle in her hand and finish undressing. No point in rushing.

She had an air conditioner in the kitchen. She meant to get another one for this room, but to tell the truth, you didn't need it that often. She thought about taking the bus to Sears and Roebuck and getting just a little one, but she always thought of it at times like this, at the end of a day, the beginning of a long hot night. She didn't mind hot days. Hot nights she didn't care for. Hot days you could share, but on a hot night, lying awake, you were alone, even if you were a little child in the same room with your brothers and sisters. If you were an old lady with your brothers and sisters all buried, even more so.

Here came the weatherman. There were wildfires burning in Idaho, some place called Ada County. That fire was started by lightning thought the weatherman; it had been dry in Ada County. Two hundred and fifty acres were burned or burning. Churches. Acres. She would like to see Idaho, but if she had to choose, she would rather live beside the burned-down black church in Alabama than the burned-down acres of Ada County. At her age, you had to stay close to what felt like home.

When the news was over, she turned off the set and went into the kitchen to get another glass of decaffeinated ice tea. She went back into the front parlor and sat there, with her plate of supper in front of her on a folding TV table. Mayonnaise seemed to be melting off her tuna salad and pooling under the lettuce. The doorbell rang.

It was two weeks away from the longest day of the year, so it was plenty light still outside. Nevertheless, Aunt Sallie thought of this as night. She was in for the night, doors locked. Not expecting any doorbells. She looked from her chair toward the hallway, and took a big drink of her ice tea. She wasn't going to answer the door with a mouthful of tuna fish. Even if she was going to be gunned down, she wanted a clean mouth, and it was more likely she was going to see some little child selling cookies, or Pastor Campbell, someone she might want to smile at.

The doorbell rang again. Aunt Sallie dabbed her lips with her paper napkin and lifted the TV table to the side. She walked to the door, listening to the sound of her own footsteps.

Now. What was the best way to do this? She could call out, "Who's there?"

But if it was somebody bad, why would they answer honestly? And if it was somebody good, they would feel as if they were interrupting or frightening her. She would have to look for herself.

Listening to the sound she was making, as if she were watching a movie, she slid the bolt above the doorknob to the side. *Kachink.* She turned the key that slid the door latch back into its socket inside the door. *Chunk.* She turned the knob and opened the door, only as far as the chain would allow, about an inch and a half. *Clink.*

No knives or guns or terrible hands came forcing their way through the crack, though she was ready to fling her considerable weight against the door to close it again if they did. She'd break fingers if she had to. But no. Now the tricky part. She had to move sideways so she could look out the door, and that would put her in the way of a blade or a bullet, if they were out there. She tried to maneuver so most of her body stayed behind the door. She craned her neck over to the right, holding her balance by keeping her hand on the doorknob and one foot braced against the bottom of the door. She got one eye all the way out and in the clear, so it could see through the crack to the doorbell ringer.

Standing on her porch, on her actual doormat, was a Negro girl. She was in shadow, but you could see that she was pale and yellow and bony. She had a lot of brown freckles on her pasty skin. Her hair had been dyed orange, but was growing out. It was brushed back against her skull and tied in back at the nape of her neck. She had been looking at the street when Aunt Sallie first clapped her eye on her, but now she had turned back to the door and was looking in at the old eyes watching her. Behind her, on the porch, there was a small, soft bag, more like a gym bag than a suitcase. A yellow leather jacket lay across it.

"Aunt Sallie?" said the girl. "It's Delia Amos."

There was a fund-raising event every day that summer in Idaho, sometimes two. Jimbo Turnbull was back. He rode an elephant into downtown Boise when the circus arrived. The local press rallied round. All three candidates appeared at the Rocky Mountain Oyster Feed and Fun Day in Eagle. The KBCI-TV crew caught up with Laurie just as Jimbo was downing his third barbecued oyster and laughing with a crowd of good old boys.

"Senator Turnbull," said the reporter, perky in her pink blazer, "there are a lot of visitors here today who might not be familiar with all our, uh, our local customs. Would you mind telling us what these are that you're eating?"

He looked at the camera rather than at her. His meat. His medium. "A little way to the east they call these prairie oysters, but this here is the place to get them done right."

"Now I understand that these are not actually—seafood, is that right?"

"You see an ocean around here?" Guffaw, guffaw. The chorus of good old boys in the background had seen this routine year after year. "No, I believe the polite way to say it is *Bull's Testicles*." Har har HAR HAR har.

"I understand they're being served in a variety of ways today . . ." The reporter played up to them.

"That's right. Used to be you'd have just your oyster grilled over an open fire. But nowadays, you've got your barbecued, got Cajun, probly can get them with hollandaise down the line. We're continental."

343

"With mole sauce," someone called from behind him.

"Yep, probably with mole sauce," Jimbo agreed. Mole sauce seemed to amuse the boys.

Laurie Lopez arrived flanked by several staffers. The reporter said, "We found Judge Lopez in the crowd and asked her to join us. Judge Lopez, are you a fan of these . . . oysters?"

"Sissy can't eat these, they'd put hair on her chest," boomed Turnbull.

"I grew up on a ranch," Laurie said, as if that meant she'd eaten them all the time. "I thought I'd try the Cajun ones." Jimbo's crew chortled with surprise and interest.

Jimbo stood back, hands on hips, wearing a huge grin. Someone handed Laurie a paper plate bearing a spice-crusted lump of animal protein looking revoltingly like what it was.

She speared it with a fork, lifted it to her mouth, and took a large bite. Hannah, the pretty blonde staffer from Idaho State, hid her eyes against the senior staffer's shoulder. "She's chewing," he whispered to Hannah. "She's swallowing . . . she's got it down."

"How was that, Judge Lopez?" chirped the reporter. She looked as if she would love it if Laurie threw up.

Laurie smiled broadly and said, "Great. I like them spicy." Jimbo and his gang were hooting. Har har har.

"Oh, Mr. Prince," cried the reporter. "We're having a caucus here, on Rocky Mountain oysters!"

Lloyd Prince was being pushed through the crowd by his ten-year-old daughter. His son was beside him, and his wheelchair was covered with campaign posters. Behind him came staffers carrying canvas bags of bumper stickers and "Prince for Senate" buttons.

"Would you care to join us?" cried the reporter. The cameras were now on Prince. He looked up at the reporter with a quizzical smile.

"You mean, would I like to *eat* one? Do you know what they are, young lady?"

"Well, yes, I do . . ." She was standing there with dead air all around her, unsure of what to say next.

"Have a poster," said Prince's daughter, and someone handed one to the reporter.

"Thank you so much," she said and giggled, and held it for the camera as Prince was wheeled away.

Laurie had to stop in the fairgrounds john and brush her teeth. Then they marched for what seemed like miles along rows of cars under dusty sun. When they finally found the campaign station wagon, someone had covered the "Lopez for Senate" bumper sticker with one that read "Jimbo = Winner." All along the rows, every car in the fairgrounds field had decided to vote for the incumbent.

"Look at that! Look, that's a *great* moment!" crowed Walter. They were watching the evening news where Laurie was taking her bite, with a smile.

"Look at that, she doesn't turn a hair! Laurie," cried Lynn, "we can use that in a spot!"

"Look at Turnbull in the background, he's gaping!"

"He can't believe she's doing it!"

"I've decided to vote for Lloyd Prince," said Laurie. "I'm going to find Amy and we're going to go get drunk." Walter watched her leave the room.

Jill walked into the lobby of the hotel Colleen referred to as "The Le Parker Meridien." It was about nine-thirty on a July night, and as always on nights when Woody played, the jazz room was packed. No way they could get a table, she was told, but she could stand at the bar. (A pretty girl alone at the bar was always good for business, as long as she didn't make commercial arrangements with other patrons.)

Jill didn't think of herself as a pretty girl, although tonight she was wearing an ancient Halston of her mother's that was downright slinky. She thought of herself as a sort of dumpling with legs. A knish. Nothing anyone was going to look at anyway. This is no doubt what prevented her from noticing that several men looked at her more than once as she made her way across the room to wait at the bar for Colleen.

She ordered a glass of wine and stood watching the door. A half hour passed; a man left with his date, and Jill got a seat. A man in a linen jacket and a shirt with no collar, a little too chic for Wall Street and a little too old for Jill, tried to buy her a drink. She explained that she was waiting for a friend.

The set began. She bought another glass of wine and thought, This, Colleen, really, is beginning to be a drag. A man moved to the seat beside her and smiled. She smiled back. Between numbers he tried to ask her a question, but after she had shouted, "I'm sorry, what?" at him three times he gave up. The set lasted forty minutes, and the applause was wild. Finally the band left the stage.

There was some turnover at the bar. Jill was nursing her drink. She looked at her watch. As soon as she finished this one, she was going. And this was the last time she was going to fall for this.

A boy of perhaps twenty, wearing chinos and a crisp blue shirt, stepped up to the bar beside her and ordered a beer. He had beautiful long eyelashes, she noticed in her brief glance. He took his beer, took a sip, and then said to her, "You look like you're ready for another."

"No. I mean, no thanks, I'm waiting for someone."

"I know. You're waiting for me."

Jill rolled her eyes. "Nice try." My, aren't we sophisticated, she said to herself at the same time. Where did that come from? I've got to get out of here.

"No," he said seriously, "you actually are waiting for me."

Something in the way he said it made her turn to stare. He nodded slightly.

"Oh, no," she said. "You're not." She dropped her head into her hands and stared at the wood of the bar through her fingers. Then she looked up at him. "Is this supposed to be cute?"

"Could we walk around the block?"

They pushed their way out through the crowd and into the bright hotel lobby. They went out to Fifty-seventh Street. "I'm sorry I was late—I couldn't talk to you once the set started; I can't hear more than one thing at a time."

She stared at him. He smiled slightly, and pointed to his ears. He was wearing fairly sizable hearing aids.

"I can't sort sound. I can hear the music with these turned up, but I can't hear anything else."

"And your name is Colleen."

"No, my name is Tom. Colleen is my sister. I started signing on with her computer because I didn't know how to change the screen name. She was major pissed when she got the bill."

"How did you know her password?"

"I guessed. It had to be either her boyfriend's address, or his phone number or his birthday. It took a while, but I had a while."

"Was I ever talking to her when I talked to Sweet2?"

"No, it was always me. She was in Europe. Her boyfriend was paying her Visa bills for her while she was gone."

They were walking in the balmy night. Amy's sleeveless dress was fluid and cool on Jill, but she suddenly had a vision of herself playing dress up. It was one thing to go meet a girlfriend who would laugh at the thought of raiding your mother's closet. Her sense of irritation returned.

"So now that she's back, how did you write to me?"

"I finally bought a pathetic old Apple with a Stone Age modem, but it took me all this time to earn the money. Colleen changed her screen name and everything. So I went on being Sweet2."

"So, you do this often?"

"Meet an on-line friend? No. Never. Well, the only other time was the time we went to Carla's."

"What do you mean 'we'?"

"I was there."

"*Where?*"

"At the bar. You weren't looking for me, and I was upset that you were so pretty. When I saw you I didn't have the nerve to . . . "

"You *saw* me?"

"In your beautiful Coke bottle coat, yes. I'd been hoping you'd be some awful dumpy thing and we could be friends."

Jill began to laugh.

"You have no idea how funny this is," she said. The laughter was boiling out of her, a little fueled by the fact that she believed him, and was beginning to remember how many long, charming, unguarded letters she'd gotten from him, how much she liked him. Him.

"We can go back to being on-line pals, if you want. I just wanted you to know, and this was the only way I could think of to tell you."

"Really," she said, still laughing. "You have no idea."

"Do you want to go home?"

"Oh, eventually. Let's walk."

W hen Carter drove up to her house after work the second week in July, she found her worst nightmare sitting in the driveway.

It was Reverend Campbell's car. Reverend Campbell himself was sitting at the wheel. Aunt Sallie Spear was sitting in the front seat beside him. There was a girl in the backseat. They were all sitting quietly staring forward like people at a drive-in movie, except what they were looking at was her garage door.

Carter got out of the Brown Bomber. She walked around to the driver's side of the waiting car, and the minister rolled down the window.

"Good evening, Reverend Campbell," she said.

"Good evening. We came to pay you a visit."

"Good evening, Aunt Sallie. Would you like to come in the house?"

"Yes, we would, if it's not inconvenient."

"Not at all. Let me just get the baby."

Carter went back to the Bomber, where Flora was strapped into her triple-A-rated crash-proof kiddie seat in the back. Carter unclasped the belts that held her in, and lifted her down. Flora took Carter's hand and walked with her up the front steps, where the three visitors were waiting. Flora was wearing little OshKosh overalls and pink sneakers. She had little pink wooden beads on the elastics that held her braids. She was bright-eyed and curious.

Carter unlocked the door, and led her visitors into the living room. Julia had been there that day, thank god, and the place was immaculate.

"Can I get you anything?" Carter asked, praying they would say no. Her heart was pounding so hard she wanted to sit down before it exploded.

Fortunately they all murmured that they wanted no refreshments. They made their way into the living room and chose places to sit. Aunt Sallie and Reverend Campbell sat on either side of the fireplace in her two good armchairs. Carter sat on one end of the couch, facing them, and Flora crawled up and snuggled beside her. The third one, the girl, sat down at the other end of the couch. Carter couldn't look at her. She didn't want to know.

"Carter," said Reverend Campbell, "we came to introduce you to Delia Amos."

Blood roared in Carter's ears. She thought she really might faint, though she had never fainted in her life. She stopped being able to see.

This must have lasted a much shorter time than it felt like. When she could, Carter turned to the girl, and saw Shanti's eyes. The rest of this girl was younger, less healthy. She had much lighter skin. Flora was looking at her, curious.

"Delia," said Carter.

"Yes," said the girl.

"They found you?"

"She appeared," said Aunt Sallie. "She's been home a few weeks, staying with me. We thought it was time she met the baby."

"Yes, indeed," said Carter. "Flora, this is your Aunt Delia. This is your mommy's sister. She was away, but she's come home."

Flora looked up at Carter. She was interested, but wary.

"Can you shake hands?" Carter asked her.

Flora looked at Delia. She looked back up at Carter.

"Can you give her five?"

Delia held her palm facing out, across from Flora. Flora turned to her, and solemnly slapped the upraised hand.

There was a silence. Carter was waiting for them to say, "So hand her over, we're taking her home." What would she do? Run for it? Her car was blocking theirs, she could scoop the baby up and pound off on foot. Beat them up? Call a lawyer?

* * *

"So, you just . . . or did somebody?"

"I just . . ." said Delia.

"She appeared," said Aunt Sallie at the same time. "She came to my door."

"Did you know we'd been looking for you?" Carter managed to ask. What was this? When were they going to get to it? She couldn't think. Her brain felt full of sand; she could feel the grinding as the cells tried to move. She could only smell Flora's skin.

"Tell her your story," said the minister. Delia looked from him to Aunt Sallie. She looked at Carter. She looked back at the minister.

"Should the baby stay?"

"Yes," he said. "I think so."

Then they all waited. Delia was wearing a long-sleeved cotton sweater over a summer dress. The dress was yellow. Her hair was cut close to her head, neat and dark. Her nails were short and clean. She wore no jewelry.

"I was in New York," she began. "I'd been there about a year."

"I'd been looking for you in San Francisco."

"I know. Shanti came up there once, looking for me. I left with a man . . . he had a car. He said he had friends in the movie business."

That you would move from L.A. to San Francisco and then New York to get into the movie business did not strike Carter as logical, but this girl was young. We all need euphemisms.

"I was working there. I was doing what I knew how to do. I made pretty good money, I lived uptown. I kept thinking at first that this was the Big Apple, where nobody knew me. Wasn't any reason things shouldn't start to go my way, you know what I'm saying? I was waiting for a break. Meanwhile, some things broke the wrong way. The man I traveled with—he didn't turn out to know much about the movie business, but he did meet Spike Lee once. Spike wasn't in town though. He had friends here and there he'd introduce me to, but . . . we were using, you probably guessed. I was working, he wasn't. I was supporting us. Soon I realized he was seeing other girls . . . you know what I'm saying? He wasn't in the movie business, he was in the pimp business. Same old business. That was what I left Ess Eff to get away from. I mean, maybe I didn't really think I was going to wake up and be Whitney Houston, but I didn't plan on spending my life supporting some pimp when it wasn't even exclusive."

Carter could understand that. Perfectly, in fact.

"So I went out on my own. I had to move—I met another guy— you don't need to hear this whole thing. I tried to get into a program, but there was a two-year wait for a bed—I don't want to make excuses. It was dawning on me that this was my life. I was in The Life, and it wasn't going to get better. It was almost surely going to get worse. I began to know people who were dying. Dirty needles, johns who won't wear . . ." She glanced at Flora and stopped. "It doesn't matter how you get it, it's not a good way to go."

"No," said Carter.

"I have to have you understand that I was not completely in my own mind, you know what I'm saying? I didn't like where I was, or who I was, and aside from the junk, getting high with the johns was part of the job most times. I did all kinds of stuff. It does very strange things to your head."

Carter was watching Aunt Sallie and Reverend Campbell. They were listening to this calmly.

"Didn't you think of asking Shanti for help?" Carter asked.

Delia shook her head, hard. "That was the last thing. The only thing I was grateful for, the only thing in my whole life, was that no one who knew me would ever see me like that. No one I used to smart off to in high school, no one who heard my big talk, would ever see me or know. Until things broke my way, you know? Until Spike Lee cast me in his movie and I came home in a Cadillac. You know?

"Then one night I got into a taxi, and I looked into the driver's mirror, and God was staring back at me."

There was a long silence. Carter looked at the two older people. They were quiet. It was Delia's story to tell. Flora was listening. Carter could feel her breathing.

"You understand—I knew that it was Sidney James. I knew it was old Sidney from high school. I didn't know how scared I'd been of that very thing, it was like, what I was doing . . . like I wasn't really doing it if no one who knew me or knew my family knew I was doing it. . . . So there it was. It had followed me, three thousand miles, down all those dark streets. I climbed into a cab with it. I was really doing what I was doing, and there was Sidney James looking at me and seeing the truth. The eyes of God, you know what I'm saying? And I thought, This is it, this is as bad as it gets. I looked at him. He looked at me. And then he opened his mouth."

There was another silence. Carter wanted to speak, but couldn't.

Finally she said, "What happened after you left the cab?"

Delia took a deep breath. "A lot of things. I tried to run, a couple of different ways. I tried to make it pass, you know, like some stone that had gotten into my system, but it was in there, hard and real. I was so scared I thought the fear might kill me if nothing else did. You don't need to know all of it.

"I went back to San Francisco. I knew someone there who'd gotten clean by herself somehow. I used to know her when I was using; she helped people like me and I knew she would look at me like I wasn't a worthless dirt sack. I thought, If she did it, I could do it, if she'd tell me how."

Carter took a deep breath.

"So . . . you did it."

"Yes."

"What'd you do for money?"

"I worked." She caught Carter's look. "I mean, I worked. They helped me get a job. First I worked in some garden, some little farm thing that hires ex-cons. Later I waited tables."

"How long have you been clean?"

Delia rubbed her mouth with the palm of her hand. As if it scared her to even say it out loud.

"Five months."

Carter nodded. She'd been off cigarettes longer than that, and she could still feel them calling to her, singing to her, four or five times a day. She'd read that there were people who still felt the craving after years.

Delia was looking at her hands. No one knew what to say next.

"I wish Shanti were here," said Carter.

*A*ll through the summer, Laurie's numbers were creeping up. EMILY's List was behind her now, and there was a Republican Women for Laura Lopez Committee. They were running steady radio and print ads and preparing for the blitz that would begin in September. Laurie traveled to fund-raisers in Texas, Iowa, Colorado, Washington again . . . anywhere people could be made to believe that Jimbo Turnbull's long run in the Senate could be broken.

The party began to take an interest. They began to urge Laurie to attack. They wanted to capture another seat in the Senate, and they especially wanted to tip Jimbo out of the important committee seats he sat in. They wanted Laurie to campaign as The Widow; they wanted her to accuse Jimbo of killing Roberto.

"I won't do that," she said. "This isn't personal. Leave it alone."

"Cronyism! Special Interests! Business as Usual!" they insisted.

"All of that," she said. "But I don't want to win that way. There's enough at stake as it is."

She campaigned at the Firebird Raceway, she campaigned at meetings of Grandparents Acting as Parents. She campaigned hard for the Hispanic vote, which no one else in the state seemed to know was there. She delivered her message. Character. Choice. No Nuclear Waste in Idaho. She rode a bucking horse at the Western Idaho Fair in August. "Let Jimbo do *that*," she said.

"We need a vacation," said Walter.

"Let's go somewhere where nobody knows us."

"Where there are no tourists."

"Where the phone won't ring."

"What do we want to do?"

"Sleep," said Laurie.

"Sleep," said Amy. She and Walter practically had their backs to each other, they were trying so hard to avoid their eyes' meeting.

"If we sleep long enough, at the end I might read a book," said Laurie.

"Mother has a friend who owns a hotel near Cabo San Lucas," said Walter. "I'll call her."

"Tell her to come with us!" Laurie and Amy said.

Rae arranged for them to use the Directors' House of the Baja Real hotel in Cabo.

"But she won't come with us," Walter said.

"Why not?"

"She's too busy."

Amy and Laurie both looked surprised.

"You know James, my Chinese brother-in-law?"

They did.

"He's got her building her own village. She can't take a vacation, she's got meetings with fourteen architects and sixteen specialists in low-income housing."

"But isn't her birthday next week? Can't she come for that?"

"On her birthday, they're knocking down the warehouses she bought to make room for her project. There's going to be dynamite. She's got her own hard hat."

They knew it was hopeless. The three of them went off for five days, leaving Lynn in charge. For that period, not even Ajax knew where to find them.

*A*ll summer, Delia lived with Aunt Sallie Spear, and worked in the church office. She learned how to use WordPerfect and how to do spreadsheets. In the evenings, she stayed in the office and took a speed-typing course on the computer. Sometimes she helped Aunt Sallie baby-sit her grandnephew, Titus. Several times a week, she would borrow the minister's car and go visit Flora.

"I like her," said Romie, in August. Delia started coming up to the office on her lunch hour. At first Romie had been suspicious. Mae Ruth and Leesa said they liked her too.

"She's a junkie," said Carter.

"I know. I know," the others said. "She's staying clean though. She isn't running with her old crowd. She's doing everything she said she would."

"I know," said Carter. Her heart was breaking. The right thing was happening, but it was breaking her heart.

"She needs a real job," said DeeAnne. "The church is paying her pin money. She needs to get out and prove she can stand up even after you take the props away."

"That could take years, you know," said Carter. "To be sure of that." By years from now, Flora would be in school. Carter would win by default; time would make the child hers.

"She must be made of some of the same stuff as her sister," said Mae Ruth. "They didn't find her under a cabbage leaf, did they?"

"Yeah, but what's her résumé going to look like? 'Ages sixteen to twenty, employed as freelance telephone operator'?"

"She could work for us," DeeAnne said.

There was a long silence. Once it was said, it was obvious to everyone that this was exactly the right solution. Delia wouldn't have to lie to them to get a job. If she started to go sour, they would know. If she succeeded, she'd have an employment record and references.

"We need a real office manager," Mae Ruth put in. "Candy can't work the computer system for shit."

On August twentieth, Delia started her new job, and that weekend the ops helped her move back into the house where she'd grown up. Jerry had sent a flunky to check the probate. Shanti had not made a will, but her father had left the house to his descendants. That meant Delia and Flora.

They mopped the floors and washed the curtains. They vacuumed, they washed the sheets, they made the beds. Delia moved into the room that had been her parents', and then Shanti's. The room that she had shared with Shanti when they were little girls was now Flora's.

Flora kept coming to work with Carter. She spent more and more time with her aunt, as Carter worked out of the office. Romie taught Delia all she knew about Flora and taking care of babies.

*I*n September, the party began running ads targeting Jimbo Turnbull. The first one showed a picture of the wreckage of the plane in which Roberto Lopez had died.

The narrator read: "Clyde Culbertson donated thousands of dollars to Senator Turnbull's war chests.

"Senator Turnbull asked the Forest Service to relax its inspections of Culbertson's Charter Fleet.

"When Culbertson's planes crash, Jimbo Turnbull says it's a harmless coincidence.

"Cronyism. Favors to Special Interests. Business as Usual. We need a change in Idaho."

Against swelling music, they showed a picture of Laurie Lopez in profile against the Sawtooth Mountains, and under the picture a banner that read "Laura Lopez for U.S. Senate."

Laurie's numbers were inching up. "I'll be," said Bliss Knox. Hunt and Bliss and Amy were meeting with the state party chair, talking through donor lists. "I'll be," Bliss said again, looking at the latest polling figures. "Laurie really read this timing right. I guess Big Jim is finally vulnerable. I got to hand it to her, I thought he had another term in him. Too bad I didn't have the sense to jump in—we might have actually *won* this sucker."

* * *

Jimbo Turnbull, meanwhile, was mad as hell. He was back in the state campaigning every weekend and he had ads pounding away on radio and TV. Experience counts. Getting things done. Jobs for Idaho. He was lashing out in two directions like a maddened bull. Laurie, a tax-and-spend liberal with no experience. Slash. Lloyd Prince, a fanatical tree-hugging carpetbagger. Slash. He made the mistake of calling Prince a "Greenie Weenie" in front of an open mike on the set of *Boise This Week*, and Prince took full advantage.

There were rumors that Turnbull's campaign had a mole in Laurie's headquarters. It was supposed to be a girl in the research office who was sleeping with one of Jimbo's strategists. Walter and Amy and Ajax wracked their brains trying to figure out who it was.

Lynn's team was working round the clock thinking up spots to respond to Jimbo's. They hammered at Jimbo's ties to special interests. His huge contributions from tobacco, from the timber industry, from the NRA. Jimbo hammered back. Laurie's campaign was funded by limousine liberals from Hollywood. By Feminazis. Laurie's numbers held steady and Lloyd Prince went on his eccentric way, appealing to a bizarre coalition of Christian and environmental extremists.

"I'm getting kind of fond of Lloyd," said Laurie. "He is pure, and he's relentless."

"See," said Walter, "that's just the problem. You're true Idaho, you're just contrary enough to like him. Look out, there may be more of you than you think."

The President of the United States stopped in Idaho to campaign for Laurie. He made a stirring speech on the steps of the capitol with Hunt on one side of him and Laurie on the other. Laurie fell four points in the polls. Idaho hated the President.

The end of September brought the Idaho Senate Debates.

There were now six candidates in the race. The Idaho *Courier* had done a Sunday feature saying Idaho was a one-party state. It had urged non-Republicans to get into the pool. This had brought out a young woman running for the Natural Law Party, and an independent, described as a monk. The monk was unable to attend the debate though; he was out of the state on retreat.

The candidates agreed to a town meeting format, with the audience asking the questions. Then there was the Crisis of the Chairs. Since Lloyd Prince couldn't stand at a podium, Laurie said they should all sit. Turnbull said it would cramp his style; he liked to stride around. Carrol Coney thought it would be cool if they all had wheelchairs. The final vote decided they would sit, but each could choose his own chair. That meant each campaign spent a week discussing Messages Sent by Furniture.

The Natural Law lady showed well. She was against political action committees, and by this time so were the voters. She supported Head Start and Transcendental Meditation in the schools. Laurie and Lloyd thought those were fine ideas, but then Lloyd got started on school prayer. Jimbo hated all of it; he sat in his big leather wing-backed chair and bellowed away about Tax and Spend and Limousines. Everyone was bored. The clear winner of the debate was Carrol Coney.

"I want the Air Force out of the Owyhee," he cried. He was sitting on a kitchen stool. "You have any idea what kind of racket those planes make? And smoke bombs! I live in a house made of hay, how would you like it if I dropped smoke bombs on your house and it was hay?" He was addressing Senator Turnbull, who was very proud to have drawn the Air Force to make the Owyhee desert a training ground. "We have California bighorn sheep—you ever seen one of those suckers? California bighorns, population's dropped in half since ninety-one. Explain *that*, Senator Air Force." Jimbo Turnbull claimed that the planes did nothing to harm the wildlife. "I moved out there to hunt and fish, to live like a natural man. But I can't hunt no bighorns if your goddamn airplanes make 'em drop dead first." The audience loved it.

"Mr. Coney," said a questioner, "my name is Marilyn Joyce, I'm a dental hygienist from Ketchum? We have a lot of airplane noise in

Blaine County too, from private jets. I was wondering if you think jets should land in unspoiled areas like that, or what you think about that."

"Hell, no, I don't think they should. I think you should shorten up those runways so the only thing that can fly in there is an eagle. Something too small to carry skis. I think you should make it take as long to get in there as it took when you went by covered wagon. You ever been to Aspen, Colorado, man?" The questioner, who was still standing, shook her head. "Go take a look at Aspen, Colorado. It's full of ghost houses. Great big houses people live in two weekends a year. What kinda community is that?"

The moderator tapped another questioner. "My name is George Garcia and I'm a schoolteacher. I'd like to ask Mr. Coney what is your position on storing nuclear waste at the INEL."

"I think it's a good idea," said Coney. He crossed his arms over his chest. He was wearing a suit coat he'd bought at the Salvation Army that morning, so you couldn't see his tattoos. The questioner, looking amazed, could only echo him.

"You think it's a good idea?"

"Hell, yes. See, I don't call it waste, I call it nuculer technology. We ought to keep it. That's the stuff that will put us on the map." Lloyd Prince was so cross he was doing wheelies.

Coney was mobbed after the debate. He went on sharing his views into the night, and when the next full-sample polls came out, he had 8 percent of the voters. The candidate who was down was Jimbo Turnbull.

lora had moved home to live with Delia the third week in September. It was DeeAnne who forced Carter's hand.

"You're thinking the longer you have her the more she is yours, right?"

"Right."

"Because the longer you have her, the more her own flesh and blood is a stranger to her."

"Right."

"So the sooner she goes, the better."

"Delia isn't ready."

"Probably not. How ready were you nine months ago? It's a job most people grow into."

"I can't do this. I can't stand it."

"Yes. You can. You saved her, honey. Nothing will ever change that. But that doesn't make her yours. Aunt Sallie will be right around the corner. She can play with Titus again. She can have a whole family, a whole neighborhood, not just one menopausal white woman."

"Who loves her."

"She'll still have you. She can keep coming to work with Delia."

Carter was stymied. It was right for Flora. It was right for Delia. She gave up the afternoon she came into the office to see Flora on Delia's lap. They were singing a song together that Carter had never heard before, not that she could sing if her life depended on it.

"You know every word of that, don't you, baby? Smart baby Flora-bug," Delia smiled at her. She looked up at Carter. "Mama used to sing that to Shanti and me when we were little."

* * *

Carter's house felt completely empty with Flora's stuff all gone. For a couple of days she kept going over to Shanti's house in the evening—Delia's house—to help feed the baby and put her to bed. But she began to feel like some sort of unwanted uncle, hanging around. Flora was comfortable with Delia. She was glad to see Carter arrive, but she didn't worry when she left. She was in her own house. She'd see Carter in the morning. Aunt Sallie was delighted to have the baby back in the neighborhood, and she let Carter know that Delia was being scrupulous about going to "her meetings."

"You think she's going to hold it together?" Carter asked Sallie Spear on the phone one night.

"I do think so, I do think so. I pray about it. She likes that job with all you."

"She's doing it very well," Carter said. This was true enough. For someone with no previous work experience of a lawful nature, Delia was doing better than anyone expected, although her number skills were weak and her spelling abominable.

"That's why God made spell checkers," DeeAnne said blithely. She was cutting Carter absolutely no slack. She didn't see any percentage in it. Rip it out, sew it up, get on with life. What other choice was there?

"So then she says to me," Carter reported to DeeAnne, "she says, 'I think Delia admires you so, she'd like to learn to be a detective too some day.'" Carter waited for a reaction.

DeeAnne was thoughtful. "You know, she's not nearly fat enough, but other than that . . . "

"DeeAnne, come on. She's got my baby, now you want her to have my life?"

"I want her to have her own. Go take a cold shower, buy a new hat, take up a hobby. How's that friend of yours doing in Idaho?"

Carter had nearly forgotten to pay attention. She went home and wallowed in cable news shows for two nights, but she couldn't find anything on Idaho. Finally she called the candidate.

One of Turnbull's researchers came up with a press clip from Laurie's visit to the senior center in Twin Falls. Back in the spring, early days of the primary. They built a TV spot around it and Jimbo started using it in his stump speech.

"Laurie Lopez is going to decide for herself if you're too rich to get Social Security or Medicare. She doesn't care how hard you worked, she doesn't know how long you'll live. That's what you get with inexperience, folks. Laurie Lopez doesn't know what it's like to be old and alone. I tell you the senior people of Idaho are scared of this talk, and they should be."

"Oh, shit," said Laurie. "It's out of context, I didn't scare anyone . . . "

"It doesn't matter, Laurie," said Walter. "We've got to respond to this."

Unfortunately, while Lynn and Walter were working on a spot to control the damage, Laurie got caught by a reporter at the end of a day, when she was wet with rain, had a headache, and was getting another cold. Asked the same question she'd answered that day fifty times, she snapped, "It's ridiculous. If I've scared any old people, I'd like to meet them."

Jimbo's people had a field day. They had quavery old people by the carloads herded into gymnasiums. Jimbo would go from one to the next with a microphone, asking what Medicare meant to them, asking what would happen to them if it were taken away. They were all coached, it was way off the point, but it hogged the campaign news for days. All Laurie could do was run her expensive rebuttal spot in as many markets as she could afford, and have every staffer who could read and write sending letters to editors and calling up talk radio shows, while she sent op ed pieces to the major papers explaining her true position.

Her numbers slipped again in the next round of polls. They had three weeks to go, and momentum was going the wrong way. Laurie's cold moved into her chest and she couldn't stop coughing.

"Go home," said Walter. "You need a night in your own bed."

"I can't, we have a town meeting in Moscow tonight."

"You don't need another night in a bad motel. Bliss will do it."

"Don't . . . it hurts when I laugh."

"He'll be great. We can all do your stump speech by now. Laurie, you've got to get a night's sleep, and frankly, you need some distance. Go home. I can't have you sick again. Where are the kids?"

"They're at Billy and Cinder's." That was except for Carlos, who was working for the campaign full-time.

"I'm going to have Carlos drive you home. I want you to go straight to bed, and I'll send someone to get you in the morning."

She lay back in the seat with her eyes closed while Carlos drove. She felt sick and sad. To come so far and screw up . . . it was too hard to bear. And it was her fault. Everyone had worked so hard and she had lost it.

The night woods were wild with yellow leaves. It was two weeks to the start of hunting season. One way or the other, it would be over. Her mind was racing.

"Honey?"

"Momski?"

"I left my goddamn briefing book."

"Where?"

"I don't know. I think where we were watching the tapes. You know what it looks like?"

"I'll tell Walter. He'll have it."

"I should be in Moscow. I was ready for them. I was going to put it together."

"Momski, shut up, please. You have to save your voice."

"Oh, thank you, Doctor," she said. She loved Carlos. He was a goofball, but deeply trustworthy.

When they got home, the house was utterly dark. It had been days since anyone had slept here. Even the dogs were with Cinder.

Carlos turned up the heat and sent his mother upstairs. He heated some water and put lemon and rum in it and took it up to her.

"Thank you, Doctor." She was in bed in a flannel nightgown.

"You look very cute. Like Old Mother Hubbard."

She took the mug from him.

"You want anything to eat?" he asked.

She shook her head.

"Do you want me to spend the night here?" Carlos asked. He had a room in Hailey, and she knew he would rather go back to town—there was a buzz about the last weeks of a campaign. It was exhausting but addictive. You'd been so out of sync with the rest of the world for so long it was like being out to sea with your own ship of fools. Even when nothing was happening, you wanted to be there.

"No thanks, buddy. I'll be fine. Just check to make sure the phones are working, will you?"

He gave a laugh. Gallows humor. Widow woman in lonely farmhouse finds her phone lines have been cut. He checked. "We have dial tone, Houston."

"Okay. Turn the lights out when you leave. Will you come for me in the morning?"

"I don't know who's staffing you, I'll check with Walter. One of us will give you a wake-up call."

This was the way she liked it. She liked to know there would be a morning call; she had nightmares about the power going out and the alarm failing.

She was so tired, she didn't even try to read. She stared into space as she drank the hot rum. Then she turned off the bedside lamp and went to sleep.

*   *   *

It was no longer pitch dark when she heard the footsteps. The moon was up; there was light between the curtains, casting shadows.

At first she thought she was imagining it. No one was here. Even she wasn't supposed to be here.

In another moment she knew it was real. She knew the noises of the stairs too well. Creak on the fifth step, then the eighth. There was someone coming up, in the dark. It was soft, creeping. As quietly as she could, she reached for the night table.

The person was looking for something. The footsteps went down the hall, away from her. She lay propped up in the dark, listening. She had her eyes stretched open wide. She didn't want to turn on the light; that would show him where she was. She wanted to get as used to the dark as she could.

The footsteps had found the twins' room. That was evidently not what was wanted. They turned and started down the hall, toward her. They stopped at Anna's room. She heard that door open. They moved on to the bathroom. She heard that door open. The steps were moving toward her. Her eyes fastened wide on the crack beneath the door, saw the glint of a beam from a flashlight. Good. He was using a light; he'd be night blind. Her heart was pounding so hard it seemed to be coming out her ears. The footsteps were right outside now; she heard her doorknob turn.

In the open door in the dark house stood the silhouette of a man. He swept the flashlight up from the floor. Toward the bed, and saw there was somebody there. The man screamed. And at the same instant, Laurie shot him.

LAURA LOPEZ SHOOTS INTRUDER

blazed the headlines.

The senatorial candidate, home for a night of rest from the campaign trail, surprised an intruder in her house and shot him with a nine-millimeter pistol. The handgun was bought for her by her late husband, tennis star Roberto Lopez, and was properly registered.

The intruder, who is in "guarded" condition, has been identified as Thomas Tickner of Nampa. A source close to the Turnbull campaign confirms that Mr. Tickner has been used by the GOP in previous years for so-called "dirty tricks," but claim they have no idea what he was doing in Judge Lopez's bedroom.

*T*he uproar was amazing. The Turnbull campaign was spinning like mad, trying to distance itself from the mess and get back on message. Lloyd Prince said nothing could have surprised him less, it was just what these brand-name party hacks got up to and always would, the perfect reason to ignore them both and vote for him. The Natural Law candidate deplored both the breaking and entering and the violent response, and pointed out that Transcendental Meditation caused people to go to a better place within themselves so things like this wouldn't happen.

As usual, it was Carrol Coney who captured the media's hearts. They charged out to Owyhee County to get his reaction.

"Aw, what a buncha assholes," said the candidate. He had to come outside and stand under the sky to be interviewed, as his dwelling was too cramped for a press conference.

"Who do you mean, Mr. Coney?" chorused the reporters.

"Those assholes who would have a guy break into a lady's house in the night . . . a person's home is their castle, man, this is America! Even if your castle is made of hay, you don't want no assholes showing up in the night and poking in your sock drawer! I'm just sorry she only drilled him in the shoulder, man. I wish she'd blown his nuts off."

"What effect do you think this will have on the campaign, Mr. Coney?"

"I'll tell you what effect it will have. I don't think this is fun anymore. As of right now, I am withdrawing from the race. I want everyone who was going to vote for me to vote for that shooter lady. Buncha assholes." He went back inside his hay house and stayed there.

"Laurie. Darling, are you all right?" Rae was on the phone from San Francisco.

"I'm fine, just tired. The papers make it sound worse than it was."

"I think I should come up there and give you a hug."

"I'd love to have you do that."

"All right, I'll be there tonight. I'll give you a hug, and then we can have some target practice."

Rae flew into Hailey on a little jet she chartered, not wanting to be away from her new project for more than a day. Amy and Laurie met her at the airport, trailed by a battery of photographers and a reporter from *People* magazine.

"Walter's with our pollster," Laurie said. "He'll be here tonight. We're having dinner at my brother's house, is that all right? You'll meet my dad, and the children." Amy carried Rae's overnight bag, and Rae beamed and exclaimed over the beauty of the mountains while flashbulbs popped. The photographers trailed them all the way back to the ranch, where Amy stopped the car, got out, and pointedly locked the gate across the road while reporters shouted questions at the car. "It makes me feel like Madonna," said Rae happily.

Dinner turned into the pure vacation Laurie had been needing—a long, noisy family gathering in which nobody mentioned politics. Bliss wasn't there; Billy said he was sulking in his tent because he had given the speech of his life in Moscow the night before and nobody had covered it. Nobody wrote about anything except the "Nine-millimeter Judge," as the papers were currently calling Laurie.

"I taught the children to shoot," Hunt boasted to Rae. "They can all shoot rifles and handguns. I remember the time when Laurie was ten, she shot the head off a milk snake that was bothering the chickens. Shot it at ten paces, and it was moving."

"I shot it at point-blank range, Daddy. Billy had his foot on it."

"I think you better teach *me* how to shoot," said Rae to Hunt. "I see now that you never know when it will come in handy."

Hunt looked down the table at Rae, who was wearing some marvelous thing made of red feathers, although everyone else was in jeans and flannel. He said, "I'd be delighted. I've got some targets in the barn, we can start in the morning."

"Why, that would be perfect," said Rae. Suddenly Walter and Amy looked across the table at each other and started to laugh. They both knew that Rae had planned to be back in California for a breakfast meeting with the Oakland City Council.

"We're back!" yelled Walter the next afternoon. The polls were coming in. It was only a half sample, but it looked as if more than half of Coney's voters had switched to Laurie, along with a lot of Turnbull's gun nuts, and an important chunk of the Undecideds. "We're going to stuff him in the killing jar!" Walter whooped. They were two points away from Jimbo Turnbull, and moving upward. Laurie's cough seemed to be cured. She did *Viewpoint, Newsmakers,* and *Boise This Week,* and was booked to do the Sunday national news shows.

*C*arter was trying to remember how to be alone. She'd spent a week of evenings just wandering from room to room. She went to the track with her brother, Buddy, a few times and hit the daily double.

"So what do you think, kid? You going to live?" Buddy asked as she left the window counting a wad of money.

"You didn't arrange that somehow, did you?"

"Kid, if I knew how to do that, would I be living in a trailer?"

She checked in with Jill. She told her that Flora had gone home to live with her aunt in a way that made Delia's coming home sound like a miracle, and Carter's losing Flora like No Big Deal. Jill was young enough that she believed her. Oddly, this made it easier for Carter.

So are we going to Fat Chance for our week? Carter wrote.

Jill wrote back a long, chatty letter. She told Carter about Sweet2.

Did you tell him he nearly got you raped and killed?

Jill wrote back that she hadn't told him that, but she had told about how John Henry Howard had heard her screaming when she hadn't made a sound. As a mostly deaf person, Tom had a lot to say about that.

How is John Henry doing?

He's getting better. He started going to my mom's church. He sits by himself. At first he wouldn't talk to anybody, he just went to the coffee hour and ate all the cookies.

Does that mean you're going to your mom's church?

I go sometimes. Last week John Henry talked to me. He's taking some new drug and also some odd vitamin therapy. He asked me how school was. He said he was thinking about going back to school himself.

Wow

Carter tapped. Another time she wrote:

How's your dad? Has he figured out where your mother is?

I don't think so. He went to Paris in August and hung around the Georges V and the Crillon looking for her.

That sounds depressing.

He said it was.

One evening just before Halloween, Carter was sorting her mail when she heard a car drive up to her house. She glanced out and saw to her surprise that it was Jerry. He was walking up the walk, bent forward, eyes on the ground, the way he usually did. He was carrying a bottle of wine. She opened the door.

"Trick or treat," he said.

"Please, no tricks. I've had enough of those."

"That makes two of us. I brought you some wine. Can I come in?"

She opened the door, smiling, and he closed it behind him and followed her into the kitchen. She opened the wine and poured two glasses. They raised them to each other.

There was a long silence. Jerry walked across the room and opened a cupboard, then another.

"Do you want to go sit down?" Carter asked.

"No, I like kitchens. Is this what we used to keep in these shelves?"

He was looking at a collection of half-used boxes of rice, sugar, and cornstarch behind one door, two shelves of mismatched glasses behind the other.

"Let me think. No, I think we had those big green plates in there on the left. Remember those? Do you still have them?"

"I remember. I think Niki didn't like them. I think she gave them to the maid."

"What was wrong with them?"

"They didn't go with her dining room."

"I never saw that dining room."

"It had a lot of swags."

They sipped their wine.

"I miss the baby," Jerry said.

"Oh. That. Join the club."

"I was thinking I'd like to set up a little trust fund for her."

"Jerry!"

"Nothing big. Just enough so that Delia can keep the house in good repair, and afford schools and camp. I wouldn't want Flora to ever know where it came from."

"I think that's a wonderful idea. I wish I'd thought of it." There was a silence. Carter said, "You sure you don't want to sit in the living room?"

"No, this is fine."

"Okay. Let's sit."

They settled down at the kitchen table with the bottle between them.

"You were great with her," said Jerry. "Flora."

Carter couldn't speak. They sat in silence for a while. Jerry crossed his long legs under the table and the chair creaked. Carter wanted to go into the living room because sitting here made her desperately want to reach into the drawer where she used to keep her cigarettes.

Jerry shifted himself all around in his chair again, and finished his wine. He poured another glass and drank half of it.

"I was wondering," he said, "if you would think about marrying me."

"Jerry!"

She started to laugh.

"I knew you'd do that," he said morosely.

"No, it's just that . . . well, for starters, aren't you married?"

"Not so much as you might think." He glowered.

"What happened to Graciela?"

"She's in Buenos Aires. My own Evita."

"Since when?"

"Since about March."

"Why the hell didn't you tell me?"

"I wasn't sure what it meant."

"You mean, whether you cared?"

"Yeah."

"Is she alone?"

"Oh, I doubt it," he said. He finished his wine again, and refilled their glasses.

"Give me some help here—did you . . . ? Or did she?"

"Quite a lot of both."

"But why? Tell me it wasn't the painting with the plates stuck in it."

"No, it was me. It was just Niki all over again. Somebody said to me lately that relationships—you know, you get in the ones you need, for some reason, karma or something, that you have to go through." He looked so darkly glum she didn't dare laugh. "The falling in love part, that's just to keep you out of your mind until you're good and hooked, then the anesthetic wears off."

"So what was it all about? With Graciela?"

"With both of them. I've thought about it and what I come up with is, I must have really needed to learn what an awful intellectual snob I am."

Carter roared. What was funny was the idea that anyone needed to learn that about Jerry. It was the most obvious thing about him.

"Fine. Laugh. I'd keep marrying these women and then about three years later, I'd wake up and realize it wasn't like having a . . . wife, I don't know, a partner . . . it was more like having one of those little poodles. Like having a gorgeous animal in the house that's too stupid to housetrain. Everyone looks at this thing prancing around and says ooh, ahh, what a physical specimen, and you're just worrying when it's going to chew your shoes apart, or piss on the rug." He glowered. Carter was trying not to laugh out loud.

"It didn't help that they kept sleeping with the tennis pro. But what did I expect? Honestly."

He reached for the bottle, but found there was not much left in it. Carter went for another one, and brought a box of crackers. Jerry wasn't a drinker and he was going to start feeling this cabernet, big time. Jerry put a big hand into the box and ate a handful of Wheat Thins while she dealt with the corkscrew and tried to think. All she wanted to do was laugh.

"I suppose you think this is easy for me," he said gloomily, as she finally poured the wine. She had never seen anyone look so unhappy and uncomfortable.

"Is it not?"

"No. I couldn't figure out whether to get drunk first and come over and ask you, or come over here while I could still drive, and then get drunk. Did I already ask you?"

"Yes."

"Oh. I knew you'd laugh at me. The others never did. They'd just get all wide-eyed and puzzled and go sleep with their tennis instructors."

"So this is really something you've given some thought to."

"Yes! I told you. Since March. I mean, since whenever I noticed that Graciela was gone."

"You could have mentioned it before this."

"No, because you'd had a baby. I thought if I asked you to marry me you'd think I wanted the baby, you know to marry the baby. I mean, you know what I mean."

"Yes."

"But it wasn't that. It did make me sorry we forgot to have children, both of us."

"Graciela could have had them . . . "

"Carter . . . aren't you listening to me? Graciela couldn't have six people to dinner without a staff of twelve and a week in Hawaii afterward to recover. What would she be like with a baby?"

Graciela had *looked* as if she was high maintenance. Carter had just figured she must have been different behind closed doors. She knew how little patience Jerry had for that sort of thing. About the same as she had herself.

She refilled her own glass. This second bottle, she noticed, was not much like the first, which had been like raspberry velvet.

"So?" he said.

"So . . . "

"Will you think about it?"

"Yes."

"Oh good," he said, and put his head down on the table. He took a deep breath. Then he sat up and looked calmer.

"I feel better now. When will you decide, do you think? Next week?"

She laughed. "Are you divorced?"

"Oh. No, probably not. I wasn't paying attention."

"Anyway, next week I'm going to the fat farm with my buddies."

"That reminds me, I think we should eat something. I'd like to take you out to dinner but I don't think I can drive. Let's call a taxi."

"I can drive."

"Oh good. Where would you like to get married? Mount Tam? That's where we usually do, but let's not. Hawaii?"

"Let's eat something, and think of someplace you've never been married before."

"Antarctica."

"I'd love that!"

"See, I knew you would! The others wouldn't. Not at all. Russian cruise ships. Ooooh, the food. But *you* would like penguins."

They went out and got into Jerry's car. He found the keys.

"I've never driven a car like this in my life," said Carter.

"You'll like it. I'll get you one."

Carter felt she hadn't completely stopped laughing for about the last hour. She had a feeling she should be serious but she couldn't seem to manage it.

"Where shall we go?"

"Somewhere they'll give us a table rather quickly."

"That's anywhere for you, isn't it?"

"I guess. Let's go to Maple Drive."

They did.

"I have to get you a ring."

"Jerry, you don't have to get me anything."

"What do you know? How many times have *you* been married? I know how these things are done, I have been trained."

"But I haven't said yes yet."

Jerry looked at her with patience. "Of course not. You say yes when you get married. When you say you'll think about it, you're engaged."

"My, the things Mama never taught me. I guess we could go shopping tomorrow."

"Yes. Exactly. Now you're getting the idea. Tomorrow, we will look at enormous rings."

"You know, this sounds like it could be fun."

"Carter, haven't you been *listening*?"

They laughed so much at dinner that the management offered to buy them a brandy at the bar, if only they would give up their table and leave the room.

"They're jealous," said Jerry as they left. And he was right.

It had been the only week of the campaign that felt like pure fun. Laurie had been on TV at least once a day since the shooting. The national press had arrived, and now there was sound and light equipment following Laurie and Jimbo everywhere. The Republican candidate for President flew in to stump for Jimbo. Old Senate campaigners and colleagues, they both got stuck in the tar pit of questions about GOP dirty tricks from the bad old days of Watergate. While they were mired and bellowing, they got hit with a good deal of splattered muck about money from foreign mining interests and using Idaho as a nuclear waste dump. "If it's not safe, why is it all right to put it here? If it's safe, why don't you put it someplace that's already ruined, like New Jersey?" Perhaps the angriest questions came from the group who wanted to know, if they had to play dirty tricks, why they kept getting such meatballs to do it instead of ones smart enough not to get caught.

The shootee, meanwhile, maintained a stoic silence. His condition had been upgraded to "good," and reporters camped outside his door reported that he seemed comfortable, now that his roommate had brought him clean underwear and his shaving gear, and a stack of *Soldier of Fortune* magazines. Walter's researchers were desperately trying to find the money trail from Turnbull's campaign to Tickner's bank account, but so far they couldn't and there were only six days to go before the election.

"We don't need it," said Walter, jubilant. "Look at the numbers." He showed Billy and Laurie the full-sample poll.

Before the shooting, the numbers stood at:

Turnbull 35
Lopez 27
Prince 19
Coney 6
Undecided 11
Natural Law 2

Now they stood at:

Turnbull 38
Lopez 37
Prince 17
Undecided 6
Natural Law 2

"Six percent undecided is still a lot," said Laurie. "And we need all our people to go to the polls—if they think we're winning, and the President is a shoo-in, they might stay home."

Amy had turned her attention to the Get Out the Vote effort. She had her college sorority sisters making phone trees all over the state. They'd call their friends, and get them each to call five more. Go to the polls. Rent a bus. Take your club. Take your church.

What they were waiting for now was the major endorsements, which would come out the Sunday before the election. The best news was that Bliss had gotten Mo Udall to sign a blistering letter. It attacked Jimbo's support of the sale of billions of dollars of Idaho mineral rights to foreign companies for a pittance; it described the time the House had passed a bill reforming the mining laws, and Jimbo had threatened to talk it to death if it came to the floor of the Senate. They were going to run a half-page ad in the Sunday *Courier* with the letter and a picture of Udall and of Frank Church, to remind the state that once in Idaho there were Democrats.

Friday, the day after Halloween, Walter and Lynn and Laurie

drove down to Boise to have lunch with the bigwigs at the *Courier*. Jimbo had been there the day before; like many papers, the *Courier* had a conservative management with a fairly liberal press corps. Sometimes one position prevailed, sometimes the other. Jimbo's seniority in the Senate, his committee positions, could mean a lot to Idaho. This endorsement might affect the Undecideds, and it could definitely go either way.

A staffer was driving the station wagon with Lopez bumper stickers and "Lopez for Senate" posters in the windows. The drive was a romp; people kept waving and honking when they saw who it was. Walter and Lynn were grinning. Light snow had begun.

"All you have to do," said Walter, "is don't get drunk or tell dirty jokes. It's going to go however it's going to go. I think they're likely to go for you; just don't be nervous."

"Let's go over it anyway. Tell me exactly who'll be there."

Walter took out his briefing book.

"The editorial board itself. You know them. George, Marjorie, John, and Hugh."

"Hugh and Roberto played poker together."

"Good. Dan Popkey for sure, a couple of other columnists. And then, I think we're going to get some VIPs from Des Moines." The paper was owned by a chain headquartered in Iowa.

"They flew in with the presidential campaign, and stayed for the meeting with Jimbo. I think they're still here."

"To see if they can rattle my cage?"

"Or Jimbo's."

"Give me names, give me histories."

"Well there's Chip Barnett, he's the son of, and grandson of."

Laurie nodded. "Have you met him?"

"I have," said Walter. "He's bright. Got a law degree. Was dragged back into the family business screaming, but he's grown into it. Then there's a cousin, Michael Ross. He's a shareholder, and sits on the board, and gives very big bucks to the Other Party. I heard Bush offered him the ambassadorship to Luxembourg."

"So I'm sure he's got an open mind about us," said Lynn dryly. "What's he here for?"

"Everyone likes celebrities." Walter looked at Laurie. There was something wrong with her.

"Laurie?"

"Do you have a middle initial?"

"Do I?"

"Does Michael Ross."

Walter looked at her hard, then riffled rapidly through his briefing book.

"W." He was staring at her. "You know him."

Laurie's nod was almost imperceptible.

"So what?" Lynn asked, mildly curious.

Laurie turned from her and looked at Walter. It took him a minute.

Then he said, "No."

She said, "Yes."

Walter slumped back against the backseat and turned his face to the roof of the car. Then he closed his eyes. "There is no God," he said.

Lunch was in the executive dining room at the top of the Courier Building. It was an imposing room, paneled in some sort of dark red wood, with huge windows and white-coated waiters gliding silently around. A large oval mahogany table in the center of the room was set for lunch. The newspaper people were standing around in clumps as Laurie's group arrived.

"Would you like a sherry?" asked the editor in chief. "Come, let me introduce you."

Laurie followed him around the room, shaking hands and smiling. All the while she heard a buzzing in her ears, and couldn't seem to get a full breath of air, as if the walls of her lungs were stuck together.

Several of the editors and columnists made jokes about Laurie's aim, about whether she was armed at that minute, and did she have a license to carry? She smiled and nodded. Walter, right behind her, made jokes about the fact that they had other issues.

Michael Ross had positioned himself so that he was among the last to be introduced. Laurie gave her full attention to each person she met as she was led around the room, so that she had not even gotten a full look at him. She moved from face to face, sensing rather than knowing for a fact that he was there.

"Yes, that's right, at the Press Club dinner, it's nice to see you. How do you do? Thank you. Welcome to Boise."

"And this is Michael Ross," said the editor in chief, and Laurie turned to him.

He was bulkier than when she had last seen him. His forehead was higher, and he had some gray in his hair. He wore a dark suit and a bright yellow tie.

"Hello, Michael." She gave him her hand.

"Laurie." He bowed slightly over the hand, rather than shaking it. "You're looking well." He smiled, but his eyes were intense and still.

"Thank you. So are you."

"And this is Helen McGowan . . . "

"I'm an old friend of your father's," said the smiling, gray-haired lady. She had edited the Local page of the paper for a million years.

They sat down to lunch, with Laurie at the head of the table. They were given clear soup, and Laurie was asked soft-ball questions. They were given filet of sole and the questions got harder.

"Judge Lopez," Chip Barnett piped up as she was taking her first mouthful of hot food, "what's your position on the balanced budget amendment?"

Walter caught his breath. He'd been coaching Laurie to avoid this question, because no matter how she answered, it would sound like hell in a sound bite.

"I'm against it," said Laurie.

"Really," said Chip, shifting in his chair and glancing at Michael Ross.

"May I explain?"

"By all means."

"I think it's an improper use of the Constitution. You can't make a document substitute for sound leadership. And if you try to, the most likely result is that you damage the document rather than solve the problem."

"Maybe a better question, Judge Lopez, is what's your position on the deficit?"

This was from Helen McGowan. A whiffle ball. She hit it over the fence. Walter passed out position papers.

"And your position on Choice, Judge Lopez?"

Laurie's heart nearly stopped. She looked at Michael Ross. After a long beat, she managed to say, "I assume you mean school choice vouchers, since I'm clear on the record otherwise."

"Fine," he said.

She answered the question. They were given a dish of sherbet and a cookie, and then they were shaking hands and out the door.

In the car, Laurie was trembling.

"I loved the little elephant pin in his lapel," said Laurie.

"Yes. Nice touch."

"I thought of reminding him that we once sat in against the war together."

"Are you two going to tell me what you're talking about?" Lynn asked.

Laurie and Walter looked at each other.

"No," said Walter, "we're not."

"Okay, fine. No problem. Just what a press secretary likes, to be the last to know."

"Next week," Laurie promised.

"Fine. No problem." Lynn crossed her arms and stared out the window. They rode in silence, replaying in their minds every minute of the lunch.

"I thought the . . . "

"When Boy Barnett . . . "

Laurie and Walter had both erupted at once.

"Go ahead."

"Boy Barnett was trying to gore your ox."

"I know. Did he?"

"I don't think so."

"And what about . . . "

"Yes. Well. That was a moment, wasn't it? As if I couldn't see what was on the table."

Laurie had looked across the table at Mike Ross and their eyes had locked. She couldn't interpret his expression.

Something had happened as the group was taking its leave that she couldn't bear to point out to Walter. There had been bowing, waves exchanged by some of the party, but more formal leave-taking between others. It seemed pretty clear that the one-on-one good-byes would be among the ranking figures. Laurie shook hands with the editor in chief, with Chip Barnett, and with the managing editor. But when she turned to Michael, hand outstretched, he had just that moment asked a question of Dan Popkey and turned his back to her.

"All it would take is one call to a reporter," Laurie said at last.

"I know," said Walter. "Don't think about it."

*S*unday morning, the Lewiston paper went for the straight Republican ticket. But the Idaho *Courier* endorsed the Republican for president, an independent for Congress, and Laura Knox Lopez for U.S. Senate.

It was Sunday night supper, the first meal of the new week at The Cloisters. Carter and Jill had been on the phone to Amy in Boise and missed the gong. Everyone else was already seated in the dining room when they came in and they had to find seats at separate tables.

A Fitness Professional, apple-cheeked and curly-haired, tinkled her little bell for their attention. She asked Rae to begin the introductions.

"My name is Rae Strouse, I'm from San Francisco, and this is my twenty-third visit."

"My name is Eloise Strouse, and I'm here with my stepmother."

"My name is Bonnie Gray, I'm from Colorado, and I raise goats."

"My name is Carter Bond, and I'm here to get in shape for my wedding."

"Carter, show us your ring!" called Jill from across the room and, vamping, Carter did so. It was the size of a chandelier.

Everyone who had been to The Cloisters before cheered and clapped, and everyone who was new wondered why the hell she had come, and remembered, too late, how much she had hated the first day of camp.

"Can I have Terri again for my personal trainer?" Carter asked Sandra as they went over her schedule.

"Terri's gone on to The Canyon Ranch. I've given you Suzanne. I don't think you met her last time; she was on maternity leave."

As she was leaving to go to Dancercise, Carter said, "I didn't see
Carol Haines last night. Is she here?"

"She's coming today. She was delayed because her mother passed
away last week."

"My girlfriend was just here and she said *don't miss* the Natural
Menopause lady," said Glenna Leisure to Eloise as they chugged
along on the Moderate Mountain hike on Tuesday morning. Natural
Menopause was one of the evening program choices. Eloise had been
planning to skip it, hoping to suggest she was too young to be interested.

"Why?"

"She tells you about this sex lubricant stuff that's exactly like your
own . . . you know. She lets you try a sample on your hand, and Trudy
says it is *too weird*. She was going straight out to get a case."

"What is it?"

"Astrolube? Aquaglide? You get it at the drugstore. And she tells
you about these little weights like lead tampons, they're sort of pelvic-
floor dumbbells, that you can exercise your insides with . . . for secks-
u-al pleasure, but also so you don't end up in Depends . . . "

Eloise was agog. Glenna rattled right on.

"I have no idea how you know what size you need . . . "

Most of Tuesday passed in a haze for Jill, she was so excited about
the election. Carol Haines had arrived at lunchtime. She wept when
she first saw Rae, but made it clear that beyond that, she didn't want
to talk about Rusty. She set straight to work polling the group and
arranging to have supper served in Saguaro for all who were interested
in watching the returns on TV.

"It's the strangest day here," Amy said to Jill on the phone from
Boise. "There's nothing to do. We voted this morning, and now we're
just wandering around."

"Where's Laurie?"

"She's here in the hotel holed up with her kids."

"And how does it feel?"

"Our last poll showed us in a dead heat. Turnbull's showed him still a point ahead. Walter's people are doing exit polls. Have you seen Solange?"

"She's gone."

"Why?"

"No one will say. Mom, why don't you come tomorrow? Both of you? Can't you?"

"Is there room?"

"I think so; I'll ask."

Laurie was as nervous as a panther. The campaign had taken a hotel suite for her and the children. Billy and Cinder were next door, and Hunt couldn't stay away, though he was sleeping at Bliss's house.

The twins were watching videos in the second bedroom. Walter kept calling.

"Our exit polls show better Hispanic turnout than ever before. This is Amy's doing, of course."

Fifteen minutes later he called again. "I've heard from Moscow and Lewiston. The women are turning out. It looks strong."

"How about the Panhandle?"

"We've got some problems there."

"Some problems means the tank."

"It's Prince's stronghold. He's hurting Turnbull worse, but he's hurting us too."

Laurie couldn't stand it anymore so she and Cinder and Anna went out for a run.

In the wet, gray, November street, people cheered Laurie when she approached. A young man on a bicycle raised his hand as he rode toward her and they slapped palms as they passed each other. "Is this a victory lap?" she asked Cinder. "Or are they saying 'Nice try'?"

By four o'clock in the afternoon she was bathed and dressed in the clothes she would wear for the last event of the campaign, whatever that turned out to be. Anna and Cara were squabbling over barrettes. The twins were overdosing on *Toy Story*. The clock seemed to be going backward and the polls wouldn't close in California for another five hours.

The President had won. Laurie knew that when he took Florida, although it wasn't official yet. That was good for him and probably bad for her. There *were* people who only went to the polls to vote for President. She gave up and went down to Walter's room, where there were four TV sets tuned to different networks. CNN reeled deliriously back and forth between election reporting and disaster coverage of a hurricane in Florida.

"Come on," said Carter to the TV for the fifteenth time. "Who cares about California, what's happening in Idaho?"

"In Idaho," said the announcer as the map behind him tumbled and clicked and suddenly the state of Idaho turned red, "we are getting word of an upset. Laurie Lopez, running against incumbent Jimbo Turnbull, has come from behind in the polls in the last two weeks to a race that right now is looking like a dead heat. A local station declared the incumbent, Senator Turnbull, the winner an hour ago. But they have just reversed themselves. Let's go to Boise."

The scene switched to a hotel room hung with tricolor banners and filled with riotous supporters. A reporter in a perky pink blazer said, "Thank you, Bill. An hour ago one of our local stations declared that Jimbo Turnbull *had* won reelection. But our own exit polls show the two candidates very, very close, and as we speak, we're giving the edge to the challenger, Laura Lopez. As you know, Bill, Judge Lopez has been very much in the news this month ever since she shot an intruder in her bedroom. In case your viewers don't know the story—"

"I'm sorry, Cindy, sorry . . ." said the famous announcer, and the viewers were returned to the national studio where some news was breaking about a tight race for governor in Washington State.

"I've just thought of what's wrong with this," said Rae.

"What?"

"This is no time to be on the wagon. I could use a great big piña colada right now. And make it snappy."

There was no more news of Idaho for what seemed like an eternity. The ladies who had eaten in the dining room began to wander in to see what was going on. There were cheers and groans as results were announced around the country. There was another disaster report from Jacksonville, now flooded after the hurricane. Families were leaving their houses in rowboats launched from second-story windows.

The famous announcer was burbling on about what it meant to the President to have won Ohio when he interrupted himself.

"Excuse me—" He listened to his earphone. "Excuse me, we have another result, from that very close Senate race in Idaho. As of now, we are showing that the challenger, Judge Laura Lopez, has beaten Jimbo Turnbull."

There were yells of joy. Carol and Rae were in each other's arms. Eloise and Glenna were wildly clapping, and Carter and Jill were giving loud high fives. When they could stand to turn their attention back to the set, they were back at Laurie's campaign ballroom. Perky Cindy was saying, "It now appears that the station had misread its polling data. We are showing that Laurie Lopez has won by a comfortable margin, and in some areas, by quite a wide margin."

"Have we heard anything from Senator Turnbull, Cindy?"

"No, not yet, Bill. Although, I am hearing now, I am hearing now, that all three networks are now forecasting Judge Lopez as the winner. As I was saying—"

"Thank you, Cindy, I'm sorry to interrupt, but we're going to switch now to Senator Turnbull's headquarters. Are you there, Ted?"

Ted was. On the podium behind him, Jimbo Turnbull, a fixture in the Capitol for over thirty years, was standing with his young wife and his pretty eighteen-year-old daughter. There were many people in rows behind him too, and tears could be seen as he lifted his hands in the two-fisted cheer with which he'd greeted well-wishers for so long. His wife and daughter were openly crying, and chanting began among his workers. He opened his palms to signal for quiet.

"I want to thank, I want to thank you all. . . . You know how much you've done, and I think you know how much we appreciate it.

This isn't the way we wanted it to end. But we fought hard, and we did the best we could. I want to say thank you, to all of you, and to my family"—here the camera went in close on the daughter, her eyes and nose red from crying—"for all you've done. You all go on home and rest up for the next fight. I'm looking forward to a rest myself, and to my first hunting season in Idaho in a long, long time." There was sniffling behind him.

"And I want to say to my opponent, the new senator from the great state of Idaho"—here he appeared to be surprised by tears himself and the camera zoomed in tight on *him*—"I want to say, Sissy, we've come a long way from the great, gray, green, greasy Limpopo River. You did good, little girl. Get out there and give 'em hell."

He turned abruptly and walked off the platform, leaving his family to trot and trail after him.

"I didn't get all of that, Ted," said the famous announcer. "Did you? What was he saying about that . . . about that river?"

"From what I understand, Bill, it's from a children's story . . . it's from a children's story that Senator Turnbull used to read to the Knox children . . . "

"Rudyard Kipling, I'm told now," said the famous announcer. "Thank you, Ted. We're going now to Judge Lopez's headquarters, where we understand she's ready to make a statement."

The camera switched back to the earlier ballroom, now a scene of pandemonium. The campaign kids were out of their minds with joy. The air was full of confetti, and Cindy in her perky blazer had one finger in her ear while the other hand clutched the microphone. She was yelling something into it, but it couldn't be heard above the din.

The platform was crammed with staffers and family and friends. Laurie, flanked by Hunt and Carlos, walked to the microphone. The rest of her children and Cinder's filled in on either side, looking toward the cameras and bumping into each other. Amy and Walter, Bliss and Billy and Lynn, were ringed around her.

In New York City, sitting alone before the TV in the den, thinking about Jill and wondering if she was watching this too, Noah Burrows suddenly learned the thing he had been trying to discover for months:

he found out where his wife was. Behind the candidate there was just a glimpse of her, wearing a dress he'd never seen before and a look of elation he'd never seen either. All these months, wondering if she were angry, lonely, who she was with, he had never come anywhere close to imagining this.

In the ballroom in Boise, Laurie held up her fists in a victory sign, and her smile was so bright and broad it seemed to glow. The cheers came in waves. She held out her hands for quiet and the roar dropped slightly. She adjusted the microphone, turned to her father, and the cheers broke out again. Three times she tried to begin her thank-yous, and three times she couldn't be heard above the joyous roar. She gave in to it and raised her fists in salute again, and the cheering crested higher. Laurie's smile was enormous.

H as anyone ever actually *killed* a Fitness Professional?" asked Margaret. She was a willowy blond from Duluth on her first visit to The Cloisters.

"We usually stop at maiming," Carter said.

"It's just Black Wednesday," said Rae.

"You've got to mainline this bran stuff." Carter was mixing another spoonful into her vegetable broth.

Eloise Strouse, chewing a slice of watermelon, came over to join them. She was wearing a silver-thong leotard.

"Look at you," said Carter. "I call that showing off."

"I bought it at the boutique," said Eloise. "Is it too much?"

"You look terrific."

"Did anyone see the news this morning, the pictures of Jacksonville?"

Heads turned to Eloise. *See* the news? Everyone knew that the one TV in the place had been off this morning. Eloise blushed.

"I just have this tiny Watchman. I've always watched the news at breakfast . . . "

"I don't know when I've been so shocked," said Rae, reaching for a radish.

"What do you know that we don't know?" Carter asked.

"First they had days and days of rain, and then the hurricane. The hurricane blew all this garbage into the storm drains; they say it's the worst flooding in thirty years. Now the sewers are full of snakes. They're coming up out of the toilets . . . "

"Don't even talk to me about snakes," said Glenna. She got up and went off to change for Water Exercise.

"It makes me so sad," said Eloise. "I used to love Jacksonville."

"Did you?" Rae asked, although she well remembered Albie telling her so. Carter and Jill were pushing their feet into their sandals and getting ready to go for herbal wraps. Eloise sat down at the foot of Rae's chaise longue.

"My grandparents lived there. Mama used to take Bert and me to visit them every winter."

"Tell me what it was like."

As the others drifted off to their classes or treatments, Rae and Eloise sat in the sun. Rae was wearing a sequined baseball cap, and she made Eloise put on sunblock. Eloise told about memories of her grandparents' house, of being taken to Ripley's Believe It or Not Museum, of picnics and outings with her uncles and cousins.

"Are you in touch with your cousins there?"

"Some. I keep looking at the pictures, thinking I'm going to see their houses up to the windows in water."

"I have an idea," said Rae. "Let's go to my room; I have something to tell you."

*a*my and Laurie arrived Wednesday evening.

"I have never been more tired in my life," Laurie said.

"Honey, I've seen tired. Tired was you, a year ago," said Rae.

"My father wants to know when you're coming back for your shooting lessons."

"Why, I didn't know I'd been invited."

"You have."

"I think I just might be able to work that in," said Rae. "I'll see if James can give me any time off."

Amy couldn't get enough of Jill. "Look at you, you're so svelte, you're so . . . what on earth are you doing for clothes? You must need new everything."

"I'm fine, Mom. Dad even took me shopping one day."

"He didn't."

"Yes, he did. Dagmar told him he wasn't giving me enough of a clothing allowance, he should go with me sometime to see how much things really cost. We spent a whole Saturday morning at Bloomingdale's."

"I can't imagine."

"Dagmar says being a single parent is bringing out the best in him."

"Hmm," said Amy.

* * *

Friday morning Rae and Carter took a class in Rollerblading.

"We sped around and around the tennis court," said Rae. "I was the best."

"You were not," said Carter.

"*We* learned the macarena," said Amy. "You should have seen Eloise."

"Please don't sing it though. *Please.*"

"Did anyone hear the radio this morning?" asked Carol, stirring pepper flakes into her potassium broth. "They had an interview with the mayor of Jacksonville. Some anonymous woman is giving a thousand dollars to every family in the whole town whose home was flooded. It's for real, there's fifteen million on deposit already. She was in tears, the mayor."

"How absolutely cool," said Glenna.

"Do you think they'll ever tell who it was?" asked Carol.

"Time for my herbal wrap," said Eloise.

Rae and Eloise sat together at dinner that night. "I like your hair like that," Carol Haines said across the table to Eloise. "I do too," said Rae. "You look like your father."

Laurie was missing from the dining room that night; she had been on a juice fast all day and was skipping dinner to have an extra massage and go to bed early. Her room was full of faxes from Walter and from Lynn Urbanski about scheduling in the coming week.

The campaign office was swamped with requests for interviews, letters of congratulation, urgent messages from realtors in Washington, D.C. Back in Boise, Walter was editing them as strictly as he dared. There was one message of welcome he thought Laurie would especially want to see, from the shyest and smartest member of the President's cabinet. There was also a letter from Walter waiting in Amy's room. It had arrived sealed, delivered by FedEx rather than sent by fax.

At Carter's table, Margaret from Duluth was arranging a blind date for her New York brother with a peppy redheaded architect. "You look exactly like his first girlfriend, the one he *should* have married. He's straight, he's sweet, he's smart. What's not to like?"

"He's been divorced for five minutes."

"Oh, yes, well, he's completely insane at the moment, but that will pass." The redhead obediently handed over her phone number.

Louise from Los Angeles, who owned several national magazines, was taking an interest in a young journalist she'd made friends with in Water Aerobics. A physician from Toronto was telling another one from Detroit about Doctors Without Borders, and a starving playwright who'd been sent to Fat Chance by her grandmother was telling a very funny story to a woman she did not yet know was a film producer.

NOVELS BY BETH GUTCHEON

LEEWAY COTTAGE: A Novel
ISBN 0-06-053905-4 (hardcover)

Beth Gutcheon takes us back to the coastal village of
Dundee, Maine. There, in a Victorian summer house called Leeway
Cottage, we witness the family drama of a 20th Century marriage.

MORE THAN YOU KNOW: A Novel
ISBN 0-06-095935-5 (paperback)

This spare, piercing, and unforgettable novel set on the coast of
Maine bridges two centuries and two intense love stories.

FIVE FORTUNES: A Novel
ISBN 0-06-092995-2 (paperback)

Funny, wise, and hope-filled, *Five Fortunes* is a large-hearted
tale of five vivid and unforgettable women who know where
they've been but have no idea where they're going.

SAYING GRACE: A Novel
ISBN 0-06-092727-5 (paperback)

Saying Grace is about the fragility of human happiness and
the strength of convictions, about keeping faith as a couple
whether it keeps one safe or not.

DOMESTIC PLEASURES: A Novel
ISBN 0-06-093476-X (paperback)

Engaging, witty, and entertaining, *Domestic Pleasures* is a
captivating tale of love lost and found.

STILL MISSING: A Novel
ISBN 0-06-097703-5 (paperback)

Alex Selky, going on seven, kissed his mother goodbye and
set off for school, a mere two blocks away. He never got there.

THE NEW GIRLS: A Novel
ISBN 0-06-097702-7 (paperback)

A resonant, engrossing novel about five friends at a girls' prep
school at the change of an era. They are being prepped for a world
of European tours, resorts, and debutante parties; what's coming at
them is the social tumult of the Vietnam War years.